BLACK ENOUGH

STORIES OF BEING YOUNG AND BLACK IN AMERICA

BLACK ENOUGH

STORIES OF BEING YOUNG AND BLACK IN AMERICA

EDITED BY
IBI ZOBOI

HarperCollins *Children's Books*

First published in the United States of America by Balzer + Bray in 2019
Balzer + Bray is an imprint of HarperCollins Publishers
Published simultaneously in the UK by HarperCollins *Children's Books* in 2019
HarperCollins *Children's Books* is a division of HarperCollins*Publishers* Ltd,
HarperCollins Publishers
1 London Bridge Street
London SE1 9GF

The HarperCollins website address is:
www.harpercollins.co.uk
1

ISBN 978-0-00-832655-5

The authors assert their moral right to be identified as the authors of their work.
A CIP catalogue record for this title is available from the British Library.

Printed and bound in England by CPI Group (UK) Ltd, Croydon CR0 4YY

MIX
Paper from
responsible sources
FSC™ C007454
www.fsc.org

This book is produced from independently certified FSC™ paper
to ensure responsible forest management.

For more information visit: www.harpercollins.co.uk/green

TO VIRGINIA HAMILTON AND
WALTER DEAN MYERS.

WE STAND ON THE SHOULDERS OF GIANTS.

Contents

INTRODUCTION

JUNE SARPONG

Any child of colour raised in the West will have been told early on by their parents or guardians that "they need to work twice as hard" in order to achieve success. Those people may not recall exactly when they had their first *"conversation"*, but they *will* remember having it.

For non-white children growing up as minorities in Europe or North America, the first uncomfortable "conversation" with their parents isn't about the birds and the bees – that comes later – it's about more pressing matters that will impact them from the moment they leave the safety of their parents' home and enter the world.

Pre-school can often be a baptism of fire for children of colour. While white children may have the luxury of waiting till their tweens before having to learn about the realities of life, children of colour are told much earlier, their "conversation" being more about the inequalities and discrimination that they will invariably face at some point in their lives. Unfortunately, this is regardless of how privileged, talented or brilliant they might be. This is a heartbreaking burden that parents of colour bear, or white parents of non-white children must face. Children of mixed-race heritage are one of the fastest-growing ethnic groups in Britain, so now many parents who themselves might not have had a personal experience of discrimination are having to have that *"conversation"* with their children.

In *Black Enough*, Ibi Zoboi powerfully weaves together a collection of short stories that examine what it means to be young and black in America. These stories bring us up close and personal with heroes and heroines who are trying their best to win on an unlevel playing field: young people refusing to give up even when the odds are stacked against them; young people who will open your hearts and minds in ways you couldn't imagine.

Like all great coming-of-age adventures, you, the reader, will leave as much changed as the protagonists. *Black Enough* will open your eyes to US injustices that are just as relevant here in the UK; *Black Enough* will provide you with a new-found appreciation for the resilience of the human spirit; and, more importantly, *Black Enough* will remind you of our shared humanity.

Whether you are a young person dealing with similar challenges faced in the pages of this book, a parent wanting to raise "woke" children, or simply an ally for change and inclusion, *Black Enough* will arm you with extra tools on your journey to make the world a fairer place.

INTRODUCTION

IBI ZOBOI

I was born in a country known for having had the first successful slave revolt in the world. Way back in 1804, Haiti became the very first independent Black nation in the Western Hemisphere. If global Blackness had a rating scale of one to ten, the Haitian Revolution has got to be at level ten, being the most Blackest thing that ever happened in history.

But none of that mattered when I first immigrated to the United States as a child. The Black and Latinx kids in my Brooklyn neighborhood didn't know and didn't care that my native country had once been a hub for freed slaves from America. According to them, I wasn't Black enough. I wore ribbons in my hair and fancy dresses to school, and I had a weird accent and a funny name. Most important, I didn't know how to jump double Dutch or separate a sunflower seed from its shell with just my front teeth, and I was off-key and off-beat when stomping, clapping, and singing to the latest cheers. These were all definitions of Brooklyn's summertime Black girlhood.

By the time I started high school, I had mastered all of those things and could easily blend into New York's particular brand of teen Blackness, even while tucking away the quirky parts of myself—my love of sci-fi, disco music, and John Stamos.

In college, my small Black world expanded when I met my first roommate, who had the thickest Southern accent I had ever heard. My best friend in high school was African American and I'd been to her big family cookouts and even to visit her cousins in a small Black town in South Carolina. I'd been a little jealous that she had such a big family and at a moment's notice could be surrounded by a plethora of aunts, uncles, and cousins. This was my first glimpse into African American culture—one with deep roots in the South. But that new roommate of mine with the Southern accent was from Rochester, New York, and her family had lived there for as long as she could remember.

Once I met new friends from Nigeria, Ghana, South Africa, and even England, my idea of Blackness began to expand. It was only then that I started to connect my own Brooklyn Blackness to a global idea of Blackness. After all, while the girls in my neighborhood teased me about not knowing how to spit out sunflower seeds, they didn't know how to properly eat a mango, or know Creole or Patois or any of the Caribbean ring games. But before long, I knew there was a fine thread that connected all of these cultural traditions to each other.

Blackness is indeed a social construct. Within the context of American racial politics, there can be no Black without white. No racism without race. But the prevalence of culture is undeniable.

What are the cultural threads that connect Black people all over the world to Africa? How have we tried to maintain certain traditions as part of our identity? And as teenagers, do we even care? These are the questions I had in mind when inviting sixteen other Black authors to write about teens examining, rebelling against, embracing, or simply existing within their own idea of Blackness.

Renée Watson's opening story, "Half a Moon," places Black teen girls outdoors, among trees, and swimming in lakes—and yes, there is the common understanding that the hair situation is already handled. Jason Reynolds and Lamar Giles fully capture #blackboyjoy in their respective stories "The Ingredients" and "Black. Nerd. Problems." There are no pervasive threats to their goofing around and being carefree. The intersectional lives of teens who are grappling with both racial and sexual identity are rendered with great care and empathy in Justina Ireland's "Kissing Sarah Smart," Kekla Magoon's "Out of the Silence," and Jay Cole's "Wild Horses, Wild Hearts." From Leah Henderson's story of appropriation at a boarding school

Liara Tamani's story of inappropriate nude pic games at a church beach retreat, the teens in *Black Enough* are living out their lives much like their white counterparts. They are whole, complete, and nuanced.

Like my revolutionary ancestors who wanted Haiti to be a safe space for Africans all over the globe, my hope is that *Black Enough* will encourage all Black teens to be their free, uninhibited selves without the constraints of being Black, too Black, or not Black enough. They will simply be enough just as they are.

HALF A MOON

RENÉE WATSON

DAY ONE: SUNDAY

Dad left when I was seven years old.

Mom thinks I was too young to remember Dad living with us, that I am holding on to moments I heard about but don't really know for myself. But I am seventeen years old now and I know what I know. Mom is much further from seven, so maybe she doesn't understand that at seventeen years old a person can still remember being seven, because it wasn't that long ago.

Seven was watching Saturday-morning cartoons and practicing counting by twos, fives, tens. I remember. Seven was fishing trips with Dad and Grandpa, and being crowned honorary fisherwoman because once I caught more than they did.

Seven was family camping trips and looking up at the night sky with Dad, pointing to the stars that looked like polka dots decorating the sky. Mom mostly stayed in the RV, and one time—the time when a snake crawled into Mom's bag—she made Dad end the trip early and we checked into a hotel.

Seven was Dad and Mom arguing more than laughing. Seven was staying at Grandma's on weekends "so your parents can have some time together," Grandma would say. At Grandma's house there was no arguing or slamming doors. Only puzzle pieces spread across the dining room table, homemade everything, and Grandma's gospel music filling the house.

Seven was Dad leaving Mom. Leaving me.

And now, seventeen is spending my spring break working at Oak Creek Campgrounds as a teen counselor for sixth-grade students, because I have to work, have to help out at home, because Mom can't take care of the bills alone.

Seventeen is knowing what to pack for trips like this because I've done this before at fourteen, fifteen, and sixteen: allergy pills, bug spray, raincoat, Keens for the walking trails, and my silk scarf so that I can tie my hair up at night. I braided my hair before I left so that if it rains, my hair won't stand on top of my head, making me look like I got electrocuted.

When I was in middle school, I was a camper at the Brown Girls Hike summit. That's one of the requirements for becoming a counselor. The annual camp is for Black girls living in the Portland metro area. Mrs. Thompson started the camp because she felt Black teens in Portland needed to learn about and appreciate the nature all around us. Every year she tells us, "Our people worked in the fields, we come from farmers and folks who knew how to get what they needed from the earth. We've got to get back to some basics. We've got to reclaim our spaces."

This is my last year working for the camp before leaving for college, so I want to make it the best one ever. But as soon as the bus full of sixth-grade girls pulls into the parking lot, I start having doubts that any good will come of this week. Out of all the girls on the bus, there's one I recognize. She is sitting at the front, all by herself. She is a big girl with enough hair to give some away and still have plenty. As soon as I see her, my heart vibrates and my mind replays ages seven and eight and nine and ten, and eleven and twelve and all the years without my dad, because the girl on the bus sitting on a seat by herself is my dad's daughter.

Brooke.

She was born when I was seven.

She is the reason Dad left Mom. Left me.

I've seen her before, always like this, as I am going about my regular life. She shows up in places I don't expect. Once at Safeway when I was with Mom grocery shopping because there was a sale on milk. She was coming down the aisle with Dad, the two of them with a cart full of things that weren't on sale, no coupon ads in hand. We said hello, but that was it.

Another time I saw her at Jefferson's homecoming football game. The whole community was out, and my aunt kept joking about how you can't be Black in Portland and not know every other Black person somehow, someway. "It's like a family reunion," she said.

Except Brooke is not my family.

She is the girl who broke my family.

During the game, I couldn't stop staring at Brooke, thinking how much she looks like Dad and wondering how it is that I came out looking just like Mom—tall and thin—more straight road and flat terrain than curves and mountains. I could tell we were opposite in personality, too. She couldn't keep still all night, full of laughter and words, waving to friends, singing along with the music at halftime. So much energy she had. Such joy spread across her face.

Not like today.

Today, she is not with her mom or my dad. Today, when she gets off the bus she is walking alone and her head is hung low and she looks completely out of her comfort zone. Maybe she is only joyful when she's with her family. Maybe she wasn't prepared to be on a camping trip with girls from North Portland. She lives in Lake Oswego. I doubt she's ever been around this many Black girls at once. I step back a bit, hide behind Natasha, the only other teen counselor I like in real life, outside of camp. We've worked together every year. Natasha's family is the kind you see in the frames at stores, the kind on greeting cards, so I don't tell her my father's daughter is on that bus. Natasha doesn't know anything about dads leaving their children.

Mrs. Thompson, the only person I know who can make a T-shirt and jeans look classy, stands at the bus waiting for the door to open. Usually as campers get off the bus, we clap and cheer and usher them into the main lodge for the welcome and cabin assignments. But I keep hiding behind Natasha, who turns and asks, "You all right?" as she claps and yells, "Welcome, welcome."

Brooke doesn't notice me. She is occupied with pulling her designer suitcase with one hand and holding her sleeping bag with the other. She looks like she is prepared to go to a fancy resort, not a muddy campground. I think about all the money Dad must spend on her name-brand clothes and shoes, her hair and manicures. This camp. She is probably one of the few girls here who paid full tuition.

Once we are all in the main hall, Mrs. Thompson gives a welcome, reviews the rules, and then tells us what our room assignments will be. Each teen counselor is responsible for four campers. She explains, "You will all have a teen counselor, or what I like to call a big sister, to look up to while you are here. If you need anything, please reach out to her."

I see Mrs. Thompson pick up her folder. She reads the master roster and begins to call out the cabin assignments. All the groups are named after a color. After she calls the Red, Yellow, and Gray groups, she says, "Raven, come on down!" like she's on *The Price Is Right*.

I walk to the front and stand next to Mrs. Thompson. Brooke is sitting right in the first row. She finally sees me. At first there is shock on her face but then her expression softens and she smiles and waves.

I look away.

Mrs. Thompson says, "Raven is responsible for the Green Campers. If you have a green folder, please come forward. That's Mercy, Cat, Hannah, and Robin. You will be in Cabin Three with Natasha and the Blue Campers."

The girls rush over to me, green folders in hand and smiling those shy first-day-of-camp smiles. I don't look at Brooke when the girls crowd around me, giving me hugs like they already know me.

DAY TWO: MONDAY

It looks like it snowed last night. The black cottonwood trees are fragrant and sweet smelling and the wind has blown their fluff across the campgrounds. The snow-like flowers stand out bright against the darkness of the fallen brown branches. I am sitting on the porch in a rocking chair across from Mercy, Cat, and Hannah, who are sitting on the steps.

We are waiting for Robin to come down so we can head over to the dining hall for breakfast. Natasha's group got to the showers first, so my girls had to wait. Natasha and I were smart enough to take our showers last night, because we know how these things go.

"I'll see you all over there," Natasha says to me as she leads the Blue Campers out the door, Brooke dragging behind them like the caboose of a train. I was relieved that she wasn't in my group, but having her this close to me, in the same cabin, is just as awkward.

We still haven't spoken to each other. What is there to say?

I watch Brooke as she walks to the dining hall and wonder what she is thinking, wonder what she knows about me, my mom. The other Blue Campers are walking side by side up the pathway, close to Natasha, who is leading the way up the steep hill. I watch Brooke trying to keep up, her plump legs climbing as fast as they can. I don't think Natasha or the other girls realize how far behind she is.

The food at Oak Creek is some of the best eating I've ever had. The head cook is from New Orleans, and everything about her meals reminds us of where she is from. The dining hall is a symphony of mouths chewing, mouths talking, mouths laughing, mouths yelling across the room. Mrs. Thompson makes an announcement that it is the last call for the kitchen and if anyone wants more, they should go up now.

The symphony continues. More mouths chewing, mouths talking, mouths laughing, mouths yelling across the room.

7

And then Mercy's voice cuts through all the noise, like a siren. "You're too fat to be getting seconds!"

I turn to see who Mercy is yelling at, getting ready to give my lecture about kindness and respect, because I am seventeen and that is what I am supposed to do, be an example. When I turn around, I see Brooke standing there with her tray, head down.

"Yeah," one of the Blue Campers says, "you think just because you got long hair and expensive things you're all that. But you're not. You could barely walk up the hill this morning. You need to go on a diet."

I don't know what Brooke's hair and belongings have to do with her weight. Sometimes, it's easier to be mean to a person than to admit that you wish you were that person.

All the girls except Robin laugh. I think maybe I should say something since I am a fake big sister to Mercy and a real big (half) sister to Brooke. If Mrs. Thompson was standing here, she'd be disappointed and tell me that she expects more from me. If Mom was standing here, she'd be disappointed and tell me it's not Brooke's fault my dad left. She'd tell me I can't go giving Brooke these feelings that really belong to Dad. But neither of them is standing here, so I don't have to do what I know they'd want me to do. Besides, before I can even open my mouth, Natasha is already handling it. "It's none of your business what she eats," Natasha says. She puts her arm around Brooke, like a big sister would.

I find the words I know I should say and reprimand Mercy

8

and the girl from the Blue group, but something in their eyes tells me they don't believe I am as upset as I am pretending to be. Once I threaten to tell Mrs. Thompson, they agree to apologize. Brooke doesn't even acknowledge them when they say, "Sorry." She just keeps her eyes straight ahead, not looking at me either.

The Green Campers and the Blue Campers walk over to the cabin where workshops are held. Robin walks close enough to Mercy and her clique to be one of them but also close enough to Brooke to say, *I see you, I know.* I notice Brooke struggling again to get up the hill. She is breathing hard and sweating.

I could walk slower, let the others go ahead and stay behind with Brooke, but instead, I walk with my Green Campers. They are my responsibility; they are the reason I am here.

Natasha and I are outside on the back porch waiting for the botany class to end. The black cottonwood trees are still shedding. It looks like someone made a wish and blew a million dandelions into the sky. I am imagining a million of my wishes coming true, wondering what it would be like to want nothing, when I hear the botany teacher say, "Black cottonwoods are also known as healing trees, as they are good for healing all types of pains and inflammations. Some say this tree possesses the balm of Gilead because of the nutrients that hide in the buds and bark. Throughout centuries people have made salves from the tree to heal all kinds of ailments."

When I hear this, I think of Grandma's gospel records and how she is always humming along with Mahalia Jackson:

There is a balm in Gilead,
there is a balm in Gilead.

The botany teacher says, "There was a time when there was no hospital to go to and people knew how to rely on the earth to supply what they needed, how to mend themselves."

There is a balm in Gilead
to make the wounded whole.

Natasha says, "You listening to me?"

I say yes, even though I am not because she is just talking about her boyfriend again, asking (but not really asking) if she should break up with him.

There is a balm in Gilead
to save a sin-sick soul.

DAY THREE: TUESDAY

For the rest of the day yesterday and all day today, at the campfire, and even as I lie in bed, all I can think about is how black cottonwoods bring healing. All I keep hearing is that song Grandma hums over and over, over and over.

Sometimes I feel discouraged,
you know and I feel like I can't go on.
Oh, but then the Holy Spirit revives my soul again.
Revives my soul, my soul again.

There is a balm in Gilead
to save a sin-sick soul.

Grandma believes God can heal *anything*. But I wonder.

DAY FOUR: WEDNESDAY

Every year of camp, day four is the day campers start getting homesick, so all of us counselors have planned a late-night talent show to get everyone laughing and having a good time. There's been stand-up comedy, Beyoncé lip syncs, and spoken-word poems. And now, Mrs. Thompson is getting the *Soul Train* line started. She sashays down the middle of the makeshift aisle as we clap and rock side to side. Each of us has a turn, all of us Black and brown girls dancing in a cabin in the middle of the woods. I imagine that underneath this cabin, the roots from trees are trembling from the bass and that leaves are swaying and dancing with us.

Mrs. Thompson thrives on nights like this. She is twirling and shake, shake, shaking, yelling, "This. Is. My. Song." Marvin Gaye's "Got to Give It Up" is the song that sets off our dance party every year. We usually play old-school music, because Mrs. Thompson says the music we are listening to these days isn't really music. "Come on now, I'm older than *all* of you in here. Don't tell me you can't keep up. Come on now." Mrs. Thompson grabs Brooke and tries to dance with her down the *Soul Train* line. "Come on, now, child," Mrs. Thompson says.

Brooke doesn't move.

Cat whispers to Mercy, "She don't look like she dance at all."

Mercy laughs and says, "Living all the way out there in Lake Oswego, she probably never even seen a *Soul Train* line."

Mrs. Thompson is so into her dancing, she doesn't even notice the tension between the Blue and Green Campers. "Natasha? Raven? One of you come help me out."

Mrs. Thompson grabs me and we dance together down the aisle doing old-school dances (that I only know because Dad taught them to me). I get to the end of the line and I am out of breath and sweating and laughing. I look back at Brooke, who is standing in the same place, like a stone.

DAY FIVE: THURSDAY

The sun has said good night and now we are sitting under an ocean of stars. They shimmer like the glitter I once used on a Father's Day card. It was after Dad left us. I never sent it.

If it weren't for the fire, it would be darker than dark out.

The rain starts and stops, but we are not going inside without at least one campfire story. Kyle, one of the other teen counselors, taught everyone the best method for roasting marshmallows. We squish the white sponge between graham crackers and squares of chocolate and feast while she whispers tales of the Oak Creek Monster.

"The spirit of a little girl who died a long time ago haunts these woods," Kyle tells them.

Mercy breaks in, "How did she die?"

Kyle rolls her eyes—she hates being interrupted and prefers to pace out the story for dramatic effect. "Well, there are many theories. Some say the girl was walking with her friends by the creek and slipped in by accident and drowned. But others say her friends pushed her in. For months, everyone mourned the little girl and shunned the friends accused of murdering her. But one year later, on the anniversary of her death, the little girl was seen walking around the woods. People believe the girl faked her death to escape her evil stepmother and that she lives in the wilderness, surviving off the land. Many visitors have spotted her hiding in the tree house at the end of Willow Road."

"There's no tree house down the road!" Mercy says.

"There is, too," Hannah tells her.

Other campers agree.

"I saw it when we got dropped off, right at the bottom of the road!" Brooke says.

Robin agrees. "Me too." Robin scoots closer to me. Brooke scoots closer to her.

Kyle looks at all of us teen counselors and asks, "Should I let them know the rest?"

This hasn't been rehearsed, so we all give different answers, nodding and shaking our heads, saying yes and no all at once.

Kyle continues, "Well, be careful, because the Oak Creek Monster gets lonely and likes to take campers to keep her company so she's not living out here alone."

Mercy stuffs the rest of the s'more in her mouth and blurts out, "This is stupid. There's no such thing." She stands and motions for Cat to come with her. "Let's go back to the cabin. These stories are boring and you're all a bunch of scaredy-cats."

"I'm not scared," Brooke mumbles.

Mercy says, "Well, you should be. You won't be able to out-run the Oak Creek Monster. If it runs after us, you'll be the first to be captured."

The girls laugh and laugh. I stand up and Brooke's eyes turn hopeful, like she thinks I am coming to tell them to stop. I wish our eyes didn't meet, that I didn't see how disappointed she looks as I walk past her, into the cabin, to get out of the heavy rain.

I hear Brooke say, "I'm not afraid."

Mercy says, "Prove it."

DAY SIX: FRIDAY

It's six o'clock in the morning and Natasha is shaking me awake, whisper-yelling, "I can't find Brooke! I can't find Brooke! Mercy dared her to find the Oak Creek Monster."

I get out of bed, put on my shoes, grab a flashlight and my phone, and throw my arms into my rain jacket. I run outside, heading to the path that winds around the back of the campus.

I am seventeen and my father's daughter is out wandering in the rain. I am seventeen and I should have taken responsibility for watching her, should have stood up for her, made her feel like she belonged so she wouldn't think she had to prove anything by taking a silly dare.

The path is slick and muddy because of the rain, and I can only see right in front of me because this flashlight isn't as bright as I thought it would be. I shine the light in all the cabins we use for classrooms, the dining hall, the game room. I can't find her. I jog down to the bottom of the hill. I flash the light all around, thinking maybe I will see her under a tree, waiting for the storm to pass. I shine the light up, moving it around and around at the sky, and then I see it.

The tree house.

The tree house is more like a tree mansion. Not only did Brooke find it, but when I knock and the door opens, she is inside sitting at a small kitchen table drinking hot apple cider with a gray-haired woman. The tree house is a cozy country cottage on the inside and is decorated with photos of smiling children and adults. The woman sees me eyeing them and tells me they are her children and grandchildren. "And you are?" she asks.

"I'm—I'm her sister," I say.

Brooke's eyes meet mine and she sets her mug on the table and stands up.

I apologize for the interruption of the woman's night and explain the myth about who she is and tell her all about the dare. She finishes my sentence, chuckling. "I know, I know. I enjoy playing along," she says.

"What do you mean?" I ask.

"Well, I'm actually the owner of this land. I manage the grounds. But I know what the rumors are and it makes for a good story, so sometimes I give a little wave there, a little howl here. You know, scare a few of the campers who come searching. But tonight, I saw something different in your sister's eyes. And when I saw her standing outside, I just had to open the door and let her in." The woman rinses the mugs in the sink and wipes her hands on her apron. She looks at Brooke and says, "You are very brave, facing your fears. I hope you are brave enough to conquer any monsters—literal or figurative—that come into your life."

Brooke smiles.

"And what a thoughtful big sister you have," the woman

continues, "to come looking for you."

Brooke blurts out, "She's my half sister."

I am not sure if she meant to hurt me or if she is just telling the truth. Maybe both.

The old woman says, "There's no such thing as a half sister." She walks over to the door, opens it. "Just like the moon," she says. "There's no such thing as a half moon either."

Brooke looks at me for confirmation and I shrug.

The woman motions us to the door. "Look at the sky. Sure, there's a half moon tonight that we can see, but the full moon is always there," she tells us. "We see the moon because as it revolves around the Earth, only the part facing the sun is visible to us." The woman stops talking and takes a long look at us. "Most times we only see part of a thing, but there's always more to see, more to know." She winks at me, says, "You understand what I'm saying?"

"Yes, ma'am," I answer. "We better get going. If I don't return soon, the others will worry." I take my phone out and see that I have ten missed calls from Natasha. I text her back, *She's safe. She's with me.*

Just before we walk out the door, Brooke says, "Wait—I need a picture. Mercy said I had to get proof."

"Well, of course. It didn't happen if there's no proof," the woman tells us. She runs her fingers through her hair as if to fix it, but it falls in the same exact place.

For the first picture, the woman tries her best to look like a monster. She doesn't smile and her eyes look lifeless, but then she breaks out into a laugh. I delete it and we pose again, taking a selfie with Brooke in the middle. After we take the photo, we say our goodbyes.

I walk with Brooke back to our cabin. Our feet break up puddles and stamp the mud with the soles of our shoes. The wind is blowing, and no matter how tight I tie my hood, it flies off. Brooke doesn't have a hood, hat, or umbrella, so her hair is a wildfire spreading and spreading. The black cottonwood trees with their healing balm release more of their white fluff, making it feel like we're walking in a snowstorm. Our faces and coats are covered.

I am walking fast so we can hurry out of the rain, but Brooke can't keep up, so I slow down, take Brooke's hand.

"Are we going to get in trouble?" Brooke asks.

"Mrs. Thompson will never know."

"Are we going to tell that there is no monster?"

"They don't have to know that. We can tell them you found the tree house, that you went in." A gust of wind blows so hard it almost pushes me forward. "I'll tell them how brave you are."

DAY SEVEN: SATURDAY

I have spent seven whole days with my sister.

Today is the last day of camp. Most times I am happy to

see the campers go. Most times I am ready to get back to my regular life. But not this time.

Word has spread that Brooke broke the curse. She met the Oak Creek Monster and lived to tell the story. No one else has done that. It is all everyone is talking about until Mrs. Thompson comes into the cafeteria. Then, all the voices fade to whispers and everyone keeps pointing and oohing and aahing at the girl who looked a monster in the eyes and survived.

After breakfast the Blue and Green Campers head back to our cabin to pack. It is tradition that the last day is a free day, which usually ends up being me and Natasha doing the girls' hair. After a week of being in and out of the rain, most of us need a touch-up, some a complete do-over. I spend the afternoon braiding and twisting. I have done Robin's and Cat's hair, and then I ask Brooke, "Do you want me to do yours?"

She sits in the chair in front of me and I start parting and flat-twisting the front. The girls orbit around her. "So tell us again what happened," Robin says.

Brooke retells the story of meeting the Oak Creek Monster. The girls respond with "Really?" and "But weren't you scared?" and "I can't believe you did that." I fan the flame, telling them "You should have seen her" and "I'm so proud."

Mercy sighs. "All this talk about Brooke conquering the Oak Creek Monster, but there's no proof. We said you had to prove it."

I take my phone out of my pocket just as Brooke's voice

rises, "You think I had time to get proof while I was escaping a monster? Besides, my sister was there—she saw everything. She's my proof."

I put my phone back in my pocket, keep our secret. Watch everyone looking at me, at Brooke, as we rotate around our sun.

"You two are sisters?" Mercy asks.

Brooke says, "Yeah," so matter-of-fact that no one says anything else about it. Natasha looks at me and, with my eyes I tell her I'll explain it all later.

Standing here with a handful of Brooke's hair in my palm makes me wonder what it would have been like to grow up with a little sister. Natasha has two younger brothers who she helped teach how to read and tie shoes and throw punches on the playground if someone was messing with them. I think about how even though I have Mom and plenty of cousins and friends, I don't know what it's like to have a sibling.

Maybe it would be like this. Me doing her hair and chaperoning sleepovers, me making sure she knows which way to walk, how to get where she's trying to go. Me knowing that I would do anything to make sure she is safe.

Just before the campers board the bus to leave, Brooke turns to me and whispers, "Don't forget to send me the picture," with a smile stretched across her face. She takes my phone and puts her number in it. When she gets on the bus, she sits with

Robin, and as they leave they wave big elaborate goodbyes. I wave back until I can't see them anymore.

I take out my phone to text Brooke the picture, but when I look at the photo, I realize it is blurry and Brooke is not even looking at the camera and half of the woman's face is cut out of the frame so you can't really tell who we're standing next to. I text the photo to Brooke anyway because I promised I would. It's not the proof we thought we'd have, but we'll always have this memory; we'll always be able to tell the story.

I head back to my cabin. The wind has settled and the branches of the black cottonwood trees are still. There are no snow-seeds blowing furiously in the sky, but remnants from last night's storm cover the damp ground. The sweet fragrance from the fallen fluff fills the air.

I breathe it in, sing Grandma's song.

BLACK ENOUGH

VARIAN JOHNSON

"Hurry up, Cam," Myron yelled from the other side of the door. "It's not like staring in the mirror is gonna make you any prettier."

"Five more minutes," I said as I checked myself out once more. My fade was a little higher on the sides than I liked, but still good. I'd convinced Myron to take me to the barbershop first thing that morning. Usually I hated going to the barbershop in South Carolina. It was always noisy—way louder than my usual barbershop back in Texas—with a lot of old men talking over each other, arguing about stuff I didn't even care about, and telling me how good kids like me and Myron had it now. But today, none of that bothered me. The three-hour wait was totally going to pay off.

My clothes were brand-new, too. I'd bought them a month

ago but was wearing them for the first time today. Everything looked great—except my shoes. After leaving the barbershop, Myron took me to the mall and convinced me to splurge on a pair of all-white retro Air Jordans. I'm sure they looked good on other sixteen-year-olds, but not on me. They made my already large feet seem extra huge. And they were super expensive compared to my usual Vans.

But they'd be worth it if they impressed Jessica Booker.

I hadn't seen Jess since last year. I had liked her for a long time, and had always hung out with her and her sisters during my summer vacations at Grandma's house here in Franklin. Last year, I promised myself that I wasn't going back to Austin without making a move. It took me up until the last day of vacation before I was able to summon up the courage, but I finally gave Jess a quick peck right on the lips.

It was the best kiss I'd ever given a girl.

It was also the only kiss I'd ever given a girl.

But then, before I could run off, Jess grabbed my hand and pulled me in for another kiss.

And that was most certainly *not* a peck.

If I had known kissing could be like that, I would have tried a long time ago.

But that was the high point of our romance. We'd tried to keep in contact over the school year—sending texts and messages through Facebook—but by Christmastime we'd lost touch. Well, if I was being honest, *she* dropped off. It took me about two weeks of additional texting before I finally realized she wasn't going to reply back with anything other than wooden, one-word replies.

I pulled out my phone and took a quick snapshot of my shoes to post on Instagram and Facebook. Then I texted my friends at home and told them to like and comment on the photo. Petty, I know, but the more likes I had, the better chance I had of my post showing up on Jess's feed.

Myron knocked again, then opened the bedroom door. "Come on, Cam," he said. "You know how Grandma is. If we aren't out the door by nine, she won't let us go anywhere." Then he looked me up and down and shook his head. "The kicks are nice, but you still look corny."

"Takes one to know one," I said, which was kind of a weak comeback, but it was the best I could do on short notice. But he did look just as goofy as I did, with his bright blue shoes. Myron usually wore Jordans, but today he was sporting a pair of KD 10s. "The finals edition," he'd bragged when he first showed them off.

Uncle Greg—Myron's dad—and my dad were twins. After college, Uncle Greg returned to Franklin to take a management job at the auto plant while Dad took an engineering job in Austin, Texas. For as long as I could remember, Mom and Dad would send me back to spend the summer at Grandma's house—and I loved it. Myron and I usually got along, and there was always a bunch of other kids running around the neighborhood.

Like Jessica Booker.

That was one of the biggest ways that Franklin was different from my neighborhood back in Austin. At home, the only time I hung with my friends was when they came over to my house to play video games or watch movies. We never went outside—Arpit was allergic to everything, and I didn't like the hot weather. But here, kids hung out everywhere. On people's front porches. At the strip mall. In the parking lot of Hardee's. Everywhere.

Maybe I was wrong—maybe kids back at home did that, too. Maybe me and my friends were the only ones stuck inside.

I followed Myron down the hallway and into the den. Grandma sat in front of the TV, flipping between stations. She worked at the small community college—she was still in her slacks and a button-up shirt, though she'd left her heels at the door. She eventually settled on a news show, then turned to us.

Or rather, she looked at our feet.

"Cameron, you're buying those horrible shoes, too?"

"They're retro, Grandma," I said.

"Hmph. Some things probably need to stay in the past." She shook her head. "But I'm betting those new clothes and shoes have more to do with trying to impress Eileen Thompson's granddaughter than anything else."

"Grandma . . ." I could feel a goofy smile forming on my face. I turned to try to hide it. "Jessica and I are only friends."

She waved her brown, wrinkled finger at me. "Boy, you've

had a hankering for that girl ever since you first laid eyes on her," she said. "Might as well have it stamped across your forehead. Your nose is so wide open, you can smell Jessica's perfume from all the way across town."

Grandma was always spouting out those old sayings. I had tried to use some at school a few years ago, but my friends had no idea what I was talking about.

"I already told Cam that he doesn't even have a shot with Jessica," Myron said. He bent down and whipped an imaginary smudge from his shoe. "She's a feminist now, always wanting to argue. Before you know it, she'll have everyone in dashikis, eating kale, and giving up pork."

"First, there's nothing wrong with being a feminist," Grandma said. "Don't you two want women to have the same rights as men?"

Both Myron and I nodded.

"Good, then you're feminists," she said. "That being said, ain't no way in the world I'm eating kale. And I've been eating pork chops for too long to give them up now." She finally turned back to the television. "Y'all have fun. Be back home by midnight."

We nodded. We'd take a midnight curfew any day. Myron's mom was way stricter than Grandma. She'd have us back at home by nine and tucked into bed by ten.

"And be safe," she yelled to us as we stepped outside. "Don't go walking around like you ain't got no common sense."

As soon as we got to the car, Myron switched out his sneakers for a pair of slip-on athletic sandals. "Driving causes a crease in the shoes," he said. "Gotta keep them fresh for as long as I can."

That was the dumbest thing I'd ever heard. What was he going to do—walk like a duck?

With his shoes safely stashed in the back seat, Myron pulled out of the driveway and cranked up the radio. An old-school rap song thumped out of the speakers. Myron leaned back in his seat and started bobbing his head to the beat. I rolled my eyes, then opened the center console.

"Hey!" he yelled. "What are you—"

"Just looking to see what else you have in here." I pulled out a CD. "*Guys and Dolls*?"

"It was for a play," he mumbled. "Plus, the theater chicks at school really dig Broadway."

"Yeah, right." I was sure that if I searched his phone, I'd find a lot more show tunes. Not that it was even a big deal. Myron was a really good singer, actor, and dancer. When he was younger, he bragged about wanting to be a "triple threat." Last we talked, he was even considering majoring in theater in college—if Uncle Greg let him.

I returned the CD and closed the console. "Okay, so tell me about Jessica again."

He groaned. "Man, how many times do I have to say it— you ain't got no shot with her. I bet she doesn't even like guys anymore. Especially not guys like you."

That last sentence hung in the air for a moment.

Especially not guys like you.

Myron turned down the radio and cleared his throat. "Cam, what I mean is—"

"No, it's okay," I said. "I get it."

And I did. I knew what kids called me behind my back. An Oreo. A Black boy trying to be white. I wasn't hard enough. Hood enough. *Woke* enough. If anything, Myron should have said "guys like us." With his love for musical theater, he fell in the same group as I did. He could try to wear fancy shoes and blast rap music, but he was who he was.

"Anyway," he finally said, "you should be more focused on Tiffany. You know she's been asking about you all year. And you know she's into smart, high-yellow dudes. Even corny, no-game fellas like you."

I just laughed. I liked Tiffany a lot—as a friend—but she was a little too wishy-washy for my tastes. Always into the newest fad—whether that be shoes, clothes, music, whatever. But she was also crazy smart. She'd only finished her sophomore year and had already damn near aced the SAT. She was planning to major in engineering in college. If Dad caught wind of that, he'd for sure try to set us up himself.

I opened up Facebook to see if the guys from home had liked my photo. They had, along with a few other people from school. No lie—it felt pretty good.

I went to Jess's page, but she hadn't posted anything in a few days. Then I went to Myron's page. It took a minute or two to scroll through the usual junk that he stuck on his page before I finally found his post about the party. Jess had mentioned that she was going to be there in the comments, but she hadn't added anything more to her original message.

Myron had told me that Tarik lived on the other side of the city. But as we pulled into the gated neighborhood and passed all the McMansions, I realized I was totally wrong about where I thought we were going.

"Let me guess," Myron said, glancing at me out of the corner of his eye. "You thought we were going to the hood just because my boy's name is Tarik and he's Black."

"No . . . ," I mumbled, clearly busted.

Myron quickly parked, opened his door, and began to switch shoes. He acknowledged a few kids as they passed by—a head nod to a group of Black dudes, and a more subdued hand wave to a group of white kids.

The house was full of people. The music was turned up loud—booming bass with rapid-fire rap lyrics on top—and I swear I could feel my teeth rattling with each thump of the tower speakers. The large, wall-mounted flat-screen was showing the game—Golden State against Cleveland. The Warriors were way up in points, and it was only the second quarter.

"You sure she'll be here, right?" I asked as we stepped farther into the den.

"She's here," he said. "Anyone who's anybody will be here. Just don't start whining and begging to leave when you crash and burn at Jess's feet."

I followed Myron and joined the group of Black kids we'd seen outside. Myron gave them daps.

"Nice kicks, my man," one of the guys said to Myron.

"'Preciate it," he replied. "Gotta step up my game for the ladies." Then he nodded toward me and introduced me to the group.

They looked me up and down. "Those are the Jordan 1 Mid Retros, right?" another boy said. "*Nice*."

"Thank you," I said.

Thank you!? Who said that? Why couldn't I say what Myron said? Or even something like plain old *Thanks*.

"Y'all hooping at the park tomorrow?" Myron asked.

They nodded. Myron wasn't a great basketball player, but he understood the game way better than I did. Me and my friends weren't into sports.

The conversation switched from basketball to football. The other guys would ask me a question every now and then, but I mostly tried to keep my mouth shut.

"Why you so quiet?" Myron whispered as everyone turned to watch a replay of a dunk on the television.

I shrugged. "I'm trying to figure out what I'm going to say to Jess when I see her."

He gave me a look but didn't say anything. Then he and I

were pulled into a nearby conversation, this time with a group of mostly white kids.

"Nice shoes, man," one of them said.

"Thanks," Myron replied. "We picked them up today. Have y'all met my cousin, Cameron?"

The change in his tone was immediate. Less bass. More enunciation. I wondered if he was even aware that he was doing it.

I quickly introduced myself. Most of them shook my hand, but one overeager guy leaned in to give me a dap-hug, saying, "What's up, brother."

And I said the same thing back, just like it was natural.

Because here was the thing—it *was* natural. This was how I interacted with kids all the time. I didn't have to code switch at my school. There weren't many other Black kids to code switch with. We lived in a very affluent neighborhood. ("A *white* neighborhood," Grandma would say whenever Dad said this.) Even though most of my friends were white, a few weren't. Arpit was from India, and Oscar was from Brazil. But it wasn't like I talked differently around them than I did with my white friends. Honestly, we didn't *want* to code switch. We were trying to sound like all our other . . . affluent classmates.

After a few minutes, Myron tapped me on the shoulder. "To your right," he whispered. "But don't turn too fast."

I waited for Myron to pull away, then slowly shifted my gaze. There was Jess, looking as good as ever. Her brown hair was pulled into a ponytail, and she was wearing one of those summer dresses that made all us guys go crazy. As our eyes met, her lips faltered for a second, before she finally offered up a small smile and waved at me. I did the same.

Before I knew it, I was crossing the room.

"Hey Jess," I said once I'd reached her group.

"Hey," she said back. No kiss. No hug. Not even a hand-shake. "Guys, this is Cameron. Myron's cousin."

"Hey."

"Wassup, man."

"How's it going?"

I took in each person's greeting, thinking how Jessica must like being around kids like this. Once the last person in the group introduced himself, I took a deep breath and said, "Wazzup, peeps."

God, did that sound as horrible out loud as it did to my ears?

Everyone else nodded back at me, but I noticed a flicker of a frown cross Jess's face.

The discussion turned back to—what else?—basketball. I waited for a lull in the conversation, then threw out the little bit of basketball knowledge I had.

"That cat Steph Curry is amazing," I said. "Best playa on the court. Breaking ankles with each step."

"Yeah, but no one has a crossover as sweet as AI, right?" one of the guys replied.

"Um. Yeah," I said. I had no idea who they were even

talking about. Was there a person with those initials on the Warriors?

I caught sight of Jess again. This time the frown was full-on across her face.

"Cam, can I talk to you for a second?" But with the way she took my arm and guided me away, it was clear she wasn't really asking.

At least she was finally making physical contact. Progress, I guess.

She led me outside, but as soon as we stepped off the front steps, she let go of me and crossed her arms.

"What are you doing?" she asked.

"Um . . . talking?"

"You sound like a fool," she said.

"I'm just . . ." I shook my head. There was no way I could explain what I was trying to do. It sounded too stupid to admit.

"And those shoes?" she continued. "Since when did you start wearing Jordans? You think that makes you hood or something?"

"Myron said they looked good."

"Myron is an idiot with too much of his daddy's money to spend." She swiped a bang away from her face. "You don't even like basketball. Tell me the truth—did you know that AI stood for Allen Iverson?"

This was not the reception I was expecting when I'd dreamed about seeing Jess again. I mean, I hadn't been holding my breath for love at first sight, but I didn't think she'd be so upset. "Jess, are you mad at me?"

"Cam . . ."

"Just tell me what happened," I said. "Why did you stop texting me? What did I do that was so wrong?"

Her eyes were warm. Kind. But not loving. More like how our vet looked when she told us we had to put down our dog. "We really shouldn't talk about this now," Jess said.

No way was I letting this go. "Just say it. I don't want to spend the rest of my summer wondering what I did." I stood up taller and steeled myself for her response. "Is it because I'm . . . *me*?"

"What does that mean?"

"You know," I said. "I don't talk the right way. Or dress the right way. Most of my friends are white. I'm not good at basketball." I glanced at the ground—I couldn't look at her while saying the words. "Did you stop talking to me because I'm not Black enough?"

She actually laughed. Doubled over, even.

"It's not that funny," I said.

"Sorry," she replied. "It's just— Cam, what does that even mean? Not Black enough?" she finally said. "Does your birth certificate say you're Black?"

"Um, yeah."

"Your school records?"

I nodded again.

"And is your momma or daddy Black?"

"Of course they are."

"Then congratulations. You're Black." Her words sounded a lot like what Grandma had said earlier about being a feminist.

I thrust my hands into my pockets. "Then what did I do to make you stop talking to me? I had to have done *something*."

Now it was her turn to look away. Those lips that were so perfect a year ago were now taut and pursed. "Do you know what happened in December? When I went ghost and fell off from all the messages?" She waited for me to shake my head. "Linton McCants was shot by the police."

"Who's that?"

"A kid from the neighborhood," she said. "He wasn't doing anything wrong. You know, other than being Black in the wrong part of town."

"I didn't know him," I said.

"You've met him before, but you probably don't remember. Anyway, he was shot in the leg, and everyone in the neighborhood was real shook up about it. I posted about it online. *Everybody* posted about it. It was all over Facebook, Twitter, and Instagram."

I thought back to her Facebook page from around that time. I *had* seen something about a shooting. But I hadn't realized the kid was from Franklin.

"And do you know what you had on your page on the same day?" This time she didn't wait for me to respond. "A photo of you and your all-white Academic Bowl team, everybody grinning like the damn Cheshire cat."

I started to reach out to her, to try to comfort her, but I stopped when she pulled back. "Like I said, I didn't know him," I replied.

"But you knew *me*. You had to have seen what I posted—you were on my page every day. Hell, even Myron put something on his page." Her voice was beginning to shake. "I wasn't looking for you to start protesting or anything. Just a simple acknowledgment of what happened would have been okay. But you were so geeked about your stupid win over whatever yuppie school you played against, you didn't even realize what happened."

"I just . . . if I had known he was from here—"

"Oh, so you care if he's from here, but you don't if he's from some other place?"

I rubbed my face. "Jess, I didn't mean it like that."

I don't know if she was even listening to me. "I mean, I knew we were different. But I didn't care about that stuff. I liked that you were so easygoing. So goofy, even. And smart. It was all really cute." Her eyes hardened. "But unlike you, I live in the real world. I can't just ignore stuff." She started pacing, twisting her hair around her finger with each step. "I mean . . . God! Aren't you mad?! Even a little bit?"

"I am!" Now I was yelling, but I didn't care. "I paid attention when Trayvon Martin was killed. Same with Philando

Castile. And all the others. And I noticed when all their shooters—"

"You mean murderers."

"Whatever. When all their killers got off. But after a while . . . it happens so much . . . you just stop paying attention."

"Hmph. Not paying attention. That's real dangerous coming from the guy living in an all-white neighborhood. I know you think all those white boys are your friends, but I'd bet anything that—"

She stopped talking as the front door opened, allowing all the noise and fun from inside to spill out. A group of kids stepped onto the porch, then closed the door behind them. They passed us, and then it was just me and Jess and the night and the silence stewing between us.

"And now you show up after a year with all the white folks. Trying to talk like you're from the hood. Wearing a pair of shoes that you don't even like. And it just pisses me off that you'd be so shallow to think that how you talk and how you dress would change my opinion of you."

She took a step away from me, moving toward the house. "As much as I like you, I can't be with a guy who doesn't understand where I come from. But look, we can still be friends."

She took another step.

She was almost at the door.

"I'll see you around, okay?"

And then she was gone.

I stood there, watching the door where she disappeared. I could feel my heart still pumping fast in my chest, in my ears, a thump loud enough to rival the music inside the house.

Was this a test? Should I follow her back into the house?

But even if I did that, I had no idea what I would say to change her mind.

Once my heartbeat had settled—or more like, once my heart had sunk all the way to my toes—I walked over to Myron's car. I sat down on the hood, pulled out my phone, and went back to Myron's Facebook page. Sure, it was full of stupid video clips and pictures of all his shoes, but he also included some real stuff. Lots of information about Linton McCants, the boy who had been shot. Myron had even helped to raise money to cover Linton's hospital bills.

I kept scrolling and eventually found other things. Quotes from Shakespeare. Langston Hughes. Tupac. Videos of Myron giving all these amazing monologues. And even pictures of him and his friends—Black, white, Latino, Asian. He looked comfortable in every photo.

I had seen all of this on his page before. I was sure that I had. I just hadn't paid attention.

Myron was right when he said *guys like you* instead of *guys like us*. He may have been a chameleon, but deep down, he knew who he was. He could code switch, but he always knew what was real beneath the clothes and the talk.

It was about an hour later when he eventually found me. He didn't say anything about Jess. He just motioned for me to get in the car.

Once he pulled away from the curb, he reached over to turn up the radio, but I stopped him.

"Myron," I said, "tell me about Linton McCants."

WARNING: COLOR MAY FADE

LEAH HENDERSON

"Almost there," I whisper, straining as my fingers grasp for the brick ledge. Flecks of fuchsia and gamboge paint crust over bits of my brown skin. A smear of cobalt shines on the cuff of my sleeve. Evidence. The window eases up without a sound as wind screams through empty branches behind me. Heat from the radiator blasts my face as I lean in from the cold. I hoist my upper body inside. My heart thuds in my ears.

In twenty-four hours, all my secrets will come out. No more hiding. Parents' Weekend and Mom and Dad can't be avoided.

I close the window against the New England chill, pressing my forehead against the glass. I've made it. I've actually made it. And no one knows what I've done—at least not yet.

The night outside is settled, silent, even with my little commotion. No prying eyes or raised blinds meet me as I stare across the dark, sparsely lit quad. I let my bag slump to the floor and flick off my sneakers. At my desk, the never-mailed early-admission application peeks out from behind a stack of books. I should've tossed it weeks ago, but I can't. Years of work went into those pages. Work I'm now willing to jeopardize.

Dad's going to find out about it at some point soon, but not tonight.

My notebook lies open. Assignments unfinished. And despite nervous adrenaline rushing through me, focusing on medieval civilizations might calm the thumping in my chest, but a hot shower in an empty bathroom sounds even better.

Peeling off my hoodie and leggings stirs up a nose burn of turpentine, my favorite scent. The three-a.m. quiet in a freshman house is a perk of being an upper-class dorm proctor—mandatory lights-out for everyone else. I wrap my robe around me and grab my shower cap and caddy.

When I step into the hall, I overlook the beams of light streaming out from under a few closed doors—the telltale signs of all-nighters in progress. As long as no one makes a sound, this is another rule I'm willing to ignore.

The motion-sensor light brightens as the bathroom door swings open. A muffled sniffle interrupts the silence.

So much for a relaxing shower.

"Hello? It's Nivia. Is everything okay?" I step into the stark white-tiled room that always smells of sweet pears and lilacs.

Finding someone sniffling in the bathroom in the early-morning hours at Caswell is never strange. It's almost a rite of passage.

And it's rarely about a crush or missing home. Pressure to meet expectations gets to all of us. Everyone cracks at some point. Mini meltdowns are the price paid for a Caswell Prep seal of approval.

I wonder if Dad or Grandpa ever bowed to the pressure when they were here. But somehow I doubt it. Mom either. Even with being some of the only Black students in a sea of white, I can't imagine any of them being unsure of themselves or what they wanted when they went here or afterward. For them, the law has been their way up from the beginning.

"Want water?" I ask, pushing away the thoughts. I reach for a cup from the dispenser and fill it without waiting for a response.

I slide it under the stall and wait.

"Thanks."

Without her saying another word, I know exactly who's on the other side of the door. "You want to talk or should I go?" I say even though the shower is calling out to me.

"I'm okay, Niv. Really."

"You know I know you're lying, right?" A hint of a smile plays in my voice. I cross my arms and lean against a sink, waiting.

Anxiety is the nastiest beast for my old roommate. But it's only ever this bad when she thinks she's failed, and she never fails.

Then the toilet flushes and the stall lock slides back.

A second later, Ryan emerges, sandy blond hair matted, blue eyes rimmed red, blotches on her pale cheeks. "Should I even ask why you're still up?" she asks, sniffling, and throws the crumpled cup in the trash.

She's always been good at deflecting questions she wants to ignore.

"Why are *you*?" I throw back.

She reaches up and scratches at the side of my face, flicking away a tiny patch of dried glue.

Her gaze settles on the tiny cerulean splotches on the back of my hand. "You been finishing your project?"

I shove my arm deeper into a fold of robe. "Something like that. You good?"

She twists on a faucet and scoops water into her mouth to gargle. Then she turns to me. Her eyes always tell a different story than the rest of her. This time I can't read it.

"Do you know your truth?"

I don't have to ask what she means. Her brain is filled with the same thing as mine—the Tri-school Jabec Beard Art Prize, which besides carrying major bragging rights comes with a prestigious summer course at the illustrious Beaux-Arts de Paris and a monthlong shadowing of an eminent artist. The prompt of this year's prize is imprinted on every senior art student's brain. *If tomorrow were your last, would you have told your authentic story? Every time you create art: Tell. Your. Truth.*

"I mean, we're only seventeen. How are we supposed to know our truth if we always do what's expected of us?" Ryan asks.

"Then don't do what's expected." This escapes my lips as if I've always believed it. As if I've always challenged expectations.

"Like it's that easy." She tucks a few loose strands of hair behind her ear, a nervous habit. "We only have two days left, and everything I show Ms. Teresi *isn't deep enough*." She throws up air quotes. "What does that even mean? You think kids from Eldridge or Alcott know how to get deep?"

"Let's hope not," I confess. Competition is steep enough between Caswell seniors. No way I want to think about what our sister schools are bringing to the table.

"I don't know what to do anymore. My entry has to be the best, Niv." She says this like there's no other option in life.

"Don't create what's expected then. Do what you want." I love how I can shell out advice but can hardly take it myself.

"It's not that simple." A slight whine creeps into her words. "You wouldn't understand."

I ignore the sting. Ryan has always carried her own spotlight. "Well, if it makes you feel any better, my truth is still working its way out of me too."

"I feel sick every time I think about it." Ryan traces a finger along the tiled wall. "They're all going to be there. I have to win. If I don't, *they* won't understand."

Her "they" is her family during Parents' Weekend. For her, art has always been the way up. Though I'm not sure how much higher she actually needs to go. While policy and legislation are my family's universe, art is her family's world. They're gallery owners, collectors, architects, and ginormous donors to everything art-related.

And she's right; they won't understand if she doesn't get the prize. It's all about the bragging rights for them. Her family's connections pretty much guarantee her entry into any art school she's interested in.

"I have to win," she says again, as if I hadn't heard her the first time. But I don't want to hear her. She's not the only one who wants to win.

White campus security jeeps create a barrier in front of Eckhart Gallery, blocking students' entry to their classes downstairs. But Headmaster Ewing hustles through in his signature navy suit and Caswell hunter-green bow tie, disappearing inside the highly coveted addition to our campus.

"What's happening?" someone asks as I reach the cluster of students decked out in their uniforms.

"Vandalism, I think," an underclassman I don't know

offers. "I heard a Jabec piece got torn down."

"No way!" My classmate Logan readjusts the faded baseball cap turned backward on his head. "The real police would be all over that. No way rent-a-cops can handle this."

The idea of *real* police has me ready to turn the other way, but Caswell would rather handle problems in-house than cast the school in an unfavorable light. There won't be police.

"Headmaster Ewing, is everything okay?" Ryan comes out of nowhere, stepping up beside me in her tailored navy school blazer and skirt, and hunter-green school tie and sweater. Her hair, flat-iron straight now, is held in place by a hunter-green scarf, the exact shade of our school colors, patterned with tiny foxes and tied like a headband. The same scarf she gave a couple of us as welcome-back presents after fall break. And of course it's school-code approved. Her perfectly arched eyebrows meet in concern. Not a blotch or dark circle in sight. Like her midnight meltdown never happened.

"Yes, yes, it's all in hand," Headmaster Ewing says. His voice is always the perfect balance of polite authority and rigid expectations. I wonder if he, like Ryan, ever tires of being so put together. He gives a nod. His ash-brown hair, sprouting gray at his temples, remains in perfect place. Then he turns to the rest of us. "Apologies for the delay, everyone. There's an unexpected addition to our gallery; however, it will not disrupt the day any further. Please make your way down to the class wing in an orderly fashion."

Everything Caswell students do is orderly. That's part of the programming.

"Nivia!" Headmaster Ewing calls out, and tips his head my way.

I nearly jump out of my skin. He and Dad were Caswell football teammates in ancient times. So him saying hi shouldn't be a big deal. But it is.

"I look forward to seeing your father this weekend."

I'm not sure if I give a smile or a grimace. Until that very second, for almost an hour I've successfully blocked out that my parents are coming, even though they've never missed a Caswell parents' event since my brother and sister went here. I try to speak, even grunt, but before I can, Headmaster Ewing moves on.

Now I'm the one who's gonna be sick.

"You okay?" Ryan asks, holding up her palm so I don't step on her foot as I sway backward.

I manage a squeak in response.

"Move along, everyone," Mr. Ivers, the art history teacher, advises in a harried tone as students file into the gallery and head for the basement classrooms. But that doesn't stop anyone from looking, especially me. I lag behind, near the railing, taking an extra moment to peer inside the main exhibit hall.

There it is. Loud, proud, colorful, and speaking some kind of truth.

"This is serious," Mr. Ivers complains to my teacher, Ms. Teresi, who stands in front of my favorite Jabec work, *Broken Reflections*. She taps the tip of her reading glasses against her lips—something she does while thinking. I linger just out of their view. "This is a definite call for expulsion."

"Perhaps, but are you even looking at the work?" She leans toward the wall.

"How can I avoid it? The transgression is right in our faces." Mr. Ivers jabs his finger at the explosion of color and brushstrokes that climb the once-white wall around Jabec's 20 x 20 canvas. *Broken Reflections*, with its shards of tile and mirrors, has birthed something new since yesterday. A larger work spreads across the wall using the original piece as inspiration, paint shining and fresh. A rainbow of cadmium yellow, magenta, viridian, and other colors splits a silhouetted body of dark fabrics. They wrap around Jabec's canvas as if scooping up pieces of mirror to construct a new whole, creating a seamless reflection.

I swear I hear Ms. Teresi breathe, "The bravery," but I can't be sure.

"This is the kind of thing Jabec would've done," she says, and stretches her hand toward the exhibit banner announcing the new permanent collection of the street-artist-turned-fine-artist's work.

"Well, I don't think we ought to applaud such blatant disregard for private property. Reckless acts warrant severe punishment," says Mr. Ivers. He's one of the most buttoned-up teachers at Caswell, and that's saying *a lot*—since most of them are stuffy, old white men who don't have time for change.

Ms. Teresi is different though. So is Headmaster Ewing. They're at least open to more.

"Every year someone pushes boundaries," Mr. Teresi says, "tries to go beyond, but this . . . this is just more literal."

"You say it as if it's to be admired?" he scoffs.

Ms. Teresi turns away from the wall, noticing me for the first time. "Nivia, is there something we can help you with?"

Yes, I want to say. *Do* you admire it? Since she was one of the Jabec Beard Prize judges, her thoughts matter. "Um, no, I'm good."

She nods toward the stairs, her salt-and-pepper hair toppling out of a messy top bun. In long graceful strides, she heads my way.

"Neither of us needs to be later than we already are," she says, reaching me. She's all but forgotten Mr. Ivers's question. "Tell me, what do you think of the new addition to our gallery?"

My brain freezes. "It's okay, I guess."

"You guess? Come now, Nivia, someone as talented as you must have an opinion."

I half smile. Her Visual Culture class sophomore year was *everything* for me. It taught me how images transform moods and relay messages deeper than even words can. That certain visual experiences challenge people to feel, notice, and continue the visual conversation. I glance back up the white marbled stairs but can no longer see the conversation started on that wall.

As if reading my thoughts, she adds, "I actually see glimpses of you in that work. But it's riskier and a bit more honest than anything you've ever dared put forth. Can you learn something from it? Do you think it speaks the element of truth that's been missing in your pieces?"

I want to tell her yes. That it holds *exactly* what's missing—but I'm still unsure. Art isn't like math. There's no right answer.

Ms. Teresi opens her classroom door. Work and supplies are spread across most of the tables as students concentrate on their midterm projects. "I'm glad to see you aren't wasting valuable time. Tomorrow morning's deadline quickly approaches." Her linen layers swing around her.

Grabbing my supplies, I head to my table, right behind Ryan's. Classmates' whispers buzz in my ear.

"Ryan, just let go," Ms. Teresi encourages, eyeing her work. Then she gives a light laugh. "Haven't you ever dabbled outside the lines?"

Ryan's brow furrows. Her work is controlled perfection. Like her. Nothing she creates is out of place or haphazard.

"It's evident you've been taught well," Ms. Teresi says. "But don't let it trap you. Explore." She taps the paper. "Stop obeying the lines and challenge them."

I don't need to see Ryan's face to know she's cracking.

"Ms. Teresi, aren't we going to talk about what happened?" Keegan asks from a front table. "Was that someone's submission?"

"Fat chance." Logan leans back on his stool. He hasn't bothered to open his folder yet. "They would've needed to take credit to get credit."

"I would," Isaiah, the only other Black kid in class, says almost to himself. "I mean, not that I'd take credit for someone else's stuff, but if I'd done it I would've signed it. The style's sick. None of us is putting out work like that."

"Okay, settle down, everyone. Focus on the work at hand. There are only a few precious hours before midterm projects are due," Ms. Teresi says, shutting down the conversation before it starts.

"But Ms. Teresi." Emily, an underclassman who has an answer for *everything*, shoots her hand into the air. "It speaks about the truth Jabec always talked about. Whoever did it is showing the weight of mirrors reflected back on us by society, filled with everything we're supposed to be for everyone, and making them something new."

"Dude, you got all that from it?" Logan asks. "You might need your glasses prescription checked."

"Hold on now, Logan," Ms. Teresi interrupts. "Great art has the ability to be different things for different people. What did you see?"

"Honestly?" Logan's front stool legs crash against the floor. "Confusion."

"That's the point," Isaiah interjects.

Ms. Teresi gives him a look to let Logan finish.

"It's a shadow split six ways, like it doesn't know what it wants to do," Logan continues.

"And the mirrors? What did the mirror mosaic mean for you?" Ms. Teresi asks him.

Logan shrugs. "I didn't think they were actually reflecting anything specific," he adds. A couple of others nod. "And things get bizarre with all those colors. Someone's pretty out of control—"

"Or torn," Ryan says, almost too quiet for anyone to hear, but I do since I sit right behind her.

"I disagree, Ms. Teresi," Isaiah speaks up. "It's not out of control at all. The shadows are trying to break free. To show their colors. To be visible."

"Who agrees with Isaiah?"

A number of hands go up around the room.

"I get what that's like," Lakshmi says. "Being in a shadow is never just as simple as stepping out of it. Shadows can camouflage a lot of things."

"Like?"

"Differences. Here we're all supposed to want basically the same things and are expected to be the same, but outside of this bubble we aren't all the same. And we aren't seen that way either. I think people forget that sometimes," Lakshmi adds. She started Caswell Prep's thirty-three-member Students of Color Alliance.

"How so?" Ms. Teresi narrows her eyes, interested.

Headmaster Ewing strides into the classroom then and everyone sits a little taller. Logan even straightens his hunter-green-and-navy-striped tie dotted with gold Caswell crests. Actually, each of us checks some part of our uniform, except Ryan. Hers is already perfect. I smooth the folds in my pleated skirt, more from nerves than anything else.

"My apologies, Ms. Teresi, for interrupting your class further. But I think in light of today's events I must." As he speaks, he looks each of us in the eye as if we're the only person in the room with him. His eyes land on me for a second, and I look down like my colored pencils are the most fascinating invention of the twenty-first century. "Though my assumptions could be wrong, I'm visiting art classes first because I assume an art student is behind this."

"We're discussing it now," Ms. Teresi says. "It's turning into quite a thoughtful conversation."

"Well, I hope you're also touching upon the severity of this action," Headmaster Ewing continues. "If the perpetrator comes forward today, maybe we'll consider taking expulsion off the table . . . but this type of leniency will only be considered if you speak up now." He clears his throat, looking out at us. "I hope I won't have to call a special all-school meeting and involve everyone in this."

There's total silence.

His steel-blue eyes settle on me again, then slip to the next person almost immediately. He doesn't even glance Ryan's way. But everyone does when Ryan's stool screeches across the polished concrete. And she starts to stand.

She pushes at the hair behind her ear even though her scarf already holds it in place.

"Yes, Ryan?" Despite the gravity of Headmaster Ewing's announcement, his face brightens almost imperceptibly. "Do you have something to share?"

My eyes bore into the back of her head, wishing I could read her thoughts. What does she know? She turns slightly and her focus darts to me before she looks back at Headmaster Ewing.

"I know who did it," she whispers.

This is so unlike Ryan—she might follow every rule in the book, but no one would ever call her a snitch. She flicks at the corner of her hair again. My heart thumps in my ears like it did the night before. She glances at me once more.

"I did it." Her words can barely be heard. But I hear them loud and clear, and instead of pounding, I think my heart stops.

"*You?*" Ms. Teresi says what I want to yell.

Headmaster Ewing studies Ryan like he's trying to imagine her scrambling through a window and defacing walls, but my mind is blank, confused, as my stomach plummets. With all the things I thought might happen, I never expected this.

She keeps pushing back her hair, and I know she's freaking out. She's not the only one. My stomach bubbles and twists.

"Well . . ." Headmaster Ewing starts, then stops, mouth wide. There's a slight twitch at the corner of his left eye.

I've never seen him this way. He's about to topple over. To be fair, we are standing in Eckhart Gallery. The world-renowned gallery the Eckhart Foundation funds because members of the family have attended Caswell since the first bricks were laid, and that includes Ryan Eckhart.

Expulsion is definitely off the table.

"Are you certain?" he asks.

I almost choke out a hack. Anyone else, including me—a rarer-than-rare Black legacy kid, and a board of trustees member's daughter—and he would've started very differently. But with an Eckhart—Caswell Prep royalty—everything is different, even the questions.

"Yes. I wanted my submission to be remembered. Like Jabec, I tried to go beyond what was expected. I hadn't really thought much about the consequences. I was so absorbed in what I wanted my work to say." Her voice barely shakes.

If I didn't know the truth, I'd believe her. She sounds so convincing, delivering her lie. But while I fume, shouting *liar* in my mind, twisting the point of my pencil into the tabletop, my lips stay cinched as Ryan voices what I've been too chicken to say. My supposed truth.

"I'm surprised to hear this, Ryan," Ms. Teresi says. "It's unlike anything we've seen from you. It challenges lines."

"What?" Ryan says before she can stop herself.

"It's all about bringing what's within beyond boundaries, right?" Ms. Teresi watches Ryan with the precision of a surgeon trying to avoid a nerve.

"Um. Yes, ma'am," Ryan mumbles. She follows Ms. Teresi's gaze to the work in front of her and slides a blank sheet over it before Ms. Teresi can search for comparisons she won't find. "I wanted to try something new."

I definitely feel sick now. This time there is no tremble in her voice, like she believes her own lie. My leg hops under the table, hammering against the stool leg. She's made a decision.

And I need to make one too.

I've been sitting on the steps outside Eckhart Gallery for the last thirty minutes, rocketing up every time one of the doors opens, waiting.

Then Ryan pushes through and stands against the doors, surprise across her face.

"Why'd you do that?" I demand, approaching her.

She says nothing, hugging her books, trying to pass me.

I don't let her.

"Answer me." I lean in. "Why?"

She avoids my eyes, then glances at me. I almost think I see regret, but that's gone in a flash.

"Why didn't *you*?" she asks.

I'm ready to yell, but her question catches me off guard.

"Don't think I didn't know you were up to something last night." Her eyes shift back and forth, searching out my secret. "When I saw it, I knew it was you. It's like the stuff in your sketchbooks you don't let anyone see."

"If you knew, then why take credit for it? I thought we were friends," I challenge. A couple students slow on a path near us.

She watches me, pushing at her hair again. "You were too scared to."

I want to tell her she's wrong. But it won't come out.

"I have to win," she says. "And this piece will win."

"What about me? You don't think I want to win too?" I snap.

"Why didn't you speak up then?" Her words are cold, but her eyes still need convincing. "You had your chance."

"It's not so simple," I say. "I have a ton to lose."

"Like I don't?" The cold creeps into her eyes now.

"Though I bet there were no consequences for you, were there?" I ask, already knowing the answer.

Ryan says nothing at first. "It will be up for consideration."

"Figures." I want to smack the entitled look off her face. "I can't believe you're actually going to do this."

Her back goes straight, like she's made another decision. "Why?" She stares at me, almost as a challenge. "It says everything I need to say to win." Ryan moves away, then looks back.

"*You* don't want it bad enough. I do."

All I can do is watch her go, feeling more than betrayal, knowing she's right. As much as I risked, I'm not sure I ever intended to confess. And now I don't know what pisses me off more—my own cowardice or her audacity.

During my junior year, my aunt Gladys, who inspired my love of art, took me on a spring-break girls' trip to Italy. And as my eyes devoured Michelangelo's *Cleopatra* sketch in the Uffizi, she casually asked: *How bad do you want this?* And by the looks of things now, not bad enough. I stand motionless in the center of my room, taking in all the sketches and paintings I've done. The ones I've actually let others see.

I pull them down and spread them across my floor. This work captures moments in my life, but it's not enough. I hesitate for just a second before pulling my sketchbooks off the shelf. The ones Ryan talked about. The ones no one was ever meant to see. They're crammed with crinkled pages of self-portraits, snips of fabric from memories, photographs, movie tickets, gum wrappers with doodles, and torn slips of paper with images painted with watercolors. My thoughts and full life spill out of these books I've always kept contained and secured with wide green rubber bands. I remember when we were roommates, Ryan peeking over my shoulder once while I was working. She didn't recognize the images were of me. And I've always wondered why. But now I think I know. It was the side of me I don't let breathe. The side that doesn't fit expectations. The side that's free.

And she saw *that* on that wall.

I scan the self-portraits and photos into the computer and print page after page. I am beginning to understand my truth, which has always been staring back at me. And now I have less than twelve hours to speak it.

For Parents' Weekend everything seems extra golden.

The chandeliers sparkle overhead in the dining room of Chatterley House, the on-campus inn, which should really be called legacy row. It's booked years in advance for every special occasion families can attend. Even before my arrival freshman year, Mom and Dad had paid four years in advance for certain dates, like they had for Mya and Reese before me. Who, unlike me, followed in *all* of the family traditions without even a grumble, both studying law. My parents couldn't have been prouder when Reese became a lobbyist and my sister a political analyst and law professor like Mom. These dark mahogany walls have been witness to many family conversations, good and bad.

"I had an interesting call from Councilwoman Myers's husband yesterday," Dad says, wiping a napkin at his lips. I fight the urge to roll my eyes at the mention of Councilwoman Myers's husband, a dean at Dad's alma mater. *Can't we have just one meal that doesn't focus on my future?* We're seated around one of the immaculate white-cloth-covered tables in the inn's dining room and my appetite is suddenly lost. "Mitch says he never saw your early-decision application come through admissions."

It hasn't escaped me that he's waited for Mom to leave the table to chat with old friends before he starts his cross-examination. At least there'll be a time limit to his storm. Though Mom has already told me where she stands. *Go after what you want.* She made it clear she isn't battling the worst of the storm if I'm not willing to myself. I take a breath.

"I didn't send it. I'm applying to art schools, general admission, instead." I don't dare tell him about my last-minute Jabec Beard submission.

Blood surges through a vein over his right eye, an impending eruption. "The answer is no." The words a hiss through clenched teeth. His expression remains blank for the sake of appearance, but I know the storm is brewing. "I'm not funding that, nor have I funded four years here for you to think painting pictures is your future. We've already discussed this."

"You talked. I didn't," I mumble before saying, "I really want to do this."

"So did your aunt Gladys, and look where that got her." The sapphire in his class ring catches the light as he smooths his hand over his close-cut beard. "My sister is a shell of who she once was. Too many doors slammed in her face, or never opened. People love brown on canvas—the bark of a tree, the shine of a saddle—but that same brown on her skin was rejected," he says, his perfectly tailored suit giving off its own shine. "This is a truth you need to know, Nivia. In this world, the brown of your skin is rarely a shelter. Here at Caswell, color may fade—for a while anyway, except when it's needed for brochures or diversity experiments—but out there, it's front and center *always*. Don't forget that. The law is where you can find a sturdy footing."

I drop my gaze, part of me knowing he's right. I'm surprised he doesn't mention me squandering Grandpa's legacy and his fight for equal consideration as one of Caswell's first Black students. He's sparing me that argument—this time.

He reaches for my hand. I don't pull away. "Mitch assures me he'll look out for your application during general admission. You can paint there in your free time. It'll be hectic with a prelaw course load, but as long as it doesn't hinder your priorities . . ."

"Such serious faces," Mom says as she nears our table with Ryan's mother. Mom's cheeks lift as loose, highlighted curls swing around her pearl earrings when she smiles. Ryan's mother reveals a perfect smile too. They look like they've sauntered out of a fashion spread.

From her table, Ryan glances at me.

I turn away.

Dad slides his hand off mine. The corner of his eye crinkles as he smiles back at Mom. He greets them warmly, then picks up his salad fork and spears a radish. For him, the matter is decided.

Latham Auditorium is alive with voices as we wait for the presentations to begin. I sink deep into the admiral-blue velvet seats. Seniors from Alcott and Eldridge are unmistakable in their maroon or gray blazers, eager as we are to know the outcomes. Four awards are given, and the Jabec always comes after community service and before the essays. I can hardly breathe as the lights dim and faculty judges take the stage.

Ryan sits two rows ahead of us, watching her grandfather onstage as he waits to give an introduction. You'd never know the lie she's holding, sitting totally collected between her parents in her Caswell uniform while the community service awards are handed out. When she keeps tucking her hair behind her ear, her mom discreetly pulls her hand away.

Mom lays her palm over my knee. The warm pressure stops my leg from jumping. She winks my way as bluesy jazz is piped in through the speakers. A self-portrait of a tanned Jabec Beard with a shaved head stares out at us, the years of his life scrawled underneath.

"Jabec Beard," Ms. Teresi begins, "is remembered and celebrated for the stunning pieces he gifted the world."

Some of his most famous works brighten the movie-theater-sized screen behind her with colors, angles, words, and feeling. Everyone drinks in the images, especially me.

"But he was more than just an artist; he was a seeker of truth in all things, and devoted his life to encouraging people to go after their inner truth and challenge the barriers put around them and the expectations suppressing them," Ms. Teresi continues. "He yearned for everyone to find his or her authentic self, and that is why this year's prize theme, Tell. Your. Truth., is so relevant for our students. These are the years where they question with open hearts, explore with abandon, and discover with amazement the courage to do so. The pieces you'll see this evening were chosen from a talented and inspiring pool, bearing witness to what he sought to inspire."

I can hardly draw in air as the lights go dimmer. A hush falls over the room as work from an Eldridge student demands everyone's attention. It's the kind of piece people sit on museum benches for hours staring at, with its deliberate brushstrokes and moody color palette of blues and grays. A scene of a lone boy in the rain. The next painting is equally as powerful—sneakers at the edge of a cliff, a lively carnival on a cloud high in the sky, fog below.

All the pieces tell an honest story.

Then I bite at my lip as Ryan's back goes rigid. Jabec Beard's *Broken Reflections* comes into focus. Ryan's grandfather nods her way from the stage as claps sprinkle through the audience when the added work is revealed.

My work!

"In an unconventional twist, one of our students has literally used Jabec's truth as a foundation for her own." Ms. Teresi's hand opens in Ryan's direction. Her parents give a wave and nod like it is their work on display. Ryan remains motionless.

But I know she is more than cracking inside.

Then a brown face, my face, with jet-black hair pulled into a high bun, fills the screen with color ribboning all around it. Glitter cascades down the cheekbones, as I bite a gag that tries to silence me. Dad's looking, but he's not focused on the image. I want to scream, *Look, Dad, look!* Look at me! The real me.

When the slide zooms in, quiet gasps poke the air as people realize the brown of the skin is made up of dozens of sepia-toned scenes, photographs, portraits, and strips of fabric from my sketchbooks.

This collage is all of me.

As I balloon with disbelief that I created this, that everyone is seeing my true world, I can see from where I'm sitting that Ryan crumples.

When the image shifts to the teeth digging into an unmistakable hunter-green scarf patterned with little foxes, Ryan flinches, turning slightly to me. But I don't have time to watch her sweat over the gift she once gave me as the focus turns to a drawing of a man hugging a little girl in bobby socks and puff-balls. Dad leans forward, his attention caught. He straightens his already straight tie, clearing his throat, blinking as if he isn't seeing things correctly. Then the complete piece fills the screen again. And everyone can see how the moments of my life weave together to create this determined, certain face. Mine. Dad turns to me and I expect to see anger, but a storm is not there. His eyes are soft.

He's about to say something when Ms. Teresi adjusts the microphone. The music goes low.

"This multilayered piece was left at my door with only a few minutes to spare, but the creator, who is obvious to some of us, still failed to sign it." Ms. Teresi searches the crowd, and then her eyes lock on mine. "It'd be a shame if this talent remained silent. And this work couldn't officially be considered."

Every part of me is shaking, but I know this is the moment I've been trying to build my courage up to for so long. I glance at my dad, whose eyes are glued to me. I nod to him. He only blinks, seeing if I'll fight.

I stand, legs trembling, then I hold my head high and say as loud as I possibly can, "This is my story. This is my truth."

BLACK. NERD. PROBLEMS.

LAMAR GILES

"*We're going to* burn this joint down, my ninja! My outfit is *fire*." We were in Foot Locker and DeMarcus popped his collar in the mirror. A floor mirror. The kind meant for checking your kicks, so he was leaning over real weird to do it. DeMarcus did everything weird.

The sharp, slightly toxic scent of fresh shoe rubber and insta-cleaner tinged the air. That *fire* outfit of his was some Old Navy jeans slashed strategically for the right percentage of exposed skinny leg meat, one shiny black patent-leather shoe, and one blinding white Air Force 1. A Drake T-shirt plus a lavender tuxedo jacket from the Salvation Army topped it off. Total swerve from the visor, polo shirt, and apron he wore daily as Chief Knot Inspector at Auntie Anne's Pretzel's.

The metal security grate was lowered, but not locked.

Beyond it, in the main mall corridor, foot traffic was low, the only thing still open to the public being the movie theater upstairs. Typical summertime Thursday in Briarwood Mall.

We jumped when multiple *somethings* crashed in the back room, followed by a bass-heavy "Fuucccck!" A moment later Amir emerged balancing two shoeboxes, peering at us over the top. "Y'all just chillin' like you ain't hear that footwear avalanche. I could've died back there."

DeMarcus said, "We would've gotten extra teriyaki chicken from the food court in your honor."

Amir's face scrunched. He scrutinized DeMarcus, aggravated. "What *is* that?"

"The chicken samples from the hibachi spot. We can't drink, no pouring one out for the homey. So we drop some chicken in a trash can in honor of your untimely—".

"Naw, dude. Your outfit!" Amir spotlighted me. "You let him do that, Shawn?"

"I didn't *let* him do anything," I said.

"This Foot Locker, man. Ain't no dressing rooms in here. He had to change in front of you."

"Actually," DeMarcus said, "I went behind the counter. Ducked down in uniform, popped up in *swag*!"

Amir set the boxes down by one of the try-on benches. "You went by my register?"

"Yeah," said DeMarcus.

To me, Amir said, "You ain't stop him?"

I said, "He's not my minion."

Amir flopped on the bench, hit us with the Disappointed Dad Sigh. "Fellas. I'm the assistant manager here. I can't allow y'all behind the counter near the till. It endangers the company's assets."

This dude. "You calling *us* thieves?"

"I'm not gonna dwell. All's forgiven." He flipped the lids on both boxes, exposing glossy new shoes. "Jordans or LeBrons?"

"LeBrons," we said simultaneously.

"Word." He removed the Jordans from their box, kicked off his workday Reeboks, and tugged cardboard slip-ins from the new kicks.

I said, "Yo. You buying those?"

"Borrowing." He worked his feet into them.

"That doesn't endanger the company's assets?"

"I need to know the product intimately if I'm to increase quarterly sales." He produced a slim roll of clear tape from his hip pocket, tore off strips, and affixed them to the soles so as not to damage the loaner shoes. "Wanna explain *your* outfit?"

I gave myself a once-over. "What?"

"There's a Care Bear on your shirt."

"Chewbacca." His ignorance was disgusting. "From *Star Wars*."

"You and that dimensional galaxy shit."

"Dimensions and galaxies aren't the same—"

"Girls gonna be there, Shawn. Ole girl from Nordstrom

gonna be there. She probably suspects you can't afford nothing from her store already. You gonna roll into the spot
looking like a five-year-old at Chuck E. Cheese's? Dumb. At
least DeMarcus can say he's a musician or something. They're
allowed to wear anything."

DeMarcus leaned into a sock display, probably checking for
one long enough to double as a headband or necktie. "Leave
him alone, Amir."

I said, "How you gonna talk? You're still wearing the Foot
Locker referee shirt."

"If this was Wall Street, I'd wear a suit. We in the mall, this
is my suit." With his shoes laced and tape applied, Amir threw
his hands up, defeated. "Fine. Whatever. Let's do it."

He powered down the store's lights and hoisted the security
gate halfway. We ducked under, emerged on the second-floor
corridor. The overhead bulbs burned at approximately one
thousand watts, though the walkways were nearly deserted.
On busy days, shopper traffic made the place feel like standing
room only, but after hours the open spaces felt as wide as an
airport runway.

While Amir locked up, I leaned on the polished teak railing
and toed the safety glass that kept untold toddlers and Apple-
bee's drunks from tumbling to their doom. From this angle,
I saw the scab-red *OP* in the GameStop sign below, waiting
for me to relight it tomorrow morning. Amir stood, the gate
secured.

There we were. The Eccentric, the Sneakerhead, and me,

the Nerd. Traversing nearly one million square feet of floor space like Masters of the Retail Universe!

Amir turned to me. "What's this thing about tonight, anyway?"

"Welcome to Mall-Stars!" Mr. Beneton, a round man with orange skin resembling the finest offerings in Wilson's Leather Shop, tugged on a braided velvet rope fixed to a drop cloth covering the restaurant's sign. When the cloth didn't come down, DeMarcus chittered a sarcastic laugh.

I stared. He mouthed, *What?*

Mr. Beneton beckoned his trio of swole-up muscular helpers, with their too-tight-in-the-arm suit coats. They yanked the rope and the cloth fell, along with the last raggedy *S* in the signage—which didn't fall all the way, just hung crooked, attached by one strained support. Electricity crackled, flooding all the letters—including that crooked *S*—with fluorescent blue light. *MALL-STARS*.

Our fellow mall employees celebrated the sign lighting with lukewarm applause. We were clustered in the East Atrium, stars visible through the skylight a hundred feet up. Thirty or forty of us from various stores were corralled next to the gurgling fountain, with its small fortune of loose wish-change submerged in greenish water. All clutching glossy invitations passed down from mall higher-ups to our managers to us, with "strong recommendations" that we attend this little party thrown by Briarwood's big boss.

Beneton slipped index cards from his coat pocket, glanced at them, said, "Thank you for accepting my invitation to the soft opening of our newest venture. We're excited to bring the 'barcade' model to Briarwood. Classic video games meet delicious food and signature drinks. As Mall Ambassadors, you will be the first to experience the magic. Put Mall-Stars through its paces. Anything that you order will be discounted twenty per—"

He frowned, signaled his least muscular helper for an eyeball debate over the notes he'd obviously not read before that moment. Then said, "Ten percent. Your discount is ten percent. Just ten."

Groans from the "Ambassadors."

"Try everything. Be sure to text any suggestions to the number posted at each table. Enjoy!" He slow-clapped, and like three other people joined in. When the applause died, Beneton's guards ushered him off like the Secret Service snatching the president from assassins.

The crowd milled in, the dark space ghostly lit by flickering game cabinets, flat TVs racked around the bar, and assorted black lights. Some eighties song I'd heard my mom sing to, by that one dead artist, blasted from ceiling speakers, drowning everyone in old-school. I lingered outside the entrance, awed by Mr. Beneton's kind-of-boss escape, and missed Amir giving me the *ninja-look* look, so he elbowed me in the ribs. "Shawn, she here."

She was Dayshia Banks. Dark brown, fine, and flawless in

a cream dress and low heels befitting the Nordstrom employee dress code. She went to Ocean Shore High, a town over. A senior, like us. Used to be a flag girl. This year she let band go to focus more on academics and saving dough for college. She didn't tell me that personally. That's off her Instagram and Twitter.

She ain't follow me back yet. It's been like eight months, but, I mean, I don't post a lot.

"Shawn," Amir said, "give me your phone."

Dayshia strolled in, hugging herself against the arctic air-conditioning. I handed my phone to Amir, no questions.

"What's your PIN?"

"1955." The year Marty McFly traveled to in *Back to the Future*.

DeMarcus said, "Why you all in the man phone?"

"Something for Beneton's suggestion box." Amir dictated while he tapped. "*Get Shawn to stop staring at women like a serial killer.*"

I snatched my phone back.

"Talk to her," Amir said with the hopeless enthusiasm of someone advising a PetSmart goldfish to towel off. "She right there."

"I will." I wasn't.

She was right there, thirty feet from us, ordering a Coke at the bar. She was by herself, and doing those do-I-know-somebody-here glances before focusing on her phone. You know what would happen the minute I crossed that divide, and tried to spit game? This:

MWARRRGHH! MWARRRGHH!

That's how Chewbacca talked.

MWARRRGHH!

That's all she was going to hear when a dude in a freaking *Chewbacca* shirt stepped to her. What was I thinking?

Black. Nerd. Problems.

Amir said, "You regretting your outfit, ain't you?"

"How'd you—?"

He tapped his temple. "I know things. Let's grab a booth."

We locked down seats with good views of the billiards table, the bar, and the Skee-Ball machines, where the dudes from the Far East Emporium—that store with mad decorative chessboards, tiger statues, incense, and a perpetual "50% OFF EVERYTHING" sale—were battling the twins, Brian and Ben, from Abercrombie & Fitch.

Brian scored a forty-pointer on a sweet roll that arced off the corner of the ramp. He high-fived his brother, then mean-mugged the competition.

DeMarcus said, "Why that joint seem so intense?"

Could've told him the beef was deeper and tougher than them one-hundred-point Skee-Ball holes. Brian and Ben were Brian and Ben *Lin*, Chinese Americans who *been* said the Far East Emporium was racist AF. Mr. Lee (like Robert E., not Bruce), *owner* of the Far East Emporium, and his sons said the

Lins were too sensitive, that the store honored the "spirit of the Orient"—also racist AF. Thus, the Lin vs. Lee Skee-Ball war.

How I know? Food court gossip on dinner breaks gets you *the whole rundown* in Briarwood. But I didn't explain all that to DeMarcus. My attention was elsewhere.

Cologne Kiosk Cameron had slithered in undetected, settled at the bar right next to Dayshia, a bulging man purse resting at his feet. A pretty boy who talked with his hands and way too many teeth, he had the complexion of a well-cooked french fry, brown and a little oily. No one was sure how old he was. Kamala from Build-A-Bear said he was a college sophomore, though nobody knew which school. Jeff, the old stoner from the vape shop, said he once saw Cameron at his aunt's bingo night hitting on single moms. Who knew?

Whatever his age, there were no characters from a Galaxy Far, Far Away anywhere on his pristine slacks, pressed plaid button-up, or blazer with those voluntary patches on the elbow. He said something. Dayshia laughed. *With* him, not *at* him.

Amir noticed me noticing. "Yo, that dude appears like Satan. I've never seen him come and go."

DeMarcus said, "I promise you a black cloud of brimstone smells better than the knockoff nerve gas he be selling at that box shop."

I said nothing. Just unlocked my phone, opened my notepad app, and wallowed in defeat.

• • •

Pia, our waitress, who used to sling frozen yogurt but said this gig paid a dollar more an hour plus tips, propped her empty serving tray on her hip. "Y'all gonna order some food?"

Amir said, "Any of it cheaper yet?"

Pia glanced down. "Why you got tape on your shoes?'

"Just bring us more water with lemon, please."

She stomped away while I slurped my third water down to the ice chips. I tapped my screen, ignoring Amir's heat-vision stare.

"I ain't sitting with you all night," he said.

"Didn't ask you to."

"I could really be checking on these shorties. I heard Chrissy from the Sprint store is a freak."

"Chrissy got a girlfriend. Stop spreading rumors."

"Oh. Shit. Look who's salty. Don't be mad at me because you too much of a punk to take your shot with Dayshia."

Naw, that didn't sting. It might if it was true, but it wasn't. Asshole. "You making a bunch of noise over nothing. She's dope. We ain't the same, though."

"Of course you ain't the same. Why would you want to be with someone the same as you? Like a female Shawn? A clone? Get off that sci-fi stuff a little bit. When you writing your books and movie—yeah, I know what you really be doing on your phone—it'll be an asset. You gonna get all that good cosplay loving at the Geeki-Con. But today, act cool."

"You're only proving my point. I love 'that sci-fi stuff.' If she act the way you act over it, why waste the time?"

"You don't *know* how she act, and you won't ever if you don't step up." He pressed back in his booth corner. Looking like he wanted to dust me for fingerprints and solve me. "So you saying it ain't a thing if I hollered?"

"Go for it. I'm cool." The lie twisted my stomach on the way up, dragging acid.

Amir slid from the booth, went straight for Dayshia, who'd drifted toward a pack of other mall girls. There was Aubrey from Things Remembered, Vicki from Victoria's Secret, and Desdemona Bloodbayne (the name she preferred; her birth name Jill) from Hot Topic.

Amir was charming when he wanted to be, so he infiltrated the ladies' convo with ease. They welcomed him with smiles.

Shit. Shit. Shit. Of course it was a thing if he hollered at Dayshia! He should know that! A clear violation of bro code.

I couldn't watch whatever happened next, so I did what came easy to me. Words.

My phone was full of them. Not the "sci-fi stuff" Mr. Know Every Damn Thing suggested. Just *stuff*. My observations about Briarwood.

Take this "soft opening," for example . . . it did not seem to be going well. Those who ordered food—like the Limited employees occupying a circular booth in the corner—grimaced on first bites and left mounds of sauce-heavy wings virtually uneaten. Dude who worked in the JCPenney men's department kept checking his watch, yet likely couldn't escape because guess who was back! Mr. Beneton, checking on the captives, making everyone as uncomfortable as the Santa Claus–looking dude from Yankee Candle who'd ordered the crab poppers and was rubbing his stomach with regret.

Brian, Ben, and the Far East Emporium took their battle to the Shoot-to-Win Free Throw machines, while the Dick's Sporting Goods crew went for like their tenth round on Big Buck Hunter—

"Hey." Dayshia slid into the booth, taking Amir's old seat. "Your friend told me about you."

I died for half a second.

"You shouldn't have been afraid to come talk to me." She smiled with perfect teeth tinted blue under the Mall-Stars black lights. My head whipped toward Amir, aiming a *Scanners*-style telepathic attack at him, hoping to either explode his head or read his mind. *What did you do?!*

He raised a fresh glass of ice water with lemon at me, winked.

Dayshia said, "If you want to take care of it tomorrow, we open at ten."

"I'm—huh?"

She pointed Amir's way. "That guy told me about the broken clasp on your mom's necklace. If her birthday was just last week, you're well within the return window. Our policy is very generous, so it won't be an issue to replace it."

There was no necklace. Was there even a mom? My short-circuiting brain repaired itself, deduced Amir *hadn't* hollered at Dayshia. He made up a story about problems with a purchase, created common ground for me and Dayshia. Chewbacca was *still on my shirt*.

Leaning forward, obscuring old fur-face, I said, "I didn't want to bother you off the clock."

"As my manager says, I'm a Nordstrom ambassador anytime I'm in the mall. I'm Dayshia, by the way."

I nearly said *I know—I follow you on the Gram*. Trapped that foolishness in my throat. "Shawn."

"You're here in the mall?"

"Yeah, GameStop."

"That sounds fun."

"It's all right. You game?"

"I have driven a Mario Kart on occasion. I also Guitar Hero'd at a party when I was ten."

"So that's a no."

She laughed. Laughed! With me, not at me. Was this actually going okay?

Glancing toward Amir, I sent another telepathic message. *I might not be whipping your ass after this. Maybe.*

When I faced Dayshia again, I nearly shit myself. Cologne Kiosk Cameron was in the booth with us, arms spread along the backrest, his fingers nearly grazing her shoulder. She curled her lip, seemed as shocked as I was.

"Yo!" he said, a spicy cloud of whatever sample he'd doused himself in crop-dusting the immediate area. "What's poppin', fam?"

". . . I was like, babe, I know it's CU homecoming weekend, but somebody else gotta use those Kendrick Lamar backstage passes. I got other plans. You feel me?" Cologne Kiosk Cameron thrust his palm at me like a karate strike.

I was slow registering his attempted high five, dazed by all his not-so-humblebrags. I slapped his palm as quick as possible, then friction-burned my palm on my jeans.

"I'm just saying," he said, "it's crazy how many opportunities come my way at the kiosk. Everybody wanna smell good, so everybody come to me. Did you know we sell women's fragrances, too?"

"You've mentioned it," Dayshia said, glassy-eyed, aiming her chin toward the bar. "Earlier. Over there."

His monologue never even paused, like a living PA announcement blaring weekly mall specials on a loop. "People drop in with concert tickets, passes to those gospel stage plays. Got my grandma on the front row of Javarius Jenkins's *If Your Man Ain't Jesus, He Just Ain't* last month." He scooted closer to Dayshia. "I got the hookup, is all. Just say the word."

He flashed a smarmy grin my way. "Same for you, little man."

"I'm taller than you."

Dayshia pressed an elbow into his ribs, halting his lateral motion. "Excuse me. I need to . . . just." She aimed finger guns in the general direction of elsewhere.

Slow, and somehow sleazy in a way basic motion shouldn't be, Cameron exited the booth, clearing a path for Dayshia. As she escaped, she shot me an I-couldn't-take-it-anymore look that got me laughing. With her. Not at her.

Cologne Kiosk Cameron sat again. "I know, dude. It's funny how I *can't keep them off me*. Hope you taking notes on that little phone of yours."

What was his deal with everything being "little"?

"I mean, unless you smashing already. I didn't get that impression because your shirt. If I misread the situation, get me up on game."

Best I could tell, this dude misread *every* situation. Quick draw with my own finger guns, I pointed somewhere—anywhere—else, ejected from the booth. I moved to midfloor where Ben, Brian, and the Far East Emporium dudes battled on Pac-Man. Did a slow spin, desperately searching for Dayshia.

Pia stomped up, lugging a tray full of waters with lemon. "Guess you don't want these anymore."

"Have you seen the girl who was in my booth?"

"Nice to see you're thirsty for something. She out by the fountain."

Beyond the Mall-Stars entrance, on the fountain's edge, Dayshia scrolled through her phone. I moved that way, a dull pinch in my lower abdomen registering. I took a few more steps, and it became sharper, more urgent, stopped me cold. Those ice waters!

Ignore my pulsing bladder to resume conversation with my dream girl? Tempting. Except she was sitting by a freaking fountain. All those spouts continuously splashing the surface, the ripples. I'd be squirming the whole time.

Maybe it was dumb—maybe *I* misread the situation—but it seemed like me and Dayshia connected back in the booth, if only for a minute. You know what would super ruin that vibe? Me pissing myself.

Quick detour, then.

The universal man/woman symbols were visible over a corridor between the Mall-Stars bar and the main gaming floor. I slipped through, took a sharp turn, and found myself in a long, darkly tiled hallway that ran the length of the restaurant. So familiar with the mall layout, I knew if I punched through the outer wall to my right, I could snatch a Father's Day card for my pops off a shelf in Hallmark. Beyond that, a hobby shop. Crafts, and paint, and artist papers. Beyond that, my jam, GameStop.

Whenever I wrote stuff about the mall, it always struck me how all of it, all of us, were connected even if we didn't know it—or didn't want it (looking at you, Far East Emporium).

A bunch of stores, and people, and reasons for being there underneath the big Briarwood umbrella.

Pushing into the men's room, I tugged my phone from my back pocket, intending to jot that down, and . . . what the entire hell?

Inside the harshly lit bathroom was a party separate from the soft-open celebration.

A couple of infamous weed heads from the Regal 14 Theater puffed a blunt right under the smoke detector that now dangled, deactivated, from a single wire. Beyond them, Amir, DeMarcus, and other guys I knew from the mall grind. DeMarcus threw a pair of dice in a way I'd never seen dice thrown—overhand, flick of the wrist, something like a Navy SEAL tossing a knife at his enemy's throat. The dice bounced off the wall beneath the plastic folding baby-changing table, settled on a piece of cardboard in the floor.

"Seven!" DeMarcus whooped over the collective groans of those on the losing end of that bet. He snatched his winnings, a loose grouping of fives and ones.

"How long y'all been shooting craps?" I asked.

Amir said, "You mean how long we been winning? Awhile. How else we gonna afford this expensive-ass food. How things go with Dayshia?"

Before I could answer, Cologne Kiosk Cameron exited the big end stall reserved for disabled customers. "Great!" He smiled, his spit-slick canines like fangs. "I think me and her really hit it off."

My head whipped toward the entrance. I'd left him in the booth. He hadn't passed me in the corridor. Where'd he come from? How?

If he wasn't the devil, he was certainly in the training program.

The bathroom was oversize. Mr. Beneton must've expected a lot of drink sales, thus, a lot of pee. I used the ninth urinal in the far corner, away from the dice game and the funk permeating the air. Not the usual bathroom funk. A toxic mix of colognes Cameron was getting dudes to sample in the accessible stall, his new makeshift kiosk.

"I'm telling you," Cameron droned, sales pitch cranked, "people sleep on Trump's Empire cologne, but a true connoisseur will recognize those velvety oaken notes as the literal smell of money. You got a lady you interested in, this be like a hostile takeover of her nose."

The telltale bottle spritz sounded like a cobra spitting venom. Jarrel from the Books-A-Million burst from the stall, clawing at his eyes and throat.

Cameron followed, grinning, holding the Empire bottle like a smoking gun. "My bad, homey. Guess the nozzle was turned the wrong way."

At the sink, Jarrel thrust his whole head beneath the faucet, frantically waving his hand near the motion sensor, with no luck triggering the water. He convulsed over to the next sink. That motion sensor didn't work either. He went for the next.

I finished at the urinal and washed my hands. Cameron watched me in the mirror.

He approached the movie theater guys, their blunt burned to the midpoint. "Let me hit that."

High and generous, they passed the stubby cigar to Cameron, who took two puffs and never gave it back. "I'll hook you up with something that'll cover the smell so you don't get in trouble with your boss. Be a shame if he caught a whiff of this, right?"

Neither of the theater workers seemed to love involuntary cologne-for-ganja barter, but Cameron moved on before they objected. "Shawn"—he jerked his head toward the stall—"come here."

"For what?"

"You want to see this." He held the accessible stall door wide, blunt dangling on his lip, its tip fiery red.

Everyone else continued their activities—craps, rolling a new blunt, eye-flushing—as if in a different reality from me and Cameron. I entered his domain cautiously.

Inside the stall, resting in the corner farthest from the toilet, was an open bag of assorted cologne bottles. Various shapes, sizes, colors, and levels of fullness. Label-gun stickers reading "Sample Not For Resale" were affixed to at least half of them.

Cameron rummaged through the bag, his goods clinking together. Streamers of earthy smoke snaked from his nostrils. He produced a white bottle adorned with a green crocodile from the stash. "She's a Lacoste Blanc lady. I can tell."

Removing the cap, he angled the bottle away and triggered a fine mist that drizzled over the U-shaped toilet seat in a citrus burst. "Smell that? That's you getting what you want. Only cost you twenty bucks. Steep discount, my dude."

Was twenty bucks for a stolen half bottle of cologne a good deal? Didn't know. Didn't want to. "Naw, I'm good."

It couldn't have been more than five minutes since I came in. That was five minutes too long. Dayshia could be gone, and I was screwing around with Bargain Beelzebub. I exited the stall, on my way out.

Cameron said, "Think you dropped something."

I turned and felt the full horror of that demonic asshole's power.

He had my phone.

Reflexively, I patted my back pocket, praying for the familiar bulge that meant what he held only *looked* like my phone. Naw. How many Rick and Morty iPhone cases were really in circulation at Briarwood? My heart bulged against my sternum, dragged me forward with my hand extended.

He scuttled back, staring at the screen. "And it's unlocked. Yo, you a writer?"

"Give me my shit, Cameron."

The rattling dice, the betting cheers, went silent.

Amir said, "Shawn."

He straightened in my peripheral. As did DeMarcus. I made

a chopping motion with one hand. I got this.

Did I, though? My hands shook. My vision vibrated with the force of my slamming pulse, making Cameron bounce in front of me. Most of my fighting was done from a PlayStation controller, but I'd never felt more like punching someone in. My. LIFE.

Cameron inhaled around the nearly gone blunt. "Why you acting so aggro? I like reading. Unless you're really frustrated about something else. Ole girl from Nordstrom?"

I willed my face still. Held eye contact past the point of discomfort.

Cameron wasn't fooled. "Wow. For real. Bro, this the mall. I take advantage of this week's coupon, you catch next week's sale. Feel me? Nordstrom got plenty for both of us."

I smacked that blunt from his mouth. The ashen tip blazed gray and molten as it flipped end over end, its trajectory unknown.

At the time.

"Ohhh!" The bathroom morphed into a fight-night crowd.

Despite his slick talk, the shady comments, Cologne Kiosk Cameron seemed uncertain. His eyes cut quickly to all the witnesses. Mine, too. The mouths that would carry this story to every corner of the mall and beyond. They were from different neighborhoods, and schools, and cities. All anticipating the birth of a new "yooooo, remember that time . . ." story.

My last fight had been on the playground in second grade.

I lost due to an inescapable full nelson, and it was horrifying to learn the ritual hadn't changed. There was a tipping point after the trash talk, after personal space had been violated, when a physical gesture so offensive was made that to not fight was dishonorable. A punk move.

"Steal on him!" DeMarcus, the most lighthearted of my friends, ordered me to sucker punch our workplace's Prince of Darkness.

"You think you got it in you!" Cameron bumped chests with me. "Swing if you man enough."

Dishonor. Shame. Punk. My right hand curled, hardened, the knuckles protruding like Wolverine's claws. My eyes flicked to Cameron's right, a distraction, intended to leave the left side of his chin unprotected, I tensed, and—

The bathroom door swung open with force, crashed against the wall.

Yankee Candle Santa Claus burst in, clutching his stomach as if being torn apart. "Crab . . . poppers."

Clawing open the first available stall, not even taking the time to lock it, he rustled loose whatever clothes needed to go . . . and . . . and . . .

Oh God! The sound. Like a pudding balloon dropped off a skyscraper. Over and over.

The exodus began immediately, not fast enough to escape the—what could only be called devastating—smell. Amir grabbed money and dice. The theater dudes collected their weed. DeMarcus grabbed my arm, and I snatched my phone from Cameron's limp grip before moving to the exit.

Not one of us thought about the bag of stolen cologne samples, or that lit blunt I'd knocked to wherever.

Cameron yelled, "That's what I thought. You ain't want none."

My desire to argue was sapped by the Crab Popper Apocalypse. We spewed into the corridor, Cameron on my heels, threatening violence where we both knew there could be none.

Fighting? Back on the main floor with everyone else? Naw. I wasn't losing my job and store discount over his bitch ass.

We emerged into Mall-Stars proper, unnoticed by the dwindling soft-opening crowd. Ben, Brian, and the Far East Emporium guys were battling on Dig Dug. Mr. Beneton had the bartender counting the till in front of him while his goons loomed. Dayshia remained at the fountain outside, like no time had passed.

Cameron kept yapping, "I'ma *take* your chick, homey. Activating all my swag. Look at you, look at me."

I looked at him. Looked at me—Chewbacca was still on my shirt.

"You don't have more game than me, Shawn. No way you winning."

Amir heavy-sighed. "Let's just take this dude out behind a dumpster."

Cameron's mouth snapped shut, weighing the odds. You

didn't have to work at Kumon to know they weren't in his favor. "So now you gonna jump me? Over a girl."

No. We weren't. Nobody here—except maybe Desdemona Bloodbayne; that girl was scary—was a back-alley brawler. Still, Cameron was insisting on a battle for Dayshia.

How do you win a fight you shouldn't have in the first place?

That's when it hit me. "Amir, DeMarcus . . . he's right."

"Pardon?" DeMarcus said.

Amir was like, "The fuck?"

To Cameron, I said (maybe in the voice of a 1980s computer simulation; I won't confirm or deny that part), "Shall we play a game?"

He rapid-blinked, unsure where I was going.

"*WarGames*? 1983? Starring Matthew Broderick and Ally Sheedy?"

Everybody in earshot shuffled, confused.

Amir leaned in, whispered, "Is now the time to be bringing up those old white-ass movies you be making us watch?"

My usual response whenever he said shit like that. "I would've watched the Black *WarGames* if anyone made it."

Cameron's face creased, confused. "I don't know what whack language you even speaking right now."

"You'll wish you did." I left him steaming, exited Mall-Stars, eyes on Dayshia. She sat her phone facedown in her lap, eyebrow arched, observing the large congregation of guys hovering at the restaurant. "What's all that about?"

Deep breath, Shawn. "Stupid guy shit."

"Ooookay? You about to tell me something that's gonna make me think of you as a stupid guy?"

"We'll know in a minute. You ever see a movie called *WarGames*?"

She shook her head. "Is it good?"

"I like it. It's about hackers and artificial intelligence trying to set off a nuclear war."

"Should you have said 'spoiler alert'?"

"Spoiler alert. The point of the movie was the only way to win an all-out nuclear war is to not have it. You win the game by *not* playing."

With a dramatic head sweep, she motioned to all the beeping, tweeting game cabinets nearby. "I don't think Mr. Beneton would agree with you there."

"I don't mean—"

Her smile shrank. "Did y'all make some kind of bet? Is that the stupid thing that got you over here to talk to me? They're all staring."

"No. Yes."

She huffed, shifted her weight as if to leave.

"Wait a second, please."

"I have been waiting. I don't want to wish I hadn't."

She was waiting? For me?

"No bet," I said fast, sensing somehow that time was not

on my side. "I wouldn't do that. There's other stupid guy stuff. Cameron wants to kick it with you. I do, too. He tried to make a thing about it in the bathroom, some let-the-best-man-win shit. I almost went for it."

Dayshia swept her phone into her purse. "I should probably go. If you want to return your mom's necklace—"

Rapid fire. "There's no necklace. Game isn't real. I have Chewbacca on my shirt."

"You're not making any sense, Shawn."

My phone was still in my hand, still unlocked with the Notepad app open. I showed her. "My thoughts get all over the place sometimes, so I write them down. My friends are always on me to say stuff and not be in my own head. Dudes like Cameron, I think, are the opposite. You follow so far?"

"Cameron talks too much and doesn't think enough. I understand and agree."

"So, like, normally I would say nothing to you at all. But Amir made up that necklace thing, and you talked to me, so I'd be stupid if I sat back while a loudmouth with not one solid thought in his head yammered at you, possibly piecing together the right combination of words to make you think he's more worth your time than I am. Whew!" I was gasping. "Forgot to breathe."

Dayshia locked eyes with me, her brow creased. "Shawn, listen to me carefully. It's important that you understand what I'm about to say."

I waited a three-heartbeat eternity for the sad trombone signaling how big a mistake me getting all outspoken had been. It didn't come.

Dayshia said, "Cameron is ass."

Inside Mall-Stars Ben and Brian Lin erupted in cheers. One screamed, "Suck it, Far East Emporium!"

My breathing stabilized, though speech was tough going. "I . . ."

"Cameron's *the worst*, Shawn."

"Somebody say my name?" Cameron sat on the opposite side of Dayshia, licked his lips. I stopped wondering how the fuck he teleported like that. He wasn't that interesting anymore.

"I did," she said. "Did you hear me call you 'ass'?"

His grin flickered. "What?"

"Look. Me and my friend are trying to have a conversation. You're being rude."

"Girl, come on. We was vibing at the bar earlier. All them grins and chuckles."

"No. I'm a Nordstrom ambassador, and you were asking me about our Shiseido skin-care products. It was funny because you obviously knew way more about the shit than I do."

Oh. She'd been laughing *at* him. Not *with* him.

And so was I.

Cameron sneered and brushed fingertips across his greasy,

baby-smooth cheek. "*This* don't happen magically."

I found my breath and words. "Bounce, dude."

Cameron rose, plucked at his lapels. "Dayshia, clearly I mistook you for someone with taste. I guess a child with a dog-man on his shirt—"

"It's a Wookiee. And Shawn said bounce."

From Mall-Stars, Amir yelled, "Go exfoliate, *ninja*!"

The laughter—from my peeps, and Dayshia, and me—gave Cameron the fight he'd been looking for; one he lost. For the first time ever, I watched dude *leave*, shoulders slumped, as mortal as the rest of us. And Chewbacca was still on my shirt. "You said 'Wookiee.'"

"Yeah, my big sister loves those movies, so I got it through osmosis. You said 'yammered.' You must've crushed your SATs."

I waved a hand in the air. "Eh."

This was banter! We were hitting it off. With Cameron finally out of the picture, nothing could possibly mess this—

Yankee Candle Santa Claus shoved through my boys hanging at the Mall-Stars entrance, barely holding his pants up. "It wasn't me!"

Then the burning smell.

Then the shrieking fire alarm.

Then hell breaking loose.

DeMarcus rushed to us. "We gotta go."

No argument from me. My only hesitation came in the

moment I offered Dayshia my hand.

She took it.

The Nerd, the Eccentric, the Sneakerhead, and the So Cool Girl executed the emergency protocol, then stood in the parking lot while Briarwood Mall burned.

Not the whole mall—thank God. We needed those jobs. Mall-Stars was pretty much a crater, scorched and boarded up. For the rest of Briarwood, it was business as usual.

Amir left Foot Locker for a manager's position at Footaction, and DeMarcus got on at Express Men. Moving up in the world.

Me and Dayshia became MeAndDayshia. Or as DeMarcus called us—once—"Day-Shawn." Amir popped him in the back of the head, and he never said it again. Which I was grateful for.

I showed her *WarGames*. She showed me *Love & Basketball*. We didn't spend much time actually watching either movie, and I had no complaints.

All the other Briarwood players kept doing their thing. Brian and Ben Lin stayed beefing with the Far East Emporium. Pia the waitress became Pia the time-share salesperson, which fit her no-nonsense attitude ("You're going to vacation anyway, might as well do it for this once-in-a-lifetime price!"). Desdemona Bloodbayne kept moonlighting as a vampire slayer, or something. I don't know. The biggest change was Cameron.

He vanished after the fire.

So did his kiosk. Like they'd never existed.

Kamala from Build-A-Bear said he was working a drone kiosk at Greenhaven Mall in Ocean Shore. Jeff from the vape shop said he conned a widow out of some insurance money and was on the run in Mexico. I believed the truth was somewhere in the middle because of what the fire chief said on the news.

According to him, the Mall-Stars blaze was caused by criminal negligence. An accelerant left too close to an open flame. Point of origin: the men's room.

Things I thought about a lot after that report: the blunt I knocked from Cameron's mouth. How it was still lit. Where it might've landed. That bag of cheap, stolen, highly flammable cologne.

Then I pushed those thoughts away. Didn't talk about them—not with Amir, DeMarcus, or Dayshia. Didn't write them down, either (at least nowhere anybody would see).

There was too much good shit to get here at the mall, I didn't need more Black Nerd Problems. Plus, when it came to the ones I had, I was doing just fine.

OUT OF THE SILENCE

KEKLA MAGOON

You died on a Friday, sometime during the night. In the movie version of my life, I would have woken up at the exact moment of impact, startled by an eerie premonition. But that's not what happened. I slept right through.

You died on a Friday. It was on the front page of the paper Saturday morning. The article stretched over the fold, the picture of twisted wreckage caught my eye. I guess I'm like that, the sort of person who wants to rubberneck, even at a still image, even after the fact. It embarrassed me, to be like that. I slid the paper closer when my mom was in the kitchen. I wasn't even going to open it up all the way, but then I saw your name.

The article contained all the scurrilous details. The sorts of information I would lap up when it's a story about strangers. You'd been out past curfew, with a reputed "bad boy." Driving too fast, not caring about the rules. Ignoring things like speed limits and stop signs. Fighting the establishment right up until the order of the universe inverted. Against the grille of a tractor trailer.

Two teens dead, two injured. Tessa Martin and Sean Ryan. Him, I didn't know. He went to a different school, like the injured kids in the back seat, who weren't named in the article.

You died on a Friday, late in the evening. Long after the football game, hours after the stadium had cleared. Hours after I caught my last glimpse of you, across the bleachers. Me in the marching band section, you entwined with the cool kids. It was the briefest of glances, really. I'm sure you didn't notice me at first. You stood out from the crowd, whereas I was dressed like all the other band kids, clutching my clarinet.

You smiled, but only sort of. At first I wasn't even sure you were smiling at me. Then you winked. And I knew. This time, like every time, I wondered if I was safe. If you were going to open your mouth and ruin everything. You only smiled, and it wasn't cold or anything. I could trust you.

I could always trust you. That wasn't the issue. The issue was, I wanted to get closer. I wanted to know how you had seen what you saw in me. How you had seen through every veneer of my heart and called me out from hiding. But I couldn't.

You died on a Friday, and my secret died with you.

• • •

I didn't go to your funeral. To remind myself we didn't know each other. At all.

We had gym class first period. One hour per weekday for six months. That was our whole relationship. It shouldn't have mattered much, should it? We were two of the four least athletic girls in class. Or really, I should say, the least interested. We did the bare minimum, and that was fine with us. Second semester of my sophomore year, your junior. It was sophomore gym. You were retaking the course, having been too lackadaisical about it the first time around. You played it fast and loose with the dress code.

"What are we, sheep?" might have been the first thing I ever heard you say.

"Huh?"

"Baaaa." You flapped your ears with your hands and bleated. You dragged out the *a*'s until you snorted and your eyes grew big beneath your bangs.

I laughed.

"They want us to look exactly alike."

"Gray sweatshorts are the look of the season," I said. "Get on board."

You pulled a tube of lipstick out of your waistband. The questionably fashionable shorts had no pockets, of course. "There have been lawsuits," you said.

For a second you held the lipstick like a cigarette and I wondered if you wished you were smoking.

"Lawsuits?"

"Dress-code lawsuits. The American Civil Liberties Union. Imposing a uniform suppresses our First Amendment rights to free speech."

The lipstick smeared on perfectly. So deep red it was more like maroon.

I tugged at the collar of my baggy blue Simpson High T-shirt. "I'd rather be *wearing* a law suit."

You stared at me, unsmiling. "You're funny."

I didn't go to your funeral. I mean, funerals are about the living and stuff, and I didn't know your family, or your friends. I wouldn't know how to stand around and spout clichés, or worse, to say something meaningful or memorable at all. *Hi, Mrs. Martin, I'm Cassie Ellison. You don't know me, but your daughter shook my life to its foundation.* Would that be comforting? *Tessa was a person who could wreak havoc with a sentence. Sixteen years doesn't seem like long, but how many lives could a person with that kind of power have ruined in her time? By the way, I'm sorry for your loss.*

I didn't go to your funeral, but sometimes I wish I'd been bold enough. I wonder what you looked like, or if the coffin was even open. You always wore a lot of makeup, so maybe if they did a good job, maybe you even still looked like yourself. But I try not to dwell on morbid thoughts. I was curious, of course, but I didn't want to be one of those people who pile on to a tragedy.

Even at school, I couldn't stand how people who hardly

knew you were sobbing and clutching each other as though a deep part of them had been ripped free. I couldn't bear to appear the way they did, like a parasite feeding on sorrow. In some cultures, I've read, there are professional mourners. Women—usually women, I think—whose role it is to wail deeply and rend their garments, to lend voice to the sadness that surrounds such a loss.

This, this was something else. This was grief rendered chic. To have been close to the girl who died . . . "What was her name again?" To be close to her, to be one of the dear friends feeling the pain most deeply, that was a coveted position. Girls jockeyed for it, while her true best friend, and fellow quiet goth, rested in silence at the lunch table reserved for freaks and outcasts. Unceremoniously. Uncelebrated.

Tessa's best friend sat alone. It was hard, but not too hard, to approach her.

"Mya?"

Her eyes were rimmed with tears. Mascara smudged. Not so much a smoky eye as the soggy dregs of a campfire pit after the flames have been doused.

"Yeah?"

"I'm really sorry. About Tessa."

Mya didn't know me from Adam. Her lashes fluttered wetly. All she had on her tray was a sad piece of pepperoni pizza and a can of grapefruit seltzer.

"Well, thanks."

I don't know what the point of it was. She clearly didn't know me, or care for anonymous expressions of sadness. I don't know why it felt important to touch your personal sphere, even if it had to be in the stupidest of ways.

"She was always really nice to me," I said. "We only had one class together, but . . ."

"Well, thanks," Mya said again.

We didn't really know each other. We came from different worlds. I was the quiet girl who never made waves. You were the actual ocean. You were goth before everyone knew what to call it. Or at least, before I did. I might have been called "preppy" if I was two shades cooler. Entirely different worlds. There were a lot of things I could have asked you, I guess, but I never thought of it at the time.

We'd sit in line and you'd take demerits for failing to appear in the correct attire for gym class. Ms. Corning stood above us, disdainfully marking it all down. "Hair not pulled back," she noted.

"I don't want a crease," you said, tossing your hair like a mane. I understood what that saying meant for the first time with you—your dark hair flew back, revealing the barely checked wildness underneath your skin, a reined creature yearning to run free.

I smoothed a hand over my twin French braids. "I can relate." My hair would hold absolutely any shape it dried in.

"Your hair's cute like that," you said. "But how come you never wear it down?"

"It doesn't go down," I said. "I could have a foot-high Afro if I wanted."

"That would be cool," you said.

I tugged the end of my braid, thinking of all the middle school boys who had teased my frizzy attempt at a ponytail. "Nah."

"There's nothing wrong with being yourself," you said. Lipstick in hand, like a cigarette.

We didn't really know each other. I never found out whether you smoked or not, for instance. I don't know if you had siblings, or if Sean was your boyfriend, or if you secretly liked one of the guys in the back seat. Maybe you didn't like boys. I don't know. I'll never know.

We didn't really know each other at all. The day it all came crashing down—on me, that is, not the accident—the day it all came crashing down, you were wearing the requisite ponytail but not the right color shorts. You weren't wearing shorts at all, in fact—it was a pair of sweats and they said "Hot Stuff" across the butt.

"Didn't feel like shaving?" I said.

You smiled. "I'm not trying to impress anyone."

"No boys you like in this class?" I said.

You shook your head.

"Me either."

"Oh." You sounded surprised. "I thought you were a lesbian."

Your words sizzled straight through me. They found a lightning rod in me that had never been struck, that I never knew existed.

"What? No."

"Really?" You raised your eyebrows. "I've seen the way you look at Angela."

My eyes cut over to Angela, two rows away. My friend and default gym class partner when we had to pair up on things. When we needed groups of four, it was Angela, me, Tessa, and her default partner, Laini.

"I don't know what you mean." I said. "How do I look at Angela?"

I could imagine the shape of her butt right then, even though she was sitting. It wasn't labeled "Hot Stuff" or anything, but when you mentioned looking at her, that's what I pictured. I didn't think it meant anything. It didn't mean anything.

"Sweetie," you said, "you might be a lesbian."

The words rolled out of you, so matter-of-fact. I'd never heard anyone refer to gayness in such a casual way. It wasn't a slur, or a takedown. It was a window opening to a whole other world I'd never imagined. A window I wanted to lean through and take in every detail of the landscape for as far as the eye could see.

"Do people look at me and think that?" My stomach knotted right up.

You shrugged. Up and down the rows, the other kids were talking or goofing around, or staring off into space. No one was listening to us.

We weren't even speaking anymore, but your words echoed off the bleachers, and the mishmash of lines on the floor, and the gray and blue cotton uniforms everyone was wearing.

I think about how it felt. I think about whether you saw it coming. A blur of headlights. The squeal of brakes. An echo of something, anything, that promised release.

I think about whether it was painful. I think about your nails clicking against the dashboard. I imagine you were laughing, but maybe you were late. Maybe that's why Sean ran the stop sign. You were trying to get home. I don't know where you lived, though. I don't know what you did with your time. I don't know whether to be jealous of everything you had going that night, right up to the tractor-trailer impact. Out late, speeding, maybe with the wind in your luscious black hair.

I didn't mean to say luscious. Your hair was simply black. Jet black. Ebony. The opposite of ice. Whipping in the wind, in the dark, it would look . . . like flames, already burned out but not knowing when to quit.

You died on a Friday. I didn't go to your funeral. We didn't know each other at all, and still, I think about you. I think about whether you saw it coming, and whether it was painful.

You died on a Friday, months ago, and still I think about you, you, you. I think about your eyes, your nails, your lips. Your red, red lips were silenced and a part of me was entirely relieved.

THE INGREDIENTS

JASON REYNOLDS

Summertime in Brooklyn means doing whatever you can to stay cool. Cool as in not becoming a melted version of yourself in the heat. Also, *cool* as in not sitting inside doing nothing, which means being outdoors, socializing in the midst of the buzz of the sun, that which serves as a heat lamp looming over the land of lizards—tough-skinned chameleon kids who blend into the browns and reds of the row homes and the jagged grit of the concrete. Kids who, in an effort to be *cool* and stay cool, can only hang out at one place—the swimming pool.

For Jamal, Big Boy, Flaco, and Randy, it's Kosciuszko Pool, a name they butcher effortlessly because they've never met a Kosciuszko—or a Polish person at all—to tell them how to pronounce it correctly. Plus, to them, it's just *the pool*. And on any given sweltering summer day, when Bed-Stuy becomes a microwave, the pool might as well be called heaven.

"It's not *really* that funny," Big Boy says, rubbing his forehead as if his skin is a smudge. "Y'all gassin' it, making it something that it ain't."

"Ain't nobody gassin' nothing," Jamal shoots back. Jamal, all head and feet, as opposed to Big Boy, who's all everything, holds the door open for his friends, each of them filing out after skipping the locker rooms. They never shower. Never rinse or swap out wet clothes. Not because they have a problem with it—locker rooms are something they're used to from years of gym class—but because they come to the pool with no baggage. No duffels or backpacks. They come already dressed in their trunks and tank tops. They don't bring towels or any extra garments. The way they see it, one of the best parts about the pool is the wet walk home. The slight breeze dancing with the damp, sending a welcome chill up their legs and backs. And they know there's no risk of yelling mothers, frustrated about the chlorinated water dripping all across the hardwood floors of their apartments, because the boys will be dry long before reaching home. Plus, they're not going home, anyway. At least not to their individual apartments. They're going to one apartment. They're always going to one. A collective dwelling, a base for postpool boyhood shenanigans. It varies by the day, but today, it's Flaco's house.

"Y'all *are* gassin' it," Big Boy grumbles. "It was a Band-Aid and y'all making it seem like it was poop or something gross like that."

"*Bruh*," Randy chimes in. "You jumped in the pool, went

under the water, and when you came up there was a dirty-ass Band-Aid stuck to your forehead." Randy brushes his palm over his head. The water has turned what used to be his freshly brushed waves into tiny onyx beads strewn across his scalp. Randy is obsessed with his waves.

"Yeah, like a . . ." Flaco tries to find the word while trying to hold in his laughter. "Like a . . . slug or something."

"Shut up, Flaco!" Big Boy snaps, swinging his arm loosely at Flaco's brittle birdcage of a chest. "You probably don't even know what a slug is."

"Yeah, I do. It's a snail without a shell, dummy." Flaco tightens his face for a moment, cocks his head back, and purses his lips into a *shut your mouth* look.

"*And* it's slimy like you was, coming up out that water," Jamal follows up. "No, like that nasty thing stuck on your head."

"It was just a Band-Aid!" Big Boy barks again as they all turn onto Tompkins Avenue.

"Yo, real talk—what if that Band-Aid had some nasty disease on it, and it seeped into your forehead and is now eating your brain or something? Tomorrow you gon' wake up even dumber than you are today." Randy's face is dead serious.

"And *that's* a shame." Jamal's is too.

"A *damn* shame." So is Flaco's.

"A low-down *dirty* shame." A smirk now splinters Randy's mug like a crack in glass.

Big Boy sucks his teeth, and even though he knows they're just jokes, he still rubs his forehead, not as if he's fearful of germs, but as if there was once a horn there, or perhaps as if there's one about to grow. "Well, if it is, maybe it skipped my brain and is working its way down to my stomach, because while y'all so busy roasting me, I'm *starving*."

Swimming always makes them hungry. They have no idea why, but it always does. Maybe it has something to do with them holding their breath. Or maybe it's due to the energy it takes to tread water, to stay afloat. Either way, whenever they leave the pool, they're always empty. Famished.

"Starving," Jamal repeats. "I could go for a sandwich."

"*Ooooh*, like peanut butter and jelly?" Flaco chimes in.

"I mean, that would be fine, but I'm thinking something even better," Jamal says. "Like turkey, with lettuce, tomato . . ."

"Some *pickles*," Randy interrupts, nodding his head as if tasting the dill.

"Of course, pickles. Some mustard. On a hero. Cut in fours." Jamal rubs his belly as they cross the intersection at Greene Avenue. On Tompkins there's a bodega on almost every corner. Each of them advertises deli meats with the same poster for the brand, Boar's Head, which is the image of a perfect sandwich and above it, well, a boar's head. And none of the boys ever notice the wolf-looking pig with the underbite. They only notice how green the lettuce is. How red the tomato.

The perfect folds of meat they've seen cut from a football of ham or chicken or turkey over and over and over again.

"Just like that." Jamal slaps his palm to the glass of the bodega. Presses his fingers against the sandwich ad. "Yum yum."

"I mean, that looks good and all," Big Boy says. "But I was thinking something like maybe . . . you know the beef you get with beef and broccoli from the Chinese spot?" Randy, Flaco, and Jamal look at Big Boy like he still has a used Band-Aid stuck to his head.

"Just, hear me out." Big Boy continues. "You take some of that beef and put that on some bread. And you put the broccoli on it too, right. Then, you put the lettuce and tomato and all that on it, but what really makes it fire is when you put the hot mustard and the duck sauce, and just a little bit of soy sauce on that thing. No mayo or mustard. Man. Oh, *and* you crunch up some of them dry chow mein noodles on it too, like how we sometimes do with the chips. Now, *that's* a sandwich."

"Yo, it's good to know that nasty Band-Aid ain't affecting your brain yet, because that sandwich actually sounds mad tasty. Like with the tang of them sauces mixing with that beef . . . *yeah*." Flaco nods.

"Exactly." Big Boy responds with a deeper, slower nod.

"Or maybe even like a . . . like some pastrami or something like that." Jamal, inspired by the beef and broccoli sandwich, revises his original idea. "And you just stack it up. Like a fistful of it, and instead of putting it on a hero or on slices, or even on a regular roll, you put it on a *challah* roll."

"A what?" Big Boy asks.

"A challah roll. It's like Jewish bread. Looks just like the back of your head, Big Boy," Jamal jokes.

"Shut up." Big Boy rolls his eyes until only the whites show.

"Anyway, they sell it over there on Bedford. Kid I go to school with let me taste it one time and I was hooked. Delicious. You put that pastrami on there, and then you add some Swiss cheese, and some coleslaw, a splash of hot sauce for a little heat, and a few corn chips for crunch, and *boom*. You got your own little piece of heaven." Jamal slows his walk as they approach the next corner, when it hits him. "A *challah* heaven!"

"Sounds like it," Randy agrees, not realizing that everyone else is easing to a stop. Randy steps out into the street. A car zooms by and almost clips him. He jumps back just in time.

"Yooo!" Flaco calls out.

"Whoa!" Jamal yelps.

"What the hell is wrong with you, Randy!" Big Boy says, now yanking Randy by the arm, a delayed reaction. "Snap out of it!"

"My bad. I'm just so hungry. Ain't even see that car coming."

"Do we need Flaco to hold your hand, bro?" Big Boy asks, his panic immediately slipping back into poking.

"Why *I* gotta hold his hand?" Flaco whines.

"Because you got hands like your mother," Big Boy says, petty, trying to clap back for all the Band-Aid jokes. "Sandwich-making hands."

"My mother got *bust you in the mouth* hands." Flaco puffs up. "And you best believe she passed them down to me."

"Fine," Jamal cuts in, extending his arm to Randy. "I guess . . . *I'll* hold Randy's hand." They all laugh, and while passing another store, Randy slaps the glass, his turn to give another picture of a perfect sandwich a five.

"I need one of *them* to hold my damn hand," he says, palm-brushing his hair again. "Maybe not one of them. But like . . . a half smoke, or a Polish sausage. With some of that kraut stuff on top. I never had it, but it's called sour kraut."

"It's *sauerkraut*. Not sour . . . kraut. *Sauerkraut*. And do you even know what it is?" Flaco asks.

"I don't care what it is, Flaco. I want it on there. I want the kraut, and some ketchup, and some jalapeños, and some jerk sauce! That's what I want, Flaco. Is that okay with you?!" Randy's voice deepens to a bass.

"Hey, hey." Flaco holds his hands up in surrender. "As long as you okay with pooping your whole heart though your butt. If you good with that, I am too."

"Exactly," Jamal adds. "You like it, I love it."

"Hey, Randy, you won't have a heart, and apparently because of that Band-Aid, I won't have a brain, but Flaco don't even have the courage to eat a *real* sandwich. He talking about peanut butter and jelly," Big Boy says. "All the delis we passing on this yellow brick road, and this fool gon' ask the wizard for peanut . . . butter . . . and jelly."

"What's wrong with peanut butter and jelly?" Flaco asks, head slightly cocked.

"Nothing," Big Boy says.

"Yeah, nothing," Randy follows.

"Nothing . . . at . . . *all*," Jamal rounds it off.

"Okay, fine. Since peanut butter and jelly ain't good enough for y'all"—Flaco adds a clap between each word—"you know what I'd like to try? One of them veggie sandwiches I always be seeing these white people get. It's like a salad sandwich or something. Y'all know what I'm talking about? Spinach, and some other kinds of leaves, maybe some kale, and then they put the cucumbers on there, some tomatoes, some onions—raw and grilled. Throw some banana peppers on it, some olives, and . . . what am I missing . . ."

"Avocado," Jamal tosses in.

"Avocado! Yeah, hit it with the avocado and some of that spicy mustard and put it on that crazy-sounding dark-brown bread. Y'all know what I'm talking about? The bread that sounds like a bad last name."

"Yeah, I know what you talking about." Big Boy taps his forehead trying to remember. "What's it called?"

"Uh-oh, it's already started," Jamal jokes.

"Shut up!" Big Boy squawks, his *shut up*s always at the ready.

"It's called pumpernickel." Again, from Jamal.

"PUMPERNICKEL!" they all shout together, then laugh.

"So, yeah, put all them veggies on that bread. Pumpernickel!" Flaco just has to say it again. "And to top it all off . . . the Michael Jordan of all meats . . . *bacon*."

"BACON!" This time only Big Boy yells, but the rest of the boys nod in agreement. They're coming up on Hancock Street, which means they're approaching Flaco's house, which sits right on the corner. Well, not right on the corner, because a bodega sits right on the corner, but next to the bodega is Flaco's house. Behind them, a disappearing trail of water, the drops becoming less frequent with each traveled block, each passed deli.

"Finally," Randy says.

"Right," Jamal cosigns as they climb the front steps. Flaco jams his key into the lock and opens the building door, and the boys, now almost completely dry, take the steps two at a time, before barreling into Flaco's apartment.

"Ma!" Flaco yells, kicking his shoes off at the door. No answer. He checks the bedroom, and repeats, "Ma!" Nothing.

Jamal, Big Boy, and Randy remove their shoes as well, then flop down on the couch in the living room—right in front of the air conditioner—and when Flaco reappears, he's holding a bottle of lotion. This is also tradition. The chlorine dries their skin out. Scales it, and covers it in a layer of uncomfortable white. The boys smear it over their arms and faces, in between their fingers, and in the corners of their mouths. They rub it on their kneecaps and up and down their ashen legs, the dryness fading like static coming into clear picture.

"So, we eating?" Big Boy asks, rubbing his hands together.

"Oh, we definitely eating," Flaco says, heading into the kitchen.

"Pumpernickel," Jamal murmurs under his breath, a grin on his face.

"What you say you wanted? Pastrami, right?" Randy asks Jamal, his voice punctured by a clanging in the kitchen.

"Hell yeah," Jamal replies. "Even though I can't front, that beef and broccoli sandwich sounded like a winner." The sound of cabinets opening and closing.

"I was all for it, until Randy started running off about the Polish sausage with the sauerkraut and the jerk sauce," Big Boy confesses. The sound of the refrigerator door, unsticking, resticking.

And then Flaco returns from the kitchen with four bowls, a box of cereal, and a half gallon of milk.

"Don't worry," he says. "I got sugar."

OREO

BRANDY COLBERT

My *little brother* is holding my acceptance letter hostage.

And I'm going to kill him.

"Ellis, do you want to live to see high school?" I snap, jabbing him in the ribs. "Stop playing around and give me that."

The problem is that at age thirteen, Ellis is already six feet two, which is a whole twelve inches taller than me. Which means that when he reaches his long, brown arm up to the ceiling, I have no chance of rescuing what's pinched between his fingers.

He squints up at the large, pale-blue envelope, holding it to the light even though the fixture is turned off. "Spelman?"

"It's in Atlanta, dummy." I stand on the tips of my toes and stretch my arm, but it's useless. He's like a tree.

"I can read," he says. "What is it? One of those Black colleges?"

"You sound like Dad." Sometimes our father says *Black* like it's a bad taste in his mouth. Which is weird since all of us who live in this house are Black, including him.

That's enough to kill Ellis's mischievous mood. "Whatever, Joni." He drops his arm, tossing the packet on the counter.

I already know I got in, unless Spelman is in the habit of sending thick envelopes when you're rejected. But I have to see the words with my own eyes before I believe it. That's what I did with the letters from the other three I applied to, though I was already well aware that a thin envelope probably meant I didn't get in.

Ellis opens the fridge as I smooth a hand over the front of the packet. I take a deep breath before I slice the letter opener across the top. This is the school that I never told my parents I was applying to because I didn't want to endure their questions; it's the school that sent confused looks across my best friends' faces when I mentioned it.

"What's an HBCU?" Mona asked, pronouncing the letters deliberately as if she was sure to forget them as soon as they left her mouth.

And after I answered that came Lydia's question. It was simple, at least on the surface: "Why?"

I didn't know how to respond. I didn't know how to explain that applying to an HBCU seemed like the right thing to do even though it scared the hell out of me. That I truly couldn't remember the last time I'd been around more than a handful of other Black people who weren't my immediate family. That sometimes, because of that, I feel like a fraud within my own race. It was bad enough admitting that to myself, let alone to my white friends. All I know is that it was a good fear. The kind of fear that made my stomach flip with excitement as I clicked Send on my application.

Ellis parks himself across from me at the counter just as I pull out the contents of the envelope. He leans over the paper, talking only after he's taken a huge bite of a sandwich. "What does it say?"

"Stop being gross. And back up. You're getting crumbs on my stuff." I look up, eyeing his snack. "Where'd you get that?"

He puts his hand up like suddenly he needs time to chew before he answers, but his stalling tactic doesn't work on me.

"Did Celia make that for you?"

He finally swallows. "Yeah. So? She wanted to."

"*So?* Ellis, you know what Mom said. We need to stop relying on Celia so much. We're too old to have a nanny now. Even you."

He looks down at the sandwich. "What's the big deal? I could've made it myself."

But he knows it's a lie because he stuffs his mouth again immediately. Celia's sandwiches are works of art. We've both watched her make them countless times over the years, and like everything else she does for us, they're created with precision and care.

"The big deal is you're going to have to get used to not

having her around anymore."

Celia is retiring in a couple of months so she can spend more time with her grandkids. And because I'll be leaving in the fall and Ellis is old enough to stay home alone now and feed himself, our parents decided not to hire another nanny.

I look down at the paper, see my name and address in the top left corner under the date. And under that:

> *Dear Ms. Franklin:*
> *Congratulations! It is an honor to welcome you to the 137th class of Spelman College . . .*

I exhale. My heart is a bass drum pounding in my chest. It's part fear, part excitement. A thrill. Because I think I'm about to do something that scares me—something huge. And that's not something I do often.

If ever.

Dinner is . . . edible.

In addition to being our nanny since I was little, Celia used to make dinners a few nights a week. Mostly because our parents work long hours in Chicago, Mom as an architect and Dad as an attorney, and sometimes they'd get home just before it was time for Ellis and me to go to bed.

They're usually home earlier these days, and they try to pretend like they're some sort of culinary wizards. Dad, especially, seems like he has something to prove. He won't start with anything easy—he's always going for a meal that absolutely confounds him, like coq au vin or paella. It's absurd and it makes me miss the nights when they were only responsible for bringing home takeout.

"How's the fish, Ellis?" Dad asks.

Ellis takes a long drink of water and gives our father a thumbs-up. He's been pushing the overcooked halibut around his plate this whole time, which is a clear sign the meal was unsuccessful. Ellis will eat just about anything you put in front of him; I don't think he's ever not hungry.

"We have some news," Mom says, spearing a piece of asparagus.

"So does Joni," Ellis says when he realizes it's safe to put down his glass.

Mom looks at me with her eyebrows raised. "You do, sweetie?"

"It's okay—you go first." I kick Ellis under the table. I am excited to share my news, but I want to do it when I'm ready, not because he can't keep his big mouth shut.

"We're going on a little trip next weekend." Mom glances at Dad with a smile I can't figure out, and I wonder if that means they're going somewhere alone.

"All of us," Dad says when he sees Ellis's hopeful face.

This is weird. They both work so much that we haven't been on a family trip in ages. The closest thing we've had to a vacation in years is a long weekend we spent in Door County last summer.

Mom finishes chewing a tiny bite of fish, tries not to make a face as she swallows, and wipes her mouth. "Mama is turning eighty this month, so we're going to Missouri to celebrate with everyone."

"Missouri?" Ellis scrunches his nose.

"It's been too long since we've all been home." Mom smooths her hand over the edge of her placemat. "It'll be like a mini family reunion."

"Your cousins will be there," Dad says cheerfully.

That's not exactly a selling point. I remember the last time we went to Missouri, though I wish I could forget. I was twelve and Ellis was seven, and our cousins teased us mercilessly—about the way our voices sounded and the music we didn't know and, it seemed, every single word that came out of our mouths. I shrank into myself until I couldn't become any smaller, learning right then and there that "words can never hurt you" was total bullshit.

"Cool," Ellis says, and he's so unbothered he even manages to get down a couple more forkfuls of halibut. He must have been too young to remember the way they mocked us.

I push my plate away. I've lost my appetite, thinking about being around my cousins again. What hurt the most was that I liked them so much: they're loud and they're fun and they seemed to know a little bit about everything—things our parents actively shielded us from, like sex and R-rated movies and violent video games.

I loved being around them, soaking up all their energy, until my cousin Junior called me an Oreo.

My friends and I had recently gotten into Broadway cast recordings, and I'd been listening to them nonstop: *Les Misérables*, *Chicago*, *Wicked*, and *Joseph and the Amazing Technicolor Dreamcoat*. I asked my cousin Della if she had any of them when we were sitting in her room one day, going through her music.

I didn't see my cousin Junior at the door until he said, "That is some white shit."

My head snapped up immediately. "What?"

"Broadway—those shows are white as hell. What about *The Wiz*?"

"Ooh, I love *The Wiz*," Della said dreamily. "I helped with the costumes last year when our school put it on."

"I've never seen it," I said quietly.

"Not even the movie?" Della stared at me in shock.

"No." My voice was even smaller.

"Bet you never seen *Dreamgirls*, either," Junior went on. Then, when I didn't answer: "*The Color Purple*?"

I shook my head.

"Damn, you really *are* an Oreo," he scoffed.

I stared at him, my mouth hanging open at the way he spit out the word. Worse than any curse word I'd ever had thrown my way. Bursting with so much venom, it stung for weeks.

Della rolled her eyes. "You stupid, Junior. You don't even like musicals."

"If I did, they wouldn't be the white ones."

I stopped responding, stopped looking at him. And, to my relief, he eventually wandered away—though the word *Oreo* lodged itself in my chest like poison.

It wasn't the first time I'd been told I was Black on the outside and white on the inside, but I never expected to hear it from my own family.

"What was your news, Joni?" Mom asks now, turning to me.

"Oh, um, I just—I got an A on my Spanish exam." I ignore Ellis's confused eyes.

"We'll celebrate with pie," Dad says, and then sighs when he sees our faces. "That I picked up from the bakery. You all are *ruthless*."

I think about the big envelope from Spelman, how it seemed like the right choice just an hour ago. But how can I be sure about going to an all-Black school when I'm overwhelmed at the thought of being around my own cousins for a couple of days?

Mom takes the train when she travels to Missouri by herself, and Nana Paulette flies when she visits us. But Dad insists on driving. He says it's good for family bonding, but I think six hours is too long to sit that close to anyone—especially Ellis, whose armpits reek constantly.

I sleep for a while, play one of Ellis's video games, text with Mona and Lydia, grudgingly play Dad's silly car games, like I spy and twenty questions—and still, the drive seems to take forever. I even look forward to the couple of times we stop at gas stations in the Podunk, Illinois, towns where everyone stares as if they've never seen a Black person in their life, because at least I can stretch my legs and get some air.

But the closer we get to Nana Paulette's house, the more nervous I feel. Maybe the best thing I can do is keep my mouth shut. I'll have to talk, of course, but the less they hear me speak, the less they have to make fun of.

Nana Paulette lives in a big white farmhouse in a small town called Bloom that's about an hour and a half west of Saint Louis. Her closest neighbors are half a mile away, and there's only one market, and one movie theater in town that shows one film at a time. I can't believe Mom grew up here.

Dad has barely pulled the car into the gravel drive before Nana Paulette is on the porch, waving and blowing kisses. She's leaning on a cane now, which she didn't have the last time I saw her. But I'm relieved that she doesn't look any smaller. My chest tightens when I think of her getting older.

Dad parks behind an old station wagon and Ellis bursts from the car, jogging up the front porch so he can be the first one to greet our grandmother. I step out, too, grateful for the fresh air and the promise that I won't have to spend the next seventy-two hours cramped in the back seat next to my brother.

Nana Paulette squeezes Ellis in her thin arms. She's not a short woman, but Ellis's lanky form nearly engulfs her as they hug. She's exclaiming how big he is as I walk up the front steps. Her eyes find mine over his shoulder and she winks at me, setting me at ease. I've always liked being around Nana Paulette. She's sweet but not afraid to tell it like it is; and when she speaks, we listen.

"Here's my sweet girl," she says, opening her arms.

"Hi, Nana Paulette." As soon as I hug her, I remember that our grandmother always smells like lavender and vanilla, and it calms me even more. Maybe I've been nervous about this trip for nothing.

"It's so good to see you, baby. You doing okay?" she asks as she pulls away.

"I'm really glad to be out of that car." I glance behind her, where my brother is leaning over the porch railing, taking in the expansive lawn. It's so big and the house is set back so far from the street that I wonder if it can still be called a lawn. "Ellis hasn't met a stick of deodorant he likes."

"Shut up, Joni." He doesn't even turn around.

Nana Paulette leans on her cane, the other hand on her hip. "Boy, I know you didn't just tell your sister to shut up in front of me."

"Sorry, ma'am," he says, suddenly remembering his manners.

"And you—don't talk about your brother like that." She taps me lightly on the nose. "Y'all go on inside and say hello to your cousins. They've been looking forward to seeing you."

I doubt that.

Ellis walks right in, but I take my time crossing the threshold, wondering who's inside. My mom's family is small; it's just her and her older brother, who has a wife and three kids of his own. Uncle Marcus—Junior's namesake—never left Bloom, and his family lives about a mile up the road from Nana Paulette.

I follow my brother's path. The whole house smells sweet, and I smile, thinking that Nana Paulette must have baked for us. But when I get to the kitchen, I see that I was wrong. Junior is sliding cake pans out of the oven, and my throat constricts at the sight of him.

Ellis is talking to our cousin Della. She's two years older than me and the sister of Junior, who's my age. I stand awkwardly in the doorway, watching Junior put two pie plates in the oven. Nobody notices me until he turns around, slipping the red oven mitt from his left hand.

"Joni?" He tosses the mitt on the counter and raises his eyebrows. "Been a long time, cuz."

"Yeah," I say. "Six years, I think."

He gives me an amused look. "You probably got it figured

out to the day, huh? Hey, Dell, look who it is."

"Joni!" Della practically squeals, bounding over. She was always friendlier than her brother, but I can't help remembering how she giggled when Junior made his cruel comments. My hug back is tentative. "How you doing, girl?"

"I'm good. I like your hair."

"Thanks, girl." She brushes a hand over her twist-out, then looks at mine. "You still doing a relaxer?"

"No, just pressing." I touch my bone-straight strands.

I don't tell her that I've been too nervous to wear my natural hair curly because I was afraid of what everyone at my super-white school would say. They already tease me enough, saying I'm "not *really* Black." Sometimes I just don't want to draw any more attention. Our hometown is only twenty miles outside of Chicago, but they're completely different worlds.

"Is all this for us?" I ask, gesturing to the baked goods.

"Yeah, it's all about y'all." Junior shakes his head as he leans against the counter. "You know you're here for Nana Paulette's birthday, right? She asked me to make her some things."

"Right." And, just like that, I already feel stupid. "Sorry. I—sorry."

"Don't apologize to him, Joni." Della flicks her eyes to the ceiling. "You want to run to the store with me? *Someone* forgot to get enough butter and is making me go to the market."

"Shoulda had y'all pick some up on the way," Junior

mumbles in the general direction of Ellis and me.

The last thing I want to do is get back in a car again, but I gladly agree to go with Della. Anything to get away from the sour mood that's quickly filling the air.

The big celebration for Nana Paulette is tomorrow, but the whole family comes over for dinner tonight, too. Uncle Marcus is still tall and quiet, with an easy smile. His wife, my aunt Virna, has the same bubbly laugh I used to love, and the same tight hugs. It suddenly hits me that Junior is the only one in his family who wasn't instantly warm to me.

Junior and Aunt Virna hole up in the kitchen to make a big Italian feast for dinner: lasagna, and mushrooms stuffed with sausage, and garlic bread, and salad. The only thing store-bought is the tiramisu from the bakery in town, and when Ellis exclaims that it's the best meal he's had in months, Dad pretends not to hear him.

"How's Emma?" Mom asks Aunt Virna.

"Still loving Vassar." It's my cousin Emma's last year there. "She's vegan now."

"You hear that, Joni?" Dad's chin dips down as he looks at me. "You'd better enjoy all my cooking now before you have to resort to nuts and berries."

My aunt raises her eyebrows. "Are you going to Vassar, Joni?"

"No," I say quickly, before she can get too excited. "But I

applied to some schools in the area."

"And she got into Smith, Barnard, and Occidental," Mom says proudly.

"And Spelman," Ellis blurts from across the table—too far away for me to kick him.

"You applied to a Black college?" Dad looks at Mom. "Did you know about this?"

I set down my fork and glare at Ellis. I really could kill him.

"Why do you sound so surprised, David?" Uncle Marcus asks, frowning at my father.

Dad frowns back at him. "We talked about where she was applying, and Spelman was never on the list."

Mom turns to me, her eyebrows wrinkled in confusion. "Sweetie, when were you going to tell us?"

"I don't know." My neck burns hot. "I found out a couple of weeks ago, and we've all been so busy, and—"

"Well," my father says, "I don't think there's anything *wrong* with an HBCU, but is it the best education you can get? Listen, I know why they were created, but do we still need them today? Sometimes I wonder if those places are setting us back instead of moving us forward."

I'm pretty sure Uncle Marcus's eyes are going to bug out of his skull. "Negro, you did not just say—"

"*Negro?*" Dad looks as if he's been sucker punched, the way I must have looked when Junior called me an Oreo years ago. "Now, listen here, Marcus—"

"Congratulations, Joni," my aunt practically shouts. She raises her glass of iced tea, glaring at my father and uncle before she gives me a wide smile. "My sister went to Spelman, and it was one of the best decisions she's ever made. It's a real sense of community—a true sisterhood. I'd be happy to put you in touch."

"Thank you, Aunt Virna." I make eye contact with Junior as I pick up my water. I can't read his expression, but I know he has an opinion about this.

I wonder where he applied. I wonder if he worries about the way people will perceive him—even a whole campus full of people he's never met.

The preparation for the party the next day starts bright and early.

It was a tight squeeze in the kitchen yesterday, and this morning there are so many people that I can barely get through to grab a pastry from the box Aunt Virna brought over. I sit at the dining room table, picking over an apple strudel as I watch them through the doorway that separates the two rooms. Junior is overseeing things, and even I'm impressed by the way he keeps so many people on task. Della is in charge of the deviled eggs, and Mom and Aunt Virna are sitting at the tiny table against the wall cleaning greens and shucking fresh corn, which I haven't actually seen anyone do in real life. Uncle Marcus and my father are setting up the tables and games outside; I guess they've called a truce for the good of the party.

Ellis plunks down next to me with a cheese Danish in one hand and a chocolate croissant in the other. "What's up with you?" he mumbles, but only after he has a mouthful of food.

"What do you mean?"

He swallows. "Why didn't you want me to say anything about that college? You were so excited when the letter showed up."

"Yeah, well . . . I don't know. Maybe it's not the right place for me."

He makes a face. "How could you know that? You haven't even been there."

"Morning," a voice cuts into our conversation.

I look behind Ellis to see Junior standing in the doorway. There's a dish towel hanging from his belt loop.

Ellis responds with a cheerful good morning and I wave, my mouth full.

"Soooo, y'all just gonna sit there or you want to help like everyone else?"

I frown at him. "Can we finish our breakfast first?" Damn.

Junior looks annoyed but nods. "Make it quick? I need someone to grate the cheese before I put the macaroni on."

"Does he have to be so pissy all the time?" I mutter when he walks away.

Ellis pops the rest of the Danish into his mouth and turns to look at Junior over his shoulder as he chews. "I dunno, I think he's kinda cool."

I shake my head. "That's, like, the last word I would use to describe him."

"He doesn't really care what anybody thinks," Ellis says. "And people listen to him. That's cool."

Whenever our parents host parties, they hire people to cook, even for small dinner parties. Mom says it cuts down on the stress of having guests and that she can concentrate on the actual entertaining. That's the norm where we live, hiring out whatever you can: cooking, childcare, housecleaning. It's weird to think that soon Celia won't be part of our everyday lives. It will feel like a family member is missing.

But there's something about this moment, with all of us pressed shoulder to shoulder in the kitchen, that makes me hope I never hire out the cooking when I get older. It's hot and cramped, but it's almost cozy. Mom and Aunt Virna are chattering away like long-lost sisters, and Della keeps cracking jokes as she tends to the eggs. Ellis is posted at the counter with three giant blocks of cheese and a grater, and I think it's the most manual labor I've ever seen him do. Junior put me to work making all the drinks: lemonade with fresh lemons and two different types of iced tea and a fizzy red punch with cut fruit mixed in.

At one point, everyone leaves to go shower or take a break or help Uncle Marcus and my father, and it's just Junior and me. I watch as he pulls out trays and party platters and organizes everything we've been making.

"Where are you going to school this fall?" I ask, setting my cutting board in the sink. It's littered with citrus rinds and lemon seeds.

His back is to me. He pauses, then says, "I'm not going."

"Are you taking a gap year?"

Junior laughs, but it's not a nice laugh. "A *gap* year? Is that what all your fancy friends call it when their parents pay for them to go travel in Europe?"

My eyebrows knit together. "I never said anything about Europe. Or my friends."

He turns to face me. "Oh, maybe they're the type to go volunteer in Africa for a few months so they can feel better about themselves?"

"What is your *problem*, Junior?"

"I don't have a problem," he says, though the heat in his eyes tells me otherwise. "I just call it like I see it."

The tension is interrupted as the back door creaks open. Della walks into the kitchen and stops, looking back and forth between us. "What's going on?"

"Absolutely nothing," Junior says before he leaves the room.

I have just enough time to shower and get ready before the guests start showing up. Nana Paulette has invited a few neighbors and friends, and by the time everyone arrives, it's a full-fledged celebration.

I guess one advantage to living in the country is that you

can play your music as loud as you want and nobody cares. It takes a while for Ellis to get the wireless speakers working, so in the meantime, Della's friend Terrence opens the doors to his car and starts blasting hip-hop ("What you know about Wu-Tang?" he hollered when he turned it up), making what feels like the entire earth shake. The car is long and old, and it would get triple takes from the neighbors where I live, but it's in impeccable condition, with a pool-blue paint job and white leather interior.

"How does he get the wheels so shiny?" I ask after Terrence has left to get a drink. I stare at the blinding silver in the center of the tires.

"Wheels?" Della laughs. "You mean *rims*?"

"Yeah." My face and neck flush. I knew that.

"This car is his baby," she says, shaking her head at the same moment Aunt Virna calls for us to put on something else or turn that mess down.

Della slides in to fiddle with the volume, then perches on the passenger seat and looks at me. "You don't seem like you like being here, Joni."

Is it so obvious?

"I guess I just feel out of place sometimes." I touch the shiny blue paint with my index finger and immediately pull it back when Della shoots me a look.

"Terrence will kill you if he sees you smudging up his car. Just got it detailed."

"Sorry."

"But why do you feel out of place? 'Cause of Junior?" She rolls her eyes. "Don't even pay attention to him. He's always mad about something."

"But it's more than that. Last time we were here . . ." I feel silly bringing up something that happened so long ago, but it still bothers me. It still hurts. Especially since he seems to feel the same way now as he did back then. "He called me an Oreo."

Della bursts out laughing, showing all her teeth.

"Thanks," I mumble, looking away.

"I'm not laughing at you," she says. "It's just—Junior has a lot of opinions, but I wouldn't listen to most of them."

"What do you mean?"

She looks behind me and I turn to see Junior walking hand in hand with a girl. She's pretty, with dark skin and long black braids that hang to the small of her back.

"He has a girlfriend?" I couldn't be more surprised. He's not a bad-looking guy, but I can't imagine anyone would put up with his surliness if they didn't have to.

"Yeah, Lita. She's real sweet." Della looks at me again. "But don't worry about Junior, okay?"

I stare at her, waiting for her to explain.

Della sighs. "He might listen to our dad too much."

What's wrong with Uncle Marcus? Of course I noticed how he didn't let my father get away with disrespecting HBCUs, but they've bickered like that before. And I like that my uncle stood up to him.

"You tell anyone I said this and I'll deny it till the day I die." Her eyes are serious as she looks at me. "But . . . Daddy's got some issues with y'all."

Issues? I stare at her.

"He thinks your mom 'started acting white' when she left Bloom." Della makes air quotes with her fingers. "That she lost touch with her roots because she wanted to go to a big city and make a name for herself. He thinks it's bougie that you have a nanny and that you live in a town with so many white people when Chicago is right there."

"I can't believe you're telling me this," I say as her words sink in.

"Yeah, me either. And I don't agree with Daddy. Neither does Mommy. Just so you know. But Junior . . . I don't know if it's some masculine thing to try to impress Daddy or if he's just not smart enough to figure it out himself. But he kinda parrots back what Daddy says, so . . ."

So this whole time it's been someone else putting ideas into Junior's head? And my Uncle Marcus thinks *all* of us are Oreos because of the way we live? I look over to the card table, where they're setting up a game of spades. Uncle Marcus is laughing at something a man next to him is saying—so hard that he's bent at the waist, hands clasped to his knees.

"Don't hate Daddy," Della pleads. "He loves you guys. And

listen, I'm majoring in journalism, not psychology, but I think he misses your mom. And maybe he wishes he'd been brave enough to leave, too."

"My dad says some messed-up things about Black people sometimes," I say after a moment. "My mom, too."

Della laughs again. "So does Daddy. I have a friend at Howard who's half Black and half Chinese. She says some of the meanest things about Chinese people sometimes. But she'd rip us to shreds if we ever repeated it—as she should." She shrugs. "It's just what we do. We're always harder on our own people."

Finally, Ellis gets the speakers set up and they start playing old doo-wop, and Motown, and slow, steamy D'Angelo and Prince songs that are entirely inappropriate for a family gathering.

When the spades game is done, we line up at the tables around the side of the house to fill our plates. We have all the food Junior organized in the kitchen, along with the meat and veggies Dad and Uncle Marcus grilled and the dishes the guests brought. The spread is admirable: deviled eggs, hush puppies, fried chicken, collard greens, mac and cheese, hot links and ribs, corn on the cob, and more. The pitchers of drinks I made are sitting on their own table, and we haven't even set out all the desserts Junior baked. Everyone urges Nana Paulette to get in line first, but she insists on standing behind the table to help serve. She looks too happy to be argued with.

Della saves me a seat at a table that just happens to be right across from Junior and his girlfriend. Even if I feel a little better knowing his comments were spurred by my uncle's feelings, I don't know that I'm ready to forget the things he's said to me.

His girlfriend smiles as I sit down. "Hi. I'm Lita."

"Joni," I say, surprised that she's so friendly. "Their cousin."

"I only have one cousin." She sighs as she forks up a bite of mac and cheese. "I wish I had more, like y'all."

"There's just five of us," Della says. "Four this weekend, without Emma."

"I guess it's nice having fewer people to leave when you go away." Lita bumps Junior's shoulder with hers. "I'm going to miss this guy a lot."

"Where are you going?" I ask.

"Georgetown. My parents' alma mater, so I almost didn't have a choice." She shakes her head, but I can see the pride in her eyes. "And I'm trying to get Marcus to apply so he can join me after his gap year."

It's strange to hear her call Junior by his actual name, but even stranger to hear his girlfriend use the same term that he snarled at me for saying only hours ago. I look at him to see if he noticed, but he's staring down at his plate, his mouth full.

"I don't know—with me in DC too, he might end up in

California or something," Della says. But even her smirk can't get Junior to look up and join this conversation. "Joni's going to Spelman in the fall."

"Probably," I say, though I know in my heart it's where I want to be.

Lita's face lights up. "You are? Oh, I'm so jealous. That was on my list, but . . . you know. Georgetown. My parents are die-hard Hoyas."

Junior finishes his plate before we're even halfway done with ours and stands up immediately, mumbling about having to go finish the birthday cake.

"You want help?" Lita asks almost reluctantly. It's clear that she's perfectly comfortable sitting here with Della and me.

"Nah, I got it." He gives her a soft smile and rubs the back of her neck before he leaves.

"Girl, you gotta tell me all about DC," Lita says to Della. "I've only been there a few times, and it's always with my parents."

They start discussing the differences between Bloom and Washington, DC, and Georgetown and Howard, and I zone out, taking in my surroundings. The song on the party playlist changes and Marvin Gaye's "Got to Give It Up" comes on— an old song I know because Dad likes to put it on while he's attempting to cook. He usually ends up dancing too much and burning things.

My grandmother starts bopping in her seat, and on the

other side of Della, Terrence calls out, "What you know about Marvin Gaye, Miss Paulette?"

Nana Paulette just laughs, one hand waving in the air as the other taps the cane leaning on the table.

Aunt Virna whips her head around to look at him. "What do *you* know about Marvin Gaye, little Terrence?"

"I'm about to show you, Miss Virna!" He leaps from his chair and pulls her to her feet so they can dance.

More people get up, including my parents. Mom usually rebuffs Dad when he tries to get her to dance with him in the kitchen, but this time she willingly lets him twirl her around the table. It makes me smile.

I get up to dump my plate and wash my hands, and narrowly miss being pulled into the dance party. Uncle Marcus taps my arm on my way to the porch and I think he's going to try to get me to join them, but he just scoops me into a quick hug and kisses the top of my head.

Inside, I use the bathroom, and as I'm walking back to the front door, I hear noises in the kitchen. I follow them to find Junior standing at the counter, carefully icing the cakes he made last night. He's almost done.

"Hey," I say.

He startles, then turns around and nods. "What's up?"

I didn't know I was going to say anything until I was standing here, but we're all alone and I feel like I can't let the opportunity pass. "Do you remember calling me an Oreo?

The last time I saw you."

His hand pauses, hovering next to the cake. I don't wait for him to answer.

"It hurt my feelings. Especially since it came from you. I go to school with almost all white people and they say really crappy things to me. Even my friends, sometimes. It's not my fault where I grew up."

"Sounds like you need some new friends." But there isn't much fire, if any, in his voice.

"Maybe," I say. "Maybe I'll find better ones when I get to college. But maybe you should think about not judging someone before you really know what it's like to be them."

Junior turns around. "What about you? Last time you visited, all you did was talk about everything that's different here. How you couldn't believe we don't have a nanny, and that it smells weird out here and it's boring and you'd hate to live in such a small town. And your dad . . . Look, I like Uncle David, but sometimes he says some weird shit."

Did I say that? All these years, I haven't been able to shake what Junior said, the name he called me. But judging his life and his home . . . Even if I didn't mean to, I get how deeply that would hurt, same as his words hurt me. And I don't remember saying it, but the conviction in his voice convinces me it's true—that maybe he's been struggling with that memory as much as I've been wrestling with mine. It makes me feel awful, that I was so careless with my words.

"We're not some poor Bamas you have to feel sorry for," Junior grumbles. "Some of us like living here."

"I don't think that," I say. "I'm sorry for what I said, Junior. All of it. But you can't judge me based on what my dad says. I don't like it, either, but he gets defensive when we call him out, so I stopped speaking up."

"Well, it wasn't cool that I called you an Oreo. Sorry about that." He's quiet for a moment, then lets out a long, slow breath. "To be honest, it's not just you that's said stuff like that about Bloom. People around here talk that mess. They can't wait to leave. Even Lita . . . I don't think she'll ever come back once she leaves."

"Her parents did, right?"

Junior shakes his head. "She's not like her parents."

"Did you ever think about culinary school?" I gesture to the cake and the kitchen in general. "All the food was so good . . . and obviously you know how to crack the whip."

He shrugs. "Thanks. It's not hard. And I guess I've thought about going into hospitality management, but that means leaving Bloom, and like I said, some of us don't want to leave."

"Couldn't you take classes in Saint Louis or at one of the other schools near here? That's not so far. Not like going to DC."

"You some kind of guidance counselor?" The corner of his mouth turns up in a tiny, quick smile. "But, yeah. Maybe I could."

I return his smile with one of my own. It's funny how my fear can push me to do something that might lead to one of the best experiences of my life while Junior's fear threatens to hold him back. And strange that I didn't see that we're battling the same thing, even though our lives and ambitions are so different.

I guess, deep down, we're not so different.

He clears his throat. "You want to help me finish up this cake? We'll burn the place down if we try to do eighty candles, but if we line them up like this . . ."

I stand next to my cousin and grin.

Nudge him in the side as I say, "Hand me those matches."

SAMSON AND THE DELILAHS

TOCHI ONYEBUCHI

Sobechi knows the power his voice has over them.

Sure, the uniform helps, though it's still a little loose around the waist and his shoulders haven't quite grown all the way into his jacket, and the khaki pants spill onto his dress shoes. But his striped tie is expertly knotted, and a silk kerchief pokes its head out of his jacket pocket to provide just the right amount of accent to the whole outfit. He's good with his hands, though he knows he needs to get better. He can do the claw to accentuate a point, can spread his arms just wide enough to highlight how far ahead his argument is from his opponent's, can do that thing where it seems he's holding the entirety of his point in one hand like a snowball, tight and succinct enough for the judges to see and analyze and nod their heads at. But it's his voice, he knows. His voice does the heavy lifting.

His mother sometimes makes him practice his speeches with his eyes closed. At first, he protested. "Mummy, if I can't see my audience, how can I tell how they are hearing my words?"

"Eh-eh, are you talking with your eyes, now? Are you see-ing with your mouth? It is called de-bate, not SEE-bate. Now, go on. Start over."

And, just like that, she had taken apart his position. And it had helped. Late at night, when he used to practice in front of his mirror, perfecting his posture and trying to keep his hands from wandering, his eyes would rove everywhere. He would get so nervous, staring at himself. When he would pause, he would look at the ceiling, and the first few times he did it in front of Mum, she had taken off her slipper and smacked him over the head with it.

When Sobechi practiced in front of both his parents, Daddy would usually have his back turned, working pots and pans over the stove, and the familiar, pungent smell of beans and peppers Mum used for *moi-moi* would fill the air. You could open all the windows in the house and fan your arms until they were about to fall off, and you wouldn't be rid of the smell.

Then, over dinner, they would critique his performance. Daddy would ladle the bean pudding, shaped like slanted pyr-amids, onto everyone's plates while Mum went straight to the chase. "You shuffle, left *oo* right, *ugu* left *oo* right, like ants ah live in your pants. You cut your hand this way; *oya*, cut it like this." Her hands and arms dance, and Sobechi wonders what on earth speech she's trying to give. "And you hunch, always. You hunch like you fi enter small small room. Stand up your back." She demonstrates in her chair, makes her spine into a pillar holding up the sky.

Daddy occasionally glances up from his fried rice and *moi-moi* to smirk at Sobechi during the critique session. Solidarity.

But it's Mummy's words that live inside Sobechi as he speaks now to his audience. He has given this closing statement enough times that the words just come out of him. He doesn't even hear them anymore.

Then the rapturous applause.

The clapping continues long enough that Sobechi knows his team has won. Even before they make the announcement, he can hear their victory. Just like Mummy taught him to.

The center judge, an older white man with a head full of silver hair, shuffles the papers before him. His face looks like it was carved out of a cliff. Sobechi knows it intimidates the others, his teammates and his opponents alike. But he recognizes that type of face. That impassive expression that betrays nothing. That waits for *you* to make the mistake. But that man is on their side. He has been converted. So has the African American woman to his right, and the older white woman to that center judge's left.

The center judge clears his throat. "The committee will

take fifteen minutes to review the arguments made by both teams, then will announce its decision." He bangs the gavel, and everyone starts moving at once.

Coach Carter emerges from the wings and beckons the team, and they huddle backstage. Angelica moves slower than the rest of them, head bowed low, and Coach puts a hand to her shoulder. "Angie, hey, you did fine."

She has her fists balled at her sides, shoulders tense beneath her suit jacket. She's practically trembling. "Fine? I botched our entire argument. I couldn't remember point number two and had to skip literally the most important part of my speech." Tears well up in her eyes, and Coach places his arm around her shoulder and pulls her in, whispering, "It's okay, Angie. It's okay."

Grayson has already loosened his tie. He smells victory in the air too, but he reacts entirely different. He lets himself go, messes up his blond hair a bit and sticks his tongue out as he drapes an arm over Sobechi.

"Not that it matters," Grayson says too loud. "Slam-Dunk Sobe put the team on his *back*. As usual!" At a sharp look from Angelica, Grayson raises his hands in self-defense. "Look, we got this in the bag. It's a Reynolds Wrap. You see how they're clapping for us out there?"

"For him," Angelica growls.

"Hey," Coach says. "We're a team, okay? We win and lose as a team."

But Sobechi pays no attention to them. He looks at the

curtain, looks past it. His lips move silently, going over the words he's spent weeks memorizing, the bits of improvisation he's sprinkled throughout, which lines landed, which ones didn't, whether that joke should have been moved elsewhere, whether he emphasized the right syllables in the right words in the right sentence. He's already thinking about the next round. Nationals.

But the biggest reason he doesn't confer with his teammates is that he has to rest his voice.

Kids stream out of the arts center into the waiting arms of their parents, some sobbing, others completely limp, unable to move their arms and hold the parents who hug them so tightly. Sobechi's mother, in a yellow-patterned gown and *gele* so bright her outfit practically glows in the night, waits by their Subaru Legacy. Her smile, when she sees the plaque in Sobechi's hands proclaiming him the best Individual Interlocutor of the Northeast Consortium Regional Debate Competition, is genuine. Even after all this time, no matter how many of these he brings home, Mummy's smile is genuine.

"Come here, my son," she says, arms wide open.

Coach isn't far behind. "Mrs. Onyekachi, your son was a wonder to listen to once again."

Sobechi's mother's dimples show when she smiles. "Why, thank you, Coach. He practices relentlessly, always so focused." Her Nigerian accent has practically disappeared. In its place is the British inflection Sobechi uses during competitions. It gives their consonants sharp edges. She switches into it so swiftly that it's like she never left England all those years ago to meet Daddy in America. "We are so very proud."

"With a voice like that, and with his skills at oratory, he'd make an excellent lawyer," Coach says.

Mrs. Onyekachi laughs with a hand to her chest. "Or a minister." She hugs Sobechi tight to her side. "His cousin is a pastor in Providence, Rhode Island. We say he learned how to talk reading the Bible."

"Oh." Coach Carter chuckles. "Well, either way, Sobechi is very gifted, but you already know that. Sobechi, make sure to have some fun next weekend, all right? We won't start prepping for Nationals until next month, so enjoy your time off, all right?" He winks at Sobechi. "A pleasure, as always, Mrs. Onyekachi."

"The pleasure is mine, Coach," she says.

The ride home passes in silence, except for the soft whispering of Sobechi in the passenger's seat redoing his arguments.

When they round the corner into their neighborhood, Sobechi sees a car, a van, and a U-Haul truck outside the house next to theirs, and a family carrying things indoors. A man and his wife struggling with a large couch, a girl holding a plastic bag full of various knickknacks in her teeth, her arms laden with totes and other assorted baggage.

"Ah, I knew they'd sold that house," Mrs. Onyekachi says as they pull into their driveway.

Sobechi stares, doesn't know why he's so entranced. It's nighttime, so he can't see all of the things the new family's moving inside.

His mother nudges him in his ribs. "*Oya*, go and help them carry their things."

Sobechi is exhausted, but he knows better than to complain, so he climbs out of car, puts his plaque back on the passenger's seat, and heads their way.

"*Oya*, come come come."

Sobechi comes back so that Mummy, through the driver's-side window, can fix his tie. "But, Mummy, I am going to carry things and sweat. Why do I need to fix my tie?"

"You never get a second chance to make a first impression," she replies.

When she finishes, Sobechi straightens his back and walks over stiffly, waving when he gets close enough. The man Sobechi assumes to be the father glances over and stops in his tracks, nearly dropping the shelves he's carrying. "Oh, hey!" he grunts with a smile. "You must be our neighbor!"

Sobechi sticks his hand out. "Sobechi Onyekachi. Pleased to meet you."

"Alphonse, or just Al." The father wobbles, manages to sneak a sweaty hand out for a quick, limp handshake. "I told Eve we weren't gonna be the only Black family on the block!"

"May I help?"

The father glances at the shelves and laughs. "This might be a little heavy. Uh, my niece might need some help with her band equipment." He pivots slightly. "Hey, Dez! Come meet our neighbors!"

By now, Mum is out of the car, and Daddy is with her, wearing a suit jacket and jeans but with the top button of his dress shirt undone. While they're making introductions and Alphonse wobbles under the weight of his shelves, Sobechi cranes his neck and sees a shape moving by the U-Haul.

Out of the shadows of the U-Haul's belly comes a girl who looks more or less his age, maybe a little older, black, hair combed down so that it covers one eye. She's dressed in all black with a chain from her belt to her front pocket jingling while she drags a big, square-shaped thing backward, occasionally glancing over her shoulder.

"Al, what is it?"

She disappears for a little, and Sobechi is left to wonder what on earth is the relationship between Dez and Alphonse that allows Dez to address him by his first name (and not even his full name, at that!) and not catch a fiery slap across the face. In a minute she's back, and she stares directly at Sobechi, sizes him up. "You sure you can help me lift that? It's heavy, and you're a little . . . skinny."

Was she going to lift it herself? Sobechi wonders, almost in shock. "I can help!" he says at last. He can't help but sound offended. *Skinny!*

"'Kay. I'll climb back in, push a little bit, then you can get the other side. Ready?"

She hops back into the U-Haul, and immediately, they're at work. Her voice is husky, deeper than any girl's voice he's ever heard before, with a little bit of a rasp, like it's being dragged over something. Maybe she needs water. Sobechi will make sure to offer her some when they've finished.

"What is this thing?" Sobechi asks, his long, narrow back already aflame from the effort of carrying it inside and down two flights of stairs.

"It's my amp. Well, one of them."

Sobechi gulps. "*One* of them?"

Dez squints at him after they set the thing down in a large room that's already a jungle of cables and what looks like pieces of a drum set and a whole bunch of other sticks and cords and instruments he's never seen before. Then she laughs with her whole body, and her voice changes, becomes thicker yet more musical. The raggedness has vanished. "Heavy, wasn't it."

She sticks her hand out. "Desirée. Or Dez, for short."

This close and in the light, he sees how beautiful she is. She wears no makeup; the skin of her face is a smooth, unblemished brown. Her hazel eyes shine. Her body, with its muscles and confidence, seems to own the air around it. It seems almost wrong to call her a girl.

"Sobechi," he manages to say, holding her hand, dry yet firm when it grips his.

"Nice to meet you." She jerks her head toward the stairs.

"Now, let's get the rest of it. It's not all that heavy." She laughs. It's too warm outside for the full black outfit she wears. Her long-sleeve T-shirt, worn gray at the elbows and with faded lettering on the front, must have been baggy on her once upon a time, but now it hugs an athletic body as tall as his but . . . fuller.

By the end, after all the moving and the overlong greetings among the adults and Sobechi brushing his teeth and showering and after his nightly prayer with Mum and Daddy, when he's lying in bed, he does not even notice how he can barely move his arms anymore or how much his back is paining him. The only thing he sees, staring straight through the ceiling, is Desirée's face. He smiles, then realizes with shock the reason she feels so different.

She's the first Black girl he has ever known who wasn't somehow related to him. Suddenly, thoughts climb over themselves in his head, a confusion of hopes and fears and wondering more tangled than the wires in the room with all that music equipment. His body is warm with a different kind of fire now.

He must see her again.

Even though it's Saturday, Mummy has Sobechi up early. First the sound—SOBEEEECHI!—and only after Mummy's voice has echoed several times through the house does he smell the jollof rice she's making.

When he makes it down to the kitchen, containers are already filled almost to bursting. Mum has brought out one of her fine ceramic bowls, a large one with flower patterns and a top that sits snugly on it.

"For the neighbors?" Sobechi asks his mother, leaning over her shoulder.

She busies herself with readying the containers. "Bring the big one over to greet our new neighbors. And tell them if they would like to come over tonight, they are welcome."

"Yes, Mummy," he says, slipping his hands under the big dish and making sure to cradle it properly in his arms.

"And speak correctly. I don't want to hear later that you were speaking all *jagga-jagga*."

He nods and assumes a straight face all the way to Desirée and Alphonse's front door.

Lifting one knee up and tempting fate, he manages to poke a finger at the doorbell. It swings open and Desirée stands in the doorway, coarse but straight hair in her face, clothes loose on her frame. So she is one of these teenagers who get to sleep in on Saturdays. Sobechi has heard of these people.

"Good morning," Sobechi says, smiling cheerily like in those Colgate commercials. "Is Mr. . . ." He panics. He didn't get Al's last name. "Um . . ." He does not dare use the man's first name.

She slaps her forehead. "Oh, duh. You mean my uncle. No, he's out. Running some errands or whatever, I dunno. Here. Let me get that."

Before he can properly protest, she's taken the dish from

him and turns to head back inside. "Wow, this smells good. Oh, hey, come on in. The place is messy, and I, like, just woke up, but it's not like I was getting ready to go anywhere."

Nothing she says makes sense to Sobechi. Why did she not let him carry the plate inside like a gentleman? How is it nine thirty in the morning and she is still in her pink pajama pants? Does she greet all strangers like this?

Inside, the place is cool and almost odorless, with cardboard boxes everywhere, and only some of the furniture is unpacked. Desirée places the dish on the kitchen countertop. "Oh, by the way, thanks for helping last night. It would've taken so much longer if it was just me and Al. Eve checked out after they brought the couch in. Al's *friend*." She opens the top of the dish and sniffs. "Hey, I got a friend coming over. Maybe you know her? Goes to school around here? Dominique Reyes?"

Sobechi's mind darts in a dozen different directions. Does he know someone who knows Desirée? Who could that person possibly be? Dominique Reyes? He shrugs.

"Anyway, we're gonna jam for a little bit if you wanna meet her."

"Yes," Sobechi manages.

She smiles at him, and it's perfect. "Cool," she says, then fetches some spoons from a drawer. She hands him one, then, with the other, starts digging into the jollof rice.

Sobechi's eyes widen in horror.

She sees his face out of the corner of her eye, then chuckles shyly, hand to mouth to catch stray grains of rice. Why does her sloppiness make Sobechi want to spend even more time with her?

"I'm a mess today," she mumbles, still smiling. "But this is really good." She stares at Sobechi for a beat, then goes, "Come on. You gotta help me with this. It's a lot."

Slowly, carefully, he digs his spoon in and takes out a good hunk of rice. Using his free hand as a safety net, he guides the spoon to his mouth. Desirée peers at him, like he's some sort of alien. He makes it without spilling a single grain, and it's the most triumphant bite of jollof he can remember ever having.

"You were literally gonna take all day," says Desirée in disbelief. Then she's laughing, and Sobechi's heart flips again so that he almost chokes on the rice.

When he finishes coughing, he starts laughing too, then suddenly, he falls into her rhythm and they begin talking and Sobechi finds that some small gate has opened in him, a single lock expertly picked.

The doorbell rings.

Even as something taps a fast rhythm on the door, Desirée is out of her seat and racing across the living room. She flings the door open and wraps her arms around the waist of whoever's on the other side. "Dom!" she bellows, pulling the other girl close. When Dom straightens, the drumsticks she holds twirl over fingers whose tips poke out through ratty gloves.

"Dom, this is . . . um—"

"Sobechi," he says, sticking his hand out.

"What up, what up?" Dom says, eyeing him up and down. Tight curls frame a face the color of sand. Then she's got eyes only for Desirée. She chews her gum with her mouth open and is always tapping the sticks on a different part of herself. Now, her thigh. Now, her collar. "So, Desert Eagle, we jamming or what?"

Desirée looks over at Sobechi, and it's like the two of them, she and Dominique, fit perfectly beside each other. Desirée with her bony elbows and wild hair and Dom with a plaid shirt tied around her wide waist and a bandanna taming her curly hair. Desirée able to stand completely still and Dom constantly moving some part of her body.

"You down?" Desirée asks.

Mummy never said what time Sobechi needed to be home, so, loosened by the risk he took with the rice, he shrugs and grins. "Yes."

"Shit yeah," Dom cheers, swaying.

"Dominique!" Desirée can barely keep the frown on her face. "Our guest!"

Dom twirls a drumstick in her fingers. Her grin nearly splits her face. "Oh, you ain't heard nothin' yet, my guy."

Dominique sits at the drum kit in the basement, moves her snares a little bit, then moves them back, checks the cymbals, and occasionally steps on her kick-drum pedal. Desirée plays with her guitar. A cord connects it to one of her amps, and a bevy of pedals lies at her bare feet. She strums idly. Her fingers dance over the neck of the thing, and she's not even looking at it, but the notes climb over each other in the air. Single trills and arpeggios, then, every so often, a CHUG-CHUG that nearly knocks him out of his folding chair. The guitar growls. That's the only way Sobechi can explain it. Something like a tiger or a dragon from the fantasy novels he sneaks into his room without his mum seeing.

Desirée and Dominique whisper to each other. Sobechi catches words like "periphery" and "system" and "August burns red." The girls giggle. Desirée shakes her head, darts a look at Sobechi, then confers with Dominique once more. They seem to come to an agreement.

"Okay," Desirée says, once again facing Sobechi. "We're a little rusty, and the song sounds a little weird without backup vocals, but here goes."

The guitar growls: chug-chug-chug-chug BRUNUNUBU-NUBUNUNUU. Dominique bangs on the drums and each kick joins forces with each stroke from Desirée, the barrage so powerful Sobechi falls out of his seat. He covers his ears. They might actually start bleeding.

Then there's only drums, then a softer melody, and a voice. Desirée's singing. Sort of.

When he can separate the sounds, he hears "Life in a bubble

jungle"—gibberish—"but I was in there for you"—what is she saying?—"life in a bubble jungle." Then . . .

BRUNUNUBUNUBUNUNUU. "Seeing you, believing"—gibberish—"THE POWER STRUGGLE, believing and healing, appeasing, THE POWER STRUGGLE."

It makes absolutely no sense. The newness of it all makes Sobechi dizzy, so dizzy he almost vomits, but after what seems like forever, they're done. It's over.

Dominique cackles behind her cymbals and snares. "Oh my God, I'm crying."

"Sobechi, you okay?"

She's back to normal. Sobechi looks up, and Desirée's face is right in front of his. She's kneeling, her guitar-that-sounds-like-a-dragon-and-a-bear on a strap around her neck. Her hand is on his shoulder.

"Hey," she whispers. "You good?"

"I . . ."

She smirks. "That was a lot. We were a little loud."

"What was that?" Sobechi manages to murmur.

"Hah! That was System of a Down."

"Best band ever!" Dominique shouts from behind the drums.

"But . . . those sounds. I've never . . ."

Desirée's eyes go wide. "Wait, you've never heard metal before?"

"What is metal?"

Desirée chuckles. "Metal, my friend, is the most freeing sound in the world." Her gaze softens. "But we kinda threw you in the deep end." She squeezes his shoulder. "Let's show you something a little softer." She's up again. "Let's do Dead Sara."

Dominique pouts. "But that's not really metal."

Desirée makes a stern face, and Dominique relents.

"'Weatherman'?"

Desirée nods. "'Weatherman.'"

Her guitar goes again, no chugs, just riffs, riffs, riffs, then drums, soft at first, snares, rising, then—Sobechi braces himself—badumdum.

"Come on!" Then it hits, but it's kinder this time, more intelligible.

The drums are slower, and he can hear her singing.

> *"Addicted to the love of ourselves*
> *I'm the weatherman*
> *And tell no one else*
> *I'm the weatherman*
>
> SO GO FOR THE KILL"

Her voice warbles and strikes, and it's got that rasp he recognizes. He can actually see that type of sound coming from an actual human being.

As she sings, she flicks her hair back, but her mouth is always pressed to the microphone in front of her. Sweat soaks her shirt, brings a sheen to her face, so that she's glowing in the fluorescent light. Occasionally, still strumming, she looks back at Dom, who smiles broadly. Then things go quiet.

Then it's just Desirée.

"I sing for the melody and I sing for a reason
. . . for all that un-American

SO GO FOR THE KIIIIIILL"

Then she's back to head-banging, dancing around in place, contained in a booth surrounding that microphone. But wild and crazy, her hair going every which way, like the music has possessed her. It has replaced her blood and her bones. She has become those sounds, that music.

By the time they finish, she's spent and looks like she just climbed out of a swimming pool, but she looks so happy. Sobechi has never seen anyone so ecstatic.

Something flutters in his chest, and he wants to freeze that moment, to stare at that smiling face and to make sure the sounds that make Desirée grin like that never, ever stop.

"He likes that one," Dominique chirps, pointing a drumstick at him.

Desirée's laugh is even more music coming from her throat.

"We're gonna make a metalhead out of you."

He has no idea what that means, but it doesn't matter. His body is alive. More alive than it's ever been. His sternum thrums from more than the echo of the growling and roaring of the amplifiers. His fingers tingle. Blood rushes to his face.

He feels like he has been struck by lightning. Thunder still rings in his ears. His insides are on fire. And he wants to do this again.

Desirée throws him right into it. Playing her favorite bands, breaking down the different genres. Explaining the difference between death metal and math metal. Turning her nose up at most nu-metal, but there are a few bands she likes. When she plays certain bands, even though they may not have the technical brilliance he recognizes in others, Desirée gets a faraway look in her eyes, and Sobechi can tell she's transported to a different place, a different time, then she'll tell him about how, when she and Al would move around a lot, Korn was always playing on her iPod. Jonathan Davis's screams held so much of what she felt.

They sit in her music room now, a week after she screamed about power struggles and a weatherman, with "Tempest" from the Deftones's *Koi No Yokan* album playing softly in the background.

"I know I was ragging on nu-metal, but Linkin Park was literally all I listened to after I went to live with Al." She smiles at the ceiling, then at Sobechi. "I used to practice Chester Bennington's screams in the shower. Aunt Eve was always banging on the walls. 'Cut that shit out!' 'Dez, if that's you howling in there . . .'"

Sobechi wants to ask what happened to her parents. He realizes with a shock he can't find the words.

"When I found out Chester had died, Sobe, I cried for the whole rest of the week." Even now, remembering it, she grows quiet, and tears well in her eyes.

It's more emotion than he has ever seen in his life, so much of it coming from one person.

"But System, that's my love right there. *Toxicity*'s easily one of my favorite albums of all time." She gets up from the carpet they're both lying on and slips her acoustic guitar's strap over her shoulder. She has that inspired shine in her eyes again. Sobechi presses pause on his iPod and disconnects it, and Chino's crooning cuts off midlyric.

Almost immediately, Desirée starts playing. He recognizes the first notes as the beginning of the title track off that System of a Down album. Over and over, Desirée plays it, extending the intro, then goes in a drumless breakdown of the chorus, singing it rather than shouting it like Serj. "Somewhere, between the scared silence and sleep, disorder, disorder, disooooorrrder," then humming.

"More wood for their fires, loud neighbours"

Before he knows what's happening, Sobechi is on his feet and singing the words, first a murmur, then something deep and rumbling coming from his chest.

> *"Flashlight reveries caught in the headlights of a*
> *truck*
>
> *Eeeeeating seeeeeeds as a pastime activity*
> *The toxicity of our city, of our city"*

Desirée, playing absently, stares in wonder at him, then smiles.

Together, they sing,

> *"You!*
> *What do you own the world*
> *How do you own disorder, disorder*
> *Now!*
> *Somewhere between the sacred silence*
> *Sacred silence and sleep . . ."*

Both of them, mouths nearly touching the microphone, mouths nearly touching each other.

> *"YOU! WHAT DO YOU OWN THE WORLD*
> *HOW DO YOU OWN DISORRDEERRRRR"*

They're louder now, shouting the chorus, but still singing, until they both get to that long, drawn-out scream at the end, and the music stops, and they're both suddenly so tired. But they can't stop looking at each other.

Desirée smiles at him, and when he lies in bed later that night, he has System playing on his iPod well after the lights in the house have been turned off.

At dinner the next day, Sobechi's head is swimming with images. After their first duet, Sobechi had downloaded every song off *Toxicity*. All night, he had listened, and the whole of it had taken Sobechi to a place he'd never been before, and the lyrics about dropping bombs on children in faraway countries and the failure of America's drug policies wouldn't let him go. At the end of the album was a hidden track, a haunting melody with a flute and different drums. There were no words, only humming and moans. Well after he should have been asleep, he'd looked the band up on the internet. They were all Armenian and they were descendants of survivors of the Armenian Genocide. People called them political. "Antiwar because they knew it in their bones," he read on one site. By the time he'd gone to sleep, the sky had started to lighten.

So Sobechi looks straight at his mum and asks, "Mummy, could you tell me about the Biafran War?" He'd heard about the civil war that had cut through Nigeria in the late sixties; he knew it was part of his mother's country's history. But nothing beyond that.

The look on Mum's face tells Sobechi that this is literally the last thing she's expected to talk about. Her eyes turn into saucers. Her ball of *fufu*, greased with pepper soup from her bowl, nearly slips from her fingers.

"You were a child then, right? Younger than me, even," Sobechi continues.

Daddy stirs in his chair but says nothing.

Mummy gets a hurt look in her eyes, as though Sobechi has wounded her.

"You lived through the Nigerian Civil War, right? I . . . I know nothing about it and I just wanted to—"

"Enough!" Her hands slam down on the table. "Enough of this. Sobechi"—she points her finger straight into his face—"if you ask me one more time about Biafra." Then a string of Igbo words he doesn't know, but the meaning of which he understands, darts from her lips. Ask her about Biafra again and she will break his legs.

"But, Mummy, I—"

"Sobechi!"

Fury Sobechi has never known takes hold of him. Suddenly, he's up on his feet and stomps away without washing his hands, stomps all the way upstairs, then does something he never thought he would ever do. He slams the door to his room. Loudly.

Why won't Mummy talk about her own history? Shouldn't she be encouraging him to learn about his country? He's too angry to think. So he plugs in his earbuds and turns the volume too high on the August Burns Red album Desirée downloaded for him earlier that day. He wants to scream but knows he can't, so he lets their singer scream for him.

During the ride to school the next morning, Sobechi doesn't say a word.

It's the first weekend of debate practice once again, and already, things feel like they're going back to the way they were. Sobechi can feel himself fighting it. He's somewhere new, somewhere freer, more colorful.

Daddy pulls up in front of the school. "Do well, Sobechi," Daddy says, smiling.

"Yes, Daddy." Sobechi's voice is so raspy it surprises him. And he coughs, but when he says, "Yes, Daddy" again, it's the same. He can barely whisper.

Daddy frowns at him. "Are you sick, Sobechi?"

Hand to throat, Sobechi says, "No, Daddy. I'm fine." Then he's off before Daddy can make him say more words. He doesn't even look back to see Daddy drive away.

Everyone is happy to see him again—Coach, Angelica, Grayson, all the others on the practice squad—until he opens his mouth to greet Coach, and everyone goes silent.

"What happened to your voice, man?" Grayson looks like someone just broke wind. "You sound way different."

Sobechi can't get it back. His fingers tremble, his heart races. A glance at Coach. A glance at Angelica. He closes his eyes, tries to will it back, then opens his mouth and . . . nothing. Just that harsh gasp that scrapes against the inside of his throat.

It's gone. His voice is gone.

He can't even pick his feet up when he walks. So when Daddy opens the front door, Sobechi merely shuffles through, holding his backpack in one hand. He stubs his toe on the leg of a chair and yelps, and it just seems like one more thing gone wrong. After he tried to practice introductory remarks—and couldn't raise his voice above a whisper!—Grayson went up and improvised his way through it all, pretending to know what he was talking about, because boys like him at school don't even really study. And he made a mockery of the text, butchered it, and every misplaced sentence and every point Grayson doubled back on and every mispronounced word— it's DEH-monstrate, not de-MOAN-strate!—made Sobechi cringe until he could barely stand to stay in the room. Angelica seemed to be the only one to improve over the break. It felt good to see her do well, but something was definitely out of whack when Sobechi wasn't the one being praised by Coach.

He's so in his own head that it isn't until he's all the way down the upstairs hallway that he notices Mummy in his room. She brandishes his iPod like a weapon. She just might hit him with it.

"Sobechi!" Her voice is an arrow cutting right through the fog in his brain. Too many thoughts fall over themselves in his head, but he knows he's supposed to be scared. She has that look in her eyes that she gets right before she twists his ear. "Sobechi, what is this?"

"Mummy, it's . . ."

"What is this DEVIL-WORSHIPPER MUSIC?! Where did you get this?" She shakes it at him, and the headphone lines flail just like he feels he's doing.

"Mummy, I can explain."

"Where did you get this? Is this what has been possessing you of late? Is this why you can barely speak? Where did you get this!"

His head slumps. "Desirée," he murmurs.

"Who? I cannot hear you! Speak up!"

"Desirée," he says louder. Still meek. Defeated. It hurts to say her name. Tears spring to his eyes. Whatever beautiful, loud journey he set off on with her, it's done now. He knows this is the end.

"The neighbor!" Mummy can't believe it. "I knew as soon as I saw how he let that young girl dress that she was trouble. Eh-HEH! Look at the company you are keeping. Sobechi, if I see you again with that girl"—then a string of menacing Igbo words—"If I catch you with that girl, you will taste fire. I will introduce you myself to the devil. Then you can scream all the *wahalla* you want. *Chineke mbere*!" She throws her hands into the air, and her voice breaks, and it's almost as if she's ready to join Sobechi in crying. But she stomps past him, muttering to herself and leaving Sobechi to stew in a silence so heavy, so unnatural, that he doesn't fall asleep for hours.

Slowly, it comes back. In a week, his voice returns to normal. In the week after that one, his confidence is completely restored. It hums in his chest, radiates warmth into his shoulders. He has it back. All of it. The morning he feels ready, he practices speaking in front of the bathroom mirror. The steam from the shower seems to help. And by the time it is his turn in their after-school practice session, he finds he can do all his regular tricks. He can modulate his voice. When he pauses, it's no longer to clear his throat or to get rid of an itch, it's to hammer home a point. If anything, his voice, when he speaks, sounds richer. Feels richer. The speech he gives that day, a short excerpt from John F. Kennedy's "Moon" speech, stuns the room into silence. Then everyone's on their feet and clapping, and they don't stop clapping until Coach's fifth try to get them to calm down. But he's smiling so hard.

On the way out, everyone claps Sobechi on the shoulder or shakes his hand or grins their thanks right at him. He can't believe how happy he's made them. After everyone leaves,

Coach slips a hand over Sobechi's shoulder. "Wherever you went . . . ," he says quietly, "it's good to have you back."

Suddenly, Sobechi doesn't know why he fought this for so long. Why he resisted. Everything feels right again. All the congratulations, the praise. People needing him again. This is where he's supposed to be.

These are his thoughts as he makes his way down the hall. But he stops short when he hears noise, muffled voices and what sounds like cymbals. Then he hears it, a guitar riff.

The door swings open to the auditorium. Sobechi sees them onstage. It looks like they're an entire world away, the stage is that far. But he recognizes them instantly. Desirée, strumming out a few licks, then directing the rest of the band through the next couple of measures; then Dominique, toying with the cymbals and kick drums while she listens; and there's someone else, someone Sobechi doesn't recognize, on bass who has a microphone in front of her too. They all seem comfortable around each other, but tired, like they've been at it for too long.

As soon as the doors swing shut behind Sobechi, the music stops, midbar, and everyone stares. Sobechi can see the emotions working across Desirée's face. The confusion, the hurt, the joy, all of it out in the open. Then a mask falls over it all, and she's saying something quietly to the girls before taking off her guitar and putting it back into its stand. She hops off the stage with practiced nonchalance and meets Sobechi halfway.

For a while, they don't say anything, Desirée clearly waiting for his explanation. And there's so much he wants to say, but he needs to say it right, needs to organize his thoughts just like in debate. However, what comes out of his mouth is simply, stupidly, "I was unaware that you practiced here."

Desirée jerks her head toward the stage. "Yeah, Dayna's in the school band, and she's got the hookup. Lets us practice here to get a better feel for our live gigs."

"Live gigs?"

"Yeah." Desirée shrugs. "Debate practice?"

"Um, yeah." He looks at his shoes. "I'm sorry. I just . . . I disappeared."

"Yeah, no reason, no talk, no nothing. For two weeks. Nothing from you."

Sobechi winces. "It's my mother. She . . . she doesn't like the music. I dunno, she's old-school, and maybe it's just too loud or not like what she's used to. But she doesn't want me listening to it anymore. Says it's devil-worshipping music."

Desirée barks out a chuckle, but Sobechi can hear the hurt in it.

"And the singing was starting to affect my voice."

"Ah, I see. And why does this mean we can't hang out?"

Sobechi wants to tell her that debate practice is going to take up more of his time, that it's where he needs to be, or that he needs to really focus on his studies, or any of the usual excuses he gives people when they ask him to be social—but he knows it's because if he and Desirée spend any more time together, he will start singing again. He loves it, he realizes. And he will scream his voice into oblivion. He knows that's what's going to happen, so he can't let himself get close to it again. That's his argument, his position, but he can't bring himself to breathe a syllable to Desirée.

"So that's it then? We're never gonna see each other again?"

"I didn't say that! I just—"

Desirée brushes him off. "Nah, it's all good. Don't worry about it. I gotta get back to practice. The girls are waiting." She storms off and doesn't say a word about what just happened to either Dom or Dayna. Just starts playing a song from the first Periphery album, all angry chugs and riffs and screaming, where the notes from the guitar become as percussive as the drums, furious beats that have replaced any semblance of conversation whatsoever.

Even though winning Nationals his junior year was supposed to be the culmination of almost an entire life's worth of effort, it still feels hollow. Everyone cheers for longer than usual. His teammates all beam at him, genuinely, basking in the glow. Angelica knocked it out the park, as they say. And Grayson knew that this was the time to buckle down. Though Sobechi was, as usual, the brightest star, his team could be said to be the best team in the nation. Future debate teams will hear of Sobechi's talent, his mesmerizing speeches, how he carried the school on his back like Atlas from Greek mythology class holding up the sky. This was what he wanted. But . . .

Even after the celebratory dinner where Mum cooks for Coach and the team, and they all finally taste that magical jollof rice, Sobechi can only pretend to be happy.

Then, it's over and everyone filters out and Sobechi is still at his seat while Daddy washes dishes and Mummy texts her friends in Nigeria using WhatsApp.

"Mummy?" Sobechi has finally looked up from his hands.

"Yes, my son." She sounds so joyful and so pleased. He's going to ruin this.

"Can you . . ." He sighs. Squares his shoulders. "Tell me about Biafra."

A cloud covers her face. Her fingers stop, and a glower sets into her eyes.

"Mummy, I know what happened. I've read about it online. I even checked books out from the library on it. I know it's part of Nigeria's history. It's part of our history. I . . . I want to know about you." He's thinking of Serj and Daron and all the other members of System of a Down and how they used their parents' tragedy to make their art. He's thinking of their political messaging and their antiwar stands, and he's thinking about what it means to stand for something in the world. And he hopes maybe there's some of that for him here too. "Mummy, it's not to hurt you. I . . . I want to be a good son." He can feel himself start to break down. "I really do, and I'm sorry. I just . . ." He can't go any further. He sniffles, then regains control.

But when he looks up, his mother's staring at the tablecloth, utterly still. "I was in kindergarten when the war began," she says quietly. "When my family and I were in hiding, we spent time in the forests, eating what we could find. When we came home, soldiers were sleeping in our house. My uncle begged and begged and begged for us to be let back in. The way they made him beg . . . . That night, we all slept in one room. There were twelve of us." Her shoulders start to shake, and Sobechi realizes it's the first time he's seen her cry. All of a sudden, she's no longer just a force of nature, a powerful typhoon or an overwhelming burst of sunlight. She's human.

Daddy joins them at the table. And Mummy talks well into the night. There's music in her voice. The more she speaks, the more it sounds like song.

It's late spring. And the sun is still shining brightly by the time Sobechi gets back from school.

As they pull into the driveway, he notices Desirée on her front porch. Then he pretends to drop something under his seat.

Mum looks over. "Eh, what is it now?"

"I dropped something. I think it was my USB drive." It's a convincing enough excuse, because Mummy eventually gets out and leaves her key on the driver's seat.

175

"Remember to lock the car when you get out."

Desirée has been watching them the whole time, silently.

Sobechi stops his fruitless search, snatches the keys, then hops out and makes a beeline for her. She makes to head back inside her home, but Sobechi catches her just before the screen door closes behind her.

"Your mom's gonna kill you when she sees us like this."

Sobechi manages a half smile. "I want to invite you and your uncle over for dinner."

"Wait, what? I thought I was a devil worshipper or something. Your mom change her mind?"

"She's being Americanized." And they both chuckle. When they settle down, he looks at her, really looks at her, to the point where she's starting to get nervous.

"What?"

"Thank you."

"For what?"

For giving me the gift of metal, Sobechi wants to say. For getting me to scream for the first time. For giving me a place where I could truly be angry or sad or have fun. For giving me music to live my life to, music that gave me the courage to unlock something in my mummy. Music that's helping me become a better son. But he hasn't quite figured out how to put that all into argument form. Instead, he smiles and says, "I'm working on a song." He kicks at a stone on the porch. "It's political."

Her face lights up when she realizes what he's saying, and he knows she can see it too. Both of them onstage, singing into microphones, screaming into them. Faces covered in sweat. Bodies weak from the effort of performing but held up by the bass drums that rock their sternums. Dez launching into a Mark Tremonti–style solo, and Sobechi watching her with what he now realizes is love. And both of them, at the end, wishing the crowd a good night in their best rock-star voices.

"I guess we're gonna have to change the band name, then."

STOP PLAYING

LIARA TAMANI

The whole naked selfie situation started on the first day of Higher Ground's Teen Beach Retreat, during the closing prayer of the opening assembly. I was sitting among the seven hundred teens in the grand ballroom of the hotel—eyes wide open, head unbowed, looking for Lucas. He hadn't seen me yet. And I needed him to see me so he could get overwhelmed by all my cuteness and take me back.

I was wearing Lucas's favorite light-pink dress over his favorite swimsuit and I'd pulled my hair up into two big Afro puffs. Lucas liked it pressed best, but salt water and sand didn't play with flat-ironed hair. Plus I hadn't worn my puffs since before I started dating Lucas. They used to be my favorite.

Lucas had broken up with me two weeks earlier over some silly shit. I mean stuff. Get this: for the beach retreat, he wanted me to room with Dara (his homeboy Derrick's girl-friend, who I can't stand) instead of with Tish (my best friend, who he can't stand). How crazy was that?

Anyway, an argument ensued. I told him he was trippin'. He told me our relationship was over. I was like, "Yeah, whatever," because he was always saying shit—I mean stuff—like that. Then after we hung up, he stopped answering my calls and texts. Not for a few hours like after our normal fights. For days! I must've called and texted him like a hundred times. Called and texted until my three usual stages of being ignored—feeling pissed then hurt then stupid—had repeated so much they rolled into one hot, crying mess. Not cute. Not even a little bit. So I stopped calling and crying. I decided that Lucas ignoring me was just another one of his stupid games, and I needed to play if I was going to win.

"We thank you for these teens, Father God, who have come here to fellowship with one another and build a closer relation-ship with thee," Brother Tony, the head of the church's youth ministry, prayed loudly into the microphone. He was standing on the stage at the front of the giant room, wiping sweat from his forehead. Looked like the combination of his long dreads and the huge chandelier overhead was getting the best of him. But no one could tell. As I looked around the ballroom for Lucas's face among all the teens, every head was bowed.

Except for this one boy. Over my right shoulder, a row back and three chairs down, I spotted him with his eyes wide open, staring at me. He had a curly high-top fade and a long face with high cheekbones. I'd never seen him before, and I figured he must've been from a different campus.

Higher Ground had five campuses, and all the teens from each campus were invited to the three-day teen beach retreat. Everybody rode down to Galveston on buses from their respective campuses in Houston and the surrounding areas that morning. Mom dropped me off before meeting her first client at the gym, so I was on one of the first buses to leave the main campus. Lucas was on the last. I know because Derrick posted a picture of them on Instagram with the caption, "Saved the best for last."

Now back to the boy. He was cute. I mean stupid cute. So cute I had to give him a pass on that yellow visor he was wearing to match his yellow shorts and smiley-face tank top. Boy clearly liked to coordinate. But I couldn't even hate, especially when yellow looked so good against his smooth dark skin, when his dimples showed without smiling, and his eyelashes curled all the way back to kiss his lids.

Hi, he mouthed, smiling, showing his straight white teeth.

Hi, I mouthed back, trying to yank the balls of my cheeks back down. I couldn't be smiling at dudes! I had a boyfriend! Well, not technically, because he was acting stupid, but I still wanted to be with him.

Lucas was my first real boyfriend. We'd been dating for almost a year, since I was a freshman. He was *the* Lucas Sykes:

the pastor's son, the all-state quarterback, the star of all of the church's big theater productions, *and* he interned for NASA every summer. *And* he drove a white drop-top BMW. Need I say more? Everybody and their mama wanted to be with him. To be honest, I never understood why he wanted to be with me. I was a year younger, never the star of anything, and wasn't blessed with beauty like Tish, who all the boys wanted. Don't get me wrong, I was cute. But let's just say I felt lucky to be his girlfriend.

But sitting in the grand ballroom that morning, I forgot all about feeling lucky. I couldn't stop smiling at that cute boy. I was straight-up giddy. Looking at him looking back at me felt delicious.

That is, until I caught the glare of Lucas. Of all of the places he could've been sitting! There he was, six rows back and two seats to the left of the cute boy. Lucas's arms were folded across his chest and he was staring at me—hard. I mean, super hard. As hard as the muscles he had popping out from his shoulders and arms.

I quickly turned back around.

"Amen," everyone said in unison.

I looked over at Tish, who was sitting beside me in a long purple sarong, and widened my eyes at her to mean, *Girl!*

She raised her eyebrows and cocked her head to mean, *What?*

I stiffened every muscle in my face and shook my head in

the tiniest movement to mean, *Can't tell you right now.*

She knocked her left knee against my right at least five times like, *I'm not having that.* Then she whispered, "What? Lucas?" with her face scrunched up. The hate between them was mutual.

"I'll tell you in a sec," I whispered back and faced forward.

"Keri!" she whispered hard.

But I kept looking forward. I knew Lucas was probably still watching.

"Now, I know the next couple of hours is beach time, but it's not completely free time," Brother Tony said into the microphone, still wiping sweat. "In each one of your tote bags, you'll find a booklet of questions we want you to reflect upon and journal about at the beach."

"Yeah, right!" Tish and I said in unison, and the room buzzed in agreement.

"I won't see y'all again until tonight's church service," Brother Tony said over the swelling voices, "so be good until then."

People sprang from their seats, ready to head to the beach.

As soon as I got up, I immediately eye-locked with the cute boy. I swear I wasn't trying to. My eyes just went straight to his. And once they got there, they snuggled up. Seriously, our eyes might as well have been sitting on a sofa, curled up together under a blanket or something.

Funny—I tried to do the same thing with Lucas once. Got

the idea from one of Tish's magazines, which said eye-gazing was a good test to see if we were in love. Anyway, we were supposed to do it for like ten minutes. Lucas didn't last ten seconds. I don't know how long cute boy and I were staring into each other's eyes. Felt like it could've been a minute. Or ten. Or a hundred.

"Now, that's what I'm talking about. Don't chase 'em. Replace 'em!" Tish said, interrupting the gaze fest.

"What? Nah, it's not even like that," I said, trying to fight the grin spreading across my face.

Tish twisted her lips. "Yeah, okay."

Damn, Lucas probably saw that, too. I looked for him among all the people exiting through the ballroom's set of double doors, but didn't see him.

We'd already raced down to the ocean three times to cool off and were almost done with our lunch by the time Lucas and Derrick ducked down under our blue umbrella with their shirts off and towels around their necks. Derrick, whose light-brown skin was bright red from the sun, sat down on the edge of Tish's lounge chair and Lucas sat on the edge of mine.

I wished Lucas didn't look so dang cute. He had a fresh cut. And something about an edge-up always made his angular face, with its hooded eyes, perfect white teeth, and plump lips, look irresistible.

Oh, so now you want to come over here and talk to me,

I thought, leaned back into the stretchy fabric of the lounge chair, and pushed my shades up the bridge of my sweaty nose. I couldn't speak because I'd just gotten red apple skin stuck between my two front teeth. I tried to get it out with my tongue but couldn't.

Derrick was the first one to say something. "You look pretty, as always," he told Tish. He wasn't lying. I was sitting on her left side, her buzz-cut side. On her right side, her hair fell down to her chin and half covered her face. Her glossy, light-pink lipstick was still holding on, and her dark-brown skin always had the fresh, dewy look of girls in ads selling makeup that doesn't look like makeup. No glow in a bottle for Tish. Her skin was just flawless like that.

"Where's Dara?" Tish asked.

I know that's right, I seconded in my head.

"Man, I broke up with that girl last week."

I didn't even like Dara, but the way he said *that girl*—like they hadn't been dating for almost two years—made me want to slide my pinky nail between my two front teeth and tell him about himself.

Tish took a sip of the canned lemonade that the church staff had handed out with the white paper lunch boxes twenty minutes earlier. "Don't tell me y'all around here synchronizing breakups."

Oooo . . . get 'em, Tish!

Derrick and Lucas looked at each other and exchanged a

nervous laugh. Then Derrick slightly widened his downturned eyes at Lucas.

"So," Lucas said, and turned to me—face, neck, and chest glistening with sweat.

I folded my arms across my waist, cocked my head to the side, pretended to have a slight attitude, and waited for him to compliment my dress and Afro puffs. Waited for him to say he wanted me back.

He did none of the above. Instead, he looked at my hair and hiked up the left corner of his upper lip. (Clearly, he wasn't a fan of my puffs.) Then he stood up, wiped his face with the towel around his neck, and said, "Well, we were just rolling through. Didn't want to be rude. Even though we're broken up, we can still be cordial and all." And they were off.

As soon as they left, Tish started in on them. "Why they always trying to act like they got so much game? And why does Derrick think he's Drake? Did you hear him? I swear, two people tell the boy he looks like Drizzy and all of a sudden he's switchin' up the sound of his voice."

"Tell me about it," I said, even though I didn't really notice, and picked the apple skin out of my teeth with the nail of my pointer finger. Then I sat up, warm breeze at my back, and fluffed out my Afro puffs. "Does my hair look okay?

"Yeah, it's supercute," Tish answered, and ate a Lay's potato chip. She still had some left.

She was right. My hair was cute. I'd gotten my mom to part

it down the middle, used a little gel and a scarf to slick down the edges, and moisturized the curls in my puffs with a little cream. I'd actually smiled at myself in my bathroom mirror before I left the house. That's how cute it was.

But my puffs didn't feel cute anymore. All of a sudden, they felt stupid. And I didn't know what possessed me to style my hair like I was two years old. I started taking my right ponytail holder out.

"What are you doing? You're gonna mess them up," Tish said.

I removed my left ponytail holder, not daring to look at her or open my mouth to reply. The tears, already heavy in my eyes, just needed any little excuse to come pouring down. And I was not about to be the one crying in front of everybody on the beach. Naw, not me.

"Man, fuck Lucas!" Tish said with so much force she sent a piece of chip flying out of her mouth. She licked her bottom lip and continued, "He ain't nobody. Miserable ass. Always got something to say about everybody, like he's the motherfucking authority on fashion. He ain't shit. Just a rich, spoiled, rude, controlling asshole!"

Tish was right, but that's not what stopped me from crying. I was too busy looking around to see if anyone else had heard all the curse words flying out of her mouth. I mean, we weren't officially in church, but Brother Tony had said we were supposed to treat the hotel and all its premises like church ground. Thankfully, no one appeared to be paying any attention. So I got busy trying to redo my hair. I wrapped a ponytail holder back around my right puff. Tried to do the same with my left, but the ponytail holder snapped.

Before I even had a chance to react, Tish said, "Damn, it's hot."

And it was. The sun had already started its descent, but that didn't mean a thing. Outside, it still felt like it was a hundred degrees. Beads of sweat pooled on my body anyplace with a dip or a crease. "Sure is," I said.

Then we looked at each other and took off racing toward the waves—hot sand stinging the bottoms of our feet. My toes touched the cool ocean first, and I kept running until I was waist deep. Then I floated on my back, eyes closed, giving the ocean my weight, until Tish caught up and splashed water in my face.

By the time dinner rolled around, my puffs were back in full effect. Tish and I'd finally made it to the front of the line, to the long rectangular tables covered with white tablecloths and topped with silver chafers. I was spooning out some blackened catfish when I heard a gruff voice say, "Hey."

I looked up and there he was. The cute boy. Standing across from me, scooping out an unreasonable amount of dirty rice. I'd just done the same thing—the dirty rice went hard.

"Hey," I said, surprised such a rough, low voice could come

out of all that cuteness . . . surprised to see him standing right in front of me. My eyes had gotten so used to looking at him in yellow that they'd missed him in line behind us in his white T-shirt and dark-blue jeans.

"Heeey," Tish said, with a little extra in her voice. She was already onto the garlic bread.

"Oh, this is my friend Tish," I said, like I knew the cute boy well.

The cute boy balanced his plate in one hand and extended the other, "Oh, hi. I'm Brandon," he said, looking at Tish briefly and then keeping his eyes on me. His smile was so big and bright, I swear I could see sparks flying from his dimples.

I put down my plate. "Hi. I'm Keri," I said, my whole body awash with tingling goodness. I placed my hand in his and held on several seconds past normal.

After I let go, we inched toward the end of the table, staring at each other and stacking up garlic bread. When there was no more table between us, we stood facing each other, overflowing plates almost kissing.

"I don't know what to say," he said, staring into my eyes.

"Me either," I said, staring back into his and then at his lips. I swear I wasn't trying to. His lips were just right there, at my eye level. That's all.

"Let's all find somewhere to sit," Tish said in a high-pitched tone, nodding and smiling, like we were kindergartners or something.

We obediently followed her to a table toward the back of the ballroom, where Brandon sat down between Tish and me.

Tish didn't waste any time. "So, why haven't we seen you before?" she said right after scooting her chair in.

"I don't know," Brandon said, and straightened the napkin in his lap.

"What campus do you attend?" I rephrased Tish's question.

"The main campus, I think. The one off of 59."

"Us too," Tish and I cheerily said in unison.

"Oh, you must go to the eight-o'clock service," I said, starting in on my dirty rice.

Brandon had already taken a bite of his fish and waited to speak until he finished chewing. "No, I go on Wednesday nights. Not all the time, though. Only when my dad brings home Indian food. Indian was my mom's favorite. My dad can't take all the spice. He only eats it when—"

"Oooh, that's why," I interrupted, talking with my mouth full and totally ignoring everything he said after *Wednesday nights*. "We always go to the eleven-o'clock Sunday service."

Tish took a sip of her sweet tea. "And sometimes the evening service."

"Yeah, but only if something's going on," I added.

"Excuse me. We're gonna get started here in a minute," Sister Chelsea, the teen girls' ministry leader, spoke into the microphone on the stage. She rocked a cute bowl cut with a silver strip coming down the middle toward her long, skinny face. "But I wanted to let you know Pastor Sykes won't be making it tonight to do the welcoming sermon."

"Bummer," Tish said sarcastically. But the room grumbled, genuinely upset. Pastor Sykes was something like a celebrity. Tish and I had been going to Higher Ground for twelve years, since it was just a small church in a shopping center off I-10, so Pastor Sykes was just Pastor Sykes to us. But ever since he got on national TV and started writing best-selling books, people started losing their minds over him, always asking for autographs and pictures and stuff. It was weird.

"There was a problem with one of the helicopter's rotors," Sister Chelsea tried to explain over the groaning in the room. She had a soft voice and didn't like to yell, but she did anyway. "It should all be resolved in time for the departing sermon tomorrow. Let's just—" And she left the rest of her words onstage and went to sit back down.

After dinner, Brother Tony turned down the lights and played *The Fighting Temptations* on two giant screens that lowered from the ceiling in the front of the room. Throwback Beyoncé was all it took to make everyone forget about Pastor Sykes. But I'd already seen the movie a million times and Brandon wasn't interested. So he broke out his phone and we laughed at memes and videos on the internet—one bud in his ear, one bud in mine. His hand touching my thigh from time to time. His smell—fresh like soap—drifting in and out of my nose. After a while, I looked up at Tish and felt guilty that she didn't have a bud (she'd seen the movie a million times too), but then she raised her eyebrows to mean, *Girl, you better get it*, and I felt just fine.

The next day, the church took us to Galveston's Pleasure Pier, a small amusement park jutting out over the ocean, and gave us each one hundred tickets. No pockets on my sundress. No pockets on Brandon's sweatshorts. So, all the tickets went into Tish's pink cross-body purse and we shared: pizza, fried pickles, cotton candy, and funnel cake. A mini water mister, rotating between us every ten minutes, because Texas's August sun didn't play. A photo booth, where we all squeezed in and stuck out our cherry-Icee-stained tongues. Two-seater rides, where we took turns being the odd one out. Our system of sharing had developed naturally, without negotiation, and was working perfectly. Until Lucas showed up.

We were in line to ride the Texas Star Flyer, a star tower with twelve double swings that whipped around in a wide circle, hundreds of feet above the Gulf of Mexico. Tish had ridden the last ride with a stranger, and it was my turn to be the odd one out. We were standing in that order—Tish, Brandon, and then me—when Lucas, Derrick, and Dara rolled up.

Brandon immediately laced his fingers with mine. Damn near gave me a heart attack, but I tried not to show it. I couldn't act brand-new. We'd been holding hands on and off all day. I'd been feeling the rush of tingles pulsing through my body all day. No tingles this time. Not with Lucas standing right there.

No compliment for Tish either. Derrick was hush-mouthed.

"What's up, Tish? Keri?" Lucas said, like he didn't even see Brandon.

"Hey," Tish said.

At first, I didn't say anything. I didn't know what to do about being caught between two boys. Then Lucas scanned Brandon head to toe (it was quick, but I still caught him), and I knew exactly what to do.

"Hey," I said, and smirked, suddenly thrilled for Lucas to see me holding Brandon's hand . . . thrilled for Lucas to see how easy it was for me to replace him . . . thrilled to let Lucas know that if he wanted to be with me, he'd better step up his game.

"You're the pastor's son," Brandon said, not in a weird star-struck way, like he was just stating a fact.

"Yeah, man. The name is Lucas." And Lucas reached out his hand with a warm smile on his face.

I can't even tell you how much that smile irked me. *Oh, okay. I see how you're playing this. Like you don't care. Boy, please. You ain't foolin' nobody,* I went off in my head.

"Brandon." He let go of my fingers and went down the line shaking hands and exchanging names.

Dara looked a little too happy to shake Brandon's hand, if you asked me. She wasn't a smiley type girl, but I saw the glee in her dark-brown eyes that traced his face. Plus she had on this light-blue T-shirt that read "Girl Power" but might as well have read "Boob Power" the way her big boobs were screaming at him, at everybody. I swore I couldn't glance in her direction without her breasts shouting, *Look at me!*

After we walked through the gates to the ride, Tish fell back so I wouldn't be the one riding with Lucas.

A curious squint told me that Brandon registered something weird about the switch.

"Don't tell me I have to ride with you," Lucas said, walking toward the swing directly behind Brandon and me.

"You know you love me," Tish said, playing it off.

The swings started at the bottom and ascended with each rotation around the star-shaped core. "Here we go," Brandon said, smiling at me.

Still low, I leaned into his thin, firm frame so he'd wrap his arm around me—just in case Lucas didn't know what was up, just in case Brandon holding my hand earlier wasn't enough. And man, did it feel good! I felt all kinds of fire shooting up my neck to the back of my head, where I imagined Lucas's eyes were burning through.

But as we moved higher, Brandon pulled me in closer and the fire started to feel like something else, something irresistible. And by the look in Brandon's eyes, he could feel it too. He pulled me in even closer and sent the heat lower, even lower. We locked eyes and went around and around over the ocean . . . around and around in the softening sky.

At the very top, our mouths followed our eyes and cozied up, curled into each other. Lip over lip. Tongue over tongue. Sliding and sucking and biting (yes, we took it there!) with the warm wind at our faces.

We unwound from each other as the swings started to head back down. And the lower we got, the more the heat started changing into something else. Something heavy, sad.

What have I done? I thought, guilt hammering me as hard as Brandon had hammered the lever in the strength test earlier, setting off all types of alarms.

"What's wrong?" Brandon asked as our feet touched the ground.

I took it too far. I should've never kissed you, I thought. But I said, "Nothing," without meeting his eyes.

We all got off the swings.

Lucas stormed off in the direction of the bumper cars.

Brandon noticed and asked, "Wait, is there something up between you and Lucas?"

"No," I lied.

"Lucas is always mad about something." Tish quickly backed me up.

"Oh, okay," Brandon replied. But his face said something different, something like, *That's a damn lie*. Then he said, "I'm gonna go find the bathroom before we have to get back on the buses. I'll see y'all."

"Okay," I said, without even trying to stop him. Then I

asked, "You want your tickets back?"

His thick eyebrows scrunched together in what looked like confusion, then relaxed . . . a little too much. He was hurt. "Naw, I'm straight," he answered, and walked off.

I felt bad for hurting Brandon, I did. But I was too sad about ruining my chances with Lucas to do anything about it. As soon as Brandon left, I started crying. It was getting dark and no one was around to see me anyway. Well, Tish, but she didn't count. Feeling bad for me, she let me have the remaining share of her tickets and came with me to try to buy Lucas something from the gift shop with them. Only found two things: a key chain and a pen that both read *Pleasure Pier*. We decided neither was a good idea.

Back in the hotel that night, my phone buzzed. A text from Lucas: **Guess that's your new boyfriend.**

"I knew he would text!" I exclaimed. Tish immediately jumped from her queen bed to mine to get up in the mix. But I was lying. Yeah, I'd hoped Lucas would text. Shoot, I'd even prayed he would text—literally on my knees in the bathroom, where Tish couldn't see. But honestly, I figured he'd never speak to me again.

I typed back an adamant **No! You're my boyfriend! Sorry . . . I never should've—**

"Oh, hell no!" Tish said, took my phone, and erased it all. "You don't have anything to be sorry about. Lucas is not your boyfriend." Then she typed, **As a matter of fact he is.**

I liked Tish's new direction. She was right, I decided. I wouldn't win Lucas's game by admitting guilt. If I wanted to make him act right, I needed to be strong. "Naw, naw," I said, thinking of something even better. I took back the phone, erased her words, and typed, **Maybe.** Hit Send.

"Ooh, that's good," Tish said, nodding her head with her eyes opened wide and an evil grin on her face.

The phone buzzed. **Is that right?**

Tish and I decided on a nonresponse.

Buzz. **Well . . . you looked pretty today.**

I replied, **Thanks.** I'd fought Tish on it but won. My rationale was that it was just a polite response to a compliment. The end.

But he continued. **Liked that little dress . . . hadn't seen that one before.**

Another **Thanks** from me and Tish moved back to her own bed and started looking at her own phone. But not before she rolled her eyes and shook her head at me. But in my mind, Tish didn't know Lucas like I did. She didn't know the Lucas who hid his face behind my shoulder during scary movies. The Lucas who agonized under the pressure of being the pastor's son to the point of having anxiety attacks. The Lucas who literally cried the time he received a B on his report card. The Lucas who, after some of his bad days, hugged me so tight and for so long that it was easy to imagine his pain was love.

After a while, Tish turned out the lights and went to sleep.

I lay under the white duvet, still texting, my phone on silent.

You still have on that dress? Lucas asked.

Yeah, I lied. I'd showered and put on my Pink pajamas soon after we'd gotten back from the pier.

Take it off.

I laughed quietly to myself. As I read the text, I could hear Lucas's trying-to-be-sexy voice plain as day. Hilarious. It was the same extra-deep, extra-fake voice he'd tried out on me the night we broke up. I'd busted out laughing after he'd asked me to take off my clothes in that same voice. Couldn't help it. And that's when he started on all the mess about me rooming with Dara for the beach retreat. And as you know, it went downhill from there.

Is it off?

Yeah. Another lie. I didn't want things to go downhill, but I wasn't about to get up and take off my pajamas. The room was cold and I was lazy.

I want to see.

How? You know Sister Chelsea got these halls on lock.

Send me a pic then.

I took a pic of myself, from the neck up—flash bright as hell—so he couldn't see my pajamas. Hit Send.

I want to see more than that.

I lowered the straps of my tank down below my shoulders. Another bright flash and Tish moaned and turned over to face the window. Pressed Send again.

More.

I'm tired. Truth. Plus I didn't wanna play the naked-picture game anymore. Enough naked pictures of girls had been spread around at my school for me to know it wasn't really a game.

Come on. For my eyes only.

No response.

I'll erase them before I go to sleep. D already snoring so it's just me.

No response.

I promise.

No response.

I just miss your beautiful body . . . haven't seen it in 4ever.

He was referring to the top half of my body. I was saving the bottom half for after we fell in love, which I was sure was going to happen the next year, my junior year. I'd imagined we'd fall in love on a Saturday evening, in the spring when the weather was just right. I'd imagined that after a long day of walking in the sun, he'd look me in the eyes and say the words—*I love you*. And I'd see in his eyes that his words were true. I'd played that scene in my mind a million times. Was playing it again when another text came in.

You know I love you, right. May not act like it but I do.

I didn't know how to respond. This was not how I pictured our falling-in-love moment. He was supposed to tell me while looking into my eyes so I could see if his words were true. I didn't feel anything soft or sweet or beautiful.

Forget it then . . . I knew this was never going to work out . . . especially after what you did today.

The guilt for kissing Brandon slammed back into my chest and made me feel low. Lower than low. For some reason, I didn't think about how Lucas had broken up with me and ignored me for weeks. I didn't think about how he always criticized my clothes and hair, hated on my friends, or found some other way to be mean. No, I'd become a pro at putting Lucas and his hurt feelings before me.

Wait, I texted.

And that was all Lucas needed to get back to his mean self. **Can't believe I'm even texting you.**

Wait, I sent again. I didn't want him to go. I didn't want him to start ignoring me all over again. **Tish asleep . . . let me go to bathroom.**

I hit the switch on the wall and bright light flooded the bathroom, making me squint. The lights whined with a quiet, high-pitched buzz. I wanted to be asleep too. I was tired and it was close to midnight. But I felt indebted to Lucas, like I owed him something. So I took off my pajamas and my underwear. *It's just a stupid picture,* I lied to myself. *He'll never show it to anyone because he wouldn't want anyone else to see me naked.*

Well? Lucas was tired of waiting.

Working on it. I stood in the dark-wood-framed mirror, held the phone down around my belly, and snapped. *Not that one,* I

thought. I put my free hand on my left hip. *Not that one either.*
I put my free hand behind my head. *Definitely not.* I hated
my boobs. They were so small. Lucas always said he wished
I had boobs like Dara. I put my foot up on the toilet. *Oh, hell
no.* I went back to my original nonpose—standing straight,
left arm at my side, looking down at the camera instead of at
myself in the mirror.

But I still didn't like the white shower curtain behind me. It
looked cheap. Tish's and my toiletries were all over the sink,
and it looked a mess. I didn't like the beige, circle-patterned
wallpaper or the Bed Bath and Beyond–looking art on the
wall, over the toilet—so basic. I opened the shower curtain
and took another pic, but it was even worse. Shampoo bottles
and shower gel flanked my naked body. I closed the shower
curtain, got rid of all the toiletries on the sink, and snapped. It
was as good as it was going to get.

I uploaded the pic to my messages with Lucas but couldn't
bring myself to press Send.

I'll show you tomorrow in person, I texted, and stayed in the bathroom another two hours pressing my hair.

Pastor Sykes was in the building. Tish and I heard the helicopter land that morning during breakfast. Between bites of
bacon, eggs, and pancakes, I looked for Lucas but couldn't
find him anywhere.

After breakfast, Brother Tony—dreads back in a ponytail

and white linen shirt on, like he was ready for the heat—instructed everyone to make their way outside. Pastor Sykes would give a sermon before he baptized ten new teens in the Gulf of Mexico.

In the hall leading outside, I spotted Lucas walking in long, determined strides. I grabbed Tish's hand and ran to catch up with him (of course slowing down right before we reached him so I wouldn't look pressed). I wanted to feel the warmth back between Lucas and me. And I wanted everyone to see us. See that we were back together. But everyone seemed to be looking at their phones.

Tish noticed it, too. "What is everyone looking at?"

I didn't answer. I was too busy trying to make the edge of my fingers touch the edge of Lucas's fingers. They kept missing, so I tried to hold his hand. He pulled away and ran ahead.

I took my phone out to text him, to ask him what the hell was going on, to confirm we were back together again. But the pic from the night before was still up. A sharp shock surged through my chest, and I quickly closed it. But not before Tish saw.

"Oh, hell no!" she said, and tried to grab my phone.

But I didn't have time for one of her lectures, so I ran off in the opposite direction, against the crowd. After I passed the ballroom where we'd eaten breakfast, the crowd cleared and I saw Brandon.

"Hey," he said loudly, as he walked toward me, like he'd forgiven me.

I was still running and slowed down a little bit. "Hey," I replied as I approached, but I didn't stop.

"I was thinking—"

"Sorry, I have to go," I said, cutting him off and running past him.

After Brandon was far enough away, I slowed down and texted Lucas. **What'd you do that for? Aren't we back together?**

No reply.

I tried calling him.

No answer.

Oh, so you don't get what you want and it's back to ignoring me?! Are we really back to that again?!

No reply.

Pissed, hurt, and confused, I found a bathroom to duck into and hopped up onto the long, wide sink. I opened my naked picture again. I hated everything about it: the shower curtain, the wallpaper, the art. Me. The way I was standing there. Naked. None of it felt right. I could barely stand to look at myself. I knew I was making a mistake, but I loaded the picture back into my messages with Lucas anyway.

Before I could press Send, I heard, "They got you to do it, too?" It was Dara. She was standing near the first stall, phone in hand, big boobs trying to bust through her boat-necked dress.

"They what?" I asked, confused. Then I realized she could see the picture of me in the mirror and put down my phone.

She walked toward me and hopped up to join me on the sink, like we were friends. I know my face had to be all kinds of twisted up, but either she didn't see or didn't care. She held out her phone to show me what everyone was looking at that morning.

Pictures of Derrick and Lucas. Cropped and placed side by side. Both of them naked. Both of them framed by the same mahogany mirror. With the same cheap white shower curtain in the background. The same boring wallpaper. And the same mass-produced art.

"Oh, shit! I mean shoot. How? What?" I didn't even know what question to ask.

"Well, Derrick kept pressing me for naked pics last night. Saying all types of stuff like he loved me and it was going to be for his eyes only. I knew that was a lie. Derrick can't keep anything to himself. And Lucas was right there. I already knew and he finally admitted it."

The words *love* and *eyes only* echoed in my ears. Same words Lucas had used on me. It was really all just a game to him. A game I would never win. He would never love me. All of it was finally so plain I couldn't ignore it, couldn't make any more excuses for it.

"Anyways, he just wouldn't let up. Kept asking and asking. So I told him that in order for me to send them one, they would each have to send me one. As collateral, you see."

"But aren't you afraid they're gonna send yours out too?"

"I didn't send that picture out. Derrick sent that picture out. I guess he was feeling himself. And I never sent them mine anyway."

"But you took one?"

"Yeah," and she swiped and showed me her naked selfie like it was no big deal. She kept swiping to show me all the ones she took. Hands on hip, foot on toilet, hands by sides—same as me.

"Girl, I tried the same poses." I opened my pictures and we held our naked bodies side by side.

"The foot on the toilet was the worst, wasn't it?"

I laughed. "I know, right. Had all the goodies hanging out."

Laughing and holding our naked bodies in our own hands, looking at the pics felt different. I didn't hate looking at myself. Sure, my boobs were small and Dara's were big, but I kind of liked mine. They were cute and they fit me. Her hips were round and fleshy, and mine were narrow and bony. But they were both all good. Her lady part was shaved in the shape of a triangle. I didn't know anything about shaping hair down there. But they were both beautiful. Too beautiful for those boys we were with. Too beautiful for the eyes of the internet. So, we erased them all.

There was a big commotion out in the hall. Then a loud chant, "Fight! Fight! Fight!"

The bathroom door swung open and the chant bounced off the walls. "Derrick and Lucas are fighting!" a girl's voice announced without bothering to come in.

Dara and I looked at each other. Then Dara said, "You better go give your boy some backup," and cracked a big smile. The only one I've ever seen on her face.

"Girl, stop playing," I said.

We busted out laughing and didn't get up off the sink. We'd had enough of Derrick and Lucas. So we stayed in the bathroom all the way through Pastor Sykes's sermon, supposedly about letting God fight your battles, entertaining ourselves with some of the funny memes and videos Brandon had shown me.

Brandon.

Sweet Brandon.

I begged my mom and dad to take me to the Wednesday service for weeks, but I didn't see him. I asked around church and found out he'd lost his mother to cancer the previous year. Felt bad I hadn't listened when he tried to talk about her. Looked him up on social media. Wasn't there. Called a number that came up for him in an internet search. No one answered. When I turned sixteen in September and got my driver's license, I went every Wednesday for a whole year. But I never saw Brandon again.

WILD HORSES, WILD HEARTS

JAY COLES

Tomorrow is the big day. Like *The* big day. The day that comes around only once every three years: the North Salem Horse Race. Our small, middle-of-nowhere town has a lot of sweet things about it and one major drawback. North Salem has fewer than one hundred residents. Out of those people, only four of them are Black and that's me and my family.

In this town things happen kinda often making us feel like real outcasts—petty things, like everyone in the town getting invited to potluck dinners or get-togethers except us. Folks make it known that we're not really liked—whether that's because we're Black or not, they make sure we feel like we're different.

It's raining lightly and I'm standing in my new boots, the sun hiding behind a few clouds, grooming up on Big Red, our oldest stallion on the farm, gnats and flies funneling around his muzzle and crest. Big Red is *my* horse—he got to the farm the same year I was born. Growing up, it seemed like Big Red was the only one to understand me. Sometimes, it still feels that way. He's a good listener, though not so much a good racer anymore. But he's the only happy thing from my childhood I've got and I'm going to be here for him, grooming him and confiding in him, like I always have, like he actually understands the words coming out of my mouth. He's sick and the vets say he's only got a few months left to live.

"It's okay, Big Red," I say, brushing his hair. "It's gon' be okay." I don't even know if he's the one who needs to hear this or if it's just for me, but saying it brings a little calm to the hurricane trapped in the pit of my gut.

He neighs like he's saying, "I know." And my heart shatters a little bit. I distract myself by looking around, blinking back tears, scanning the farm to see if anything needs to be done, like picking up goat poop or stopping two hens from squaring up—anything to give me a reason not to think about Big Red not being here anymore.

A sadness creeps on me that's more than just the idea of Big Red dying. It's also imagining what it'd be like if things were different for me. If I could actually show happiness for things that I'm happy about. If I could live out the things I've been dreaming. If Momma and Daddy would put away their Bibles and see the real me. If I could believe—just believe—they'd love me the same if I told them who I really am. If I told them the truth about who Tank Robinson really is.

This farm, these fences, this life. It's all I've ever known.

Acres of land in the middle of nowhere—a plot adjacent to the Smith family, who've hated my family since the last North Salem Horse Race. There's a ditch as wide as Dad's truck that stretches for yards between our properties that my dad filled with bricks, a literal red line separating the exact spot where the Smiths' territory ends and ours begins. Personally, I think the feud is ridiculous, but I can't say nothing about it without the risk of getting my ass whooped. (Momma's ass-whoopings ain't nothing to mess with.)

The Smiths think we cheated when we won the last race. But I know that's not what it's really about. They have Confederate flags hanging outside their house. To my parents, the Smiths are racist atheists who need Jesus and don't know what the hell they're talking about.

Though our farm is only a few dozen acres and feels like a fenced-in backyard to a medium-sized house in the city, it's a lot of hard work. Last night, after collecting the eggs from our chicken coop, I lay out in front of Big Red's corral shelter wrapped in a couple blankets and gazed up at the stars, squinting at them, using my fingers to trace their shapes. Then, I heard a familiar voice—all sweet and low. It was my neighbor's son, Skyler. Skyler Smith.

"Tank." He called my name softly, like a whisper. "I brought you something."

He had a couple of cans of IPA, stolen from his dad.

Standing on the other side of the large crater between us, he tossed me one.

Hesitating, never having drunk anything, I opened it anyway and took a slow sip.

I probably made the world's most unattractive face, and I hoped that he didn't see it, until I looked at him trying desperately to suppress his laughter. If I was on the other side of the divide with him, I would play-punch him, but I can't. I'm stuck over here.

I ran into him one night a few weeks ago while doing chores out in the pasture, and we've been meeting at the ditch secretly since then, mainly to talk about the stupid beef between our families. But it started evolving into something else.

I'm standing in the exact same spot we've been meeting, waiting for him to show up tonight. I look at the time on my phone. He's late and suddenly, I'm worried.

Four, five, six minutes slip past and I watch Skyler in the distance come closer, the sun almost completely out of the sky yet still shining enough for me to see the freckles on his face and arms.

I walk over to the edge of the ditch, facing him on the other side. He gives me a small smile and then nods at me. "Sorry

I'm late. Big fight with my parents. What's up over there?" he asks.

"Nothin'" is all I say, my head hanging low. I can't look at him in the eye for some reason. I'm trying and trying, but I just can't. "Fight? You okay?"

"Oh yeah. And I'm peachier than the finest Georgia peach." He's smiling, but it isn't reaching his eyes.

"Sure?" I can only speak in short sentences. Hell, they're not even sentences. Just bits and pieces of my running thoughts. It's hard forming the right words when I'm around him.

"They're just so stupid," he says, sighing. "In addition to this stupid, racist feud they have with your family, they've got all of these Make America Great Again posters plastered over our windows, and while we were in the living room watching a movie together, they just kept making really shitty homophobic comments. And I had enough." He sighs again. "And you know, they had the nerve to threaten me, saying if I cost them the race tomorrow, they'll send me to Texas to live with my grandparents."

"I'm sorry," I offer. There are so many other things I want to say to him.

"It's okay. I just don't know how to deal with their ignorance," he says. "I kinda just laid some news on them, and now my dad is inside consoling my mom, who's crying."

"News?" We face each other.

He takes off his cowboy hat, showing his thin, short, curly blond hair. My gaze shifts and follows the tiny red freckles spaced out like constellations from his chin down his neck against his ivory-white skin. I watch him slide down onto the ground and then stretch out across the grass, his half-buttoned baby-blue plaid shirt probably getting a little muddied. But he doesn't care.

I follow his lead and lie down on my side of the divide.

He changes the subject. "Ever think about how weird the sun is? It's literally a giant dying star, but it's still so full of light and never leaves the earth." A pause. "Look at how beautiful this sky is."

I furrow my brows trying to keep up. I look at the sky and nearly gasp. The sky is a gorgeous mural of oranges and yellows and pinks.

Last night when we met, we talked about simple things, like how online school is working out for me and how homeschooling is going for him with his dad as his teacher and all. We talked about mosquitoes and heroes; horses and our dreams; our obsessions and fandoms—mine being all things Britney Spears and his being country music and making up his own tunes with his acoustic guitar. We talked about how we both really wanna go to college—maybe someplace far away from North Salem. Tonight, despite everything going on with him and his parents, he's wanting to just escape in the sun. Here. With me.

"I think it gets lonely sometimes though. That's why it goes into hiding," he says, still staring up at the sky.

"Yeah," I say. "Maybe."

He turns to me and lets out a small, playful giggle. There's a pause. I watch him squint and point up, making shapes with his hands. "This is one of the only things I love about being out here in the country—how crazy, insanely beautiful the sunsets are."

"Yeah," I say. I can only think of one-word answers. I'm just so nervous.

"I'm having way too much fun," he says.

"Me too," I say, nearly blushing, picking at the mud stain on my pants. "Not to be weird, but I think hanging with you is my favorite part of the day."

He grins and I can see his dimple showing from across the ditch. "Has anyone ever told you that you're not like anyone else?"

"No. Is that something I should aspire to be?"

"Not necessarily. But you are. You ever feel like it?"

"I don't know. Maybe. What about you?" I ask.

"I do. Every time I look at myself in the mirror." He says the word *mirror* like it's just one syllable. "I've realized that I'm a lot like the sun—the way I hide myself in the darkness. I'm tired of hiding."

"What do you mean?"

"I . . ." He lifts up and I can tell he's trying so desperately to reveal something by the way he pauses, looks at me, and then looks away. "I like boys. And only boys. And I like you."

A gasp nearly slips out of me.

Here I am, wearing a white hoodie and tube socks, wrapped in blankets, and I feel suddenly cold.

"That's what I told my parents. There's no more lying to myself or to them. I'm taking back my happiness."

"I think I might like boys too," I say back to him quietly, like I don't want God to hear me say such a thing out loud. "I mean . . . at least, I like you. *That*, I'm sure."

I'd only discovered this desire two weeks ago, after the first night we hung out at the ditch, when I dreamed about him and woke up with the world's hardest erection and sticky boxer briefs. I'm slowly starting to accept this new fact about myself, contemplating why I've only ever dated girls. (Well, just two girls. Both from middle school.)

I plugged in some Britney Spears, listening to the *Glory* album for hours on repeat, danced along to the choreography of the music video to "Toxic," and then I realized that I had dated girls just because of what people expected of me—what people told me was right for me—what was godly. My whole life people had been telling me who I should be, who I should like, and even where I should put my dick. But I wasn't listening to them anymore.

We stay on the ground, staring up at the sky together. Everything is so still and feels so perfect for this little while, I can almost feel the whole world move in front of us.

Eventually, he says, "I wish I could hold your hand. But that would be too soon. Right?"

I shake my head. "No. It's not too soon. I really want that."

"This stupid ditch."

My phone rings so loud in my pocket, buzzing against my thigh. It's Momma. I press the button to silence it.

"I gotta go," I say to him after a brief pause. "Meet here at midnight?"

Skyler agrees and we hold each other's gaze for a moment.

Walking up the hill toward home, I replay everything that Skyler told me in my head, holding on to the feelings for as long as I can, a smile probably stained to my face. Then it hits me as soon as I see Momma coming from the direction of our house. No matter how magical the last forty or so minutes felt, he's supposed to be my enemy.

No matter what my heart feels like, I have to remind myself that tomorrow he's my competition and I'll have to do everything in my power to win the race and bring home this year's trophy.

I stop by the pastures to check on the horses for a moment. Momma's with my nine-year-old little sister, Natasha, who's eating a hot dog, mustard all over her face.

"How's Big Red lookin'?" Momma asks, and zips up her purple jacket. "Poor thing. Lord have mercy on his precious soul."

I shrug. "He's okay. He's as good as he can be right now, I guess." Maybe this is just a lie that I believe, but the words fly out my mouth fast.

"Well, I was just talkin' to your father and he . . . well, he thinks we should put him down so he ain't suffering and all."

"What!" It feels like someone just punched me, and I want to throw up.

"We ain't got the money or the space to keep him around," Momma says, cupping my chin in her palm. "And waiting for him to die is too damn hard on all of us. Big Red was a nice horse and he's had his run. Gotta let him go, son. It's clearly what God wants."

God?

An awkward pause.

God?

Why would they talk about this without me? I hurt all over. I'm pissed—way more pissed than when Momma and Daddy told Natasha and me that we didn't have the money for Big Red's medication a couple months ago.

God?

"Anyway, I came to tell you that dinner's ready, if you want some," she says. "I made something easy today—hot dogs, so I can make a big feast tomorrow after we win."

I don't know what to do. I don't know what to think. For the longest time, I stand still, watching her walk away in the distance, holding Natasha's hand as the moon slides into the sky.

When I get back inside the house, Natasha's already gone to bed and it's just Momma and Daddy sitting at the dinner table with glasses and a bottle of golden-brown alcohol in front of them, the Holy Bible on the table between them.

One look at each of their facial expressions and I can tell they've been waiting for me.

"Your father has something to say," Momma blurts out, sipping on some of the golden-brown alcohol in her glass. "Say it, Victor."

"Lisa." I watch Daddy roll his eyes a little bit, lifting from the table, his beer gut hanging over his belt, leftover relish still in his long beard from the hot dogs he had for dinner. "Listen, son. Take a seat."

I sit at the table. I don't know if this is about the race tomorrow or about Big Red, but the way they're acting makes me feel like they're about to tell me Grandma G just died or something.

My palms are clammy and I brush them on my camo pants. "Yes?" I look into Daddy's big, dark-brown eyes.

He walks around the table and closer to me, placing his hands on the table. "You know what tomorrow means to your mom and me, right?"

"Yeah, Dad," I say. It's all they've talked about this whole week. Hell, it's all they've talked about since the last race three years ago.

"Good. It's as important to us as Big Red is to you. And it seems like you've been distracted lately, so we wanted to make sure you're goin' into tomorrow with a clear mind." He coughs a little. "We don't want you to mess this up for us, son. It's tradition. This would be our sixth trophy since you were born. We need to get out there and show them white folks what we're capable of, that we belong 'round here. They can't keep treating us like we ain't a part of this town. Your granddaddy used to say, 'White folks can't hold you down if you're coming up.' And look at how good another trophy would complete our trophy case in the living room."

I just nod.

"Big Red will go to a better place. He'll be back in the Kingdom of God, where he was once with Adam and Eve."

I roll my eyes, still nodding.

"Speaking of, uh, Big Red . . . I just got a text from Dr. Lonnie." Dr. Lonnie's been taking care of our animals for years. He's a short, old fella from the Midwest whose beard is probably longer than Moses's was after walking in the desert those forty years. "After we bring the trophy home, we're gonna have Dr. Lonnie come and put him down. We'll let you pick where he's buried at in the backyard and all that."

Tears cascade down my cheeks and dry at my chin. I feel like I want to scream, but I don't. Natasha's sleeping.

He picks up the Bible, flips through it, and reads a passage. "Therefore if any man be in Christ, he is a new creature: old things are passed away; behold, all things become new." At this point, I'm just so numb, so shocked. It's like my feelings don't even matter to them at all, like always.

Fuck this. Fuck them. Fuck whatever they just read from the Bible.

I want to throw up.

I don't. I can't. All that can come out of me are these hot tears. I just lift up from the table and storm upstairs to my room. I've never done this before, but it feels kind of nice. It feels kind of needed, and though I can't place any of my thoughts, I know what I have to do tomorrow for me, for Skyler, and for Big Red. For all of us to finally break free.

I pull all my blankets over myself and plug in my headphones, blasting Britney Spears, listening to her sing about what freedom means and what it looks like to be stronger than yesterday. Britney calms my nerves enough for me to think rationally about everything. But I'm still excited to see Skyler. I count the minutes, no, seconds until I can sneak out and hopefully see him. He'll understand how I feel.

Midnight finally comes around. I slip into my hoodie again and I leave out my window, heading down the hill to wait at the ditch. The air is stale and smells like a blend of poop, freshly cut grass, and flowers.

I watch the time go up on phone, staring at my lock screen, which I changed to a picture of Big Red earlier today—then suddenly, I look up and see him. Skyler is walking toward me.

Instantly, I lose my breath. I don't know if I'll ever stop getting so nervous when I see him. There's just something about the feeling I get in my gut when I'm in his presence. I forget the world.

"Hey," Skyler says softly.

I wave and stammer. "H-h-hey."

He puts his arm behind his head and I look away. A pause lingers between us.

I'm supposed to hate him. *But I can't stop imagining his touch, his taste.*

"Everything okay?" Not sure where this comes from. Maybe he senses something on my face. "Did I freak you out earlier?"

"No, no," I say, swatting away mosquitoes. I explain to him everything that's happening with Big Red and my parents.

He just nods, and in his deep Southern accent says, "Well, I'm just sorry to hear all that, T. I know how much ole Red means to you."

I nod *thanks*.

"Y'know, I really know how hard it is to lose something so close, like a childhood companion," Skyler says. "Ruby was my pet pig. I got her as a little tiny baby, played with her, grew up with her, everything. Then, one day, my parents put her up for sale, she got bought during one North Salem animal showing competition, and became bacon months after, last I heard."

"That sucks" is all that comes out, even though there's so much I want to say, so many words I want to offer.

He walks closer to the edge. "If I could help, I would."

Having him here to walk me through this is enough. Skyler plus Britney Spears sounds like the perfect combination to get me through this broken moment in my broken life—the dread knotting in my chest of having to put Big Red down.

"I need to be with you right now," he mutters. I watch him take more steps forward and my heart is beating so hard in my chest. His toes dangle on the edge.

Oh my God. He's crossing over the ditch. He's crossing over no-man's-land, showing the kind of bravery I used to pray for. I blink back the shock, my heart thudding in triples now. Suddenly, he's on our side of the divide. He's standing in front of me—so close I can reach out and touch him.

"Can I hold your hand?"

I nod at him.

His hand grips mine and the warmth is everything.

"I've been wanting to do this."

"I have too," I say softly.

His hands move to my cheeks and his lips are so close to mine, but he pulls back just to look me in the eye, my chest heaving. "Tank Robinson, can I kiss you?"

"Please," I say, my heart feeling like it's about to pound its way out of my chest.

He presses his lips against me, soft and easy at first and then hard and firm. Everything in my head goes quiet, and I feel like I'm floating on a cloud far, far away from North Salem. When we pull apart, the taste of his cherry ChapStick is left in my mouth and I can't help but smile at his smile.

If Momma or Daddy came out to see this, they would kill

me. Hell, they would kill the both of us and then blame the Smiths. And I don't know why, but I'm also suddenly realizing that part of me actually doesn't care. Part of me kinda wishes one of them came out and saw us. It would make things easier for me. I would no longer have to think about how to come out to my God-fearing parents and especially not have to think about explaining how the first boy I've ever kissed was their enemy's one and only son.

I kick at a fly buzzing around my legs, taking in everything, not wanting this night to end.

Before long, Skyler tells me he has to go and get some rest for tomorrow. I watch him walk away, still feeling like I've been split at the seams and stuffed with rays of sunlight. I do a last-minute inspection of the horses. Tomorrow I'll be racing Lima Bean, who's just plain gorgeous, with her white, silvery hair. I end up letting Big Red out of the shelter to run around in the open field.

Ignoring the coyotes singing in the distance and shielding the glowing full moon from my face, I watch him go so freely under the expanding night sky, how happy he looks, not knowing what's going to happen to him.

I wake up the next day with his name repeating over and over again in my mind. The dream I had last night was about him and it's too embarrassing to talk about right now, but I'm gonna need to change my boxers for sure.

I end up showering, grabbing a bowl of Cocoa Puffs with Natasha, and helping Daddy load his pickup truck and trailer for the race today. The sun is so bright and yellow, pinned in the bluest, stillest sky I've ever seen. Something about it is like a reminder of hope, a reminder of Skyler.

Suddenly, I look up in the distance and Skyler's helping his folks load their trucks, too. Sheep, goats, and hogs getting loaded in the back of one. Horses in the others. It's all actually kind of adorable, but the tension that lives on this road kills away all of that feeling after a while, with Momma and Daddy side-eyeing the Smiths so damn hard.

After they're all loaded, I look over and watch Skyler's parents drive away, leaving him there. He calls me over sneakily.

I take a deep breath and tell Momma that I'll be right back. Daddy's in the back of one of the trailers.

She waves me off.

I walk behind the house and down the hill in our backyard to the pasture. I stand in front of the ditch, feeling electric volts run through me, like I'm one and the same with the earth's center or some shit, thinking about crossing over the ditch for the first time. Sure, it's a great *fuck off* to my parents, but the adrenaline is overwhelming. So overwhelming, I can feel my heart beating in my chest. It's my turn. I should be able to cross this ditch, like Skyler did last night.

Then it hits me—what Skyler said about taking back his

happiness. This isn't about Momma or Daddy. This is about me and what I want. This is about having the courage to tell myself that it's okay to love him. It's okay to be strong and brave and daring in the name of love.

He's waiting at our usual spot, a slight grin easing on his face.

I take a deep breath and jump over the ditch, like I'm crossing through the golden gates of reality into a brand-new life or something.

"Hey, you," he says so sweetly, hugging me tight. "You smell ready for today."

"You too," I reply, grinning.

I take a whiff of myself. *He's right.*

Somehow we end up going to his house and he takes me upstairs, almost giving me a minitour of it. I've always wondered what it would be like to be inside the place where someone as interesting and different as Skyler lives. His parents own Confederate flags and MAGA posters, but Skyler has reminded me that he doesn't believe in any of that, that he knows his parents are racist and have been contributing to the hatred of me and my family in this town since we've been here. He makes it a thing to remind me that he's not like that, that he'll always be here to stand with *and* for me, never against me.

We laugh small laughs. "Why did your parents leave you?"

"I told them I would meet them there. I told them I had some last-minute things to do before heading out to the race.

Truth is, I just wanted to do this."

He leans in and kisses me soft on the lips.

Instantly, I feel like there's a lit match in my gut. I half smile.

I'm supposed to hate him. But when my lips touched his for the first time and we collided, every butterfly in a hundred-mile radius fluttered in my stomach. And I felt at home for once. And all of this just happened again. Just now. Wow.

Days ago, I imagined kissing him for the first time.

Yesterday, we actually did.

Right now, in this moment right here.

It hits me. One thought repeating in my head, squeezing past every happy thought I can have right now.

My parents would kill me if they knew I was here in the Smiths' house. They would bring me back to life and kill me again if they knew I had kissed Skyler. Skyler's parents would do something drastic, too, like force him never to leave his room or send him hundreds of miles away to Texas, if they knew he liked and kissed someone with my skin color—dark brown like somewhere between umber and cocoa. That's the nature of this town.

I end up sneaking back over to my side, hearing my name being screamed. "Tank. Tank. Taaaaaank!" I know that tone, that voice, whenever I hear it. And it's a pissed-off Lisa Renée Robinson.

Turns out, I accidentally left the pen open and the goats got out.

• • •

It's usually a tradition for us to eat at Mother Mal's Pancake House before we go to the race, but not this year. This year, we go straight to North Salem Park, where the race and animal showings are hosted every three years. Maybe this is my parents' way of showing me just how serious they were about me winning this race for them? Maybe this is their way of saying they don't really care about my feelings toward this race, just winning? I don't know, but I'm only salty I don't get those signature hash browns that I like with the sautéed onions.

At first, the air smells like shit and tastes kind of dirty and bitter once I get out of my dad's truck, where I have headphones on listening to Britney's "Hold It Against Me," avoiding what could've been the most awkward ride of my life. I look down and realize that I'm stepping in a fresh, mushy pile of horse crap in my brand-new boots.

Fuck.

I keep walking, wiping my feet as I go, going across a parking lot and through a series of barns. I end up stomping my feet on a concrete slab near the registration table as we get signed in. I see the medium-sized gold horseshoe-shaped trophy that looks like this year's updated version of the trophies we already have at home from previous years. It's cool to look at. Some white, bald man in a gray suit, who looks as if he'll be dying of a heatstroke in a matter of time, shows us where our assigned spot to set up is.

If everything indeed has a bright side to it, like Britney's "Stronger" and "Break the Ice," then I guess the bright side to being here at the North Salem Park for this year's race and animal-showing competition is that there's a lot of free food. The air smells like pizza and funnel cake and everything reminds me of a carnival, except without rides, just animals behind tiny fences and trailers full of hay.

There's a fan blasting near the area where we get set up at, saving us from this blazing heat as we start unloading Lima Bean from behind the back of the truck, and then we unload all the other animals for the showing.

I look left and right, then right again. Conveniently for me and inconveniently for our parents, our main competition is setting up next to us. Skyler waves and smiles, like he doesn't care at all that he's been caught with me. His mom catches him and swats his hand away, giving him the dirtiest look and then giving the same one to me.

Skyler looks away, focusing back on brushing a horse—probably the one he's using to race with. He's a really tall, all-black horse with one silver stripe going around the top of his head like a crown, like he's royalty and destined for victory. He's a beauty.

I remember seeing speakers all over the place, and suddenly a loud voice starts blaring out of all of them. "The triennial North Salem Horse Race will start in approximately seven minutes." The voice is low, smooth, and relaxing. The whole time, my eyes don't shift away from Skyler.

"Tank!" Momma and Daddy both call out for me in different tones, reining me back in from my daze.

I turn around to walk over to them.

"Lima Bean's all ready to go, son," Daddy says to me. "If we win, we'll buy you a new horse that looks exactly like Big Red. Maybe you can name him Little Red."

I don't say anything back, just look into his eyes and feel how strangely detached we both are in this moment.

He places a hand on my shoulder, leans in, and kisses me light on the forehead. "You got this." An uncomfortable, tight-lipped smile. "You got this."

Do I?

I don't want this.

Momma comes over and kisses me on the forehead, too, kissing into the creases of it how proud she is of me.

The two of them stand at my sides, and out of nowhere, they begin reciting a prayer. They pray for my heart, they pray for my mind, they pray for Lima Bean, and they pray for victory.

An overwhelming wave of nausea hits me, and my hands get really clammy.

The same loud voice comes over every single speaker in this open park again. "Attention, all horse racers! We'll begin in approximately one minute."

"Hurry, son, go get him," Daddy shouts in a voice somewhere between excitement and anxiety.

I get saddled up and ready on Lima Bean, nudge her at her

sides lightly in the direction of where everyone's lining up for the race. There are individual lanes drawn on a field that I didn't even see when I got in. I don't know where Skyler is now, since there are over thirty racers, but I hope he's out here and I hope he wins.

So many thoughts flood my brain and I'm having a really hard time sorting them. It's like I'm two halves of something. Part A of me wants to win this, get my parents the trophy, so they can stop bugging me about it for the next three years. Part B of me, though, wants to do everything I can to have Skyler win, and then I can finally stand up to my parents and also to his.

Last night, I spent a lot of time thinking about this and talking to my three Britney Spears posters about it as well. *To win or not to win?* I know if I gave this my all with a clear mind, I could definitely win. Especially now that I'm looking at some of these other horses that look like they've been starving for months. But I'm not sure if I want to.

The same bald white guy in a gray suit stands in front of all the horses with his hands behind his back. I can barely hear him, but he's explaining all the rules for this race, things I grew up reading and hearing about from Daddy.

My whole body clenches, and I feel the muscles in my legs and arms rise up, the same muscles I use to control thousands of pounds of thundering horseflesh.

I almost forget I'm wearing a hat. I pull it down over my low fade, so it feels tight and secure. I don't wanna lose it. It was a birthday gift from Grandma G.

The bald man whips out his hands from behind his back and I see a gun. I gulp as he points it into the air. I watch him so closely, licking his lips. I look around and grab onto the reins around Lima Bean.

"On your mark," he says.

I swallow hot spit.

"Get set."

I lean in forward a bit.

And then, BOOM! "Go!"

We're off and I'm tied for third place. Not sure who the two are in front of me, but I know that their horses look like they won't make it past the first lap with how hard they're working them.

I jerk my head back, the wind slapping me in the face hard—so damn hard. I end up passing everyone by the time it gets to the second-to-last lap. I'm in first.

Big Red dies today. The thought enters my head in the most fucked-up way. I don't even realize I'm fucking crying, until everything blurs and I feel Lima Bean go off the track a little. I wipe my face on my sleeves and suddenly, I've gotten passed by two people. One of them, I think, is Skyler.

It starts drizzling a little bit, giving us all some temporary relief from the heat.

I try to get Lima Bean to go faster to catch up. After a while, it's just Skyler and me neck-and-neck. I can see the finish line approaching and I can tell by the look in his eyes that no matter how this ends, we will have each other.

It's in this moment that I finally man up, something Daddy's always telling me to do, and I pull Lima Bean back. Skyler crosses the finish line.

Once Skyler wins, my stomach flips, but I'm smiling hard. The crowds of spectators all erupt in a series of different sounds. Some of them are cheering, like they're really excited that he won. Others are not. I can feel the anger coming from my parents and I can't even make them out in the crowd yet.

We all get off our horses once everyone crosses the finish line and walk through the crowd to our stations.

When I get to mine, Momma and Daddy have huge scowls on their faces.

Daddy walks over to me sternly. "What the hell was that?" The anger is leaking from his voice.

Skyler comes over with the first-place trophy and sets it down. "It's for you."

Everything stills. Daddy takes a step back. Momma holds his arm.

"Skyler—"

He interrupts me, walking past me and toward my parents with the trophy in his hands, giving it to them. *What the hell is he doing?* "I know how much this means to you."

"Why?" Daddy says on repeat even though Skyler just basically explained why.

I walk over to Skyler, to stand at his side, and he says, "I have something to say to you. I know you won't like it, but—"

"We kissed." I finish his sentence, wanting to have this moment. My heart is pounding so hard in my chest and now the rain is picking up. I hug myself.

Momma looks shaken. Natasha smiles while eating cotton candy.

"You kissed?" Momma asks, giving me a strange look, like I just said I killed someone.

"Yeah." I look away to sort through my thoughts and stop being an anxious mess. I breathe in and out, repeating my favorite Britney Spears lyrics in my head.

"I know you won't like it or whatever because of God or the Bible or because the world thinks all boys should like girls or whatever, but—"

I'm interrupted.

"Absolutely not," Daddy goes. "Jesus. God. No, no, no, no. What have you done to my son?" He approaches Skyler and Skyler takes a few steps back, flinching.

I jump in between them.

There's the longest pause that lingers between all of us.

The Smiths arrive to get Skyler, but he tells them that he's staying right where he is.

Momma chews on her lip, then nods, her head in her hands, and she's now crying, holding her hands together like she's about to begin praying, asking God for a cure for me.

Skyler's dad grabs him by the arm forcefully and pulls him back. He yells so loud, everyone at this competition probably knows what's going on. "We're going home, packing your bags, and you're going to spend some time with your grandparents in Texas!"

"No!" A yelp emerges from my gut. "Leave him alone," I shout at his parents, my voice inching higher as the words come out. I feel a rush of adrenaline shoot up my neck. Things slow.

Skyler reaches for my hand and I give it up, lacing my fingers with his.

Speakers blare to life in all directions and an announcer's low voice booms, robotically, "One minute until the triennial group competitor photo. I repeat, one minute until the triennial group competitor photo."

"We have to go," I say, walking away toward the track where all the horse racers are gathering for the picture.

The rain finally stops and the sun comes out from hiding behind the clouds, shining rays of light on us.

We walk away, and the whole time, I make sure not to let go of him.

WHOA!

RITA WILLIAMS-GARCIA

I get like this when I'm anxious. Sleep. Wake up. Sleep. Wake up. Since I'm up, I start my preshoot ritual early. It usually does the trick—lets me relax, feel face-worthy. Empowered.

Some of the other freshmen, like my roommate, have college funds. My great-granny Mae gave me a white enamel basin. She said it was older than her mama, so you know that's old. It's not exactly a college fund, but I make good use of it. Once I get the water steaming, I sit the basin in the sink, drop in a few blades of fresh rosemary, and let the water fill it. I'm about to hood myself over the basin with a towel and let the steam and herbs do their thing, but when I look down into the steamy water, past the blades of green, a face stares up at me. It's not mine.

"WHOA!" I jump back. Turn around. I couldn't have seen what I thought.

I'm just anxious. My nerves have nerves. Got me seeing things. I take a breath, step up to the sink, and peer down into the basin. Okay. Nothing but hot water, some rosemary. Steam.

I'm back to breathing normal, thinking about the shoot. I want them to like my face, maybe see *this* face as *their* face. Not just for this shoot, but for an entire fall fashion campaign. I don't intend to make print-ad modeling my life. I have designer dreams of having my own label before I'm twenty-five. My own fall line. Right now, I fill the call for the Pretty Boy Next Door look. But check back in a few years, and I mean just a few. Once these family features kick in, the eyes, nose, lips? Goodbye, Pretty Boy Next Door. I'm out before I do urban. The money's in iconic brands, upscale catalogs, and I plan to work this look while it's selling. At least through undergrad.

I laugh at myself to myself. Imagine telling anyone about being scared by your own face. Roommate wouldn't let me forget it. Great-Granny Mae prays enough as it is.

Again. I lower my face and raise the towel to create that sauna, but then, I see it. And then, I don't see it! *Where's my reflection? Where the fuck is my reflection?*

As if to answer, a dark mass appears beneath the steam, in the water, slowly, revealing itself. Thick, ungroomed hair. A forehead, frightened eyes, a nose—both broad and sharp—and well-defined full lips. Nothing but fright looking back at me.

What kind of shit is this?

We're having the same thought, or close to it. The face in the basin shouts, "I rebuke thee, demon! I rebuke thee from the master's well, in the name of the Lord!"

Oh, shit! It talks! I look up to see if there's some kind of projector. This would make the ultimate prank, but no one I know, including my roommate, has that kind of energy. I feel around the basin. No buttons or things. Just a blue-rimmed white enamel washbasin.

I ask, "Who you?"

"Get back, demon! Get back!" His nostrils flare. He's a combination of fright and ferociousness.

"Who you calling demon? You're the banshee-looking thing, trapped in my great-granny's basin."

"I know a demon! Yes, suh! Shaved 'round the head like Beelzebub—a multitude of demon's horns sproutin' out the top of yo' head like a wicked crop."

"I'm no demon," I say to my imaginary water friend. "And these aren't horns. It's hair. My hair is locked."

"Who shackles hair but a demon?"

"Shackle? Are you for real? Not that kind of locks. Dreadlocks. You never seen locked hair? Everybody else got 'em. The trick is maintaining them." I know the concept of hair maintenance is lost on him. We check out each other's hair. His: no-style thick matted bush. Mine: a crown of product-rich short locks that stand up like black daggers, with sides shaved low from temple to temple. It's a signature look that gets me modeling jobs. It says different things depending upon how I smile. If I smile.

"Demon. Get out of the master's well. I can't bring back water with a demon."

"Who's this master?" I ask him. "There's no masters."

He laughs. Maybe it was water distortion, but I never seen teeth that big.

"You's the demon, all right! Telling me there's no master when I know Master Jacob'll tan my hide to the bare bone if I come back with demon water."

He's making no sense. Still, I study him. By the looks of him, he's studying me. I don't know what he's thinking about me, but I slowly put him together. The look. The speech. The fear. The master.

To be sure, I ask, "Where you at? I mean, I know you're at the master's well, but *where* are you?"

He answers readily, like it's obvious. "Where I been since birth. The Cosgrove Plantation."

"Quick: What year is it?"

"Year?"

"Yes. Year. What year is it at the Cosgrove Plantation?"

"Only years I worry about are my years. So far, I'm eighteen years old," he says to my complete disbelief. Through the steam his skin is sun-beaten tough. His large nose and lips belong on someone much older, like my dead father. How can eighteen look like that?

"My wife's sixteen. I worry about her years, too."

Wife? Don't get me started. I put all that aside and ask, "Who's the president. In Washington?"

"Master Jacob cast his vote for President Ban B'yoon. He says to me, 'John, as long as you votes Democrat, you won't have to fear where you sleep, what you eat, or what you do with all your days. The Democrat is the farmer's party!'"

"Ban B'yoon." I say it over. I got it. "Martin Van Buren."

"Can't you hear, demon? I said Ban B'yoon."

"Don't get so agitated. I'm only clarifying things." All I know about Van Buren is that he was a president, they named a high school after him, and back in high school the boys on Van Buren's track team looked fine leaping over hurdles in blue short shorts. I say, "Martin Van Buren" into my phone. Glance. 1840 something? I look in the water. Can't be. Can it? "No."

"Don't you 'naw' me. I'm wise to you, demon."

"Will you stop calling me demon. I'm Danté."

"That's a demon name if I heard one!"

I ask what I already know. "So . . . you're a slave. That Master Jacob person owns you."

He gives me the "obviously" face. "You free?" he asks. "You got papers?"

I know I'm dreaming. I feel awake, but this must be a dream. I should know. I've had a few dreams like this before. Dreams so real I couldn't believe they were dreams when I'd finally woken up. And then I'd release my breath, put things back in order, and get on with my waking life.

Still, this dream is different. I feel the hot steam from the water. I wipe my forehead and brow. Moist. Yes. Real. Or, feels real.

Why panic? I'll awaken the second I touch the water. All it takes is for one thing to break through the dream barrier and my eyes will pop open. To prove it, or end this dream, because, let's face it, talking to a slave is depressing—I go to stick my hand in the water but only get as far as the fingertips.

"OW!!!" How did I forget it's scalding? And, if this is a dream, would I feel heat like this? I suck my fingers to soothe them, and I look down into the basin. He's still there.

"What you do to yo'self? You all right?" Before I can answer he's laughing again, all toothy. "Lord! I ask the demon if he's all right!"

"The water's hot. I burned my fingers. And I'm no demon. I'm Danté. I'm just waiting to wake up from this dream. I have things to do, starting with getting ready for my photo shoot."

So, this is weird. I'm the one with burned fingers, but his eyes buck. His jaws clench, and although I only see his face, it's clear he crouches like he's been hit.

"Yo, yo! You all right?" I ask him.

It takes him a while to recover. He's not fully upright and seems confused. "Demon, you fit to be shot?"

It's my turn to laugh, and come to think of it, my teeth are kind of big, so he must think I look like a jackass.

"Sorry, Slave John. A *photo* shoot." This shouldn't be so hard to convey. They had photographs back in the 1800s. I study period clothing for my History of American Fashion class. There were a lot of drawings, but there were actual photographs too. Daguerreotypes and whatnot.

I don't blame him for not knowing that. It's not like slaves were lining up to get their photos taken.

He shrinks a bit. "FO-toe . . . shoot?"

The way he puts an accent on "photo," it's clear we're talking about two different things.

"I know you're a demon, but you ain't harm me, so I don't wish no harm on you. Listen, demon. Don't let them shoot yo' FO-toe. Steal away long before they take aim."

"Whoa. Whoa. Whoa. I don't know what 'FO-toe' is to you, but I need to do this photo shoot. Tuition's due."

A look of anguish comes over his face. He's shaking his head. "I know why yo' master shoots you. It's to tame yo' pride—with that strange talk and hair in shackles. Demon, just repent! Say you repent from your pride and maybe yo' master sell you, but he won't shoot you. You settle in yo' ways. Take a wife, like John, here. Have some young'uns."

I say, "I don't have no master, Slave John. And trust me. I won't be taking a wife." I laugh. I just don't have time. "And a *photo* over here is when they take your picture."

"Yo' pitcher? Why they take yo' pitcher, demon? I s'pose

even the devil get thirsty."

I say it to myself the way he says it. This 1840s talk is work! Pitcher. *Pitcher.* Then it clicks. Only because my great-granny Mae believes summer is for pitchers of lemonade and great-grandsons are made for squeezing lemons. I try again.

"Pick-shure. Pick-shure! Like when they draw or paint a picture of your face and hang it on the wall."

He slaps his thigh—I can only see his face, but his arm makes the motion of thigh-slapping. "Pick-chah! Pick-chah!"

We're both relieved. But now I have a question. "What does 'FO-toe' mean on the Cosgrove Plantation?"

He grins. Looks around. "FO-toe don't come from Cosgrove. The word come from my grandmama, along with a few other words she kept when they caught her."

"Whoa. Whoa. Africa. You're talking the motherland!"

"Mama's land is here on the plantation. Got a small plot for her vegetable garden."

I remind myself, if I don't want to be explaining and translating, I better keep it simple. I ask, "And what is FO-toe?"

He shows all his teeth and whispers. "It's the wife's property."

What?

He sees my confusion and whispers, "That's Grandmama's proper talk for where us mens make water."

"I got it. I got it." We share a laugh.

Usually by this time in the dream, he would morph into

someone I knew, a mythical being, or food I've been craving. But nothing has changed. Slave John is still looking up at me from the mist. Like he wants something from me.

"Someone think you so big to draw you up? Only one I know with a picture is Master Jacob's pappy. Hangs over the fireplace. I know it because I'm the one hang it."

It isn't worth the trouble of telling Slave John I had a fall spread in a magazine and I'm looking to be part of the brand. I can hear it now: *Demon, they brand you like cattle?* Instead, I try to speak his language, or close to it. After all, I'm acing History of American Fashion.

"I wear these new gentlemen's clothes. Waistcoats, mourning coats, britches. Top hats. And they make pictures of me for mag—uh, for everyone to see. Then the masters like how I look and they buy the clothes for themselves." That wasn't exactly right, but it was as close as I could get. "That's my job. That's the work I do."

He laughs loud. "That's what you call work? Letting folks make pictures of you in fancy britches and top coats?" He can't stop laughing.

"Are you laughing at me? You laughing at me, Slave John?"

"Tell you what, demon: you quit your crazy talking and I'll quit my laughing."

"They make pictures of me because I look fly—good. I look handsome. And I get paid. Good money. You pick cotton and get paid nothing."

"I see I gone and hurt your pride, demon. Maybe that's good for you. It's true: I don't get more than a pig and some whiskey come Christmas, but I make my money as a carver. That's my freedom money."

"Freedom money?"

"Don't you know nothing to be so fancy? Freedom money. Money I work for to buy my freedom. Master rent me out, I earn a good sum carving furniture, fancy walking sticks. I make enough to one day buy my freedom. Keep carving bed-posts and such and I'll earn enough for my wife, Mama, Pappy. My sisters, my brother. Grandmama too!"

"Whoa."

"Why you keep sayin 'whoa'? I'm no horse."

"It's because I need you to slow down, Slave John. The things you say are like a fast-running horse. So fast I have to say, 'Whoa.'"

He says, "If I say 'whoa' when you speak, I'd say nothing but 'whoa.' Like wearing fancy clothes is a day's work."

"Don't sneeze at my work, Slave John. You make a pig and some whiskey. I get two grand—uh, two thousand dollars to wear fancy clothes."

He takes his time laughing at me. "No need telling tall tales, demon or not."

"That's for real, Slave John."

"Just John."

"If you call me Danté."

"Danté, Danté. Tall tales as sure as you born."

"What are you? Some kind of slave rapper?"

"I don't know slave wrap. Missus wears a wrap. Cook wraps ham sandwiches in paper. I don't see no sense in wrapping a slave. How a slave wrap a slave?"

"We not communicating. We're just talking."

"I'm plain-talking, demon. Danté. You the one telling tales. Two thousand dollars to have someone draw yo' picture in fancy britches. Why, I could buy my wife, Mama, and one of my sisters for that money. I might can't read but I can figure on some money."

What do I say to that? *What?*

"I don't get it all," I tell him. "It's less after I pay the booking agent and taxes. The rest is for room and board."

"You stay in a boarding house?"

"A dorm. For college."

"College? College? You? Whoa!"

It's his turn to see my big teeth. We're kind of rubbing off on each other.

"Slow yo horse, Danté. Master sent young master up north to college. Granny said to yelling college, though I don't see a need to learn yelling."

"Yelling college? To yell?" I start to coach myself as I dream, because that's what I do. And then I get it. "You mean Yale."

"Open your ears, demon. Danté. That's what I said. Yell. Is that the one you go to? Your yelling is fine to me. You learning good."

Yell. Yale. I'm not going to try. "I don't study yelling.

I study making fancy suits and ball gowns for rich people."
More like sportswear and dresses. But this way is easier. "My
great-granny Mae is my inspiration. She recognized my talent
and encourages me."

He does his best to keep up with me, but now his eyes glint.
"Mae's my mama's name! That's your great-granny's name?"

"Mae on my father's side. Aletha on my mother's side."

We study each other through the mist, which is now cooling. "Naw!" he says. "We don't favor."

I don't know how long the steam will hold up. Even as I look
at him and he looks up at me, I can feel him fading. Something
in his eyes tells me to do something, but I don't know what
that is. In every time-travel movie I've seen, the rule is to learn
from the past but don't disturb it. But the steam is clearing and
he's really leaving me now. I want to give him something. Tell
him something about what life will be like. Besides, it's just a
dream. I can tell a dream about things that might to him sound
like a crazy dream.

"Look, John. I'm gonna tell you something. You'll be the
only one to know, but you got to promise not to tell anyone
what I'm about to say."

He shakes his head. "No, demon. I don't bond myself to no
demon."

"I'm no demon. I'm just a man. Eighteen. Like you. Got different hair. That's all. And I'm free."

"I figure you free—proud and fancy as you is."

"That's what I'm trying to tell you. But what I want to tell you won't happen if you tell anyone else."

John is quiet. I take that as my cue.

"You ready?" I ask.

"Go on, d—"

"Danté. My great-granny Mae named me Danté."

He nods. Looks around.

I say, "The Democrats, like your master, are for slavery. The Republicans want to end slavery. The Republican president will. Hang on—you'll live to be free. Not just you. But all of us."

"Publikan president?"

"That's right." Why bother to correct it. I keep telling him, since the water seems to be cooling. "Man's going to fly to the moon and back."

He almost shouts.

"We will have a Black president of the United States."

All I can see are big horse teeth.

"And if I get married, I'll have a legal husband. Not a wife."

"Say *what*?"

"John, John. Just don't tell."

He can't stop laughing and slapping his thigh. Maybe I told him too much, but once I started, the horses kept running.

Then I swear I hear the snap of a whip. Another snap. And another.

I spring up. Look around. Blanket. Desk. Wastebasket,

dresser, chair. Textbooks. Sketchbook. My makeup case. Roommate.

"I knew it," I say to my roommate, entering my waking life. "Dream."

"Again?"

"It was surreal. But real. Except for the fact that I was talking to a slave in my great-granny Mae's basin."

"I don't know what that means. Don't want to know. But seriously, Danté. This is like the fifth crazy dream. You should talk to someone."

He means the counseling center.

Maybe I do need to talk to someone, but what do I say? How do I explain that I can actually feel the weight of him—of John? How do I even start?

I don't close my eyes to get those last winks of sleep. I'm up and have to get my head right for the shoot. I shower, steam—this time without John staring up at me—dress, grab my makeup kit, and catch the train.

Usually my dreams fade to nothing when I wake up. Or, when I wake up I remember only one thing. And barely. But I can't stop thinking about John, seeing his teeth, hearing his laugh, or the snap of that whip.

The photographer tries to get me to smile. "More, Danté. More. More teeth, Danté." And then I lose it. And lose the gig.

On the train ride back to the dorms, my phone buzzes nonstop. I glance each time, but never answer. I'm in no mood to talk to the booking agent. I mean, what do I say? What? I can't talk about the shoot without talking about John. And that's not a talk I can have with the agent. Or my roommate. Or just about anyone.

That night I try to conjure John again. Tell him how he cost me my tuition. Hear what he had to say about that. John never shows. And I just sleep. Wake. Shower. Dress. Grab my sketchbook. Go to class. Draw sketches of John instead of the cuffs, collars, and sleeves I'm supposed to draw for my History of American Fashion class.

Besides John, Great-Granny Mae is on my mind, so we FaceTime.

It's clear that I get my fashion sense from Great-Granny Mae. She wears a silver wig, huge square glasses, and a pearl necklace, and is dressed in a light-green suit, stockings, and orthopedic pumps, even though she's not going anywhere but inside her apartment.

Her aide, a hunched-over woman who could probably use an aide herself, wraps a shawl around my great-granny Mae's shoulders and sits away from us to give us some privacy. Well. It's never quite private. She's always there.

I start with the bad news first. That I got fired from the modeling shoot and won't have my tuition money together. Then I tell her all about my dream and John. Great-Granny Mae laughs so long and so hard, I see where I get my teeth from. Her aide takes her time getting out of her chair but makes it over to her, to pat her back. Great-Granny shoos her away.

The first thing she tells me is not to worry. Seeing her laugh like that makes me feel a little better. From there, it's easier to tell her the rest, which makes her laugh even harder.

"Never saw him," she says. "He was long gone before I was thought of, but they called him Laughing John Carver. Story goes he went to the well to draw water for the master. He looked down the well and couldn't stop laughing. Master came to see about the water since John was taking too long. Master whipped John, but John kept laughing and saying, 'Whoa!'

"John wasn't ever the same since. He picked cotton, plowed, laughed. The Civil War came, he laughed. And every other time he'd look down the well, or up at the moon, and he'd just say, 'Whoa.'"

GRAVITY

TRACEY BAPTISTE

You are dancing in this club where the music is loud and everyone has launched into the air en masse and perfectly on the beat. Voices are wrapped around the last word of "We Here for That," one of the latest Bunji Garlin Carnival anthems. His deep tone fills every space in this hot second-floor room. It covers every writhing body, every flung strand of hair, every curled mote of cigarette smoke. You have finally let loose, hands in the air, wining bigger, and those hip swings have a life of their own. (Wining is a dance that works the waist and hips particular to those born at latitudes approaching zero.) Your hips get close enough to brush the inside seam of the ripped jeans on the boy you are dancing with. You pump your fists higher and lean close enough to his neck to smell the sweat mixed with vanilla-scented cologne that pools at his clavicle.

You had to be convinced to come, but your cousins were right. The music is sweet, the crowd is energized, and it's nice to be at a fête. Maybe you will give this boy your phone number.

You land and jump up again.

A microsecond into this midbeat jump and you feel the pressure of his fingers against you. Hard. Between your legs.

Time slows to infinitesimal units, like you and everyone in this place are being stretched by the mouth of a black hole, making this moment a millennium.

You have only just met this boy. You didn't catch his name or where he's from. You only know him in that way you know any boy who asks for a dance in a loud, crowded club.

The boy is grinning with delight at his coup. Maybe he's even amazed that he has gotten away with the palming of your crotch in this crowded place.

The smile rips from your face with a roughness matched by the tip of his finger.

It is dark in here. So dark that the neon lights looped along the walls reflect off bodies, plastic cups of liquid, and the exposed pipes on the ceiling in a way that makes them seem otherworldly. In this darkness and light, the boy glows purple and orange. Bright. Not dangerous at all.

You notice his perfectly straight, brilliant teeth and wonder how he manages to keep them so white. Your own teeth are crooked and yellow and your parents don't have the money to get them fixed. Not right now anyway, when you've all just arrived in this country and you're still sleeping on Aunty Alicia's living room floor on air mattresses. Your father, who can barely fit the bulk of his body on what he has been calling "the plastic raft," sends reverberating snores through the house every night. Your mother has been sleeping upstairs, since Uncle Andre has not been home. When your cousins are out, calls of "Clara bring me . . ." and "Clara girl, why you taking so long?" come from inside the sealed envelope of your aunt's bedroom. When you get close enough, your mother opens the door a sliver, takes what they've asked for, and gives you a smile that is all tiredness at the edges.

Why Uncle Andre isn't home is a big secret, like all the rest of the secrets, of which there are many. Family secrets never remain so. Over time, enough whispers get snatched from the air to declassify even the most shocking of them. They cross a threshold into cautionary tales and anecdotes that cast meaning into stories nobody has all the pieces to. Over half-cooked pots of fish stew or partially cleaned bowls of rice, someone will say, "You don't remember how Celeste get thin, thin, thin after the surgery?" to explain why Cousin So-and-So was suddenly slim. Or "How you ent see what Jodi do to Mannish car when she catch him?" would fill in the gaps of why This One or That One's car had been by the mechanic for so long. The secrets of your family stretch from the south of Trinidad all the way to a thin-walled bedroom in Brooklyn, New York, where you can hear your aunt sobbing, and your mother saying, "You know, you better off."

This long-limbed boy who *you yourself* chose to dance with after scanning the room and skirting the edges for thirty minutes has gripped you. It's a surprise. You are only steeled against the possibility of assault on Carnival Monday and Tuesday in the heat and crowds of Queen's Park Savannah. But there, you have your defenses in place: a phalanx of friends, somebody's older brother, and failing either of these two options, there is always the defense of keeping your wining behind at home in front of the TV. This pussy grab—for now—is one more secret. And what is one more secret, eh?

You know that girls who run their mouths get the spotlight turned on them. Quiet girls go unnoticed. Loud ones get called *fast*. Slow girls have their own problems. They are too slow to realize, to get out of the way, to avoid the things that will turn into secrets they have to keep.

In this moment that has stretched out to infinity, fresh beads of sweat spring from your pores. It's an involuntary evolutionary response designed to prevent you from overheating, from succumbing to a moment of danger. The chill of your own sweat causes your entire body to constrict: muscles, mind, thoughts. Everything presses in as if the black hole dilating time is you yourself.

This is when you remember, wasn't it you who smiled at him first?

Your toes are just off the floor, defying gravity with this

jubilant crowd, still headed upward as you try to think of a way to separate his hand from your body without making a fuss, without causing an incident, and without everyone in this club seeing beyond his fingers to what they always see—a girl who is fast, who asked for it, who likes it that way.

You want to avoid alerting your cousins Xavia and Zora, who like drama, who you have only known for three short weeks, and for whom this incident could go in unpredictable ways.

But nearing the tip of the jump, you realize that Xavia's head is thrown back in laughter, and that Zora's box braids are midwhip. Neither of them has noticed.

Yet.

Midjump, you are still the girl they thought you were: a nice Catholic girl, fresh off the boat, real country.

Your body and this boy's are still locked together, hovering in that moment at the vertex before gravity takes hold. Bunji's gravelly note holds in midair with you. Everything you know about physics tells you that where you go from here is a prede-termined arc. Unless some new force changes your trajectory, your destiny is to fall back to the sticky floor with this problem still firmly in place.

Is it possible to wrench yourself free? Twist somehow and come loose? You calculate the danger of this. You have seen rejected boys' backlash marked across the faces of girls. And what if your movement isn't smooth and silent? One of the cousins might turn. Look. See. Then what? Their part of the equation has too many unknown factors. You cannot solve for X or Z.

The fact of his hand between your legs on a crowded dance floor is a complicated matter, but only for you. For him, it is simple. Pleasure. Delight. For you, there will be questions. If not from the cousins, then from any and everyone else. Why did you wear a skirt? Why were you at that party? Were you talking to him before? Why would he just do that to you with no provocation?

It will not matter that this is the first time you have been in this situation. His hand will say something about you before you can say anything at all about yourself. You have seen this before.

There was the time that Myesha, crushing on Devon, let him lead her behind the cricket pitch off San Fernando Hill, past the row of bike racks, to the space underneath the stairs, so he could kiss her. That was her first time, too. She had loosened her uniform tie and unbuttoned the top button of her crisp white shirt, and boasted that Devon was going to kiss her that day. Right in front of everyone. But when it came to it, he had requested privacy. And she had said yes. She went off, and all you were thinking was how did she manage to keep her shirt so crisp in the hot Trinidad air, when you were a sodden mess every morning before first bell. But when they came back, her crisp white uniform shirt was torn at the shoulder, with a streak of dirt across her chest, and there was a brightening hibiscus-pink bruise at the side of her lip that bloomed brilliantly against her skin.

You ran toward her, but she shook her head and lowered her eyes in a way that made you stop in your tracks. Then the two of you walked home, pushing your bikes in the kind of sudden rain that leaves you soaked and then dries up instantly in the beaming sun, and you didn't talk about it again between you. But the next morning, someone leaned over during assembly and said, "You hear about Myesha behind the cricket pitch?" It was almost like she had been there alone, like she had assaulted herself. So you tried to explain and they laughed and said, "Is she own fault. Why you would go back there with a boy?" And the truth was, you knew you wouldn't. Good girls like you in your starched uniforms of pleated plaid skirts, white shirts, and ties didn't do things like that. So then who was really to blame?

Maybe if Myesha had stayed with the rest of you, then Devon would have taken someone else under the steps. And then everyone would be talking about her instead. That other girl would have been the shield that protected the rest of you. A sacrificial girl. You figure this was probably why Solange and Fatima whispered when Myesha and Devon disappeared the day before, lowering their eyes and keeping their conversation behind their hands. The next day, they side-eyed you both and refused to say anything at all. At lunchtime you discovered someone wrote "Devon is a pig" on the bathroom wall, and it wasn't Myesha who put it there. First, you know her handwriting, and second, you asked her. When she followed you into the stall and saw it, she cried. It was no comfort to her that someone else knew and hadn't told. So you asked if she was going to tell, and she just ran out into the hallway, leaving you there to add "Yes he is" on your own.

"Yes he is" slingshots you to the present, with the weight of your situation crashing into you. You who were convinced to put on Xavia's tight red T-shirt. You who slipped on Zora's skirt that was inches short of regulation length. (You checked. It did not come as far as your fingertips when you held your hands against your thighs.) You who cannot break free of the pressure of this pinpoint in time and space.

You return to the past, to how you and Myesha collided and fell apart. You didn't want the stain of her mistake, so for days, a week, two weeks, as Myesha settled into her new role, you steered clear. Then one day your mother said, "Show me your friends and I'll tell you who you are," which made you realize that the fact of Myesha and Devon under the stairs was not something just the Saint Theresa's girls and the Saint Michael's boys knew. The whole of San Fernando knew. This secret was all up and down High Street, heard in the choking exhaust of after-school maxi taxis, and spinning off the fan blades in every store. It was another one of those secrets that was anything but.

Myesha would become a cautionary tale. An anecdote.

You became extra careful. When the Saint Mike's boys went right, you toggled left. A zig for a zag. You buttoned your short-sleeve uniform shirt all the way to your sweaty throat and pulled your hair back into a single French braid that even Myesha called the "unsexiest hairstyle" she'd ever seen on the one occasion she tried to talk to you since you started avoiding her.

But then she started wearing her hair like that, too, and then you switched to two cornrows just to be different, just in case anyone thought you two were still friends. And when she called you a "C U next Tuesday," Fatima and Solange said, "That's how these kind of girls are." You knew different. But you said nothing.

Then the visas came through and the whole family was leaving for the States, so you started to count down the time and wear your hair the regular way again, down around your shoulders. Things would be different in America. You could make other choices. Better ones. Start fresh.

But here you are, hovering over this dance floor, and the only thing that has changed is the location.

Even before you left Trinidad, before this awful moment, you were awash in guilt. You left a note for Myesha and slowly began to lose hope she would respond to it, up until your last day of class, when you found a folded piece of paper in your bag, and you smiled at her. Even though she looked away, you decided to save it until you got home. But the moment you read it, you wished you hadn't waited. Still unfolding in your fingers, you read the words, "Good luck," and the email address Solange_cutie02, and the curvature on the letters, the upswing of the loops, were just like another set of writing you'd seen in a bathroom stall a few weeks before.

So you left the country without a word from Myesha, and with the understanding that Solange had used your friend as a sacrificial lamb.

In Brooklyn, with no school uniform and no regulation-length skirts enforced by nuns, you stuck to jeans and baggy tees that read "MAY THE $\frac{d}{dt} \implies_{(mv)}$ BE WITH YOU," or "$\sqrt{-1}$ 2^3 $\Sigma \pi$ and it was delicious" and kept to yourself. But tonight you are at a club, about to come back down to earth, where all things fall apart. Another fact of physics. Because it is the hardness of the floor, and the abrupt halt in momentum, and the unyielding nature of the surface, that causes a thing to crack. Even if it is not that thing's fault. And then we talk about this thing being broken, or it needing to be fixed, and not what part the floor has played in the matter. Never the part about the floor being a constant threat. Even if it is a nice floor. Even if everybody wants one just like it.

Heading back to the ground, gravity presses your weight into him. You squirm. The idea that he might think you are participating makes you want to vomit.

But you have one chance. There is one slim fact in your

favor. While gravity pulls you down, as the earth spins on its axis, and the solar system hurtles through space, and the entire universe stretches, all invisible forces acting on you, well, who can stay steady in all that?

Your toes touch first, pressing into the floor as the song thuds out a drumbeat. Then your heel comes down. Your knees bend, wanting to bounce back. But instead you succumb to the forces tugging at you. You fall. No, you genuflect. It's a moment of prayer that this will work. His hand slips away. His nails scrape your skin and you wince, then feel relief as he detaches. All eyes turn as Xavia's and Zora's arms reach to catch you. Others watch. They are a combination of surprised and amused.

You see that the smile slips from his face. He has lost his handle on the situation. He doesn't try to help you. He watches you crash to the ground.

Only, you do not crash. Your leg shoots out from under you and collides with his. The force of the impact is enough to throw him off-balance. The shock of it leaves him with no time to break his own fall.

Time resets to its usual speed.

You rebound to your feet, and as you watch him tumble into people nearby, you wonder if that little flick of your leg seemed like an accident, or if it looked deliberate. You smile and narrow your eyes. He sees it. He pulls in his lips between his teeth and spits out, "Bitch." Xavia screams, louder than the brass section behind Bunji Garlin's next soulful note, "Watchu say 'bout my girl?"

Her words rain daggers on him and draw the eyes of a small circle of dancers. The man he has jostled is angry. The boy struggles to get his feet under him. No one offers help. Embarrassment pins him there for a second until he finds his legs and straightens right in front of your face. His lips curl as if he is going to say something again. But your cousins are behind you. They are spread at your left and right like vengeful archangel wings. His defeat is a matter of simple math. You have the numbers on your side. Right now.

You leave. Your ears are still buzzing from the music, but at least it is much cooler out here and no one gets too close. You want to get to a bathroom. You want to check for damage. You and your cousins walk the seven blocks down and one block across to home, just off Flatbush Avenue. When you turn the last corner, you see someone exiting the front gate.

Xavia reacts first. She runs down the street calling, "Daddy!"

You and Zora approach slowly. Uncle Andre waits to hug both of his girls. He waves at you. Aunty Alicia watches from an upstairs window. It is the first time you know her not crying. Uncle Andre's eyes trace a path to his wife's. It is like watching a magnetic field form. You are all caught in it.

You wonder if all encounters of attraction are meant to be collisions. If there is no way anyone walks away unharmed.

THE TROUBLE WITH DROWNING

DHONIELLE CLAYTON

This spring they dragged three bodies from the Potomac River. I started counting at the end of April. Now I often visit the places where they washed up. I like to climb down under the bridge that connects Washington, DC, to Virginia and listen to the cars rumble overhead. I like how the water hisses as it licks the bridge's concrete legs.

I'm nervous about drowning and I'm afraid to swim. That plays into all the stereotypes about Black people. But the idea of big water makes me want to never leave my room. Not even for the temptation presented by the fried catfish and hush puppies our housekeeper, Bea, makes. Not even to shop for church hats with Gram. Not even to get sheet music from Melba's Blue Note when they have their yearly sale.

My twin sister, Madeleine, would hate how I've gotten more scared now, and she'd say to me: "Lena, stop being Chicken Little. The sky isn't always falling."

But that's how it all feels.

I keep coming back to this place. Like the gravel on the boathouse shore needs me to stand there. Like it won't really look right unless my shoes press into it, smooth it out for all the people who come to rent paddleboats. Like maybe those dead people might not have died if I'd been standing in this very spot.

I scramble up onto a nearby rock and sweep away cigarette butts left there, letting them fall like snowflakes into the waters below. Madeleine always smells like cigarette smoke. She says the scent and the smoke clouds help her think, help her paint. I've been getting older men who think I'm pretty to buy me cigarettes for the past two weeks. They stand in front of the corner stores in Adams Morgan, and all I have to do is take a cab down there and smile.

They help me smell like her. So I can think like her.

I've tried all different brands: Newports, Camels, Lucky Strikes, Marlboros, American Spirits. I like the shape of the boxes and their colors and how if you didn't know any better, you'd think they were full of the most wonderful candy imaginable instead of just cigarettes that can give you cancer or cause birth defects if you are pregnant.

My favorite are the little black ones. Cloves.

They come in an all-black box and carry the scent of Christmas, and watching the stick burn down to a nub calms my brain. Even though that's weird, and people buy cigarettes to smoke and I don't actually do that. But I couldn't tell anybody why this happens, why I feel better afterward. Because the words to try to explain it just don't make sense anymore.

Nothing does.

The cigarettes drift off in the water below. And I watch them, wondering if dead bodies float so effortlessly.

I stretch my arms out into the sun. I didn't get any browner this summer. We didn't go to Martha's Vineyard because of all the things that happened.

My uniform skirt whooshes, filling with the air from passing cars and becoming a bell curved around my legs. I like to feel the breeze whipping up through my panties, whistling inside me, reminding me that I'm awake.

That I'm here.

Madeleine plugs in Mama's old stereo. Paint specks freckle her neck and hair. We're identical, two little yellow-brown Black girls, but everyone can tell us easily apart now. Ever since we started high school last year, she wears her hair all natural and curly and frizzy, a cloud around her face and neck, while I get mine blown out straight every week when Mama's hair stylist comes to the house. Madeleine says I'm too much like Mama and not enough like myself.

We rest on our backs, attic dust everywhere, gazing upside down at the wall and ceiling.

Her canvas.

Our ritual.

She paints all over the loft, in the tight corners, the pointed ceiling when she can get to it, the floor panels at times. The wood is awash with portraits full of different hues of blue, her favorite color. When we were seven years old, she declared the attic her studio, where she'd become her own version of Picasso or Dalí.

I wish I could hide the piano in a secret room away from our mother's listening ears and commentary. Where I could play any melody I wanted with no one to correct me about it. Where I could become my own version of Miles Davis or Duke Ellington.

Thin streams of smoke create a gray cloud between the walls, the junk, and us. She lights dozens of cigarettes in ashtrays she stole from public places. They're smoking lily pads dotting a lake all around our brown legs.

An early spring heat wave warms the wood beneath our bodies. An air-conditioned breeze struggles through the small vent, and the tarot cards pinned on the wall rustle. I changed the arrangement today, sorting them into two T-shaped patterns, trying to divine some good luck.

I tap my fingers along the floor, plunking a melody across the wood while we gaze up at her painting. A gigantic hand stretches over our heads, consuming sections of the ceiling. The fingers are dangling branches of a demented willow tree with sharp, scratching petals. Last month, a beautiful dogwood grew over the wall, its flowers changing whenever Madeleine didn't feel well. Bad spells, our gram calls them. Attitudes in need of correcting, Mama labels them. I used to stay up here and whistle her a tune until she calmed down; then she'd transform the color of the petals and come out of the confusing place. I made her feel more like herself, and she made me feel not like myself. Confident, less afraid.

Madeleine whispers close to my ear, "Do you like it?"

"Can we turn the radio down?" I ask.

"You know Mama's always listening. Answer my question."

I don't remind her that Mama is getting her nails done.

"Wait, don't answer yet. Hand me the bowl near your head," she says, her voice high-pitched with the excitement of finishing a piece. Her rare cloud of happiness drifts around me. Everything about her is animated today: her footsteps across the wooden floor, her frequent smiles, the light movements of her brush on the painting. She always folded herself inside the attic, never worried about all the things outside its borders. I want that feeling, to finally start writing my own music and play more jazz and less classical. Despite Mama's protests.

I don't want to ruin her excitement by telling her that her

hand scares me. It makes me think of the bodies that have been washing up all summer.

I pass her one of Mama's teacups filled to the brim with gray paint. If Mama catches her with the good china, she'll be punished for the rest of the school year.

She spreads a skinny line of color across the wall with her fingers. I watch her as she moves back and forth in front of the hand. Her tattered cutoff shorts are smudged with color, barely recognizable as denim. A valley of scabbed blisters covers her inner thigh where she sometimes snuffed out her cigarettes and anger. We argued a million times over why she wouldn't stop.

She rejoins me on the floor. A streak of gray lightning now cuts through the black thumbnail.

"Now, what do you think?" She watches my expression. I avoid her eyes. They remind me of marbles with storm clouds trapped in them.

"It scares me," I admit.

"You're scared of everything." She pokes me with her paint-covered fingers.

"Am not," I reply.

She flicks the brush at me. A gray fleck sprays onto my cheek and another on my linen shorts.

"Maddie!" I rub away the drop before it dries.

"Lena!" Madeleine mocks me. "Don't be so fussy."

"I don't like being dirty," I say.

"You'd put plastic down under your head if I let you."

"No."

"Yes. Clean and virginal Lena Marie Hathaway."

"Dirty and bad Madeleine Sarah Hathaway. Whatever."

"Will your shorts be okay? Can you still supper with Mama at the country club?" she taunts.

"Mama and Daddy don't belong to a country club."

"Our house might as well be one," she replies.

I snuff out a few cigarettes in the ashtray nearby.

"Hey, you know those help me focus," she says.

"They give me a headache. Mama will kill me if I come down smelling like smoke."

The word *kill* stretches between us and I regret using it.

She cracks open one of the four circle windows, the eyes in her attic. They look out onto our neighborhood. "The Gold Coast doesn't look that gold." She moves the smoking round-abouts to the room's far corners and creates a circle of scented candles and incense around me. "Now you'll smell like Egyptian musk and vanilla. Stop being so afraid of Mama."

"You used to be scared of her."

When we started tenth grade, a small crack split the platform we both stood on. She got into more and more trouble— outbursts, skipping school, running away. I thought it'd just be a phase, like in eighth grade when she locked her hair after she claimed to channel Bob Marley through our old Ouija board. I was confident the crack would seal up, the wood fibers stitching back together, the platform remaking itself anew, and we'd go back to doing all the things we used to. Midnight movies, diaries full of secrets, and eavesdropping on all the dinner parties Mama would host.

But it got worse, and Mama and Daddy kept arguing about what to do about it. Mama didn't want their business out 'cause everybody at church and in our community always had something to say.

"Give me your arm," she orders.

I extend it. We face each other, our knees touching. A cornrow snakes along her hairline and purple beads hang from it, grazing her light-brown cheek. The hairstyle Mama hates. Blue veins bulge in her temples and her small hands from the attic heat. Her face reminds me of the homemade butter Gram used to churn when we were on the farm in Mississippi. Cool yellow.

With the tiniest brush she draws a stream of orange around my wrist. The liquid feels like yogurt on my skin.

"I'll be careful not to splatter on those precious shorts," she whispers.

I tap her hand, noticing wounds on the underside of her forearm. Fresh red gashes, like lines drawn with a teacher's red pen, mark up her skin. A train of painted red beads circles her wrist and covers sections of the cuts.

I grab her arm. She switches the brush into her other hand, not pausing her work. She lets me examine the barely scabbed marks.

"I thought you were done with that. You promised both me and James."

She doesn't answer. Her eyes fix on the attic's latch door.

It vibrates from a series of knocks. The stereo tumbles over as it lifts upright.

Mama doesn't poke her head all the way in. All I hear is her voice: "Turn that music off and come downstairs, Lena. I told you to stop coming up here."

The idea of drowning scares me. I was surrounded this summer: stories about the bodies on the radio in Daddy's car; headlines staring up from the newspapers; TV reporters trying to find patterns in the cases on the tiny kitchen TV that Bea watches when she makes us dinner; phone calls soliciting Mama's opinion on the matter.

Those bodies really didn't have much to do with me, but I couldn't help wondering what it would be like to let your insides die by filling yourself with water. To soak your heart, letting the empty spots flood. The pain of punching the waves. The fight to keep your head above water. The burn of gasping for air. I think it might be the worst thing in the whole world. So many had done it this spring, and everyone was talking about it. I guess everyone . . . except my family.

We eat in silence now. No more arguments. No more tears. No more threats of punishment. Not even any more *we-aren't-talking-about-sad-things-right-now.*

Mama flips through her schedule book, planning a fund-raising memorial, and Daddy has his eyes fixed on the newspaper. Dark spots ring their eyes like two pairs of crescent bruises, and Daddy's light-brown nose is bright red and blistered with broken blood vessels.

Bea sets out breakfast dishes between us—warm biscuits and honey, country ham and grits, and steaming mountains of home fries, the potatoes glistening with onions.

You'd never know anything was wrong.

We could be frozen in a snow globe. The perfect family. If someone was watching us, if someone even shook up our ball, the little flakes would swirl around us, but we'd still be in these exact positions. And no one would ever think bad things happen in our family.

Gram says a pile of money can make a barrel of sins disappear.

But what about sadness?

My stomach growls and I know I should feed it, but I have no interest in even chewing, really. Madeleine sits beside Daddy. She doesn't reach for a plate. She stares at the stack of biscuits on the table.

"It might be time to clean that room," Daddy says.

"I don't want to," I reply.

"Lena." Mama says my name in a way that means this isn't a choice. She bats her disappointed eyes at me; they're the color of two honeybees. She looks like she stepped out of one of the black-and-white photos that hang all over our house or from the pages of a vintage clothing catalog. Sleek chignon bun, a bloodred lip, her skin a cool yellow like a slivered almond, and always in expertly tailored dresses. Gram says she belongs to a different time. "This is not a discussion."

Mama hasn't always been this dissatisfied with me. I used to do everything perfectly, without even being asked. Madeleine was the one who argued and did the opposite of what she said. I didn't know how to *not* do what she wanted. But nothing makes Mama happy these days; she finds every out-of-place hair on my head.

"Let's adjust our attitude, shall we?" Mama lifts a perfectly arched eyebrow.

I've never had an *attitude* before. I rarely pushed the line. I wasn't the bad twin, the one who did anything out of the ordinary. I wear my hair the way she wants, my school uniform skirt is always the right length, I never overdid it on the makeup she let me use, and I'm still a virgin.

Madeleine crosses her arms over her chest like she's ready to say something to them and start trouble.

"Not right now," I say to her.

She shrugs.

"What was that?" Mama asks.

"Maybe we should discuss this while at the Vineyard house over the long weekend," Daddy says.

"I think we put this conversation off a while longer," Mama says to Daddy before turning her gaze back to me. "The cotillion rehearsal is tonight."

My body clenches.

"I don't want to do it anymore," I mumble. "I don't even have a date. Brett moved away. Did you forget?"

"Well, James will be without an escort," Mama says. Whenever she says James's name, she puts her excitement about him into each letter of it.

"I think under the circumstances no one would blame us if we canceled," Daddy says, flattening the paper in front of him.

Madeleine stares at me. Her gaze heavy, almost hot.

"You and James would make a beautiful pair. The dress is already made. It was delivered this afternoon," Mama says. "I don't think we should stop doing the things we planned to do."

"Let's discuss this later," Daddy says.

"There's nothing to discuss. We honor our commitments in this family. Right, Lena?" Her eyes sting, and a blue vein pulses in her temple.

Madeleine winks at me.

"Of course," I mumble.

The first body that washed up this spring was a white man. A paddleboater found him on April 28. The man's jacket got caught on a rusty hook, and he just floated there for days until somebody spotted him, face down, legs stretching out from under him, bloated like a dead fish. I want to look for that hook. I want to press my finger against it, see how strong it is, see how it could catch that body and hold on to something so heavy.

I take the newspaper clipping out of a shoebox. I smooth it out on top of my comforter and think about ironing the page if the paper gets wrinkled again.

His name was Jeremiah Flanagan, and he was from what Mama calls one of those Virginia towns with three people and a stoplight and a cup of racism. I wonder if people smile when they remember him or if they say good riddance. I wonder if you don't know how people really feel about you until you're dead. Would they wish you back? Would they think the world was better off without you in it?

Would people cry if I jumped?

How would Madeleine feel?

My sister's boyfriend, James, lives next door. Our houses sit like perfectly tiered cakes on a glittering tray, far away enough away to not touch like the other houses in Washington, DC, but close enough to look pretty together. Gram calls our area the Gold Coast. She said it's always been called that, since her own grandmother settled in the house. A place where rich Black people got away from the poor ones. But still didn't have to live with white folks.

You'd think the houses would be dipped in gold, though. Instead, the driveways hold expensive cars, the flower boxes burst with exotic roses, and only certain people with the right kind of money belong. Mama said, "Different people had different kinds. Old money, new money, illegal money, sports money. But we had money from the dead." Which has always been the most important.

I move a brass telescope in front of the window. We used to always peep at James through it. Daddy bought it for us when we turned eight, after we told him we planned to be the first twins to go to outer space.

When they first started dating, Madeleine liked to look each night to make sure he didn't have another girl in his room, even though he has the type of parents who don't allow girls to come over. She would climb across the thick tree boughs that reached from his window to ours.

I watch him now, pivoting the telescope to avoid the tree's new spring leaves so I can see him clearly. I catch parts of him. He has his shirt off. Daddy calls him "the scrawny boy next door" and thinks he's a little too soft. Mama just thinks his mother should feed him more. He's all freckled, even his light-brown chest. Madeleine said she would play a game where she'd try to connect the dots on him with one of her gel pens.

James catches me staring at him from my window and he flinches as if I've touched him. He yanks on a T-shirt, then sheepishly waves.

I lift open the window, and he does the same.

"You good?" he shouts, then scratches his head. "I mean . . . like . . . I know you couldn't possibly . . ." He drops his gaze.

"It's okay," I lie. "Can I come over there?" I yell back, and sound more like Madeleine and less like me.

He looks surprised by my question but then he nods. "Sure."

I do what my sister always did—climb into the arms of the tree and tiptoe across the boughs like it's a tightrope. I stop on his window ledge. He helps me inside, his hands warm from a shower and their heat pressing through my shirt.

"You smell like cigarettes," he says. "You smoke now?"

"No." I glance around his room. It's so different than Madeleine's and mine. A large bed is tucked in the corner and video game posters cover the walls. He's even got two small, glowing aquariums full of colorful fish. His DJ equipment is piled into one corner—turntables and speakers and albums and headphones.

I inhale the scent of his room and try to identify all the components.

"So how's it been?"

"Fine."

"You still coming tonight?"

The cotillion rehearsal.

"I guess." His gaze follows me as I walk around his room. I run my fingers over the items on his desk. I let my leg graze the beanbag chair in the corner. I wonder if this is where Madeleine used to sit when she came over here. Or was she bold enough to get on his bed? Yeah, she probably just plopped right on his blanket.

"My mom said that you were going to be my date."

I stare up at a clear piggy bank on his shelf, fat with coins. His dad is a banker.

"You know I'm sorry, right?" he says.

"About what? You didn't do anything."

"I didn't say anything. I could've . . ."

I turn around to face him, then close the gap between us. Tears slick the surface of his deep-brown eyes.

"She always does what she wants," I say.

His eyes comb over my face. "You both look so much alike. It's so weird . . . like . . ."

I lean forward and press my lips into his, pushing whatever he's about to say back into his mouth. He grabs my shoulders and steps away. His brow furrows with confusion.

"What're you doing?" he asks.

"Don't you miss her?" I say, moving closer again.

"Of course . . . but . . ." He puts his arms out to block me.

"Then why not?"

He catches me before I get too close again.

"You don't want me?" My bottom lip quivers and a hot wave of embarrassment warms my insides. My head gets light and the room spins around me.

"Lena . . . this isn't right," he replies. "I know things are hard, but—"

"You don't know anything." I shove him and head back to the window. "I'll see you tonight. I *guess*." I start to climb out and look up.

Maddie stares at me from our bedroom window.

• • •

We all stand inside Ballroom C in the Hay-Adams Hotel. It's one of Mama's favorites in the entire city, where she does most of her own private fund-raising events. If she and Daddy don't go to the Vineyard house, they come here for long weekends, leaving Maddie and me home with Bea.

"You okay?" James whispers as we stand in a pocket of noisy kids waiting for the cotillion dress rehearsal to begin.

Even if I did answer him, my words would be lost in the boom of voices echoing off the high ceilings. The faces of the other kids are a tornado of brown, most hailing from other DC private schools, some from Maryland and Virginia. We've seen each other at these events throughout the year. But now, we're all sixteen and are dressed up like we've escaped a group wedding.

Mama likes to call it our very own secret society: a group of wealthy Black people who have their membership-only club to ensure that everyone finds the right person to marry or the right network for the right job or the right people to be friends with. Women with perfect smiles, pearls, and pretty dresses, gentlemen in fine suits, swathed in the best fashions. They were people who set up the Black middle class and distinguished a high society for us, according to my mama.

And now we're here to be presented.

I smile at a few of the girls I recognize as their eyes comb over my dress. I feel like I've caught a fluffy white cloud, its rippled layers of tulle and satin and crinoline swallowing me in a corseted storm. It all feels stupid to be dressed up to practice. It all feels silly now.

I look for my sister, but she's not here. Parents and volunteers watch us from the side and flash me pitiful smiles if I catch their eye.

"Ladies and gentlemen, may I have your attention? Please locate your partners," Mrs. Moore, one of the cotillion organizers, directs. "We're going to practice the entry and go straight into the first waltz."

My eyelids droop in the dim light. The noises wax and wane in my ears, like someone is turning a radio dial up and down, up and down.

"Places," she says. "When you hear your name, come to the center of the room and step up onto the platform. Find your mark and stand there until I've called everyone."

The names drone on. There's a fly in the room. I watch it whiz over the beautiful treats set out for the parents to eat. It seems to dance from one cupcake to the next. It could almost be a bee. If only it were more beautiful.

James jostles my arm. "Let's go."

"What?" I say, too loud.

A nearby girl chuckles under her breath.

"They called us."

"Now, presenting Lena Marie Hathaway, daughter of Mr. and Mrs. Bernard Hathaway. She is escorted by James R. McKinley, son of Dr. and Mrs. George R. McKinley," the cotillion announcer says.

James tugs me forward like a doll.

I try to smile, but I can't. My mouth won't soften. My lips won't part.

We stand like mannequins on our marked spot as the other debutantes and their escorts are called one after another: "Tamara McDonald, daughter of Mr. and Mrs. Samuel McDonald, escorted by Michael Pinkney III, son of Dr. and Mrs. Michael Pinkney II . . . . Emilia Jenna Mullen, daughter of Mr. and Mrs. Stephen Douglass Mullen . . ."

I feel Mama's gaze on me. Out of all the eyes, I know the heat of hers the most. I can hear her say, "Lena, push your shoulders back. Soften your face. Look graceful. This is practice for the big event. It will be *the* event. Act as if it's the real thing."

The dress hem of one of the other debutantes drags when she waves at her mother and breaks her arm link with her date. Her mom stands almost on stage, taking prohibited photos of us all. They look just alike, both their shoulders curled over, and they have moon-pie-shaped faces.

I spot Mama shaking her head at her; she'll gossip about her on the car ride home.

We're led off the platform. The stage lights dim, and thousands of tiny lanterns glow from within the fake trees planted all over the room. A waltz begins. James grips the small of my back. The tiara glued into my hair bounces from his jerks. His shoes leave gray footprints on my dress hem.

"I need you to pay attention. You're messing up the steps," he whispers. Beads of sweat appear on his forehead.

"It's just the dress rehearsal," I snap.

"Still," he complains.

"Ugh, I can't. I need a break," I say, leading him to the side. I glance behind me to make sure Mama wasn't watching. She has her hand cupped to a woman's ear, no doubt whispering the latest scandal in our small community.

"What is it?" James says.

"Come with me somewhere." I squeeze his hand.

He doesn't say yes, but he doesn't say no.

I yank him forward.

The second body didn't really wash up at all. Police boats fished out a Black lady still wearing a church hat. The news said her leg hung from her body like a broken twig. The radio said that her husband barely recognized her. Called her pale. Said she'd lost most of her skin color. I guess you can jump into the water as a Black person and die, and be discovered later having lost some of your pigment. You can become white after death—if you start out light enough. The dusty brown color I got at the Vineyard house would fade fast. I'd be the yellow like the butter Gram always served at the Mississippi house. Like Madeleine.

The construction workers putting the new addition on the Williamsons' house wouldn't call me a "red bone" girl anymore. When I asked Mama what the term meant, she said it was some old-timey term left over from slavery. That our bones must be red 'cause we were fair-skinned Black people instead of dark brown.

This church lady became one, too. From the water.

Reporters kept shoving microphones in her husband's face, asking what happened and balking at the fact that a grown woman couldn't swim.

The man cried so badly, his tears glittered like constellations of stardust.

Her name was Bernadette Jackson, and she was sixty years old. Her husband said neither of them had learned to swim when they were kids because pools didn't allow Black folks in North Carolina to enjoy the water.

He said she'd left a note that he wasn't ready to talk about.

I'd love to have read it.

I ask the bellhop at the hotel to get James and me a cab.

"Where are we going?" he asks.

"You'll see." I pull out a pack of cigarettes from my clutch and light one. I take one puff just so it will start disintegrating, and watch it burn. I hate the way they taste but love watching the clouds of smoke dance in front of me.

The cab pulls up, and we get in.

"We shouldn't be leaving," he says, because he always follows the rules, like I did.

"We won't be long, I promise."

"Where to?" the cab driver asks.

"The Key Bridge."

"That's not a destination," the cab driver replies.

"The boathouse," I snap.

"Okay," the man replies.

"This isn't a good idea." James frowns.

"Nothing is a good idea anymore. But no one asked me how I felt about it. Maddie sure didn't. My parents didn't."

"Okay." He sits back and stares out the window, then slides earbuds out of his pocket and puts them in.

My sister gets into the front seat. Like the smoke called her right to me.

The cab driver makes a left out of the parking lot.

"You know you should go back, right?" Madeleine stares at me, but I don't look at her. She shouldn't be here. But she doesn't startle me. She hasn't left my side since the last week of March.

"Lena, you're missing the last parts of rehearsal. Mama will be mad," she says. "You hate making Mama mad."

"I don't care."

The cab driver glances up at me. He raises his eyebrows.

"I'm not missing anything important," I say. "Why you so worried?"

James takes out his earbuds. "Who are you talking to?"

"Madeleine," I reply.

"Are you okay?" he asks.

"You don't like it when Mama and Daddy are upset with you," she says.

"You didn't have to come," I say.

"You dragged me along," he says.

"I didn't mean *you*," I say to him.

I look away from him and at her.

"I did have to come." Madeleine stares back at me. The beaded cornrow along her hairline grazes her cheek. Her curls frizz a little from the humidity. Pale-blue veins raise in her hands. One appears down the center of her forehead, and I know she's hot. I feel hot, too, just because she does. Just because we're always supposed to feel the same things.

The cab pulls up to the little boathouse. I give the man cash, and we get out.

James walks beside me, and I feel him watching me.

Maddie lingers behind us. "You have to go back," she calls out. Her voice is desperate.

I flinch.

"Why did you bring me here?" James asks. "And why are you being weird?"

I ignore her, and him. She never used to act scared of anything: always breaking curfew, not afraid to show Daddy a bad report card or kiss boys in the basement or say curse words at Mama's benefit luncheons just to be embarrassing.

I am the scared one.

I watch the water.

"You're too close," she warns, and now she's right beside me, her hand reaching out, trying to pull me back to safety. Her nails and fingers are painted purple, and I think one day the colors will seep into her bloodstream, and her sweat and tears will change colors.

"We shouldn't be here," James says. "This is weird."

"You sound like her, you know," I say.

"It's time to go. Too much time near the water. And thinking about the water." She reaches for me again. The moonlight makes her hand see-through.

I don't take it. I can't take it.

"Are you going to be okay?" he asks.

"Are you going to be okay?" I spit back.

"I lost her too." He looks away as a tear falls.

The third body that washed up this summer was my sister's.

James and I light cigarettes and throw them in the water. Their slender bodies bob in the cold and angry waves. I watch the water soak into the filters and stamp the light out. It makes me think about Maddie and what it might've been like for her.

The sadness drowning her like the water. Her heart stopping. Her mind going silent. Insects nesting inside her. Her blue veins and red bones exposed to the light.

"I wish she was still here," he mumbles.

"Me too."

I cut my eyes at her. Each time we light a cigarette and toss it, a part of her disappears.

A leg.

An arm.

One of her ears.

Her neck.

Like a candle flame extinguished in the dark.

"Did you know she was going to do it?" he asks.

"No," I say, but it feels a little like a lie.

"What do we do?"

"I don't want to let her go."

"I don't think she's gone." He tries to smoke one of the cigarettes but breaks out into a fit of coughs. "Whenever I see you, I'll also, always see her. You carry her with you."

He doesn't realize she's standing right next to us. Well, what's left of her. I watch as she slowly disappears.

"I feel like I drowned with her," I admit.

He looks at me. Then touches my arm. "We all did."

Closing my eyes, I tell my sister I will always love her. Then I take my pack of cigarettes and throw it into the water.

Turning to James, I say, "I'm ready to head back now."

KISSING SARAH SMART

JUSTINA IRELAND

It's the first day of summer vacation, and I stand on the edge of my grandmother's front porch wishing that I could disappear into the wooden boards. Or maybe I could just vaporize into mist. Anything would be better than this.

"It isn't serious, I'm just tired," my mom says to my grandmother. It's become her mantra. Tired is better than "mentally ill," better than "nervous breakdown," much more comfortable than "severe depression."

In my family we skirt the truth like a minefield.

"Tired people don't have themselves committed." Grandma Rose stands in the doorway with her arms crossed. Her face wears a scowl of disapproval mixed with delight in seeing us. My grandmother looks like an older version of my mom: pale skin, dark hair sliding to steel gray, and a bracket of lines around her mouth from a life spent pursing her lips in disapproval. Mom's lines are just a little less deep.

Mom deftly dodges Grandma's point. "It was just a few days in the hospital. Exhaustion. Anyway, Tony and I thought it would be good for me to spend some time back home. Things are so stressful that close to the base. Besides, Devon missed you," she says.

She hadn't decided anything. It was my dad who had decided that my mother's breakdown in May was due to fatigue, and that what she needed was some time back home in Maryland. Mom had spent an afternoon taking too many muscle relaxers for her back. She said that she'd forgotten she'd already taken her medicine and taken another dose. Dad thought she was just being overdramatic, that it wasn't a big deal.

I didn't know what I thought. I was just glad I'd found her before anything too bad had happened.

But it was the perfect reason for Dad to get rid of us. After all, he'd said, it would give him time to work out the kinks of his unit's upcoming deployment. He somehow didn't think Mom's health issues could be related to his unit getting sent halfway across the world to fight in some war no one wanted. Again.

But that was my father. Country first, army second, and the rest of us somewhere after that.

I sound bitter, but I'm not. Resigned is probably closer to how I feel.

Grandma Rose still doesn't budge. "It isn't that I'm not happy to see you, Annabelle. It's just that I would've expected to get a call first. We haven't talked since early May."

I shift from foot to foot. I told my mom to call Grandma before we left. It was a nine-hour drive from Georgia to Maryland, so it wasn't like she didn't have an opportunity.

"I want it to be a surprise," Mom had said, flipping through my playlist as I drove.

"Not all surprises are good," I said.

She ignored me.

Now, here we were having an awkward family reunion. No one asked for this.

Mom sighs. She still hasn't answered Grandma's accusation. "I texted you."

Grandma Rose harrumphs. "A text isn't a conversation, Annabelle." She looks from my mom to where I stand at the edge of the porch. "What does Devon think of this? This is her last summer at home before she goes to college. Doesn't she want to spend it with her friends?"

"She's fine with it," Mom says, shooting me a nervous look over her shoulder. I could blow up her spot so easily if I wanted, but it just seems needlessly cruel. The past few months I've been trying not to think about what'll happen to her after I leave for college and she's all by herself. The least I can do is give her this small bit of backup.

I smile at my grandma, as though that can make Mom's

lies reality. I'd begged to stay in Georgia, had even treated my mom to a week of silence to prove how serious I was. But then my dad looked at me and said, "Your mother can't drive the car by herself. Someone has to get her to Maryland. Maybe this will change your mind about being a nurse." And I knew the conversation was over. My declaration that I wanted to study sociology instead of nursing had been a well-trodden battleground over the winter and spring, and I had no desire to revisit it. Either way, I could tell by the set of his jaw he'd already removed himself from the situation, and there was no way anything was going to change his mind.

It didn't matter. Once I got to college I'd be free. In a little less than two months I would start college in New York, and once I was there I could do whatever I wanted.

It was the dream.

But first, I had to survive the summer in the backwoods of Maryland. Cecil County wasn't exactly open-minded and welcoming to Black folks. And even though I was used to seeing Confederate flags dotting the landscape, they seemed more ominous this far north. I didn't want to be here any more than Grandma Rose wanted us to be here, so I stood there silently as my mother tap-danced around the truth.

My parents were getting a divorce. It was just that neither of them wanted to say it out loud. But anyone could see the train hurtling down the track toward its inevitable crash.

I watch wearily as Mom spins her web of lies in the early-morning heat. She crosses her arms and sighs heavily, like Grandma is the one being unreasonable. "Look, you won't even notice us here. I'm going to finish a project for work and Devon is going to start getting ready for college. If it's too much of an inconvenience, we can get a hotel, come back and spend some time with you later this week."

My mom quit her job right after her hospital stay. And we don't have money for a hotel. But I say nothing. My phone buzzes, and I dig it out of my back pocket, surprised I have a signal in the middle of God's country. It's a picture of Amy and some of our other friends by the side of her pool.

miss you, the text reads.

Ugh. Now I miss her, too.

Barely ten a.m. and already sweat trickles down the small of my back as I stand on the porch daydreaming about being back home, away from this awkwardness. Not that it would be any cooler in Georgia. But right now I could be swimming with my best friend Amy in her pool. Amy in her bright-red bikini that made me feel some kind of way.

That gets me to thinking about her and the way she'd kissed me after one too many beers the night of graduation.

"I hope you don't think I'm a lesbian or anything, but you're my best friend, Devon. I just love you so much," she'd said. And because I'm a great friend I'd taken her home immediately.

But that didn't mean I hadn't thought about that kiss, and Amy, ever since.

"I suppose you two had better come on in," Grandma Rose finally says, jolting me from my memory and back to the here and now. She stands back from the door. "I'm letting all the cool air out. I hope you aren't expecting breakfast, because I don't have anything to eat. If you'd have called me, I would've gone to the store."

"We're fine, Mom. Besides, Devon can go to the store. It'll give her something to do," Mom says, kissing Grandma Rose on the cheek as she walks by. As for me, Grandma Rose just gives me a long look before patting me awkwardly on the shoulder.

"Sorry about your summer, kiddo," she says, just low enough so that my mom can't hear.

I guess Mom's tap-dancing isn't so effective after all. Even Grandma Rose knows the truth.

When I was younger, we used to come to Grandma's house every time Dad deployed, spending the summers here in Parrish Point, small-town, middle-of-nowhere Maryland. It's about an hour from Baltimore, but we rarely visited the city because Grandma Rose always complained that the one-way streets were too difficult to navigate.

I know now that *one-way streets* is code for too many Black folks, but as a kid I never knew that. The time I spent in Parrish Point was magical. I loved climbing trees, chasing fireflies, and drinking not-too-sweet tea in the evenings while

Grandma and Mom gossiped about distant family members and complained about the mosquitoes. Sometimes we would even ride bikes the three miles into town to get burgers and shakes at the town's lone drive-through, Chuck's Creamery. I have a lot of memories of this small town, so being in Parrish Point feels like returning to visit an old friend.

An old, racist friend.

I'm hyperaware of my dark skin as I push my cart through the grocery store, people giving me hard looks if I spend too much time in one aisle or another. Most likely none of them remember Rose Davidson's Black granddaughter. I hear their whispers and comments, but it's easy to ignore them. Shopping while Black. Well, half Black. But it's not like it matters to anyone white.

All they see is the high melanin content of my skin.

Of course, I guess it's partially my fault. I'm damn near a stereotype. My hair is down, a frizzy halo of curls around my face, and I'm wearing short shorts and my Black Lives Matter shirt that Dad threatened to burn when I brought it home. "We aren't thugs in this family. We respect the police," he'd said. Like BLM was about respecting authority, not demanding the right to live. But he's always been more comfortable being the "Good" Black person, as though it's possible to be better than racism.

It had taken hiding the shirt at Amy's house to keep it in one piece, and the last thing I was about to do was to let Parrish

Point make me feel bad about it.

I swing the cart around to the cereal aisle, staring at my options for a bit too long. I've just about narrowed it down to two different high-sugar cereals when a white woman comes around the corner, pushing her baby in a cart.

"Oh, I just love your hair," she says, her eyes going wide at my curls.

"Oh, thanks," I say. I stare really hard at the cereal, hoping she'll take the hint and leave me alone.

She doesn't.

"It's just so amazing. How do you get it like that?" The woman touches her own straight brown hair, as though she's imagining how she'd look with an Afro.

I blink. "This is pretty much what it does."

"It looks so soft . . . ," she says, and for a moment I'm afraid she's going to reach out and pet me like I'm a labradoodle.

"Please, for the love of God, tell me you are not about to try and touch her hair."

Behind the woman stands a girl who looks close to my age. She's what my mom would call "pleasingly plump" in order to avoid saying *fat*, like it's a crime to carry around extra pounds. The girl's hair is the same brown as the woman with the baby, but cropped closely in an aggressive pixie cut. She wears a shirt with a unicorn that says "Trample the Patriarchy," and a pair of board shorts with work boots that are completely inappropriate for the heat. Her lip is pierced and she wears an expression somewhere between rage and embarrassment.

She is, quite plainly, the hottest white girl I have ever seen.

"Sarah! Of course I wasn't," the white lady says with a laugh, hands nervously adjusting her baby's bib. She looks embarrassed, so I know that's exactly what she was going to do.

"I'll grab the cereal if you want to go get some bacon? You know Mom will lose it if I bring home the vegetarian stuff again," the girl says, and the woman with the baby shoots me a wan smile before beating a hasty retreat.

"Sorry about that," the girl says once the woman's gone. Her voice carries the hint of an urban area, her words slightly more clipped than the slow vowels of rural Maryland. "That's my sister, trying to prove she isn't just another racist white person. If you would've talked to her long enough, she would've told you how she voted for Obama."

I shrug, because I want to play it cool and but I'm also trying to check the girl out without looking like I'm checking her out. I fail miserably.

"It's no big deal, I'm used to Parrish Point," I say, like I'm so cool not even awkward white nonsense can bother me. "It is what it is."

"You aren't from around here," the girl says, glancing at me out of the corner of her eye as she peruses the array of cereals. At first I think maybe she's checking me out as well, but when I look in her direction and our eyes meet, I convince myself that I'm just making it up, that it's all in my head.

"No, I live in Savannah. Well, outside of Savannah. My mom and I are up here visiting my grandmother. You might know her—she's the librarian here. Rose Davidson?"

"Oh yeah, I totally do. I'm always at the library. Well, I was before I went away to school. Rose is . . . Rose. I'm Sarah, by the way. Sarah Smart."

I smile at her avoidance of classifying my grandmother as anything other than what she is and grab a box of super-sugary cereal, the kind I can count on my mom not to eat. And then I grab a box of something that looks boring and healthy as well. "I'm Devon. And I guess if you're always at the library, then I'll see you there? Since it's the only thing to do in this town."

She smiles at me, and I'm surprised to see that her front tooth is slightly chipped. Somehow it makes her even more appealing.

"Definitely," she says.

I walk away to do the rest of my grocery shopping, feeling buoyed by the possibilities.

My first crush was a white girl named Leslie Salinger in fifth grade. She had a blond ponytail and smelled like strawberry bubble gum. She was obsessed with being a good kisser, because her older sister had told her that the only thing boys cared about were boobs and being a good kisser. Leslie used to practice on me, because, as she said "you have puffy lips and are a better kisser than anyone else. Plus, you always smell a little like chocolate."

The chocolate smell was cocoa butter, helping a sister out.

Our kissing lessons went on for a couple weeks, until a teacher found us practicing one day during recess and that was the end of that. Another girl had ratted us out, and I like to think it was because she was jealous. Either way, Leslie's parents decided to send her and her sister to Catholic school and my dad threatened to send me to boarding school if anything like that ever happened again.

"That's disgusting—you don't kiss girls, you understand? We don't have gays in our family," he said. Mom eventually got him calmed down, but I never forgot the way his eyes bulged as he yelled "GAYS."

After that, I never kissed another girl until my friend Amy's drunken advances.

That doesn't mean I didn't think about it, though.

I'm daydreaming about kissing Sarah when she walks into the library a week after our first meeting in the grocery store.

I stop the shelving I'm doing for a few seconds and stare stupidly, because I'm only partially sure I didn't conjure her out of my imagination.

When I'd agreed to help my grandma out at the library, I'd done it half because my mom was working my nerves and half because I was hoping I'd see Sarah again, but now, here

I am looking right at her and I'm not sure exactly how to feel besides ecstatic.

"Hey," she says. She's walking straight toward me, and suddenly I don't know what to do with my hands and my heart is beating too hard and I'm also trying to remind myself that there is a possibility that she is not thinking about me the way I'm thinking about her. I don't want to be a creeper and my brain is like, "SMILE, SMILE!" So I do. But not too wide.

"Hey," I say. I slide a book onto the shelf. Cool. I'm the chillest ever.

"That's nonfiction, Devon. It goes on the other side of the library," my grandma calls from the front desk. I don't even know how she can see where I put the book this far back into the building.

My face heats as all of the blood in my body rushes into it. "I knew that," I mutter. Because I did, until Sarah fried my brain circuits.

Sarah grins. "The Dewey decimal system makes zero sense," she says sympathetically.

"Right? I mean, why make things needlessly complicated? Letters or numbers, pick one," I say.

Sarah laughs, and not in that fake way people do when they're trying to be polite, but like she actually thinks I'm funny. "So, are you working here now?"

I shake my head. "Just helping out. It's better than HGTV."

She widens her eyes. "Are you a fan of those tiny-house shows?"

My heart sinks. Dammit, and here I thought she was perfect. "Actually, I hate them. I spend most of my time watching them and waiting for them to say something ridiculous like, 'Oh, I thought there'd be more space in here.'"

She claps her hands over her mouth, her brown eyes somehow even wider with excitement. "YES!" she says, loud enough that Grandma, who is the loudest loud talker that ever uttered a syllable, is shushing her from the front desk.

Sarah ducks her head and says in a quieter voice, "My favorite part is when they're always like, 'Where are we going to put the baby and the dog,' and I'm like, 'Not in that tiny-ass house.'"

I snort, and cover my mouth to keep from laughing too loudly.

"Hey," Sarah says, sobering suddenly. "I actually had a reason for stopping by."

"Need something to read?" I ask.

She grins lopsidedly. "No, I was wondering if you wanted to hang out later tonight. Some of my friends in town are having a barbecue, and I thought it would be cool if you came along. Since you don't know anyone and all. I figured the Dollar General has just about lost its charm by now."

"What are you talking about, I haven't even been to the Dollar General yet," I say with a smile. "But yeah, that would be cool." I don't mention that my other option is listening to Grandma Rose and my mom bicker over every single tiny thing until Mom retreats to the guest room and buries her face in a romance novel. Sarah's party sounds way better.

"Great!" Sarah says, looking a little relieved.

I dig my phone out of my pocket and we trade numbers. It's all I can do to keep my hands from shaking.

"Should I bring anything?" I ask,

She gives me a Cheshire cat smile. "Just a swimsuit and a smile." I can't quite tell if she's just being friendly or if she's actually into me.

But it doesn't really matter. I am smitten.

It turns out the barbecue is at Sarah's house, which isn't all that far geographically from my grandma's house and yet a complete world away from what I'm used to. Maryland is all rolling hills and deciduous forest, while in Georgia we'd lived in a giant house on a postage-stamp lot. One look at the traffic speeding by on the rural highway out front and I decide driving is the better option. Nothing good is going to come of a lone Black girl walking along the highway in the middle of nowhere. Mom surfaces from her laptop just long enough to point out where her car keys are when I ask to borrow the car.

Escaping Grandma Rose's house is like running away to Neverland.

But once I'm to Sarah's place, I lose my nerve. After parking my mom's car, I get out and spend a few long minutes trying to build up the courage to go inside. Sarah's house is nearly three times the size of my grandma's, and from what I can tell she doesn't just have a pool, she has an entire swimming complex. Bass can be heard from the end of the driveway, as well as girlish screams and splashing.

"What am I doing?" I mutter. I'm so far out of my league that I'm not even playing the same sport. Sarah is too pretty, this house is too fancy, and I don't belong here. I should just go back to my grandma's house. I could watch HGTV with Mom while she talks about how she wants one of those bright-orange accent walls, which is my dad's least favorite color.

"Hey, you aren't planning on flaking on me, are you?"

I spin around and Sarah is standing behind me.

"Okay, that's creepy."

She laughs. "You said you'd be here around four, and I wanted to make sure you didn't get lost. Sometimes people try to take the private road instead, and if you did that, you would've ended up in a field of cows."

"Well then, thank you for saving me from the cows."

She bows gallantly. "My pleasure. Come on, everyone is dying to meet you."

She takes me by the hand and pulls me up to the house, and my nervousness fades into the background. As we walk around the house to the pool area, she keeps ahold of my hand, glancing at me very quickly. "Is this okay?" she asks. My heart trips a merry rhythm.

"Yes," I say, and her answering grin is everything.

The party is a blur of activity. I meet her friends, some from Parrish Point, others up from Baltimore for the day. Sarah is heading into her sophomore year of college, and most of the people there go to Towson University, which is also where Sarah goes. I am relieved to see that I'm not the only Black person there. She knows so many people, and they're all super friendly, but I can't remember most of their names.

We swim, we eat, and a few folks drink, but I don't. Sarah is never far from me, and when someone asks her in a low voice, "Is that your girlfriend?" I'm delighted to see her turn several shades of red.

Once everyone is sufficiently tired and full, we hang out around the fire pit. Like at most parties, the chatter breaks into several conversations, and the words drift by me without really making any impact.

"Your parents have a really nice house," I murmur. Sarah and I are sitting close, shoulders touching, and her hand is almost on my leg but not quite. It gives me all kinds of thoughts, which should be silly since I just met her, but also feels completely natural.

"Yeah, the murder machine pays well." At my raised eyebrows she clarifies, "My dad does contracting work for the army." She says this almost apologetically.

"Oh, no worries. My dad is in the army. So murder is also his business. Where are your parents, anyway?" I ask.

"Upstate New York. We have a cabin up there and my parents and my sister, who you met at the store, spend most of the summer there. Which is why I stay here in Parrish Point," she says with a mischievous grin. "The scenery is much better."

The compliment sends my brain into panic mode. Suddenly I'm thinking about my mom, wondering if she took her medicine and if she's fighting with Grandma Rose and what kind of mess could be waiting for me when I get home. "I should get going. My mom doesn't like me staying out too late. And I have important library business to attend to in the morning." I give her a half smile in apology for both bailing and the weak joke.

"I'll walk you out," Sarah says.

I wave goodbye to everyone as Sarah and I pick our way through the cool grass. "Thanks for having me over. It was a lot of fun."

"I'm glad you came," she says. Both of us fall silent, the reality that our time together is about to end dampening my good mood. Then we're stepping into a shadow and she's grabbing my hand and turning me around.

We don't say the word *crazy* in my house. Not anymore. After Mom had her incident last winter, it was erased from our family's lexicon, like we can rewrite reality by changing how we talk about things.

But it doesn't work, because the first thing I think when Sarah Smart kisses me, touching her soft lips to mine, is *This is crazy.*

Followed closely by *Dad would lose it if he found out.* Then *He won't know. He isn't here.* And *There's no way this lasts beyond the summer. Is this what I want? A summer fling?*

Or could this be more?

I don't have an answer. But I also don't much care. Because when a pretty girl kisses you full out, it's time to stop thinking and start doing.

So I ignore all of the panicked thoughts whirring through my brain and kiss Sarah back.

My days take on a pleasant pattern.

I get up and eat breakfast with Mom, who has retreated into her books. I worry that she's trying to replace reality with dashing dukes and swooning ladies, but it's the first time she's seemed happy in a long time, so I make a point to check out new books for her and just make sure she's keeping up with her prescriptions. A couple times she drives down to Baltimore to "have a tune-up," as she calls it, an appointment with a local psychiatrist. I always ask her how those appointments go, but she usually just gives me a smile and picks up her book.

Afterward I drive Grandma to the library to open it up. At some point in the morning, Sarah comes by, usually with coffee, so that Grandma starts to look forward to her visits as much as I do.

Sometimes Grandma Rose gives me a sly look, but I don't think she knows what's going on. I'm pretty sure there aren't any lesbians in Parrish Point.

And if there are, I can guarantee they aren't hanging out with my grandma.

At lunchtime, after most of the shelving from the library's night drop has been done, Sarah and I sneak away to be together. Sometimes we go swimming at her house. One day we drive down to Baltimore and walk around Inner Harbor, holding hands and grinning. We go to the aquarium and steal kisses in the shadows between the exhibits, giggling whenever we're nearly caught.

Sarah is the happiest person I've ever known, and smart as hell. Her humor matches mine, and we spend entire after-noons watching terrible TV and cracking each other up. Being around her makes me feel like someone's turned a light on inside of me, like I was a vacant house and a family has finally moved in. Even though I know this is only happening because my mom seems too distracted to notice and my father is five hundred miles away living his own life. If any of that were to change, it would break this fragile thing I'm building with Sarah.

And I'm not sure any of that even matters. At the end of the summer she'll go back to Towson and I'll go to NYU.

Sometimes, when I'm lying on the couch in Grandma Rose's living room, thinking about that makes me feel a bit panicky. The inevitable end to my time with Sarah.

But when I'm kissing her, everything else fades into the background.

And of course, by the middle of July we're doing more than just kissing, our hands and mouths finding the places that make each other sigh in delight. I learn the landscape of her body, and she navigates mine just as well. Sometimes we're awkward, breaking into nervous giggles when things feel too serious, too heavy. But then we find our rhythm and fall back into sync.

I don't have words for the way she makes me feel when we're messing around up in her room. Happy just doesn't seem adequate; alive is much closer to the truth.

After my time spent with Sarah, I go back to my grandma's house and dodge my mother's questions and my grandmother's knowing looks. Because I want my afternoons and evenings to be mine alone, and if I put a name to what Sarah and I have, if I call her my girlfriend, then I'll have to have an entirely different conversation. One that I'm just not ready to have.

And so I become two versions of Devon: the old one, who tucks her feelings away under polite smiles, and the new Devon, who knows exactly what she wants and isn't afraid to say so. Because while we skirt every topic imaginable at

Grandma Rose's house, Sarah and I talk about everything.

Except for what will happen when summer ends.

"Have you ever been with anyone else like this?" she asks one afternoon as we float in her pool, limbs tangled around one another, breaths short from too many kisses.

I shrug. "Not since fifth grade," I say.

"You had sex in fifth grade?" she says in amazement.

"No! I had sex last year, with a guy I dated for a while. But it wasn't great. I think I did it mostly because I felt sorry for him. Fifth grade was the only time I kissed a girl. Well, that and my best friend earlier this summer. But that didn't really count." I fall silent as something occurs to me. "Wait, what are you talking about, sex?"

Sarah gives me a sidelong look. "You do know that's what we're doing, right? You and me?"

I pause, trying to put the things we've done together into the concept of what I consider sex. "We're not having sex. We're just messing around," I say.

As soon as the words are out of my mouth, I know it was the wrong thing to say. Sarah frowns, her hurt carved into her features, and disentangles herself. She swims back a few feet so that I am left without her body heat. I'm suddenly chilled, and I wrap my arms around myself as my feet find the bottom of the pool.

"We're having sex, Devon. The stuff we do, that's sex. You need to get rid of your heteronormative standards that sex is only penis in vagina." She isn't yelling, but her words come out in a rush and her face is suddenly red.

I hold up my hands in surrender. "Okay, okay! I'm sorry. This is new to me and . . . I don't know. I don't want to mess it up. But I also have no idea what I'm doing. I'm not going to always use the right words, but that doesn't mean I can't learn."

Her anger fades away and she sighs. "I know. I'm sorry. I just—sometimes I get so mad, at how everything revolves around what other people consider to be the truth, you know? Like the experiences of someone like me don't matter."

I give her a bit of side-eye. "I'm Black, Sarah. I think I know what that's like."

Sarah opens and closes her mouth a couple times. "Oh God, now I know how my sister must feel."

And then we're laughing at the ridiculousness of it all and talking about how terrible the world is.

As I drive home a couple hours later, I smile, realizing that we've just had our first fight. And we made it through okay. We are officially a couple. Maybe with a better understanding of each other.

I don't think either of us wants to ruin this.

But neither of us can stop the summer from ending.

Two weeks before I'm scheduled to go to New York to move into my dorm room, my dad calls to say his deployment schedule has been moved up.

"I'm not going to be taking you to New York," he says over the phone. He called Grandma Rose's landline instead of my cell phone, which is weird. Like he wants to make sure she knows he called. "I have some extra training they want me to go to, so I'll be out in Washington State. Your mom will buy you what you need, and I'll see you over Thanksgiving and Christmas break. I'm not shipping out until February."

He hangs up and doesn't talk to my mom.

"Predictable," Grandma Rose huffs when I tell her why he called. But honestly, I'm relieved. I can't imagine him in a place like New York, let alone on a college campus. He's still annoyed that I want to be a sociologist and not a nurse.

But for once, I just don't care. Much.

Mom and I sit down a couple days later in the kitchen and decide what I'll need for my dorm room, and Mom gives me a credit card with my name on it.

"Does Dad know you're giving me a credit card?" I ask.

"No, because this is on my account. I got a job in Baltimore. That's where I've been, going on interviews."

"Oh," I say. "I thought you were just going to the doctor."

"I was, but I was also looking for a job. I didn't tell you because I didn't want you to worry about things." Mom takes a deep breath and lets it out. "Your father and I are getting divorced. There's no more sidestepping the conversation, I suppose." Mom looks down at her hands, and I notice for the first time that her rings are missing. "He was supposed to be here when I told you, but like with everything else, he seems to have his own agenda."

I nod. There's a part of me that's devastated, and I suppose I'll cry later, but mostly I'm just relieved that it's finally done. That we're finally talking about it. "Why, though? I mean, I know Dad seems to be volunteering for more deployments and he's gone a lot, but I thought you were happy until you got sick."

Mom smiles sadly and drinks her coffee to give herself extra time to consider the question. "I guess I was just tired of always being second to everything else. It wasn't like that in the beginning. But lately . . ." She trails off. "I deserve to be happy," she says.

"I know, Mom."

"You deserve to be happy, too," she says with a knowing smile. "What are you and Sarah going to do after the end of the summer?"

"What are you talking about?" I sputter, but Mom just raises her eyebrows.

"Aren't you dating? Because it looks like you're dating."

"I don't know." I pause and look at her. "Maybe?"

Mom shakes her head sadly. "You should talk to her, because at some point there won't be time to say all the things you feel. And feelings have a way of coming out one way or another. It's better to control how those feelings manifest." Mom stands and kisses me on my forehead. "Your grandma used to always tell me that just because something is over doesn't mean it wasn't successful. All things end at some point."

Mom walks out of the room. I'm not entirely sure she's talking about me and Sarah, but the advice is good all the same.

I spend the next couple of days agonizing over how to bring up what happens next between me and Sarah. I don't know that it makes sense to have a long-distance relationship, but I also don't want to just ghost on her when it's time to leave.

Finally, as we sit in front of Chuck's Creamery eating greasy cheeseburgers and salty fries, I bring it up. "Hey, I leave for NYU in a couple of days," I say.

Sarah puts down her burger. "Yeah, I figured it was coming up soon. I'm actually supposed to go down to Towson tomorrow to start moving into my apartment with my roommates. I guess I've just kind of been putting this off."

I take a deep breath. "I don't know how you feel about leaving things as they are, but I don't want to lose you as a friend. But I also know that the odds of a long-distance relationship surviving aren't good."

Sarah nods, even though her expression is sad. And maybe a little relieved? "Yeah. I don't know, I kind of just don't want to talk about it. Can't we just let things continue on until they don't work for us anymore?"

"Is that how it usually works?" I ask.

Sarah shrugs. "I have no idea. Let's just live in the moment.

We can keep making out and figure things out as we go."

And old white lady carrying a couple of vanilla cones walks by, and she looks at us with an expression of horror and utter disgust.

"Not you, no one wants to make out with you," Sarah calls after her.

The old woman quickens her step as we burst out laughing.

"You're going to love New York," Sarah says with a grin that seems a little bit forced. "Hey, do you know the story of how Central Park was built? It's wild." She's changing the subject, and I let her. Maybe we will keep seeing each other, especially since Mom will be working in Baltimore. There's always Thanksgiving and Christmas, and New York isn't that far away.

But maybe I'll start school and fall in love with a hot New York girl the first week. In that moment, I realize that anything is possible.

And I decide to do just like Sarah asks and live in the moment.

HACKATHON SUMMERS

COE BOOTH

NOW

The banners on the wall in the giant well-lit reception room read "Welcome, Incoming Computer Science Students," along with the New York University logo on either end. Garry smiles, staring up at the big white letters, and it's like he finally feels like he's where he's supposed to be.

This reception is a lot nicer than he expected. He's imagined a room with folding chairs and a Spotify Top 40 playlist trying too hard to loosen everyone up. But all the computer science students would be standing around awkwardly, not sure how to interact with anyone.

Exactly what *he's* doing right now.

There's a buffet with hot and cold food, and even servers

walking around with hors d'oeuvres and sparkling apple cider in champagne glasses. Garry silently thanks his father for dragging him to Men's Wearhouse a couple of weeks ago so he could have "dress slacks and a button-up shirt for college like every young man should."

Early in the morning, he and his dad drove down to Manhattan and moved him into the freshman dorm. Garry felt different being back in New York City. This time he wasn't here for only thirty-six hours. He was here for four years.

Now, at the reception, all he can think about is how much he wants to see her again. Scanning the room over and over, he's starting to fear she's not here. But she *has* to be. That was their plan.

"Garry, my man!" He turns around to see Marc, from their team. Marc is all height and dreads and smile. They bro-hug.

"NYU let *you* in?" Garry asks him.

Marc laughs. And they talk about everything, how they both applied early admission, and how much they couldn't wait to get back here but for real, not just for one weekend every summer.

Finally Garry asks the only thing that's on his mind. "You see Inaaya?"

"Nah. You trying to pick up where y'all left off last year?"

Garry shakes his head. "I told you, man. It wasn't like that."

"Okay. All right. You sticking with that?" Marc looks at

Garry like he's being ridiculous, and maybe he is. "I was there, remember?"

"Just let me know if you see her," Garry says. He can't deal with Marc and his questions. Not when he can hardly make sense of things himself.

He met Marc at his first hackathon the summer after freshman year, held right here at NYU, and they ended up being teammates every year. And even though they found out they didn't live that far from one another—Garry in Rochester, Marc a little outside Buffalo—they never saw each other during the school year. Just in the summer, for the hackathons.

Now they walk around the reception for new computer science students, drinking cider and eating mini egg rolls, sharing dorm information and class schedules, but Garry can't help scanning the room. Maybe she's late. Maybe that's why he can't find her.

One thing he doesn't do is consider the other possibility, that she chose a different college. He can't think of that because, if he does, he knows he'll never see her again.

THE FIRST HACKATHON

The first time Garry saw her was three summers ago. It was the first time his dad let him come to the city by himself and stay for a whole weekend "with absolutely no supervision," even though Garry told him a million times there were going to be adults there. He had left home early in the morning, before his father woke up for work, and gotten to the Greyhound station on his own. The bus took over seven hours to get to the city, stopping in every small town in Upstate New York nobody's ever heard of. But to Garry, the whole thing was an adventure, proof he could do things on his own, even get to New York City.

That Friday evening, after he found the right building and checked in at the registration table, he watched as all the kids arrived. He was looking. Not looking for *her*, specifically. But someone else Black, someone whose presence there would tell him he was in the right place, that he wasn't going to be the only one.

And then there she was.

He stared at her as she walked into the lobby of the computer science building with her mother, a tall woman wearing a long dark-blue dress and a light-blue hijab. The girl was tall, too, slim with dark skin and natural hair pushed back off her face with a red headband. She wore jeans and a "Will Hack for Chocolate" long-sleeve T-shirt.

Garry watched as they waited in line at the registration table and as she got her name badge and a tote bag filled with snacks and travel-size toothpaste and lotion—stuff they were giving out to everyone. And he watched them walk toward the auditorium. He knew this wasn't her first hackathon. She hugged kids she already knew and introduced them to her mother. More than that, she looked comfortable. Unlike him.

In the auditorium, she sat with a bunch of kids and their parents during the opening remarks, where the NYU students who had organized the event discussed the goals of the hackathon, how they had gathered brilliant young minds together for thirty-six hours of innovation and collaboration and fun. Then the corporate sponsors spoke for a few minutes, talking about how excited they were to see so many talented high school students there, and how they were looking forward to what they would create with their software.

By then, there were several Black kids in the auditorium, so that helped a little, but still, Garry couldn't help but feel nervous. He knew he wasn't the only one there for the first time, but maybe he was in over his head. What did he know about any of this?

Another thing was becoming obvious. He was the only kid there without a parent. There was no way his father would miss a day of work to bring him all the way down to Manhattan. And then what was his father supposed to do? Wait there the whole weekend so he could drive him back to Rochester?

Of course, there was his mother, who lived close by. But no, that wasn't an option. She didn't even know he was there. And that was the way he wanted to keep it.

The hackathon officially began at nine o'clock that night, so after all the welcomes and pep talks, and after the parents went home, the NYU student volunteers got on the stage and started breaking everyone up into three groups, depending on the area they had signed up for—HealthTech, EdTech, or Social Justice.

One after the other, names were called for the HealthTech group and those kids left the room. The girl was still there, though. He hoped she'd chosen Social Justice like he had. But her name—Inaaya Saddiq—was called for EdTech, and then she and her friends were gone. He'd picked the wrong group.

After an hour-long hands-on demo with the new software package they had to use to create their app, and after another pep talk by the Social Justice mentors, telling the kids how injustice was a growing problem and the world needed young people like them to come up with solutions, they were brought into the large atrium, with round tables everywhere. The other groups were already there, on other sides of the room. Garry started to get excited. He had seen hackathons online, but there he was. This was what he wanted. He was really doing this.

For the next few minutes everyone in the Social Justice group had to form small teams. One of the other Black guys came up to him and said, "You a developer?"

Garry nodded.

"You good?"

Garry nodded again.

"Be on my team then," the guy said. "We need someone who can kick ass."

Garry swallowed hard. He kicked ass at his tech high school. But that was Rochester. This was New York City.

"I'm Marc, by the way," the guy said.

"Garry."

"Cool."

They walked over to a table and Garry met the three girls on their team. Hannah was a developer, too, but she'd only been coding a couple of years. Lisa was a designer like Marc. And the other girl, Christine, was going to be the project manager and the spokesperson for their presentation.

For the next few minutes everyone pulled out their laptops and plugged them in. While downloading the new software package, Garry opened an energy drink that was in his tote bag and drank a little. He was feeling the effects of leaving home so early and traveling all day. He was tired, but he couldn't give in to it. With his laptop logged into the Wi-Fi, he settled into the chair and tried to relax with his team.

"Okay," Christine said after everyone was ready to get down to work. "What kind of app can we create in thirty-six hours that will change the world?"

It was after two in the morning when Garry finally looked up from his screen. Their app in progress was going to be a kind of alert you could send out to those nearby if you were being threatened by a police officer. People could be on the scene right away to witness the interaction, and the app would even record video that would immediately upload to its servers. So even if the cops took away someone's phone, they wouldn't be able to delete the evidence.

"The police are going to hate this," Hannah said.

"Not if they're doing the right thing," Marc responded. "Anyway, we don't hate the police. Only the ones who shoot people who look like me for no reason."

"I like that it's people looking out for each other," Garry said. "It can't hurt to have other people there to keep the police in line."

They all nodded.

"We need something else, to make our app stand out," Garry said. "I'm gonna check some APIs and repositories. There has to be something we can use."

Hours later, Garry's eyes burned from searching through the open-source code on GitHub for something he could build upon, so he closed his laptop for the first time. He noticed some of the kids were taking a break, walking outside, and he needed some air, too.

All night, his fingers had flown over his keyboard, writing line after line of code so fast, it felt like he was playing music. That was the thing about coding he loved. He could lose himself in a project. It was like he could already see the finished product in his mind. He just needed to tell the computer how to get there.

"I'll be right back," he said.

"Take a half hour," Christine said. "Eat something. You too, Hannah. Give the designers time to figure out some of their details."

Hannah got up and headed for the table where they had some sandwiches and soda and chips. But Garry headed for the door. As he walked outside, he found himself in a group of kids all leaving together.

And she was there, too.

They all walked down the street and into Washington Square Park. It was after two o'clock in the morning and so dark outside even with the streetlights on. The weather was warm and perfect, and it felt good being out there with Manhattan surrounding them.

It was his first time being back in the city. He'd spent the first ten years of his life in Brooklyn, but that had seemed like a lifetime ago. He was a different kid then. Sad, scared, tired.

He lived with his mom in a tiny apartment in the basement of a house on Parkside Avenue. There was only one bedroom, so he had to sleep on the pullout sofa. Every night, he heard mice scratching their way into the kitchen from the backyard. When he found their holes, he plugged them with steel wool, but it was a never-ending battle. They always found their way back in.

The only time he couldn't hear the mice was when his mother was in the bedroom fighting with a boyfriend, or crying over another broken relationship. Garry would lie on the sofa bed, hoping she'd stay in the room and not come out and take everything out on him. Blame him for why she could never keep a man. His mother never hurt him, at least not physically, but he'd been on the wrong end of her rages too many times. They terrified him, made it so he couldn't wait until the next morning when school started. He would stay there all day if he could.

And he tried. He joined just about every club at school—the math team, the coding club, even the trivia bowl. Anything that kept him away from home. Those teams and clubs helped him realize he was smart—the exact opposite of the words his mother called him on a near-daily basis.

At school he came alive. At home he died.

One day, he called his dad in Rochester and begged him to come and take him away from there. His mother was getting worse, angrier, and even school wasn't enough to keep him from sliding into his sadness.

But his father came through. He told his mother about a school in Rochester, near his house, for kids who were good at tech. He said it was his turn to take on the burden of raising Garry. As if he was a burden. But Garry figured his father was saying whatever he had to say, just to get him out of there.

And it worked. Two weeks before middle school started, Dad drove down to get him. Garry was waiting in front of the house. He didn't want to even say goodbye to his mother, but his dad made him.

He hadn't spoken to her since then.

Being back in New York City for the hackathon, he leaned

against a lamppost in Washington Square Park and looked around. Even though he had grown up just a few miles from there, he had never known the area around NYU. He felt like a tourist in what used to be his city.

There in the park, he watched the other hackathon kids run around, laughing. Two guys tried to climb a tree. Nobody knew what to do with their energy. Time was running out. Their break was almost over.

He saw the girl, standing not too far from him, but she was with two other girls, and they looked like they were already friends. He wanted to talk to her, but he couldn't figure out a way to interrupt them. And what would he say, anyway?

So he just watched her, averting his eyes every few seconds so she wouldn't see him staring at her. But there was something about her. Yes, she was pretty. Beautiful. But he was drawn to her smile, the way she covered her mouth when she giggled with her friends. He loved the way she seemed so present in the moment. Happy. She looked like she didn't want to be anywhere other than right there.

Before he could work up the courage to say anything to her, to maybe ask her what her team was working on, they were all headed back inside the building. And they were back to their own teams—laptops open, heads down.

And that's where they stayed for the rest of the hackathon, on opposite sides of the room, siloed in their own projects. Every so often he would look at her, see her huddled with her team, watch her grab a sandwich or a cookie from the food table, see her laughing with her friends on the way to the bathroom. He wanted to know her, but thinking about how to talk to her was taking up too much space in his brain. He needed to focus on his team, on their app.

That was what he was there for, right?

THE SECOND HACKATHON

If he were being honest with himself, Garry would admit part of the reason he made sure he came back the next summer was so he could possibly see her again, maybe even work up the courage to talk to her. He had kicked himself more than a few times in the year since he'd first seen her, but now he was going into junior year. He should be able to say hi to a girl, at least in theory.

Inaaya was there at NYU before him this time. Her mom was there, too, in a yellow hijab and long purple dress. Inaaya was dressed for the hackathon. Jeans, sneakers, long-sleeve T-shirt that said "I Code Like a Girl."

Garry couldn't help but smile. He liked her style. Who knew? He might even like her personality if he could ever *say* anything to her.

As things unfolded, Garry started to feel like he was living the previous year over again. They were broken into categories, and once again, they were in different groups. She'd chosen

HealthTech that summer, while Garry had picked Social Justice again. He liked his team, and he was happy when Marc and Hannah were back. They rounded out their team with two new kids, who looked as overwhelmed as he'd probably looked the year before.

Even though they were crazy busy, this year creating a browser extension using the sponsor's web tools, that didn't stop Garry from glancing at Inaaya on the other side of the atrium whenever he had the chance.

The whole first night went by, and there was no time for a long break, only a couple of short naps right there at their table. There was a room set up with cots, but who had the time to sleep? There was so much to do and only thirty-six hours to do it.

It wasn't until the second night, just a few hours before the corporate sponsors would start walking around to hear their pitches, that Garry felt he was too bleary-eyed to function. It was four in the morning, and if he didn't get some air, he wouldn't be able to think through the finishing touches.

While Marc and Hannah worked on the logo and the branding, he stood up and said, "I'll be back." And he grabbed a brownie on his way out the door.

Even though he hadn't noticed her leaving, he actually ran into Inaaya and two other girls in Washington Square Park, taking their break at the same time. This was his chance.

Shaking off the heaviness of exhaustion, he walked right

up to the group and said, "Hey, y'all needed some air, too?" It was the best he could do in the state he was in.

But it worked.

Inaaya turned to him and smiled. "You were here last year, right? I remember you."

Garry forced himself not to show how happy he was that she'd actually noticed him. "Yeah," he said, as cool as he could. "That was my first hackathon."

"I've been doing them since middle school," she said.

The voice in Garry's head was screaming, *C'mon, man. Say something!*

"I remember you, too," he said, and he tried to ignore the way one of her friends elbowed her.

"You do?" she asked.

He couldn't tell what she was thinking. Was she flattered? Or just irritated? But he kept talking, the sleepiness quickly being replaced by sheer terror. But he was too far into this already. "Would you like to take a walk around the park with me? I promise to get you back to your friends in a few minutes."

Her friend elbowed her again and whispered way too loud, "Go. He's cute."

Inaaya hit her friend on the shoulder. "Stop it, Kenya." Then she turned to Garry and said, "Okay."

Walking away from the other two girls, Garry felt so unsure of himself that for a minute, he didn't say anything. They just walked. Finally he said, "I love this park."

"Yeah," Inaaya said. "It's beautiful. Especially at night."

"I know." He looked up at the sky through the thick trees. "It doesn't even look like New York City when you're here."

They kept walking and he asked her how she got into hackathons.

"I've been coding since I was a little kid," she said. "Nobody in my family understands how I got this way."

"Your mom, she's real supportive, though. She always comes with you, and she's always all dressed up and—"

"*Everybody* notices my mom," Inaaya said, laughing. "She's beautiful! And she loves color—the brighter the hijab, the better."

Garry wanted to tell her *she* was beautiful too, but instead he asked, "Why don't you—I mean, do you ever—?"

"I wear it sometimes," she said. "At the mosque, for prayers, and, like, when we visit my relatives. But I don't think I need to wear a hijab to be a good Muslim. It's in my heart. It's who I am."

Garry smiled. He liked how confident she was, how much she already knew herself.

"Your turn," Inaaya said. "If this is too personal, don't answer. But why do you always come by yourself?"

"That's not too personal. It's just that I live with my dad all the way up in Rochester. He can't come with me because he works security at a mall, and he has to work on weekends."

"Does he get all the stuff you do?"

Garry laughed, shaking his head. "Not at all. But he knows it's a good thing, something smart."

"It must be weird for our parents." She giggled, covering her mouth with her hand. "It's like we're coding Martians to them."

They walked from one crisscrossed path to the other, passing a couple of people walking their dogs at that time of morning. They eventually found themselves under the huge arch.

"Wow," Inaaya said, looking up at the monument. "You know what I have a sudden urge to do?"

"What?" He was intrigued.

"Watch!" Then for no reason Garry could figure out, she started spinning around with her arms outstretched, laughing the whole time. There were a few men hanging out by the arch, probably getting high, and even they looked at her like she was crazy.

Garry yelled, "What are you doing? You're losing your mind." But her joy was contagious. He found himself laughing right along with her.

A few seconds later, she stopped spinning. "I needed that," she said, still giggling. "Being cooped up in that room was getting to me. You should try it, Garry."

"No, I'm good," he said. No way would he let her see him acting a fool, not when their walk was going well so far.

On the way back to her friends, Garry found out a few more things about her. She was from Long Island, she had an older sister, and her father had died when she was little. She got a little sad when she talked about him and Garry thought about reaching out to touch her hand, maybe hold it so she knew he understood her feelings. But he resisted. He didn't want to scare her off.

When they rejoined her friends, she told them, "Garry was a complete gentleman."

"See," Garry said. "Just like I promised."

On the way back to their building, it was all Garry could do to hide his smile. He waved goodbye to them and headed back toward his team. "Where were you, man?" Marc asked. "You left us to go hang with the competition?"

"Not the competition," Garry defended. "Inaaya."

Marc shook his head. "Damn, it's sad, watching a smart guy like you let a girl mess with his head."

"She's not like that."

"All right, watch. While you're sitting with your head in the clouds, thinking about her, you know what she's gonna be doing? *Winning*, that's what!"

Of course, when Inaaya's team won later that morning, Garry had to hear Marc laughing at him, telling him how he knew what she was up to.

Garry didn't believe him. As he watched the winning team leave the college with the sponsors, off to tour their corporate building and then have a fancy lunch somewhere, all he could think was "Why didn't I get her number?"

THE THIRD HACKATHON

Inaaya was different at their last hackathon.

Her mom wasn't with her this time. She was there with her friends, but there was something about the way she looked while they all checked in, the way she stood, arms folded in front of her. She was dressed in jeans and an oversize gray sweatshirt that said "Keep Calm and Hackathon." But when she talked to her friends, her smile wasn't the same as it was the year before.

There was a news crew on-site that day, doing a story about the hackathon. Marc practically jumped in front of the cameras, and Garry watched as he talked about how important these hackathons were and how much he looked forward to it every year. Meanwhile, Garry noticed he was doing a lot of posing for the camera. The boy had no shame.

The reporter asked Garry only one question, where he was from. "Rochester," Garry answered, not even thinking to say Brooklyn. He was a Rochester kid now.

As they walked into the auditorium, Garry approached Inaaya. "You gonna be in Social Justice this year?" he asked her. He knew she liked to try new things. Maybe they'd finally get to work together.

"I have to," she said, and there was a little half smile on her face. "I need to give you a chance to win."

"Hey, that's not right." Garry shook his head.

By eleven o'clock that night, after all the teams had been formed and the projects begun, everybody huddled around a few laptops that were streaming the news live. The hackathon story came on at the end of the broadcast, of course. Garry sat next to Inaaya, and he felt happier than he had any right to be.

The atrium got quiet as the reporter who had been there talked about how the brightest kids from all over New York had gathered at NYU for the weekend. And sure enough, Marc's comments had made it on air. And Inaaya was introduced as a member of the winning team from last year. She told the reporter that the hackathon helped her land an internship at a software developer that summer. Then there was a montage of kids telling the reporter where they were from. Garry made the cut, right in the middle of all the other kids. When the segment ended, everyone cheered.

"I looked good," Marc said.

Garry crumpled up some paper and threw it at him. "You got a face for coding, man."

Everyone laughed, and after a few minutes, they were back at work. He loved working with Inaaya, looking at her code, watching the way her mind worked. He knew she was going to be good, but he didn't anticipate how well they would collaborate. They spoke the same language.

It was about a half hour later when Garry's cell buzzed. It was a message from an unknown number, but when he read it, he knew who it was from. His mother.

i saw you on the news, called your dad. don't be mad he gave me your number, i want to say i'm proud of you, that's it.

He didn't respond. Inside, he felt nothing but anger—at his dad for betraying his privacy and at his mother for thinking a message like that could change anything. Like the ten years he spent with her could be undone by one "I'm proud of you."

He was glad he had their app to keep his mind off the text. He focused, wishing he hadn't let it get to him. There wasn't time for that.

Just like at the previous hackathon, Garry worked straight through the first night and the next day, surviving on short naps and warm energy drinks. Inaaya was quiet, and so was he.

At two in the morning on the second night, Garry sat back in his chair and felt his heavy eyes closing. That was when he heard, "Wake up, Garry. Time for our walk through the park." It was Inaaya, and she tried to flash him a smile, but it was forced. "Let's let the designers make this app look pretty."

Garry sat up, suddenly alert. "We'll be back," he told the rest of the team.

As he and Inaaya walked away, Marc and the other teammates started hooting and making kissing noises. "Sorry you got stuck with a bunch of sixth graders," Garry told her.

"They sound more like fifth!" Inaaya wasn't upset, so he

tried to relax as they made their way outside together.

It had rained, and the trees cast dark shadows across the park. They walked instinctively to the path they had walked the year before, toward the arch. They were quiet. Garry hoped the cool night air would help him release the tension he had been holding on to ever since he'd gotten that text.

His mother was proud of him. So what?

"You okay?" Inaaya asked, her sneakers making a slapping sound on the wet ground.

"I'm good. What about you? You're kinda different, like not really yourself."

She shrugged. "You know. People change."

Now *she* sounded like his mother, who was good for three or four phone calls to his father a year. She always wanted his dad to tell him that she had changed, that she had done a lot of work to be a better person. But Garry never wanted to talk to her. If she had changed, fine. That had nothing to do with him.

They walked without talking until they got to the arch. And when they got there, he half expected her to spin around and laugh all the stress away again, but that didn't happen. They stood silently in their own separate worlds.

They were alone there. The rain must have driven out the regulars. Inaaya leaned against the arch and looked around. "I love it here," she said.

"Me too." Then he told her something he'd been thinking about, something he hadn't told anyone else. "I'm gonna apply here. I can't even think of another college I want to go to."

She smiled. "Same. I'm doing early admission. You?"

He hadn't thought about that, but this was where he wanted to be. "Definitely."

They stared at each other.

"Plan?" Garry asked.

"Plan," she said.

Hearing that word, Garry could already see himself there next year, being a college freshman, having some of the same classes with Inaaya, working on projects together. It was going to happen. They had a plan.

For a few seconds, he felt good. Then the real world came back. She looked as far away as he was. Finally, he said, "C'mon, Inaaya. Tell me what's wrong. I'm a good listener."

"So am I," she said. "You first."

So he told her about the text and how he'd thought about it all night and all day. "I'm not gonna respond," he said. "I don't owe her anything."

"She's that bad?"

He nodded. "Yeah." Then he filled her in on his mother and all her problems, how he spent the first half of his life afraid something would set her off. "I'm not over what she put me through. I know she probably had a lot of undiagnosed mental issues and I'm supposed to understand that and let it go, but—"

"You're not supposed to do anything. You didn't do anything wrong. Just remember that."

She understood. The first person he told understood.

He leaned against the arch next to her and put his hand on hers for a few seconds. "What's going on with you?"

"It's kind of hard to explain," she said. "It's my mom. She and I, we used to be so close. Don't get me wrong. We've always been different, but it didn't matter. I always looked up to her, still do, and I thought she respected me for who I am, too."

"Did something happen?" Garry asked. "She didn't come with you this time."

Inaaya shrugged. "I told her I wanted to come on my own. I'm almost a senior. She doesn't need to bring me everywhere all the time. Sometimes it's like—it feels like she's trying to control me. Like if she holds on tight enough, she's going to stop me from being my own person. But it won't work. She should know that by now." Inaaya folded her arms in front of her.

Garry could feel her frustration. He wanted to say something, but he didn't know what. So he just waited for her to keep talking.

"Most parents give their kids more freedom when they get older. My mom is the opposite. But at the same time, she wants me to make all these decisions about my whole life. Like, I have to choose who I want to be *now*."

"What kind of decisions?"

"That's the thing. She wants me to *decide* to be just like her.

Traditional. *She* did everything her father wanted her to, but I don't have a father, so . . ." Her voice trailed off.

Garry stared at her face as she tried, and failed, to control her emotions. "You okay?" he asked.

"I'm all right." She got quiet again for a little while. Then she said, "It's not just my mom. It's me, too. It's like, sometimes I don't know who I'm supposed to be. I'm not a kid anymore. But I can't figure anything out if everyone is constantly telling me what I should do."

"I hear that," Garry said. He really liked her honesty.

"I think it's because I'm a developer," she said. "I have a developer's mind. I have to try things to see if they work. And if they don't, *that's* when I make changes."

Garry smiled. They had twin minds.

"My mom doesn't understand. She keeps pressuring me to make these big decisions about my life when I haven't experienced anything yet. I haven't run them to see what works." She turned away from him and looked around the park. For a few seconds, she looked like she was very far away. Then she turned back to him. "I couldn't wait to be back here."

Garry definitely understood that, the need to be there. To be back. The thirty-six hours at NYU were the only thing he looked forward to every summer. Being in the city, surrounded by his kind of people, these hackathons felt like a magnet pulling him back every year.

And he knew as soon as he got back to Rochester he would

be teaching Fun with Computers to five- to eight-year-olds at a day camp near his house. It was a decent summer job. But there were only so many ways to pry the kids away from YouTube long enough to get them excited about introductory coding projects. Anyway, he didn't want to think about that now. This weekend was for him. "Can you believe this is our last high school hackathon?" he asked.

Inaaya shook her head. "When you say it like that, it seems so final."

"I know," he said. "This time next year, we'll be getting ready to go to college."

The small smile on her face was the most genuine one that night. "Don't forget the plan," she said. "I'm holding you to it!"

On the way back to their building, Garry took her hand again. And they walked back holding hands the whole way.

As Inaaya headed to the food table, Garry decided he actually did need a nap. He peeked into the room they had set up with cots, but it was crowded, not what he was looking for. He wanted to be alone, to decompress. He walked down the hall and around the corner and found an unlocked storage room. It was filled with a bunch of furniture and lamps and fans and easels. Garry set a sofa right side up and got comfortable on it. Then he closed his eyes.

• • •

Something woke Garry. It was Inaaya leaning over him. "How did you know where I—"

She whispered, "I was looking for you."

And then she kissed him. His body was instantly awake. Garry opened his mouth and felt the heat between them, the intensity.

It was a while before she pulled her lips from his and whispered, "You're the first guy I kissed."

His lips were only a half inch from hers when he asked, "You sure you want—? I mean, I don't want you doing something you're not supposed to." And he meant it.

Inaaya put her mouth to his ear and whispered, "I told you. I only do what I want."

He sat up on the sofa, so they could be eye to eye, put his arm around her, and brought his mouth back on hers. He hadn't known how much he wanted her until now.

He had to remind himself to breathe.

Inaaya's hands made their way under his shirt, touching his stomach and back and chest. And in the dark, they fumbled out of their shirts, breathing hard and giggling in between kisses.

"You're so beautiful," he told her, his hands running up and down her arms and across her stomach.

He had never gone this far with a girl before. And he couldn't believe it was happening with Inaaya. He also knew it couldn't go any further.

Inaaya was too special.

The kissing and touching and giggling only lasted a few more minutes, until they had to scramble back into their clothes and get back to their team.

He needed to go over the last-minute details for their app, and Inaaya had to get ready for the presentation.

Garry knew those few minutes were ones he would never forget.

A little later, sitting in the auditorium with the rest of their team, Garry watched her on the stage—smart, confident, so incredibly beautiful. He waited for her eyes to find his, for them to have a shared moment, just the two of them, in the midst of everybody else.

But she never looked in his direction. She presented their app and then sat in the audience with her friends on the other side of the auditorium while they all waited to hear the winning team.

And when their team wasn't called, and the hackathon was officially over, Garry sat there, not knowing what to do.

She'd never even looked at him.

A tap on the shoulder shook him out of it. He turned around and came face-to-face with his mother. He hadn't seen her since that day he left home. He stood up and realized he was taller than she was now.

She couldn't intimidate him anymore.

She looked different, dressed in a print blouse, black slacks, and flats; she looked like the other mothers in the room. And she smiled, actually *smiled*, and said, "I told you I changed. I'm here to show you."

They talked for a few minutes, about nothing. He tried to explain about the hackathons. She told him she had taken a computer course at the community center. He told her about his job with the kids. She said she was working at a nursing home.

Garry listened, staring at her the whole time. Her face, especially her eyes, were softer now. They used to look wild, always searching for something to spark her rage. Now, they were just settled on him.

The conversation ended when she told him she had to get to work.

"Um, thanks, you know," Garry stammered. The words felt strange coming out of his mouth. Was he really thanking her?

"Seeing you on the news," she said, and laughed. "I couldn't believe it!"

Garry shook his head. He'd only said one word on the news. Did she really come all the way from Brooklyn just for that?

"Now that you have my number," his mother said, "if you ever wanted to talk, *really talk*, call me." She took his hand,

and he watched her face as tears quickly filled her eyes. "I know I wasn't the best mother to you. I was in a bad place back then, and—" Her voice cracked and she looked down for a few seconds. Then she looked at him with those soft eyes and said, "I'm sorry, baby. Sorry for all of it. Everything."

All he could do was nod. It was too much for him. Too much had happened in the past six hours. Now his mother was back.

After she left, Garry walked over to where Inaaya had been sitting with her friends. The auditorium was emptying out, and all around them, kids were hugging and taking pictures with each other.

That was when he realized Inaaya wasn't there. His eyes searched the whole auditorium, but she was gone. Just like that.

NOW

Garry scans the NYU computer science students' reception again, still looking for her. Thinking about everything that happened makes him wish *for the one billionth time* he had gotten to talk to her that day, after everything was over, that he had gotten her number.

He hasn't heard her voice in over a year.

He hasn't seen her face either. He's spent way too much time searching for her online, on all the apps, everywhere. But it's as if she's disappeared.

Garry watches as more kids arrive, but none of them are her. *She's supposed to be here with me*, he thinks. *That was the plan.*

His phone buzzes in his pocket. A text from his mom.

you move into ur dorm? if you need anything call me or text.

Garry writes back, ok

Then he adds, thanks

Marc comes up to him with a whole tray of scallops wrapped in bacon. "One of the servers hooked me up," he says, grinning. "You have to meet the right people around here."

Garry reaches for a scallop.

"Dude, you have to use a toothpick," Marc says. "Don't they teach y'all anything in Rochester?"

They laugh. And they eat. It's so good to be back.

A few minutes later, the director of undergraduate studies is in front of the room, speaking to the incoming students. Garry stands next to Marc, listening, still having a hard time believing he's here for the next four years.

That's when he sees her.

Inaaya.

She's across the room with a friend. She might have been here the whole time, but he hadn't noticed her. But now their eyes meet the way he hoped they would have that morning last year when she was on the stage.

He stares at her. She's wearing a long denim skirt and an

"I <br/> for Coffee" T-shirt. But he can't see her natural hair anymore.

She's wearing a blue hijab.

Garry and Inaaya look at each other and he can feel himself stop breathing.

The sound of applause shakes him back into the room. The director has finished speaking. Marc elbows him and points to a server walking around with chocolate-covered strawberries. But Garry shakes his head.

He looks back to Inaaya and takes a few steps in her direction, but her eyes—they lock on his and he knows what they're telling him.

Not now.

He takes a few more steps, then stops himself.

Everything that happened between them comes rushing back—their conversation under the arch, the pressure she was feeling, how she couldn't decide her life when she hadn't even lived yet, how she kissed him, the way she touched him.

It takes a while, but Garry looks away from her and turns around. He won't talk to her. Not now.

He thinks he gets it. Gets *her*. She was struggling. She was trying to figure out who she wanted to be. She just wanted to know.

Garry slowly walks back over to Marc, who's enjoying his strawberry way too much. Garry laughs. "Something wrong with you?"

"Me? You the one asking about Inaaya all night and you find her and won't go talk to the girl."

"I'll talk to her," Garry says. "Just not now." And it's true. They'll probably be in a class together, or they'll run into each other at the library or the cafeteria. Or maybe he'll see her at some CompSci student meeting or something.

Maybe they'll be friends again, the kind of friends who meet and talk under the arch in Washington Square Park.

But that's all. He knows he has to let her go. She made her decision.

And it wasn't him.

INTO THE STARLIGHT

NIC STONE

When Makenzie Taylor was younger, she promised Mama she'd never go into the Starlight. She was ten, eleven, something like that—she's too distracted to remember right now—and they were passing it on the way home from Aunt Trish's new place on the Eastside ("Still the damn *ghetto*," Mama said). The letters S-T-A-R-L-I-G-H-T were placed vertically on a tower-type thing at least as tall as Mak's three-story house, and beside it, *Six Drive-In Theatres* glowed red above a list of movie titles.

Mak's face lit up almost as bright as the massive marquee.

"Whoa!" she gasped, leaning toward it as if drawn by a string. Her nose hit the cool glass of the back passenger-side window. "What *is* that place?"

"Somewhere you're never to go," Mama replied. "It's a

place where gangbangers deal drugs and fast girls like your cousin get pregnant." She turned around to look Mak in the eye then. "It's not a place for *nice* young ladies like you. Promise me you'll never go in there."

And Mak did. Promise.

She's breaking that promise right now.

In fact, at this moment, Mak's not only parked inside the Starlight. She's in the back seat of the Audi Mama insisted Daddy buy for Mak's sixteenth birthday, with Kamari Funderburke's amazing lips all up on her neck.

"You smell good," he says, dragging his beautifully wide nose up under her jawline to her ear before nipping at the lobe. His long dreadlocks tickle the exposed skin near her collarbone. Whatever kind of oil or pomade or butter he uses to keep them so neat? *That* smells good. All natural and nutty, but kinda sweet and spicy too. Nothing like the artificial serums and burnt-hair smell she's used to from getting her coils pressed bone straight at the salon every Saturday.

Just got it done this morning, and she's totally sweating her edges out right now.

Mama is going to flip.

Kamari's massive hand—Mak will never forget the time she saw him palm a basketball—slides beneath the hem of her top and around her waist. "Damn girl, you burning *up*," he says. "We need to crack the windows a little more?" And he laughs.

"Oh my God, shut up," Mak says.

"Make me," And his lips latch onto hers.

The first time Mak saw Kamari Funderburke, he was leaving the Starlight on foot with his arm draped around some girl. Mak was driving her cousin Crystal back to Aunt Trish's house, and they were stopped at the traffic light by the drive-in entrance. There was no ignoring the tall and slim but *clearly* solid, mahogany-skinned boy on the corner whose long locs swung as he turned to say something to someone behind him.

When he faced back forward, he was smiling. Big, bright (though dark) eyes twinkling in the light from the marquee. Dimples so deep, Mak instantly wanted to put her fingers in them.

She gulped.

"There *that* nigga go," Crystal said from the passenger seat, yanking Mak back to the present. As Kamari and the girl passed in front of Mak's car on their way across the wide, five-lane road, he turned and looked into the windshield. Crystal flipped him off, and he rolled his eyes.

Then he looked at Mak.

And looked away.

"Punk ass," Crystal said as the light turned green.

Mak wanted to let it go, but she couldn't. "Who is that?"

"Girl." Crystal waved her hand like the question was a waste of time. "Some fuckboy I go to school with."

"Ah."

"His name is Kamari, and he's triflin'. Knocked up one of my homegirls last year, then basically *made* her get an abortion."

Mak had no idea what to say to that. While a good number of the kids at her snobby-ass school on the Northside were "sexually active," as adults liked to say, every girl *she* knew was on birth control. Mak's best friend, Tess, had a scare a few months prior—condom broke, she said—because Tess sometimes forgot to take her pill, but that was the closest Mak had ever been to a teen pregnancy.

"All the niggas around here are exactly the same," Crystal said as Mak turned onto Crystal's street. "They get in, get off, and get out. That's part of the reason I can't wait to leave this place."

As Mak pulled into the driveway of the three-bedroom ranch house where, at seventeen, Crystal shared a bedroom with three of her five siblings and a bathroom with those three siblings *plus* her older sister, Divinity, and Divinity's three kids (all of whom lived in one of the other bedrooms), Mama's warnings—and judgments—rang through Mak's head the way they always did when she came to her auntie's place. *Just look at Trish for what* not *to do; All them kids in that tiny-ass house; You would think she'd want to get off government assistance; It's no wonder Divinity repeated the cycle; I know you and Crystal are close, but you be careful, Mak.*

Bad company corrupts good character, and I won't have my
daughter acting all ghetto . . .

That last one always tripped Mak up. Crystal had been
accepted early to Duke on a full academic scholarship, and
was smarter—book *and* street—than Mak could ever dream
of being. Yeah, she cussed like the very concept of verbal com-
munication depended on it, and tossed the *n*-word around like
a Frisbee, but in the grand scheme of things, did that actually
matter?

Mak took in the surroundings: house to the left was unin-
habited—if the broken windows, sagging porch roof, and
shin-high grass/weeds were any indication—and the one to
the right had a blue tarp on the roof and three cars parked in
the yard (one of them permanently, since it had no wheels) in
lieu of grass. Even Aunt Trish's house looked a little worse for
the wear. The formerly peach paint was faded and peeling,
and there was a big hole in the screen door. (Divinity's son
had "lost his muthafuckin' mind and kicked the shit out of it,"
according to Crystal. Mak can only imagine the whoopin' he
got. Mama didn't "believe in corporal punishment," but Mak
knew it was the go-to at Aunt Trish's house.)

The one thing all three houses had in common were the bars
on their respective windows. Aunt Trish's were decorative-
ish. Kinda swirly, fleur-de-lis vibe. But the first thing Mama
said when they pulled up to this house after Trish's move was
"Look at them damn burglar bars. How she supposed to get

all those kids out if there's a fire? You'd think she'd want better for *them*."

Mak will never forget the time she asked Crys what they *would* do if there was a fire since they couldn't go out the windows. They were both ten, and Crys looked Mak dead in the face and said, "Go out the door, stupid."

That's when Mak knew they'd be close forever. Everybody else always talked to Mak like she was some princess. Yeah, Daddy was a bigshot banker, and Mama had a JD from Emory and had never lost at trial, and yeah, the Taylors were one of the most well-respected families in North Atlanta, but the way people handled Mak like fine china—Mama included—got on her nerves. Crystal didn't have time for that. She'd let Mak *know* that living in a fancy house in the expensive part of town didn't make Mak better than anybody else.

Then they'd played Barbies (which they both secretly loved despite being fifth graders), and Crystal put cornrows in Mak's hair.

Of course Mama lost every ounce of her shit and made Mak take them out.

At any rate, it never ceased to amaze Mak just *how* close she and her cousin were despite how differently they were raised.

"You *sure* you don't wanna just come to my house and sleep over, Crys?" Mak said as Crystal gathered her stuff to get out of Mak's car. Mak liked when Crys slept over. She felt way less alone inside her unnecessarily large house. Mama talked about the bars on Aunt Trish's windows, but the concrete wall surrounding Mak's family's acre of land—accessible only by the motorized wrought-iron gate at the end of the winding driveway—made her feel just as trapped as she assumed Crys felt inside Aunt Trish's house.

"No, ma'am. You know I can't deal with the way your bougie-ass mama looks at me. Like I drug a dead cat all over her imported Moroccan rugs or something. Besides, I have a movie date." She flipped her braids.

"With who?"

"Nunya."

"But I thought you said all the guys around here are trash?" Kamari's dimpled face popped into Mak's mind unbidden.

"Who said he was from around here?"

"Oh."

"Hmph. Presumptuous ass." And she opened the door.

"Crys, you ever been in the Starlight?" Mak asked.

"Huh?"

"That drive-in we always pass."

"Umm . . ." Crystal was well known for her withering side-eye. "Of course I have, Mak. The hell kinda question is that?"

Mak shrugged. Took a deep breath.

Thought about seeing the Kamari guy and what Crystal had said about him.

"I've never been," Mak went on. "Mama says it's not a good place. . . . But I've always secretly wanted to go."

"Girl, bye," Crystal said, rummaging around in her bag for her keys. "No offense, but your mama talks a lotta shit about stuff she don't have a damn clue about."

And Crystal got out of the car.

Two days later, Mak's friend Tess—the one who'd had the pregnancy scare—wrecked her car. Rear-ended one of her volleyball teammates whipping into the senior lot a bit too swiftly (as Tess was wont to do). Which meant that if Tess wanted to go somewhere, Mak was on the receiving end of a grossly pleading phone call or gif-filled series of text messages.

Like the night when she and her boyfriend Trent were in a fight and Tess *had* to go over to his house so they could "work through it like almost-adults." Mak rolled her eyes at this one but was in Tess's circular driveway within fifteen minutes— Tess's fam lived in a minimansion right up the street from Mak's (no gate to get to hers, though).

They drove across town—Trent's house wasn't too far from Aunt Trish's—and as Tess got out of the car to head inside, Mak grabbed the book she'd brought, took her shoes off, kicked her seat back, and settled in for the long haul (aka one hour: the amount of time Mak told Tess she'd wait before going home whether Tess was ready or not).

Mak had read exactly two pages when the passenger door opened and someone got into her car.

"'Sup?"

Mak yelped and threw her arms out. Book went flying, and her hand smacked the horn. Which honked. Probably a good thing too—if nothing else, someone would've noticed. Maybe Tess would come out thinking she'd left something in the car and Mak was trying to alert her. She thought maybe she should honk it again, lean on it real good so *anyone* inside Trent's house would know that she was in distress and maybe about to be robbed and killed (*why hadn't she locked the doors? Mama would die if she knew Mak had been so careless in* this *neighborhood*).

She eased her body toward the steering wheel, trying not to make any sudden moves—

But then she saw the locs. And the shoulders. The big hands, fingers spread out over *clearly* solid thighs.

She froze, and her eyes lifted back to his face. His eyes, sparkling the same way they did the first time she saw him outside the Starlight.

His dimples.

Which were disappearing as the smile melted away and those eyes narrowed like he was confused. "Wait, do I know you?" he said.

Which . . . was he serious? "Oh, *now* you wanna ask if you know me? *After* you climb into my car without permission?"

"I technically *dropped* into your car, considering how low to the ground this shit is," he said. "It's real nice though. Supple-ass leather . . ." He wiggled his butt in the seat.

Which was disarming. Mak almost smiled.

Almost.

"For real though," he went on. "Do I know you? You look hella familiar."

Mak gulped and looked out the windshield. "I think you know my cousin. Crystal Rogers?"

"Oh, that's right! You the girl Crystal was in the car with outside the drive-in that one night. Damn, Crys ain't tell me she had a gorgeous cousin. Like . . . you're *really* beautiful. That's your real hair too, ain't it? All long and shit."

Mak couldn't think of a single thing to say.

"I'm Kamari, by the way."

"Yeah, I've heard."

"Ah, here we go, Crystal out here slandering me again?" He shook his head.

That was when Mak noticed his T-shirt. It was orange and had a Pegasus beneath the words *Camp Half Blood*.

"You're a Percy Jackson fan?" Mak said.

(Mak *loved* Percy Jackson. It was basically her whole childhood.)

"Why you sound so surprised?"

"Oh. Umm . . ." Yikes.

"Nah, I'm just playin'," he said, clearly enjoying the look on Mak's face as she fumbled around for words. "If Crystal told you what I *think* she did, your shock makes sense." He shook his head again. Added a heavy sigh. "Anyway: yes. I am a Percy Jackson fan. Kane Chronicles, too. And Heroes of

Olympus. Magnus Chase is also pretty lit so far. Really any-thing Uncle Rick writes—"

"Uncle Rick, huh?"

He grinned shyly. "Whatever, man."

Mak looked him over again. He was certainly hot, no denying that. Smelled really good too. Definitely a little rough around the edges, but there was also something softer about him than she would've expected. And it wasn't *just* the Percy Jackson thing.

Something in the way his index finger nervously tapped his thigh as he sat next to her. And how he kept glancing at her out of the corner of his eye and clearing his throat. She expected a guy like him to be more . . . sure of himself?

But what even did "a guy like him" mean? A guy from the hood?

"Why you looking at me like that?" he asked.

Mak hadn't realized she was staring. She swallowed. "Umm, how'd you get into 'Uncle Rick's' books?"

Kamari shrugged. "I started reading the Percys to my little brother 'cause they were more, like . . . educational, I guess, than the Harry Potter books. Liked the fact that he was basi-cally learning Greek mythology and shit just by listening to me read."

Mak felt guilty for being so shocked. Why would him being an amazing brother be a surprise? Her big brother used to read to her when she was little. . . . "How old is he?"

"Now? Nine."

"Wow."

There was a pause and then: "What's your name, by the way?" he said. "We sitting here talking about books and shit, and I don't even know who I'm talking to." With a smirk. That exposed one of the dimples.

It made Mak . . . feel things. In her chest and stomach. A swoopy, fluttery sensation that moved from behind her ribs to her belly button and on down to . . . Yeah.

She had to look away. "My name is Makenzie."

"*Makenzie?*" He sucked his teeth. "You would have some bougie-ass name."

"Oh my God, shut up."

"*Oh mai gahd, like totally shut UP!*" he mimicked.

"Excuse you, I do *not* sound like that."

He laughed. It was a very nice laugh. "Well, it's a pleasure to make your acquaintance, *Makenzie.*"

"Stop saying it like that! And besides, my friends call me Mak."

"Oh, so you saying we friends now?"

At that moment, Trent's front door flew open and Tess came storming out of it.

"Welp, guess Operation Reconciliation was a bust," Mak said to Kamari. "You should probably hop out so she doesn't detonate on you for being in her seat."

"Oh damn," he said, scrambling to exit.

"Mar, tell your friend he's an *ass*hole!" Tess shoved past Kamari and flounced into the passenger seat.

"Uhh, yeah, I'll do that. It was nice to meet you, Mak—"

But Mak would never know if he said her whole name then, because Tess slammed the door.

Right now though? At this drive-in she promised she'd never enter, in back seat of this car her parents bought her? Kamari is *definitely* saying Mak's whole name.

Just all broken down.

"Ma . . ." *Kiss.* "Ken . . ." *Kiss.* "Zie . . ." *Kiss, kiss, kiss, kiss.*

Chin, jaw, earlobe, neck—

The sound of the movie cuts out in Mak's car as her phone rings over Bluetooth.

She can see "Crys" pop up on the LED screen in her car's center console.

"You need to get that?" *Kiss.* (Collarbone this time.)

Mak sits up straight, pushing Kamari away a little more forcefully than she intends to.

"Damn, it's like that?" he says. "Who even is—" He looks at the screen. "Oh."

And now Mak doesn't know what to do. She's never brought up the stuff Crys told her about Kamari—frankly because she does her best to just push it out of her mind. (Isn't that what you do when somebody you like maybe has some kinda problematic shit in their past?)

The phone continues to blare—when the hell is it gonna *stop*?—and Mak glances at Kamari out of the corner of her eye. Crys would lose her entire mind if she knew Mak was with him right now. And truth be told: it's *Kamari's* safety Mak's concerned about. Mak will never forget seeing Crys take a baseball bat to the driver's-side window of a grown man's car after the man tried to touch Mak's butt at a barbecue in Crys's neighborhood.

Kamari is now sitting with his hands clasped in his lap, jaw clenched so tight, Mak can see the muscle ticking there.

Could he really have done what Crys said he did? Forced a girl to make such a heavy decision about something going on inside *her* body?

She'd never say it aloud, but Mak finds it a little hard to believe. This is the same guy who came to *her* rescue when she got a flat tire in an area she wasn't familiar with just a week ago. Tess had asked Mak to take her to Trent's again, so Mak dropped her off, planning to go hang out at Aunt Trish's until Tess let Mak know she was done.

It was a six-minute drive according to GPS, but four minutes into it, Mak's car started driving funny. A yellow light glared at her from the dash, and soon, a loud beeping noise took over, like the vehicle itself was panicking.

Looking back, Mak's not proud of her immediate reaction: she was scared. Mama always rambled on about crack houses and murders and "gangbangers" when she and Mak would cross beneath the bridge that put them in "the *ghetto*."

She pulled the car into a bright patch of sunlight in front of a kudzu-swallowed house and locked her doors. Scrambled for her phone and opened her car insurance app so she could request roadside assistance.

Discovered a series of new text messages:

Sup MAKENZIE Lol.

Dis Kamari. Tess put ur number in my phone

(swear I didn't ask 4 it!)

Just finished the new Magnus Chase. Shit was LIT.

Save my number (if u want 2 that is)

Before Mak realized what she was doing, she'd hit the Call button. She'd known it was Kamari before reading the second message because she'd stolen *his* number from Tess's phone when Tess wasn't looking the night after Kamari and Mak met.

He answered on the first ring. "Hello?"

Mak swallowed and looked out her window. "Hi, Kamari."

"Makenzie?"

"Yeah."

"Well damn," he said.

Mak laughed and the tension went out of her shoulders instantly.

"Umm . . ." *Was she really about to do this?* "Not to be all damsel in distress, but I'm kinda stranded with a flat tire on your side of town—"

"*My* side of town? The hell is that supposed to mean?"

"Oh . . ." Crap.

"I'm just fuckin' with you, Makenzie. Where you at?"

"You're really awful, you know that?"

He laughed. Which made Mak smile.

"So you gonna tell me your location, or . . ."

"Oh. Yeah, sorry. I'm on Barfield Ave just past Wingate Street?"

"All right. I'll be there in ten minutes, cool?"

"Mm-hmm! I'll see you then."

He hung up.

Mak put her head on the steering wheel and silently freaked out. She wasn't sure her heart had ever beat that fast. What the hell was she doing, calling this guy? If Crys knew—

There was a knock on the window, and Mak jumped, smacking her knees on the underside of the steering column.

Kamari threw his head back in laughter, and as much as Mak hated him in that moment, seeing him standing there in a tank top and basketball shorts with his rich brown skin gleaming in the sunlight, his muscles displayed in all their glory, and his long locs swinging slightly in the breeze . . . it made her head spin.

Which scared her almost as much as being stranded in the hood.

"I thought you said ten minutes!" Mak yelled as she rolled the window down.

"I was lying!" Kamari laughed some more and pointed over

his shoulder. "My house is right down there. I wanted to sneak up on you 'cause you cute as hell when you get all startled and shit. It's what I remember most from that night we first met."

"But you almost gave me a heart attack! *Twice* now."

"Ah, you'll be a'ight," he'd said with a wink. "Pop the trunk."

Mak did as he asked, then got out to watch him work.

"Need any help?" she asked, more as a courtesy than anything.

"Nah. Wouldn't want you to drop a lug nut and jump out of your skin when it hits the ground."

"Shut up."

"So what brings you to *my* side of town today?"

"You're not gonna let that go, are you?"

"Never. Bougie ass." He looked over his shoulder at Mak and grinned, then turned back to the task at hand. "*Beautiful* bougie ass, mind you, but still bougie as hell."

Stung, and feeling a little guilty, Mak took a deep breath. "I'm sorry about how that came out," she said.

"Nah. Nothing to apologize for. Trent told me about that school y'all go to and where y'all live and all that. I know you don't come across a lotta dudes like me." He removed the flat tire and set it aside, then hefted the spare into place. "Just hope all this *work* my ass is putting in is unraveling some of them preconceived notions you got up under all that hair." He looked back at Mak again, and her eyes dropped to his hands. "I *am* a son of Hephaestus, after all. Which prolly means I should stay away from *you*, since your trifling-ass mama cheated on my daddy with half the population of Mount Olympus *and* earth. Tuh."

It was the nerdiest, most backhanded compliment Mak had ever gotten, Kamari suggesting that Aphrodite, Greek goddess of love, beauty, and pleasure, was Mak's mother.

That Mak was a demigod(dess).

Soon he was returning the jack and flat to her trunk, slamming it shut, and dusting his hands off. "Hate to cut this li'l rendezvous short, but I'm officially gonna be late for basketball practice."

"Crap, I made you *late*?"

He smiled. The whole world could've been ablaze at that moment, but Mak wouldn't've noticed. "Few extra suicides never killed anybody." And his eyes traced over Mak's whole face.

She felt like she might be dead.

"So can I get a hug, Makenzie?" he said, spreading his arms.

"Umm. Sure . . ." Mak stepped forward and gasped a little as those arms swept around her waist and lifted her from the ground. She held on to Kamari's neck as he squeezed her around the middle. Just tight enough to make her feel like the only person in the universe who existed in that moment. She'd never experienced anything like it.

Mak had been involved with boys before, but they were usually really rich, really white, and really only trying to get in her pants—they all wanted to add "banging the Black girl" to their list of unlocked achievements in the pursuit of taking as much as they could from the world.

But this was different. As she floated there in Kamari's arms, Mak was reminded of how just a few days prior, she and Mama drove past a group of boys, Kamari included, sitting on someone's porch steps en route to Aunt Trish's. Said boys were laughing and passing something smokable among themselves. Kamari had waved at Mak, and she'd made the mistake of waving back.

"Girl, don't you wave at them thugs!" Mama had said. "Got the nerve to be sitting outside smoking marijuana in broad daylight."

Mak's mind immediately flashed to a party she went to with Tess in her own neighborhood, and to the neat little lines of white powder she'd seen on the polished marble of a kitchen countertop before they disappeared up the noses of some National Honor Society students via tightly rolled hundred-dollar bills. ("*These* are the people you need to surround yourself with, Makenzie. They're going places," Mama was always saying.)

Yeah, she came from the other side of the proverbial tracks, and her world *looked* cleaner, shinier, safer, less chaotic . . .

But was it really?

All Mak really knew for sure at *that* moment was that she'd be fine if Kamari never set her back on the ground.

Of course he had to, though. He was late for basketball practice.

He let her go and started walking away backward. All swaggy and stereotypical. "You should use that number every now and then," he said. "You know. When you're on *my* side of town and all."

And he turned and jogged away.

The whole encounter had her messed up for days. That this boy her mama (and cousin) would've never approved of came to her rescue despite the fact that she'd basically insulted him.

The sound of the movie cuts back in as the phone finally stops ringing in the car, and Mak looks from Kamari's jawline to those massive twiddling thumbs. Could *that* boy, the one who reads books about Greek mythology to his baby brother, the one Mak has spent the past couple weeks talking to into the wee hours of the night and then texting all day, the one who makes her feel more beautiful and desirable than anybody ever has, and who came to her aid when she needed him. . .

Could he be bad? Could he have done what Crys said he did?

Mak turns to look at him. He's nibbling on the cuticle of his right thumb.

She takes a deep breath.

"Hey, Kamari?"

"Yeah, Mak?"

He picked a hell of a time to drop the enzie . . .

"Is it true you got a girl pregnant?"

He sighs. Almost like he knew the question was coming. "You really wanna talk about this *now*?"

Mak shifts her focus through the windshield to the massive movie screen. "I know it's none of my business, but—"

"Yeah, I did."

She freezes. Blinks. "Huh?"

"I did get a girl pregnant. My *ex*-girl."

"Oh." A part of Mak hoped he'd tell her everything Crys said was untrue. But if *that* part of the story was accurate . . . "Did you really force her to . . . take care of things?"

He shakes his head. "I wondered if that was the shit Crystal told you. Thought maybe it wasn't since you let me get at you, but . . ." Now he sighs. "It was complicated, Makenzie."

Mak doesn't respond.

"I wanted her to keep him—or her, I guess. Raise the baby together. My dad ain't never done shit for me, and I didn't wanna be like him, you know? I was ready to man up." He looks out his window.

Mak clears her throat. "So what happened?"

"She . . . well, her folks weren't real happy, as I'm sure you can imagine. And then when she started getting sick to her stomach every day and it hit her that, like, her whole *life* was gonna change . . ." Now a defeated shrug. "Can't say I blame her. And we couldn't recover from it, so we broke up."

Mak opens her mouth to respond, but nothing comes out.

"Don't nobody know that though," he says. "When it got out that she'd been pregnant and had an abortion, somebody assumed I'd made her do it, and she didn't correct them. So then *that* got around."

"And you never told anybody what really happened?"

His eyes narrow for a second. "Nah. I already had a rep and she clearly wanted to save face. So now most girls at my school think I'm an asshole and stay away from me." Shrugs again. "Which means I stay focused on school and ball. I been scouted by a few D-Two schools, so we'll see what happens."

"Who was that girl you were with when I saw you the night I was with Crystal?"

His eyebrows furrow. "Huh?"

"You had your arm around a girl as you crossed the street."

"Oh." He sucks his teeth and waves his hand. "That's my homegirl Dasia. We known each other since we was five. She don't even like dudes."

"Ah. Okay."

They fall silent, and one of the characters on-screen says something about cauliflower. What the hell even movie are they parked in front of?

"So I guess you hate me now, knowin' I really did get a girl pregnant?"

Mak thinks for a moment. About cauliflower. Which she likes even though Tess and Crys both think it's gross. One of the few things they have in common, those two. "No, actually," she says, "I don't hate you."

He looks at her then. "You know, I was wrong about you," he says.

"Huh?"

"I knew who you were when I got in your car that one night. I been seeing you around since we was little kids, Crystal's prissy li'l cousin, who clearly had money 'cause her mama drove a Jag."

"Oh, so you lied then."

"Yep," he says without hesitation. Though he won't look her in the eye. "I was nervous. Girls like you don't usually mess with dudes like me."

Mak doesn't reply.

"I thought you would be kinda judgy and standoffish. I shot my shot 'cause avoiding a beautiful woman sitting in my homeboy's driveway with a book in hand seemed straight-up *wasteful*."

Mak laughs.

"But you really surprised me," Kamari continues. "You have this . . . *openness* about you. Shit's dope."

Kamari turns to Mak and grins, and her carefully constructed world unravels. She looks at his face. His hair. His big brown hands clasped in his lap. His nerdy T-shirt (this one has Yoda on it).

She slides closer and smiles. "You're pretty dope, too, son of Hephaestus." And then she leans in for another kiss.

THE (R)EVOLUTION OF NIGERIA JONES

IBI ZOBOI

I've been waiting for this night my whole life. Maybe even before I was born. My father, Dr. Kofi Sankofa Jones, tells his followers that we choose our lives while we're in the spirit world. We choose the time and place to be born. We choose our family and parents. And therefore, we choose our race. So, according to him and everybody else in the Movement, I *begged* to be Black.

But I swear on all my African ancestors that I didn't ask to be *this* Black.

I'm the only daughter of a Black nationalist revolutionary freedom fighter. At least that's what my father calls himself. This afternoon, there'll be about three hundred of his followers gathered in the First African Presbyterian Church. He's presenting his final lecture, called "There *Is* No Table," before he serves time at a correctional facility.

I'm in the back of the church as the Young Warriors, the teen boys of the Movement, place pamphlets onto the pews. I'm holding a stack of those pamphlets in my hand that showcases my dope graphic design skills with the Movement's logo—an *M* in the middle of a black silhouette of Africa—but no one ever notices that. They read about the Movement's history and my father's bio. Dr. Kofi Sankofa Jones is the great-grandson of Garveyites and his father was a Black Panther. He had me write that up. He never mentions my grandmother—a strict Baptist who's been trying to get me out of the Movement since the day my mother died four years ago.

We're not Christian, but the Movement rented this church for the lecture. My father says that as liberated Black people, we're not supposed to believe in a white Jesus, a white god, or any white savior. Still, it's the only place that would host us because they believe half the stuff my father says.

I'm wearing a pair of Chuck Taylors along with my usual ankle-length denim skirt deconstructed from an old pair of jeans from a thrift store. My feet hurt from standing all day. This morning, I spent four hours in front of the Old Navy on Chestnut Street handing out flyers for this lecture to any Black person walking by. My best friend, Kamau, was with me, but he stood on the opposite corner. We get more recruits that way.

I could hear him from across the street reciting his spiel

with a big, bright smile. "Do you know who you are, brother? Do you know your history?" He made eye contact and stepped closer to the stranger. "Well, history is our story, and Dr. Kofi Sankofa Jones will tell it like it is!"

His hype is way more convincing than mine. Not one person took a flyer from me. A man who recognized me even blurted out, "Your daddy needs to pay his taxes, Nigeria Jones!"

I shift my weight from one foot to the other to ease some of the soreness just as someone touches my shoulder. It's Kamau, and he's wearing his signature Young Warriors custom-made red dashiki and black pants. "Geri, I put your bag under the blue minivan in the parking lot," he whispers.

"Is the book in there?" I ask.

"*The Great Gatsby*," he says.

"Jeans and a wig?"

"Shredded at the thighs just like you wanted and blond ombré!"

"Ombré?" I whisper-yell, turning my whole body to him. "I didn't ask for all of that, Kamau."

"Trust me. It'll look good on you," he says.

"Fine. Then did you pack deodorant? And not the chemical-free stuff we usually wear, 'cause I'll be sweating like a hog under that wig."

"Even better. Antiperspirant. The kind that gives you cancer," he says with his eyes moving about, making sure no one is watching us.

That joke stings, but I don't tell him.

When Kamau is around the Young Warriors, his whole body changes from when he's around me. He raises his chin, pokes out his chest, and tightens his fists like the rest of those boys. He's supposed to be a warrior for his people—that's why his parents named him Kamau, meaning "silent warrior" in Kikuyu. I'm the only one who knows that Kamau is a lover, not a fighter.

My father named me Nigeria because it's the richest country in Africa. I guess his dream for me is to be like an oil-rich country on a third-world continent. But trying to jack poor people for all their paper is the last thing on my mind. Unlike my father.

"Thank you," I say, looking around as well. It's no big deal that we're talking to each other. But it's a big deal that Kamau is helping me plan my one-night escape.

"Awww! Nigeria and Kamau!" Mama Afua sings as she approaches us. She's the eldest member, who, at sixty-two, knows how many times the Movement has tried and failed to be a sovereign people like the Amish, or the folks down in Texas, but Black and with more sense. "Geri, don't you worry. You know we've got your back while your father's away. And Kamau will take care of you. How long until the wedding? Y'all turn eighteen in a few months, right?"

Kamau puts his arm around my shoulders, pulls me in, and kisses my forehead. I wrap my arms around his thin torso.

We're supposed to be boyfriend and girlfriend.

"You'll be the first on our guest list, Mama Afua," Kamau jokes, and I pinch his side.

Kamau and I were homeschooled together along with the eight other children our age who were born into the Movement in the same year. Homeschooling us was the Movement's way of reaching back for something old, traditional, and maybe African. Public schools were closing all over Philadelphia, and charter schools were full of young white women from the Midwest thinking they could change the world and save the poor Black kids.

So our entire schooling, from the age of five up until now at seventeen, was within the four walls of my father's house on Osage Avenue. There, we ate vegan breakfasts of oatmeal and almond milk, cubed tofu and brown rice for lunch, and on the days we memorized the names of all the Black freedom fighters dating back to the uprising on the *Amistad*, and even Mansa Musa, 'cause my father says Black history didn't start with slavery, we were allowed one organic vegan sugar-free lollipop from Whole Foods.

The very best days were when we got to visit the zoo—not to pet the animals, of course, but to protest. The Movement didn't believe in keeping animals in cages, much less eating them. A few members would stand outside the Philadelphia Zoo chanting and shouting and singing for the freedom of all living things: Black people, native people, disabled people, immigrant people, tree people, and animal people.

A couple of years ago, on one of those seasonal trips to protest at the zoo, Kamau leaned toward me and asked, "But what about the freedom of gay people?"

"What about it?" I repeated, holding a picket sign that read *If You Can Name Them, You Can Free Them!*

"What'd they ever do to us? We're not oppressed by them," Kamau had said. His freeform locs were tied into a bun on top of his head. His T-shirt, with the words "Black and Green," hung loose over his thin frame.

"Right!" I said. "There must have been plenty of gay people in Africa." We've been having this conversation since we were twelve. In that moment, I tried to make Kamau feel better, even though Kofi Sankofa has never mentioned anything about gays in his lectures. But with all that talk about preserving the traditional Black family and bringing more Black babies into the world, Kamau made his own assumptions. And those discussions with my best friend always ended with the words "Such bullshit."

Kamau doesn't let go of me until Mama Afua limps her way to the front of the church. And it takes her a while because of her bum knee.

"She was the one who snitched on you the last time," I whisper to Kamau. "You think she knows something about what I'm doing tonight?"

"I wouldn't be surprised if she does," he says. "She must've already read it in the cowrie shells and sage smoke, or the ancestors must've whispered it to her. If that's the case, *they're* the snitches." He flashes me one of his half smiles and walks away to help the Young Warriors with the setup.

I shake my head as I watch Mama Afua scold Kamau for not draping fabric over the crucifix on the pulpit properly. That's how the Movement has managed to keep us teenagers in line. We're led to believe that the Movement's elders' eyes have eyes, and their ears have ears. So being disrespectful in any way, openly questioning the Movement's philosophies, or even tasting a piece of bacon is never an option. We can't even listen to trap music because my father says it's the white man's way of helping us to enslave ourselves with an endless cycle of celebrating sex, violence, and drugs.

But Kamau and I have been secretly poking holes into this thing since we were twelve: when my mother got sick. We question, Google, fact-check, smirk, and roll our eyes at just about everything the Movement says and does, even though the mastermind is my father. And Kamau managed to fool them for a whole weekend when he went to New York City for a party, until Mama Afua figured it out. She read it all over his face, smelled it on his breath, and saw it in his eyes. Still, there was one thing they haven't figured out about Kamau. And that's how I knew that the elders of the Movement are just like everybody else. They're not magical. And they can't keep us trapped in this life forever.

With each passing minute, my breath shortens and my heart races. I have to pay attention to the time and keep a poker face, as Kamau says. He's done this before, and even though he got caught, he thinks I can pull it off since I'm Kofi Sankofa's daughter and all. No one would expect it from me. But I'm sweating and my hands are clammy.

Soon, some members will be coming in with their children and my job is to usher the little ones down to the basement, where the Sisters in Sisterhood, the teen girls of the Movement, will have a kente-cloth-covered table full of vegan food and keep them engaged with songs and games while their parents listen to Kofi Sankofa's lecture. The Movement is organized in that way. Everyone has a role, a job. Everyone looks out for each other. Kofi Sankofa always reminds us that this is our little three-hundred-member African village in a big white city.

I keep an eye on the doors in front of the church and behind the pulpit, even though the Young Warriors are part of the security team. There's no telling what type of people my father will attract this time. Some of his former students from Temple University usually came through, if they were not part of that petition to kick him off the faculty for spreading hate speech. Usually, it was longtime followers of the Movement who came from all over the East Coast, or newbie high school and college kids after they've binge-watched all his YouTube videos, especially his most popular lecture, "A Seat at the Table."

Word on the internet was that my father had gone soft. He used to travel all over the country lecturing white folks on how they needed to not only make room for Black people at the table, but they had to give up their seats. They couldn't hold on to their power and only give us a little bit. They had to let it go completely so we could make all the decisions around this proverbial table. Then he raised the bar by telling Black folks to "Get Up from the Table and Flip It"—to overthrow power and not seek it for themselves,

But now they were saying that my father was having an existential crisis with all this "there is no table" mess. He said that the best way to handle white supremacist bullshit was to not only get up from the table, but walk away and forget it was even there in the first place.

And just as my father said he was done fighting white people, they finally got him for tax evasion. They couldn't lock him up for spreading "hate speech," inciting riots, and telling hardworking people to leave their good-paying jobs because he says they're like modern-day plantations. Getting him for not paying taxes was a way to shut him up for a while.

But people are still coming to hear him speak about how he hates what white people have done all over the world. He doesn't trust them, neither. And as his daughter, I'm supposed to be his most supportive follower. But all Kamau and I keep saying to ourselves is, *Such bullshit.*

Plus, I have my own dreams, especially since finding out that I got a perfect score on the SATs when I took them three years ago.

I want to go to college—a really good one like Columbia

University—to study paleontology. And deep down in my heart, I really like white boys, especially an older one named Dr. Ross Geller—a paleontologist and young Columbia graduate. Thinking of Ross and how cute he is on that old TV show *Friends* is the only thing to keep me from bailing out on *my* friend. Kamau made me promise that I would do what he did—live out my dreams for one night. Only for one night. And then we both could start planning our Great Escape, he calls it. We both have less than a year before we turn eighteen and we can do whatever the hell we want, including leave the Movement for good.

My father manages to fill the whole church, and it's standing room only with all the wooden pews packed with warm Black bodies. The audience applauds and cheers when he makes his way up to the pulpit to the sound of djembe drums and the sight of raised fists. Dr. Kofi Sankofa Jones, in his long, graying locs and shimmering white-and-gold embroidered boubou, only has to raise one hand to silence the audience. Then he shouts with a deep, booming voice into the mic, "Power to the people! The Movement is ours, the path is clear, and our freedom is near!" Then he leads his followers to begin the opening song, "Lift Every Voice and Sing."

This is my cue to meet Kamau in the parking lot of the church. Before I leave, I take a look at all the people who've come to hear my father speak—all brown faces, some smiling, some pissed, and everything in between. They're here because they want freedom from oppression, and they think my father will lead them to some kind of promised land. As for me, I just want freedom, period. And it doesn't involve my father or no promised land. I discreetly make my way out of the church and around to the parking lot. My heart is beating so fast, I might as well be a walking djembe drum.

Kamau is standing near the blue minivan. He motions to where he hid my bag. I kneel down to retrieve it and hoist it onto my back. When we're finally facing each other, we both take a deep pranayama breath just like we were taught in yoga since we were toddlers.

"You ready to have the time of your life?" Kamau asks, pursing his lips and trying to hold in a laugh.

"Stop making fun of me, Kamau," I say.

"Are you sure you don't wanna check out that ball I went to? Even if you don't like it, just take all that good fun and put it in a paper bag for me. Better yet, a video and some pictures will do."

"You know I would if I had more time. And are you sure you don't wanna come with me? We can still get a bus ticket at the last minute."

"No, Geri. If I leave tonight, I'm never coming back. I've had enough of this bullshit. We gotta do this right. Save some more coins, say goodbye without saying goodbye. You know? And please, I wouldn't wanna go sit in no café just to read a Dead White Man book and . . . *assimilate*. Or whatever the hell you're trying to do in there."

I exhale deep and look up at the warm, late-afternoon sky. My father's shouting can be heard from outside even with the giant AC system blasting from the church. He's going on and on about not ever needing the white man's help and how we've got to do this or that on our own. "Weren't you trying to *assimilate* in that vogue ball, Kamau?"

"I wasn't *trying*. I fit right in." Kamau does his dance, flinging his wrists from side to side, perfecting his tutting and clicks.

I turn around to glance toward the church's back door, making sure no one sees him doing this. No one knows that the party Kamau went to was a kiki. A vogue ball. And when he turns eighteen, he'll be competing to join a house in New York City—House of Ninja or House of Xtravaganza, hopefully. He's that good. But his parents would disown him if they knew. The Young Warriors would turn their backs on him.

"Okay, it's time for you to bust the hell up out of here, Nigeria Jones," Kamau says, and I cringe.

"Don't call me that," I say through clenched teeth.

"It's your name, girl. Claim it!" he snorts. "Okay, fine. What you want me to call you now? Becky? Once you put on that wig, you'll have *all* the good hair."

I roll my eyes hard at him and sigh. "Where'd you put the bus ticket?"

"Front pocket along with your wallet, your cheap-ass

phone, and some cash," he says, and extends his arms out at me to give me a hug. "I'm a text and a phone call away. The bootleg revolutionaries in there will be at this all night, so I'll cover for you. You weren't feeling well and you went home to sleep. And since I'm there, they won't suspect a thing. You wouldn't go running off to anywhere by yourself. Especially not to New York City. Perfect plan."

"Perfect plan," I repeat.

"Okay. The return ticket is for midnight on the dot. So you got seven hours, Blackerella. If the Ross of your dreams shows up, make the first move. But don't go up to nobody's dorm room or apartment no matter how much they know about *Tyrannosaurus rex*. And since you wanna have this white-girl experience and all, please . . . I'm begging you . . . do not get white-girl wasted."

"Oh, shut up, Kamau!" I shove his shoulder, laughing.

"And don't forget that Harlem is one subway stop away. Just get to 125th Street and ask the closest brother selling incense, shea butter, and your father's books and DVDs for help if you need it."

We hug each other one last time, and he holds me even tighter. "You are so brave, Becky Jones," he says. "I don't get you, but we've always been the two unicorns up in this place."

Kamau watches me as I leave the parking lot and discreetly pass the closed bright-red front doors of the church and walk to the corner of West Girard and Belmont Avenues to catch a cab to the Greyhound Terminal on Filbert Street.

But I end up at the McDonald's on North Broad Street instead. I'm here for two things: the bathroom mirror and a bacon double cheeseburger. Kamau suggested that I try it. If I'm doing this one-night-of-fun thing, I might as well go all out.

I'm in the bathroom tucking my shoulder-length locs beneath the blond ombré wig. It's dark brown at the roots and blond at the ends—as if I'd been a brunette and wanted to be like the girls who have more fun. I have to admit, there's something about the wig against my deep-brown skin that makes me look neater, almost. Nicer, even. I smile different smiles in the mirror and practice saying my name with different voices, tones, and codes. Geri. Geri? *Geri.* But never, ever Nigeria.

I change out of my skirt and into the pair of jeans Kamau put into my backpack. I've been wearing skirts my whole life because the Movement believes that young women like me should protect our womb energy. Jeans are stifling. We need to keep the "portal of life" free and clear for all those new Black babies coming into the world. I don't even want babies. As usual, all of that nonsense is bullshit.

I think of throwing the skirt into the trash, but I have to be on the midnight bus back to Philly and play it cool. I have to be Nigeria Jones, the princess of the revolution, when I return. Like Kamau said, we have to plan this right.

I step back away from the mirror to take a good look at myself wearing a regular white T-shirt, torn jeans, and a messy wig. I look . . . regular. I push back some of the hair behind my ears like I've seen the girls on *Friends* do. Rachel has the prettiest hair, but still, she isn't smart enough for Ross. I wonder if Ross would approach me if he saw me sitting by myself in Central Perk.

But my phone pings in my backpack and a text from Kamau reads, **Don't forget the bacon double cheeseburger and a Coke. Live a little!**

You just got out of the Movement jail yesterday and you're talking about live a little. Whatever. I'm on it! I text back with a series of food emoji and a smiley face.

So I take a window seat on the five-o'clock Greyhound to New York City and pick apart the bacon double cheeseburger. I nibble on the bacon and burger and savor every single salty, oily morsel—the white man's mass-produced plastic food, as my father calls it. I've been a vegan my whole life, except for the times Kamau and I secretly had ice cream, had pizza, or had mistaken a hamburger for soy.

But I spit out the last bit of bacon into the paper bag. I can't finish the rest, not even the soda. So I eat the fries and sip my water. My stomach disagrees with my taste buds.

When I reach into the bottom of my backpack for my book, I discover that Kamau has packed his tablet. On it is a sticky note with a password to a Hulu account. "So you can watch your stupid show," it reads.

My heart leaps and I squeal on the inside. "Thank you, best friend," I whisper. In no time, I'm logged on, and even though I've seen every episode of every season, I decide to watch my favorite ones to prepare for this trip. I'm on the episode where Ross and Rachel are breaking up. "She doesn't appreciate him," I say as I put in my earbuds.

The older Black woman sitting next to me scoots over and closes her eyes.

"What do you see in those white boys, anyway?" Kamau asked me once.

"The same thing you see in them," I said. But he assured me that he doesn't like white boys. He likes the Jaden Smith type—Black boys who look like him, I guess. I wonder if the Movement would be more tolerant if they knew I liked white boys or if they knew Kamau liked Black boys. My father sees everything in Black and white. There's hardly anything or anyone in between. Or if he ever did mention Asians or Latinos, it was to remind us that they've never experienced the transatlantic slave trade. According to him, Black people are the most oppressed people in the world.

I pause a scene where Rachel and Phoebe are having a heart-to-heart, place the tablet on my lap, and hold my head in my hands. *Friends* was the only TV show Mama watched when she was sick. It made her laugh a little and let her take her mind off things. But my father disapproved, of course. He did of anything that had to do with white folks' nonsense.

The thing about my father's way of seeing the world in black and white is that there are no gray spaces. Everything is a fight. Black against white. White against Black. And while I didn't grow up surrounded by actual walls, my father's ideas and words have created an invisible wall.

So I have to break past the fact that even though I got a perfect score on my SATs and could've gotten into an Ivy League by the time I was fifteen, my father said that I couldn't let these white institutions capitalize on my genius. He had me take that test to prove something, to show off, to make his point. And it did. But I had my heart set on Columbia. I dreamed of going to the most remote places on this earth to dig for old bones, older than people. Before humans and their stupid ideas. Before hate. Maybe even before love, too. Dinosaurs just existed. No lectures, no books, no language. No world-conquering Europeans and no defeated everybody else. Just those powerful, unrestrained creatures roaming the planet.

I sit back up in my seat, hold my head high, inhale, and push my blond ombré hair behind my ear. Tonight, I'm not the daughter of a Black nationalist revolutionary freedom fighter. I'm a freshman studying dinosaur bones and geology. And since there's no actual Central Perk anywhere in Manhattan, any café near the university will do. I'll be relaxing on a warm Saturday evening in May just as finals are over, and be immersed in classical literature about white people and their problems, while sipping on my iced latte.

I end up watching three episodes by the time the bus pulls into Port Authority.

The number one train takes me to Columbia University. All these memories start to swim around my head as I stand on the crowded train headed uptown—the times I'd come up to Harlem with my parents to buy fabric from the Senegalese shops and Black books, incense, shea butter, and oils from the street vendors. And on a few occasions, my father would lecture at the historic National Black Theatre on Fifth Avenue and 126th Street. I'm told that he once sold out seats for a lecture at the Apollo Theater when I was a toddler. That was about fifteen years ago, when the Movement was at its height. But fifteen years have passed and nothing has changed. The people who believed in every word my father was preaching, their lives didn't change. Philly didn't change. This country didn't change. But everything changed for me when Mama died, 'cause I realized that the Movement couldn't save her. And I decided I needed to be in control of my own life.

More people squeeze into the train car at Eighty-Sixth Street, and I can't unsee what I've been taught to see by my father—the differences in people, how polished or poor they are, the look on their faces, what kind of phones they have, how they speak and what they talk about. Who has more and who has less. A young Black guy, maybe a little older than me, has on giant headphones, nods his head, and shouts out the words to his rap every so often. Three white women are huddled around a pole giggling and talking. They could be

Rachel, Phoebe, and Monica. An older Black woman, Latina maybe, is sleeping in her seat—head tilted back, mouth open, eyes weary even while they're closed.

"Can you move your bag?" an Asian man says to me.

I take off my backpack, place it on the floor in front of my feet, and hold on to another pole. My phone buzzes in my bag, but it's way too crowded to reach down and take it out. We're all squeezed onto this train as if it's the end of the world. I wonder how we'd act toward each other—all of us: Black, white, and everything in between—if this train stalled right in this tunnel. I wonder if we'd all help each other and love each other for just a moment, and disprove everything my father has built his life on: that white people are hell-bent on destroying the world and everyone in it. Then my own life—with all that homeschooling, vegan diet, homemade clothes, and books upon books about Black everything—would've been for nothing. And maybe Mama's death could've been prevented. She would've trusted white doctors instead of trying to green-juice and kale-salad away her cancer.

The train's doors are about to close when I notice the stop for Columbia University. I squeeze my way off just in time, and the train speeds out of the unbearably hot station. I rush up the stairs and out of the subway with all the other people headed toward Broadway—college students and professors, maybe.

The warm early-evening air wraps around me and I stand there for a moment gazing up at the architecture—the tall, wide buildings that look as if they've been there since the beginning of time. But not in the time of dinosaurs, of course. They didn't kill trees to build cities. My father says that this is the white man's idea of civilization: destroy to build, build to destroy. Still, out of the rubble of destruction—the bowels of white supremacy, he calls it—ideas are born.

I can't get him out of my head. Two hours and a hundred miles away, Kofi Sankofa's words bounce around my mind as I make my way to the café on Amsterdam Avenue.

There isn't another brown face in sight as I walk down the two blocks. No one makes eye contact. No one seems to notice me. My hair brushes against my shoulders and the back of my neck the way my locs do. This wig is a layer of protection, a disguise. Even if someone looks my way, it's not really me they're seeing.

The café will be my spot for now. I've seen the pictures online, studied the menu, and read the Yelp reviews.

"Why can't you just go sit in a café near U. Penn?" Kamau had asked. "This'll be your one night in New York City and that's how you want to spend it?"

He didn't understand at first, but Kamau is the only person in my life who knew that it all started with boy bands, just like for any other nine-year-old girl, I guess. White boys were like forbidden fruit because I'd heard how my father called them the devil, the Destroyers. First it was Justin Bieber, then the boys in One Direction, every single last one of them. The Jonas

Brothers, the cuties from Big Time Rush, and once I realized that I preferred them a little more mature, Shia LaBeouf. Until the day I sat with my mother while she was in bed watching a nineties TV show where white people were not sitting around plotting the annihilation of Black people—they just talked about nothing at all in their big New York City apartment.

Later, I would hide in my room under the covers with a borrowed tablet or my cheap phone and laugh at all the friends' nonsense. I liked Phoebe the most. Rachel annoyed me. And I fell in love with Ross. He was the one who got me into paleontology in the first place. He was the one who got me to dream about Columbia University and sitting in cafés reading literary classics.

The place is crowded and the ice-cold AC make goose bumps rise on my skin. Still, I play it extra cool and smile. Before I even get a chance to take in the whole scene, the white boy behind the counter asks how I'm doing.

"Iced latte with regular milk and a cupcake, please," I immediately say. I've been practicing.

There are no Black people here, just like I expected. But no one is giving me looks that make me feel as if I don't belong. My father has protected me from those looks my whole life. I've never been the only chocolate chip in the batch, ever.

A couple gets up from a small round table near the counter and I immediately grab the empty seat. Before I can even settle down, the white boy comes over with the latte and cupcake.

"I'll be right here if you need anything," he says, flashing me a bright smile.

Something warm settles in my belly and the goose bumps disappear. I keep my eyes on him, and he glances back at me, still smiling. He doesn't smile that brightly at the other people in front of the counter. He's no Ross, for sure. He's taller. Wider, even, with a head full of dirty blond hair, almost like my wig. He's wearing a plain black T-shirt with a simple illustration of a spaceship. I can talk about space, too. Dinosaurs, space. Same thing. If he's not a paleontology student, then he's a budding astronomer, for sure. Astrophysics, maybe. I'm cool with that.

He quickly looks my way again, and this time, I smile back and wave. I actually make the first move, just like Kamau told me to. He waves back and smiles brighter this time. I look around the place. No one notices my budding love affair with the white boy behind the counter. No one cares.

I watch him closely as he serves the customers, makes small talk, and glances at me, still smiling. The warm feeling in my belly turns hot. And if it wasn't so cold, I'd definitely be sweating under the wig. I take a sip of the iced latte, which makes me colder, and I bite off a piece of the cupcake. I have to text Kamau that I found him—the Ross of my dreams.

I reach behind me for my backpack and grab nothing but cool air. I touch both my shoulders and my back. Nothing. That hot feeling in my belly quickly solidifies and my whole body feels like it's collapsing under its weight. Slowly, I check my lap to see if my backpack is there. Then the floor. Then I look up toward the counter. Nothing. Everything around me—the voices, the laughter, and even that white boy's bright smile—all come to a stop.

I left my bag and everything in it on the train.

The tall glass of iced latte is half full now, and a quarter of the cupcake is gone. I don't have any money to pay for this.

It's only wishful thinking that makes me check the pocket of my jeans for my phone or some cash. Still nothing.

"Shit!" I say out loud.

The white boy glances over at me. His smile has faded.

And as if someone turned up the volume really loud, I can now hear the exact words from the voices around me. The clinking of knives and forks, the swinging door, the grazing chairs on the wooden floor, and even the tiny seconds of silence. My breath and heartbeat are louder, too.

Harlem is not that far away. I could walk there and find someone selling my father's books and DVDs. I'd have to tell them that I'm Nigeria Jones, daughter of the Black nationalist revolutionary freedom fighter from Philly. I need money for a bus ticket home, that's all. I'd have to answer questions when I get back. My father would make me promise not to pull this ever again while he's away, or else.

I don't want to lose you like I lost your mother, he'd say.

I'd be going back to the life I didn't ask for—the one that I didn't choose while in the spirit world.

Kamau would get in trouble, because of course he got me to do this. And there goes his plan to live the life of his dreams. Our plan.

"You want anything else?" the white boy asks as he smiles down, as he wipes his hands on a white towel. His eyes are ocean blue.

Blue-eyed devil—I can hear my father's words echo in my mind.

My throat is so tight and dry that I can't find the words to say yes or no. So his smile is completely gone now and he walks away. He doesn't look in my direction again.

Still, the voices get louder and louder as I think of how to leave this unpaid-for latte and cupcake behind. There are people by the door and the white boy would definitely notice me leaving without paying. And he'd call me back in. Everyone would turn to look at me, and of course the Black girl with the fake hair couldn't pay the ten bucks. Of course she'd try to break out of here.

Your very existence is a crime, I hear my father preach.

I've never been in a closed space with this many white people. So I watch their faces the way I've watched *Friends*. Kamau wanted me to get into *Living Single* instead. They did it first, he said. But they were too familiar. So with each new episode of *Friends*, I felt as if I'd solved a mystery about white people. My father talked about them too much. I needed to understand them, step into their lives, and maybe get a taste of all that freedom and power. But Ross, Rachel, and the crew weren't trying to take over the world.

I make eye contact with one of them in this café. An older man. He doesn't turn away and neither do I. He's not smiling and he purses his lips. And for the first time since being in here, I know what he's thinking. So I turn away and drop my head.

They want nothing more than to see us wiped off the face of this earth, I hear my father shout.

I can say that I've lost my bag. I can just get up and walk away and flip my middle finger on the way out. My mind races with all these possibilities, but it's as if my body doesn't want to lose my seat at this table. This is where I want to be. I've gotten this far. This is where I belong.

So I take another bite of the cupcake, a sip of the latte, and try to remember the plot to *The Great Gatsby*. I read it when I was thirteen, right after my mother made me read *The Bluest Eye* before she died, and for the same reason I started watching *Friends* on my own.

You're already ten times as good, I hear my father whisper.

I inhale and try to savor this moment.

You take all that genius, stay right here, help your people out, and build our own damn table! I hear my father say.

The white boy keeps glancing my way, but I look in every direction but his. I can't help but feel other eyes on me, too, and the voices have quieted a little, almost whispering.

Your body is free, but your mind is still enslaved! I hear my father yell.

"Is this seat taken?" a white girl asks.

Out of the corner of my eye, I see the white boy watching closely.

"Is this seat taken?" the white girl asks again, louder this time. She leans in closer to me, her hair hanging over my latte and almost grazing my cupcake.

I don't answer. So she takes the chair anyway. I call her Rachel in my mind.

I don't need your help and you're gonna have to kill me first before I let you take my daughter away, I hear my father say to the people from the Department of Human Services. They'd come to take me away months after my mother died. They said my father wasn't feeding me well and wouldn't allow me to go school. But Mama Afua had gathered all the elder women in the Movement and they squeezed into our living room forming a protective shield around me and dared those people to come take me away.

I sip and eat slowly as I watch the white boy wipe his hands on the white towel again. He's looking in my direction, but he's avoiding my eyes, even as I stare at him. He comes around the counter, not smiling, and he starts to make his way toward me.

I take another sip, slurping up the last bit of ice water through the straw. I push my hair back behind my ears. My hands are shaking. I don't know if it's from the cold or from something else.

He's in front of the table now and I look him dead in the face, not smiling. My body is tense, my teeth are chattering.

He leans in slowly, glancing down at my empty glass and the last piece of cupcake before I take it, put it into my mouth, and chew it slowly, savoring the sweetness while staring up at him.

"Do you need anything else?" the white boy asks.

I slide off the blond ombré wig, letting my locs drop down over my shoulders, and place it on the table next to the empty glass and small plate of cupcake crumbs. I close my eyes for a long second and exhale. I shake my head no and watch the boy walk away with the glass and plate, and leave me alone.

I sit back in my seat and let myself settle into this moment. I'm miles away from home with no money, ID, or phone. I'm the only Black person here.

But then it dawns on me that except for a minor setback, I pulled this off. I actually pulled this off.

I look around and catch his eye. Then I raise my hand to call the white boy back over to my table.

"I'll get another one of those cupcakes, please," I say with a smile.

AUTHOR BIOGRAPHIES

TRACEY BAPTISTE is a *New York Times* bestselling author best known for *Minecraft: The Crash* and the Jumbies series. She has written several other fiction and nonfiction books for kids and the adult short story "Ma Laja," which was included in *Sycorax's Daughters*, a Bram Stoker Award finalist for excellence in horror writing. Her works for children have received starred reviews from *Kirkus* and *Publishers Weekly* and have been named Junior Library Guild selections. Find her online @traceybaptiste on Twitter, or at www.traceybaptiste.com.

COE BOOTH earned an MFA in creative writing from the New School. Her first novel, *Tyrell*, was published in 2006, and it won the *Los Angeles Times* Book Prize for Young Adult Literature. Her novels *Kendra* and *Bronxwood* followed, and both were selected by the American Library Association as Best Books for Young Adults. Her first novel for middle school readers, *Kinda Like Brothers*, was published in 2014. You can find Coe online at www.coebooth.com.

DHONIELLE CLAYTON is the *New York Times* best-selling author of *The Belles* and the coauthor of the Tiny Pretty Things series. She earned an MA in children's literature from Hollins University and an MFA in writing for children at the New School. She taught secondary school for several years. Clayton is a former librarian and cofounder of Cake Literary, a creative kitchen whipping up decadent—and decidedly diverse—literary confections for middle grade, young adult, and women's fiction readers. She can be found online at www.dhonielleclayton.com.

BRANDY COLBERT is the Stonewall Award–winning author of *Little & Lion*, *Finding Yvonne*, *Pointe*, and the forthcoming *The Revolution of Birdie Randolph*. Her work has been named a Junior Library Guild selection and a Book-of-the-Month Club selection, and included on ALA's Best Fiction for Young Adults list, as well as best-of lists from *Kirkus*, *Booklist*, *Publishers Weekly*, *Vulture*, and more. Brandy lives and writes in Los Angeles. She can be found online at www.brandycolbert.com.

JAY COLES is a young adult and middle grade writer, a composer with ASCAP, and a professional musician residing in Indianapolis, Indiana. He is a graduate of Vincennes University and Ball State University and holds degrees in English and liberal arts. When he's not writing diverse books, he's advocating for them, teaching middle school students, and composing music for various music publishers. Coles's debut young adult novel, *Tyler Johnson Was Here*, about a boy whose life is torn apart by police brutality when his twin brother goes missing, was inspired by events from the author's life and the Black Lives Matter movement. You can find him online at www.jaycoleswriter.com.

LAMAR GILES is an author, speaker, teacher, and founding member of We Need Diverse Books. His novels *Fake ID* and *Endangered* were Mystery Writers of America Edgar Award finalists, and his novel *Overturned* was named a *Kirkus Reviews* Best YA Book of 2017. He resides in Virginia with his wife. Check him out at www.lamargiles.com or follow @lrgiles on Twitter.

LEAH HENDERSON is the author of *One Shadow on the Wall*, an Africana Children's Book Award notable and a Bank Street Best Book of 2017, and starred for outstanding merit. *Mamie on the Mound, A Day for Rememberin',* and *Together We March* are her forthcoming picture books. She mentors at-risk teens and has an insatiable travel bug, and her volunteer work has roots in Mali, West Africa. Leah graduated from Phillips Andover Academy and received her MFA from Spalding University. You can find her at www.leahhendersonbooks.com.

JUSTINA IRELAND enjoys dark chocolate and dark humor, and she is not too proud to admit that she's still afraid of the dark. She lives with her husband, kid, cat, and dog in Pennsylvania. She is the author of teen novels *Vengeance Bound*, *Promise of Shadows*, and *Dread Nation*, a *New York Times* bestseller. You can visit her at www.justinaireland.com.

VARIAN JOHNSON is the author of nine novels, including *The Great Greene Heist*, which has been named to over twenty-five state reading and best-of lists. His books for older readers include *My Life as a Rhombus* and *Saving Maddie*. Varian's newest novel, *The Parker Inheritance*, was released in spring 2018. You can visit him online at www.varianjohnson .com.

KEKLA MAGOON is the author of eleven novels, including *The Season of Styx Malone*, *The Rock and the River*, and *How It Went Down*. She has received an NAACP Image Award, the John Steptoe New Talent Award, two Coretta Scott King Award honors, and the Walter Award honor and been long-listed for the National Book Award. Kekla holds an MFA in writing from Vermont College of Fine Arts, where she now teaches. www.keklamagoon.com.

TOCHI ONYEBUCHI is the author of the young adult novel *Beasts Made of Night* and its sequel, *Crown of Thunder*. He holds an MFA from New York University's Tisch School of the Arts and a JD from Columbia Law School. His fiction has appeared in *Asimov's Science Fiction* and *Omenana* magazines, his nonfiction in the *Harvard Journal of African American Public Policy* and on Twitter @tochitruestory.

JASON REYNOLDS is a *New York Times* bestselling author. His award-winning work includes *When I Was the Greatest*, *The Boy in the Black Suit*, *All American Boys*, *As Brave as You*, *For Every One*, the Track series, and *Long Way Down*, a Newbery and Printz Award honoree. You can find his ramblings at www.jasonwritesbooks.com.

NIC STONE, author of *Odd One Out* and the *New York Times* bestselling and William C. Morris Award finalist *Dear Martin*, was born and raised in a suburb of Atlanta, Georgia. After graduating from Spelman College, she worked extensively in teen mentoring and lived in Israel for a few years before returning to the US to write full-time. You can find her online at www.nicstone.info.

LIARA TAMANI is the author of *Calling My Name*, a PEN American Literary Award finalist and SCBWI Golden Kite Award honoree. Liara's forthcoming novel is *All the Things We Never Knew*. She holds an MFA in writing from Vermont College and a BA from Duke University. She lives in Houston, Texas, and can be found online at www.liaratamani.com.

RENÉE WATSON is the author of seven books for children, including *This Side of Home* and *What Momma Left Me*. Her *New York Times* bestselling novel *Piecing Me Together* received the Coretta Scott King Award and a Newbery honor. She has given readings and lectures at the United Nations, the Library of Congress, and the US Embassy in Japan. She is the founder of I, Too Arts Collective, a nonprofit dedicated to preserving the legacy of Langston Hughes and nurturing voices from underrepresented communities. Visit Renée at www.reneewatson.net.

RITA WILLIAMS-GARCIA is the celebrated author of ten novels for young adults and middle grade readers. Her most recent novel, *Clayton Byrd Goes Underground*, won the 2018 NAACP Image Award for Literature for Young People and was named a 2017 National Book Award Finalist. She is most known for her Coretta Scott King Award–winning Gaither Sisters novels. She can be found online at www.ritawg.com.

IBI ZOBOI holds an MFA in writing for children and young adults from Vermont College of Fine Arts. She is the author of *Pride*, the forthcoming middle grade novel *My Life as an Ice Cream Sandwich*, and *American Street*, a National Book Award finalist, a *New York Times* Notable Book, and best book of the year as listed by *Publishers Weekly*, *School Library Journal*, *Booklist*, and *Kirkus Reviews*. You can find her online at www.ibizoboi.net.